VALLEY OF SHADOWS

J. R. Biery

Cover created with Gimp 2 using background image from Pixabay.com photographed by Christopher Kuszajewski and a photo of an archive painting "Oregon or bust" of a wagon train from the Great Platte River Road Archway Monument, Kearney, NE taken by http://debandjoeontheroad.blogspot.com.

ABOUT THIS BOOK

Compelled to write more about the three factory girls who started together in From Darkness to Glory. Bonnie Magee is tall and shy, the hard-working eldest in a family of ten. When she meets Tarn Micheals she believes love will change her life. Then he betrays and beats her so badly she loses their unborn child.

Bonnie decides to join Claire's family as they travel west to a new life. Crossing the country by wagon train is a long hard journey full of danger. She keeps being saved by Calum Douglas, a handsome lieutenant. Wary of trusting another man, she must remind herself and him that she is a married woman.

DISCLAIMER

DEDICATION

Dedicated to Jerry, my rock. Also, thanks to the members of Cookeville Creative Writers' Association who prodded and nudged me forward. Special thanks to those who have read the previous two books and written to ask for another. I hope you realize how much you touch and motivate a writer when you praise their work. Bonnie's story is dedicated to all of you. Thanks especially to readers Linda Lattin and Joann Black.

CHAPTER ONE

1876-Outskirts of Boston, Massachusetts

Bonnie Magee Micheals waited until her petite friends scurried over the rough boards that crossed the swollen creek before stepping after them. She felt choked by the sweet vapors of starch laden steam that followed them through the factory door.

Cautiously she placed one long foot in front of the other, gasped as the board sagged when she reached the middle of the stream, then hurried across. It wasn't just the growing weight of the baby inside her that made her feel ungainly. At five eight, she was four inches taller than Lynne McKinney, nearly eight more than Claire Wimberley. Before, they had teased that she was their tall willow tree. But now she felt anything but graceful. Where both of her dear friends were slim, she was solid. Her shoulders and hips now felt too broad, her breasts even fuller than before the pregnancy.

Together they turned the corner and the fog was left behind. Bonnie was determined to leave her gloomy thoughts as well. Lynne was teasing the giggling Claire and Bonnie leaned over to see what new bonnet or gown had excited her friend. She tried not to feel jealous of Claire, the way she spent every dime she earned on something new each payday. Claire had no large family like Lynne and she had, people hungry for every penny they could earn. The Wimberleys had only the golden haired Claire and spoiled her rotten.

Friends since their first day in school. Lynne had been the scholar, Claire the class pet, and Bonnie their brave defender. Lynne loved to learn. Claire enjoyed the extra attention and the excuse to dress up. Bonnie loved the chance to escape the crowded slum apartment, whether she learned or not.

When Lynne's father died, along with three other McKinneys during the terrible Cholera epidemic of 1873, Lynne had to leave school and find work. Bonnie had been thrilled to leave the slate and chalk behind and work in the factory. Claire had no need to work, but didn't want her friends to move on without her. They had remained inseparable, at least until Tarn last year.

For just a minute she couldn't see the magazine ad, instead she saw Blanche Sawyer's smug face. All week she had been aware of people gossiping around her, hushing when she walked by. Today Blanche had waylaid her near the privies to tell her in person.

"What do you think, Bonnie?" Claire asked.

Bonnie shook away that image and stared at the unmentionable item before grinning. "I wish there were a corset strong enough to make this flat." She curved a hand beneath her rounded belly and Claire laughed. Lynne placed her hand on the curve and smiled when the little one inside moved.

"Two months to go, then you'll be a mother." Lynne whispered the words as though it were a holy miracle. Bonnie felt a chill of fear creep down her back instead of the joy the thought usually brought.

When the three girls passed the pub, the idle men outside whistled and called to them. Lynne straightened and tucked Claire's arm in hers and reached for her, but Bonnie hung back. "You two go on, I've got to wait for Tarn."

Lynne cast a last pitying look her way and Bonnie bowed her head. Did they know too? Had they heard the gossip? Her cheeks flooded with color but she raised her head, holding her chin proudly. It wasn't true, Tarn loved only her.

It couldn't be true. Didn't she work hard at the mill, standing over the hot vats of starch to dip the finished garments, then working the big presses to flatten the newly sewn seams? Hour after hour, shaping and pulling hot cloth through the press until the garments were crisp and perfectly formed. Sixty hours a week on her swollen feet, her stomach churning from the smell of the starch.

Anxiously she looked for the tall handsome man in the crowd. The man who was her husband, the father of her unborn child. The man she loved. True times were hard. It was difficult for a man to earn a living wage and that was why she still had to go to the factory six days a week. It was why they were living with her parents, sleeping on the closed in porch, a place Tarn had finished just for the two of them.

She loved him. Tarn who was so tall he made her feel small. The handsomest man in Boston with his dark wavy hair, thick chest, deep dimpled cheeks. She loved how his sooty black lashes framed his flashing blue eyes when he whispered love words to her. Each time he swept her into his arms, she felt her heart race, her bones melt. Where was he today? Had he gotten a good job finally?

Bonnie was tired of waiting, her feet and hands numb with cold. Most of the men who had gathered to wait for wives or sweethearts had already linked arms with them and headed home to a warm fire or to the pub for a full glass.

Well enough, if he didn't care to meet her, she would take the money home to her mother. Or maybe she would buy some ribbons to trim the flour sack gowns she had cut out ready to sew for the little one. As Lynne had said, she would be a mother soon.

Still she waited.

In the fading light she thought she heard a woman laugh. For just a moment she thought the voice sounded like Blanche. Bitterly she turned to walk home through the shadows, stopping to pick up a discarded two by four. She needed it to ward off anything evil lurking in the dark. As she walked, she thumped the board against her hand and imagined it was Blanche's face.

The flat was full with Magees wedged from front door to back, the noise deafening. The press of all the bodies raised the temperature of the small space more than the small fire in the standing heater. Her mother was busy ladling thin stew into cups and bowls and Bonnie stood over her and held out the last big cup for her share. Her mother held the ladle over the chipped brim. "Tain't enough left for that black Irish husband of yours if'n I fill it."

"Good." Bonnie shrugged out of her damp cloak, dropped the small sack with ribbons and a penny worth of candy on the table. Quickly her sisters moved back to leave her a box to sit down to the make-shift table with them. She bowed her head, said a silent prayer, and then raised her eyes to stare at her family.

Proudly Bonnie held out two coins to her mother. She had decided after stopping at Sanders to give her parents the larger part of this week's pay. Mum dropped the coins in her pocket. When Da stood and held out his hand, Bonnie was pleased to see her mother hand him a quarter. He shook his fist at her but her mum clutched the pocket tight.

"There's enough for a dram. Let me keep the other to get food and coal for you and all your babbys."

Da seemed to shrink as the children looked up at him to beg. Bonnie held her breath as he kept his fist clinched over her Mum.

When she didn't flinch, he swore and grabbed his ragged coat to disappear into the cold.

Bonnie exchanged a stolen glance of shared triumph with her mother. Later, after the candles were snuffed, she would give her mother another quarter so she could hide the two bigger coins. That way if Da tried to take it away later, her mum could surrender another quarter. At least what she gave her mother wouldn't go down Tarn Micheal's throat tonight.

The little ones were settled. Ranging in age from Bonnie at seventeen down to Clyde at three, there was a child for every two years of her parent's marriage. Until last spring when the boy had been born dead. This loss had put a pall on her parent's relationship. Maybe it was because Mum was relieved and Da sad, but all the teasing and loving seemed missing. Da wasn't the best provider, yet Mum had always seemed happier whenever he was around. Part of the reason Bonnie had succumbed to Tarn's charms was because she wanted that same happiness. Instead of humming hymns and smiling, her mother seemed lost in gloom and despair and her father fled to the pub with every penny he earned.

Normally after eating Bonnie would rush, merely helping move the make shift furniture to the walls and hang blankets before disappearing to her own teasing husband and their small room. Tonight she took her time, talking with each of her brothers. Ian and Shawn were proud, they had each earned a little money carrying lumber for builders for a new tenement on Adams Street. Closest to her in age, Ian was nearly as tall as Bonnie. The boys needed no help to unroll their mattress and settle down to play with baby Clyde.

When she reached the girl's side of the room, they were glad for her help. Brigid, Darcey, Meara, and Reagan were stair-steps in height with only Brigid much over five feet. Brigid at eleven was the next oldest girl. Bonnie hugged her when Brigid told her she was thinking of taking a job at the chocolate factory. Hadn't she been just as frightened and excited about going to work at the Mill? But her younger sister's happy giggles and chatter annoyed her instead of making Bonnie want to join in.

Until a year ago she would have settled down with whispered secrets and giggles in this small area, separated from their brothers and their parent's corners near the door by the hanging blankets, and felt as though she were where she belonged. All shoes stacked on the crates or chairs beneath the bent nails on the wall where their clean clothes and coats hung. Everyone crawled under thin blankets and cuddled to keep warm. In winter, still wearing all their clothes. Some nights they needed to spread all the other clothes and coats on top. Tonight, she bent and kissed each cheek, then slipped away.

After silently pressing another quarter into her mother's hand and accepting a soft caress to her cheek, Bonnie fled. She forced the sticking door open to the enclosed porch and quickly forced it closed behind her. The cold emptiness of the room made her shiver. She unfastened her shoes and hurried barefooted over the quilt covered mattress to put them on the shelf Tarn had built on the house wall to hold them. The space was long and narrow, ten feet by five. She remembered how the landlord had complained when he saw Tarn had sealed the porch completely with unpainted boards.

Tarn had just stood there glaring at him until the fat man ran out of breath. Her husband had conceded to paint the outside so it wasn't as noticeable, but only if the man provided the paint. Later when the season changed, they had made flour paste and used it to glue layers of newspapers on the inside of the boards. When they had four layers, some places more, the cold air stopped seeping through the gaps. Bonnie had wanted to paint it too, but Tarn argued he liked to have something to read before falling asleep. Had they really laughed about the joke? Later she realized the papers had been stolen since the events and news were the same from one wall to the next. Had the lumber been stolen as well?

The landlord had been right. There were three other enclosed porches on their block now, living space stolen and inviting open porches lost. Bonnie had been thrilled that Tarn was so clever, that they had a place to live for free but still had some privacy. But tonight he wasn't inside here, waiting for her, kissing her and more, wheedling until she turned her earnings over to him. Bonnie relaxed onto the thin mattress, wrapped herself tightly into the quilt. She inhaled the familiar scents of Tarn and the musky reminder of last night. Tonight there would be no escape into bliss at his love-making, no matter how rough and hasty. Tonight she was alone.

Bonnie covered her mouth, let the tears leak onto her pillow.

CHAPTER TWO

Bonnie walked home from late mass with her mother and the other children. Only her father had stayed home, complaining of his head and the bad weather. Bonnie sniffed. After the beautiful cathedral it was hard to return to the cold narrow streets of the slums. The choir had sung hymns to lift the soul. Even though they were above the pews at the rear of the church, Bonnie knew by listening that Lynne's clear sweet voice was absent. She had also missed the Wimberleys and her friend Claire. Knowing the family, she figured they had attended early mass.

Tarn's not coming home had been too much for her to bear last night. Even after praying about it in church she still wavered between jealous rage and confused worry. When they first wed he stayed out drinking late and went home with friends or even back to his parents sometimes. That had only happened once since he built their little room, their love nest. Maybe he had been in a fight and was hurt somewhere. Then she would remember Blanche's smirking face, hear her boasts, and twist in misery.

The day was gray, as sullen looking as she felt after the sleepless night. All she knew was she needed to talk to someone about her fears and doubts. She didn't dare talk to her parents. She didn't want to hear her father remind her Tarn was the husband she chose, her mother talk about a wifes duty to suffer and toil. Although she wasn't sure what to say, or how to begin, she needed Lynne's wisdom, Claire's happy encouragement to not worry.

What if he was mad at her for something else? He had complained the other night when she wanted to stay up a little later and cut out gowns with her mother's help. But hadn't they made up that quarrel in bed? She had tried to lure him back into a jolly mood which always led to one thing. Maybe it was because she had asked him to go slow, to be gentler with her now that the baby was growing larger inside her.

During her sleepless night that had loomed as the biggest reason. He had accused her of not ever wanting to make love. She hadn't answered him then, couldn't come up with an honest answer now.

Was that what led him to such a tramp as Blanche Sawyer? But was Blanche a tramp? Hadn't Bonnie committed the first sin by going out with Tarn Micheals? Wasn't it her fault about what happened?

She knew he had flirted with Lynne first, then Claire. Lynne ignored and insulted him. Claire giggled at everything he said and that annoyed him. Then he settled his attention on Bonnie. Tall and shy, she had never had a boy notice her before. Tarn wasn't a boy, he was the handsomest man in the world. She loved looking at him, hearing the lilting timbre of his voice, but could never find her voice to speak. Decided, he pursued her.

Bonnie had felt excited to see him there every day after work. When he told her he was waiting for her to cross the factory bridge, to run up the path toward him she blushed. Then he said he couldn't be happy until he saw her lovely face. She had lost her breath and heart. He was there the next day and the next. He would bow to her, offer her wild flowers or penny candy. She had wanted to have him hold her hand, to kiss her, to whisper words about how pretty and sweet she was. She wanted someone to love her the way her father loved her mother.

She had been besotted with him, talked about nothing but Tarn Micheals to her friends, to anyone who would listen. As he told her later, after he had pushed her to the grass and torn her clothes to get at her, what was a man to think if a girl willingly asked him to walk beside the river and then let him kiss her the way she had?

Almost home that day, she realized she had also lost her purse. Terrified, she didn't dare go back to look for it. She called herself a fool and ran home to her parents, at least having enough sense to dry her eyes and wipe her nose before going inside. She had told no one. Not her parents, her sisters or brothers, or her best friends. He wasn't at the bridge the next day. She had seen him standing, laughing with the other men and was afraid to so much as look his way after that.

Later, when her mother complained about missing her own monthly and swore and cried because she was pregnant again, Bonnie had started to shake. No, she told herself before turning to comfort her mother. Just one time, one mistake. That couldn't happen as well.

But when the second month came with no curse she had pulled her mother aside and told her, told her everything. Her father and oldest brothers had found Tarn Micheals outside a bar. He had laughed at them, told them they were crazy. The next day he had waited for Bonnie to get paid and then come up to take her arm. Fear had washed through her. He insisted they go for a walk, that she let Lynne and Claire go on home. All she could remember was the pain and humiliation of their other walk. She had wanted to run home again. It had taken all her courage to tell her friends to go on without her.

This time there was no haste, no rush to reach the shadowed path beneath overhanging branches. He had taken her arm, hooked it gently in his and tugged her in the direction of the river. For a moment she forgot her terror as he talked to her sweetly, finally asking her to explain what she had told her parents.

Then he called them lies. Infuriated, Bonnie had pushed him and he almost slid off the path and into the river. Tarn had scrambled up to pull her into his arms and force her down against the bank. Exposed where others walking nearby could see them, terrified, Bonnie slapped at his ears.

"I'm in the family way. I've been with one man, one time, and that man is you. Now if you've no shame and want your baby to be born a bastard, I've nothing else to say."

At his shock she shoved hard to break free. She heard a splash and his oaths as she hurried down the path toward home. Laughing he had caught up with her, swung her into the air, getting her all wet before kissing her. "No, my brawny cailin, I'll not be having your arguments, nor hearing your nays. Besides your father has promised to fetch the magistrate if we don't wed."

It wasn't what she wanted to hear, but she had been too overcome by emotion when he lifted her off the ground so easily, when he pressed her so close, to push him away again. Whatever he felt for her, it would never be as much as she felt for him. She knew it even then. Quickly she answered yes and held her breath as she kissed the wet giant.

It was only natural that they found the shadowy path again and made love. At least this time it wasn't as painful. It had seemed okay too to join him in the pub for a pint to celebrate their engagement. When he invited friends over to share a drink and meet his bride to be she had blushed at the attention. Later he borrowed her money to pay for the drinks, reminding her that when they wed they would share everything. For a moment she wondered, but what choice was there?

They exchanged vows before the priest with their happy families and her best friends as bride maids. Five months later, surely it wasn't all over between them.

◇◇◇

Ian and Shawn left them at the corner, running to where other boys were already playing stick ball in the street. Brigid took the toddler into her arms and the other three girls danced a circle around them, making the boy laugh at the game of peek-a-boo. Lost in her thoughts, Bonnie ignored the drone of her mother's voice beside her. Mum was still talking about what they would have for dinner as they turned the corner toward the blank front of their tenement.

Unlike the ones they passed walking home, there were no faces peering at them from a narrow porch. Instead, there were two men leaning against the outer wall, passing a bottle between them.

Her heart hammered against her ribs, as Bonnie relived all the emotions she had felt last night. Hurt, fear, rage, betrayal. This morning when she put on her clean dress, she felt despair. All Tarn's clothes were missing. It had made her weep again. Why, why would he be here now if it wasn't to gather his belongings?

Tarn smiled at her and Bonnie leaned down to whisper to her mother. "You didn't leave the money at home?"

Her mother hissed and shook her head as she grabbed her daughter's arm. "Stay here."

"There she be. Don't doddle daughter, your husband has been waiting for you," Da called.

Tarn grinned and held his arms open. Bonnie looked about the nearly empty street and raised her head. Shaking free of her mother she strode forward.

"I was afraid you were hurt somewhere when you didn't come home. Then this morning, I thought I was rid of you when I saw your belongings were gone. Have you no shame, carrying on openly with Blanche Sawyer, wallowing in her bed all night? How dare you show up here now?"

The blow surprised her. He cuffed her so hard she staggered from it and sat down on the damp street. Her mother screamed and rushed forward but her father pulled her away. "Nay, don't interfere. They need to work it out."

"Work it out, you're going to let him beat her?"

For a moment her father looked confused and turned toward Tarn. "See hear, there's no need for that. You said you only wanted to talk to the girl."

"Aye, we're talking." He leaned down, grabbed her arm and jerked her to her feet. Fiercely he tugged her into his arms. "Bonnie, my sweet, isn't that what you wanted. Didn't you tell me to not be so demanding of you now the baby is growing bigger? You know the kind of man I am, the needs I have. What did you expect?"

Shocked, Bonnie shook her head, answered in a horrified whisper. "I never turned you away, only asked you to be gentler."

"Is this gentle enough for you wife?" He whispered fiercely in her ear, twisting one arm behind her as he forced her cloak open. His big hand moved over her and she realized what he was searching for as he patted down one pocket then the other. His grin was malicious at her gasp of pain.

Despite her efforts, Bonnie felt tears filling her eyes. He tugged, and she heard the pocket rip as he nabbed the half-empty purse. Before she could react he shoved her back into the arms of her parents, pausing just long enough to take the half empty bottle from her father.

"I'll see you next week, wife," he hissed at her.

When her startled parents barely caught her, Bonnie hiccupped in fear. As he disappeared around the corner, she was hurt again to hear her sisters calling hellos to the handsome man. Then she heard the boys shout his name. Had they heard the fight and chosen Tarn's side? Or did they still think the handsome devil with his Irish tunes and funny jokes was part of their family? Before the tears could fall, she rushed into the house.

She held onto the door, swayed inside. Behind her she heard her parents arguing. "Stay out of it wife. A man has rights and Bonnie needs to learn what happens when she denies them. She's lucky they were living here, or she'd be out in the street and you know it."

"He's an adulterer, you heard him admit it."

"Aye, a sin. But one the church pardons and a woman who wants to keep a man will learn to forgive as well. If Bonnie wants to be stubborn and proud, she'll lose her husband, that's what. You should have raised the girl to know her duty, not yell when the man returns to beg forgiveness. Mind you, she'll lose him and none will blame him for leaving."

CHAPTER THREE

Bonnie tore through the house and into the cold little room, slamming the door. Furious, she paced from one end to the other, ignoring the muddy tracks she was leaving on the quilt. She raised a hand to her face, turned to stare into the small metal mirror nailed to the wall. Da had taken Tarn's side, would have understood if he'd cast her into the streets. She shook with white hot anger. And Mum, she had argued with him, but only for a minute. Had she agreed that Tarn was in his rights to beat her?

There was a red mark and her eye throbbed where he had struck her. She felt the baby inside squirm and kick and slowly she stood cradling her belly, drawing in ragged breath after breath until her temper cooled. Calmer, she gasped at the marks on the quilt and sank down to unbutton her shoes. As she set them aside she brushed at the scuffs but the wet clay clung to the old quilt. Bonnie gulped air to fight the tears. She opened her cloak, moved it to cover her lap and brushed at the old plaid wool but it too was stained from the street. As she moved it, she gasped at the ripped skirt.

The thief. First he stole her heart, then her virginity, and now her money. Was she to sacrifice her dignity and sanity to the brute as well? He had not come to beg forgiveness as Da said. He had come to take her pay. She had two dresses, and he had ruined the good one.

Swallowing hot tears instead of shedding them, she found the little gown she'd sewn, then used the threaded needle to try to mend the thin brown wool of the dress her mother had loaned her. Even with the hem let down all the way, the skirt barely reached her shoe tops. She hated the baggy top, the dingy brown material, but it wasn't as tight in the bodice and had room for her and the baby to breathe in the skirt.

She needed it for work next week. She brushed at her eyes, winced as she touched the bruised one. He had hit her. Angrily she jabbed the needle through the worn cloth, lifted her finger to suck the drop of blood away. He had handled her roughly before, if she were honest, had raped her. The first time on the path and then later, when she had objected to his being drunk, he had taken her with force. But he had never struck her before.

Cautiously she worked the needle slowly through the fabric, catching the pocket back in place and carefully moving it just enough to hide the mended rip. Finished, she stuck the needle back in the baby gown and moved enough to raise the quilt. Shivering, she covered up, then reached and moved the cloak over top of the quilt. She snuffled, but was surprised that she didn't want to cry. She had cried over Tarn too much.

Mum called her name and Bonnie lay still, not answering. As expected, her mother came to the room, opened the door without knocking. Bonnie held her breath, lay with the covers pulled up to hide her face. Through slitted eyes she studied the emotions sweeping over her mother's face, saw the pity there and felt her throat tighten again.

Then Mum ducked back, pulling the door closed. "Brigid, Darcey, I need you girls to help."

Exhausted, Bonnie finally slept.

◇◇◇

Lynne stood waving her handkerchief at her friends, stepping up on the boardwalk out of the worst of the downpour. Bonnie smiled grimly, holding her rain cloak over her head, hoping Lynne wouldn't see her face. She had heard her friend complain often enough that Tarn was a devil and if Bonnie ever did anything to make him angry, he would be the worse husband imaginable. She had also made Bonnie promise that if he ever laid a hand on her she would tell Tarn Micheals where to go.

It was Claire who stopped and called to Lynne. "Hurry up, it's cold but you won't melt in the rain."

Lynne leaned forward, holding her cape high to deflect the cold drizzle. "I'm not going to be there today. Tell the foreman my mother is sick with fever, and the children and I have been quarantined."

Claire's brow puckered and both women stared anxiously at their slender friend as others crowded past them down the muddy pathway. "Good grief, Lynne," Bonnie leaned forward to call, "It's not a good time to be missing work."

Lynne made a face. She might as well have said "I know, I know." Bonnie wasn't the only one to appreciate how tenuous their positions were, obviously would never go to work in her condition if the job wasn't at risk.

"Are you all right this morning? Has Tarn gotten out of line again?"

Bonnie stood still, glad the swelling on her cheek and eye had gone down a little. She knew the black eye made her eyes look as dark as her hair in the cold drizzle. Again, reminded her of the first time she and Tarn had quarreled. She had refused to give him her money. He didn't strike her, just knocked her to their mattress and held her while he forced himself on her. Afterward, he laughed while she cried, then methodically rummaged through her clothes until he found her small pay. She had complained bitterly to her friends.

Long after Tarn asked for forgiveness and their lives were back on track, her friends were still attacking him and reminding her he was a brute. "I sent him home to his mother. If he doesn't straighten up, I'm through with him."

She saw Lynne wince, read the disbelief in her eyes. Bonnie felt a sweep of shame flush across her face with the lie. She knew if she spoke, her pain and fear would fill her voice and she would be crying again. Bonnie didn't want to listen to her pity as Lynne asked her about the baby, about what caused the argument, whether he hit her before or after she told him to leave. "There's no time to talk. We can't be late, we'll get sacked."

Claire looked up the path at the backs of the retreating women, then whispered something to Bonnie. Lynne watched as Bonnie waddled cautiously forward after the departing group. "I've got to be going too, Lynne. Perhaps I can come by this evening with news," Claire called.

Lynne waved at her, "Go on, hurry, but don't bother about tonight. There's sickness in our building, you'd best stay away. I'll come back this afternoon to talk from here if I can."

Bonnie stood just outside the factory door and looked back to wave at Lynne as Claire hurried across the board. Together they entered the mill and their day.

Bonnie sneezed as she walked across the gray floor, the dust from all the fabric floating away with each step. "Bless you," someone called from the sewing machine nearby. Bonnie sneezed even louder and this time heard three blessings. She smiled even as she pushed the hamper of damp garments toward the big steam press. From the corner of her eye she saw a pair of women whispering as she unloaded the first garment.

Instead of bowing her head and looking embarrassed, she raised her face to stare at them until they looked away. The swollen eye, already changing from red to purple, had shamed her when she first arrived. It made her want to steal one of the stave bonnets they made to cover her head and shade her face but she knew it would just call more attention to her black eye. Now, she just stared people down.

Satisfied, she took the first shirt and quickly ironed it into stiff perfection. She passed it to a small girl beside her who quickly ran clean fingers across the hot cloth to shape and fold before securing it with four steel pins. A second later, Bonnie pressed the narrow pieces that formed the separate collar and cuffs and handed them over for the girl to position and pin into place. One done, forty seven to go.

The girl placed the stiff rectangle on the side board to wait for the boxing girl to come through. She would inspect each garment, box it with five others of the same size for shipment to department stores across the country. Bonnie saw the child point to her own eye while staring at her shiner.

"Ran into a door-knob."

The child nodded but from one of the machines Bonnie heard a woman laugh and yell to her neighbor. "I'd like to see a door that tall."

By the time the whistle blew for lunch, Bonnie felt as though her back would break and her stomach scream. She had spent the weekend shut away in the small bedroom, too busy sulking to come out to eat. Now she couldn't wait to open her lunch pail. Bless Mum, she had packed a large boiled potato and a hard-boiled egg. Had she gone upstairs to the Henneseys to borrow it or crept through the alley to steal it from the hens caged by Barnaby's tavern? Bonnie peeled the precious treat, grateful either way, then alternated tiny bites of egg with the cold potato.

Claire smiled when she joined her, carefully opening her pail.

"Sorry. I was too hungry to wait."

Claire smiled again as she set out a tiny salt shaker, bread, tomato, and a piece of roast beef between them on a checkered napkin. She bowed her head and Bonnie almost choked as she coughed guiltily, hastily crossing herself, food in each hand. Together the two girls prayed.

Claire generously held up the shaker and at Bonnie's nod, sprinkled both the egg and brown skinned potato. Bonnie took a bite of each and gave her friend a contented smile. As usual, there was no time for talk.

Bonnie finished first and walked over to drink deeply before filling Claire's collapsible cup at the fountain. When she straightened, Blanche Sawyer was standing in front of her, smirking. All Sunday afternoon, Bonnie had imagined this encounter and what she would do. None of the smart things she had rehearsed to say came to mind. Luckily for the straw haired girl, she didn't have her two-by-four with her.

Bonnie waited for the girl to say something mean or boastful. She had planned to call her harlot, slut, and worse. As the girl looked gloatingly at Bonnie's eye, hands on hips, a hush fell over the room as everyone leaned forward to listen.

Bonnie suddenly felt a strange feeling of peace come over her. In a calm, loud voice she spoke. "Aye, you've Tarn, but what've you got? An adulterer who'll beat you for your pay and leave you for a little trollop when you're carrying his babe. You're welcome to him. You deserve each other."

At the girl's astonished look, Bonnie elbowed past her. Grinning, she walked back toward her friend and the bench full of cheering women.

CHAPTER FOUR

At closing time, the foreman called the women to a meeting in the center of the floor. Claire was already pulling on her gloves and looking through her magazine's ads.

"Just keep you a minute. As you know, orders are down. Means more cuts." He waved his hand to hush the collective groans and complaints. "I'm looking at production, will announce seamstress cuts tomorrow. You little ones, pin girls. Today's your last. See me for your pay."

The other girl who starched and pressed, dared to ask about who would do the additional work. But Bonnie could have predicted his answer. "You can fold and pin, nothing stopping you."

She pushed past the others, eager to be clear of the stuffy floor and out into the fresher air. Claire caught at her arm. "Wait, don't you want to hear."

Bonnie didn't shake her arm free but did shrug. "Didn't make a difference when he let go the women dipping or managing the mangle to wring out the starch. He added that to our job as pressers, made no allowance for the added time it took. Just paid us the same and demanded more work. Quota numbers stayed the same so there's never any piece work bonus anymore. This will be the same. I've no choice, I'll be back as long as they'll have me. Especially now."

She let the hand reaching for the door slip to rest on her stomach. Claire stared at her friend, as though amazed at her calm. Bonnie smiled wryly to push down her other emotions.

◇◇◇

Outside, Bonnie let Claire cross then followed closely behind. She just needed to reach home, to crawl back into bed to rest a little before dinner. The last few days had been exhausting. Even though it went better than she had hoped, the confrontation with Blanche had left her drained. As though thinking of her caused it, the girl appeared out of the mist. Blanche and Tarn stood together on the other side of the stream.

Bonnie stopped in shock, then stared at the couple a little closer. For once she ignored the handsome physique, the dimpled cheeks. She saw instead his hard glare as Tarn stood over the shorter girl who was yelling up at him and crying. She watched the volatile exchange, watched the girl storm off. Then she realized Tarn was staring at her. The rest of the street seemed empty as his eyes locked with hers.

She was aware he was moving toward her and instead of running away she stepped forward at the same time. People were all making noise as they approached and suddenly Tarn extended a hand to grip her arm and jerk her closer. "What did you say to her, Bonnie?"

Bonnie tried to pull her arm free, realized the futility of it and looked into his face to yell. "Told her the truth -- that you're no prize."

He started swearing. This time when he swung his fist at her, she ducked and he connected with air. To make her point, she used her free arm to connect with his chin as he stared at her in disbelief. Claire screamed in the background.

"Wife beater, that's what she'll have, a lazy do-nothing boozer waiting to drink up her pay."

This time the swearing was vile. Bonnie's face flamed, and Tarn grinned in triumph. "Where's the rest of the money? I know you hid it from me."

Bonnie twisted, trying again to get away. "Nay, I gave you all that was left. I spent most of it on food for the children, things for our baby."

In disgust he shoved her away. Bonnie had to struggle to keep her feet but managed to save herself from a fall. As he turned the glare of his piercing blue eyes away she gave a shuddery sigh of relief. She turned to stare ahead at Claire, trying to hold back the cocky grin of her double victory today. Claire was raising her hands to clap. Bonnie watched the hands freeze in mid-air, saw the girl's smiling eyes fill with horror. Behind her she heard a woman's gloating laugh then she felt the slam of his fist against her shoulder.

The blow spun her around into the next fist which punched against her breastbone. Bonnie felt the air gush out of her chest, a fierce tight squeeze of pain and then she was falling.

No scream or sound would come out, there was just the sound of his fist slamming against her. She felt its sting along the top of her arm, bouncing off her neck. Even while falling she realized in horror that he was raising his thick boot and she curled to try to protect her stomach. The sickening thud of his heavy kick slammed into her belly and reverberated in her soul. As she heard Claire emit a high scream behind her, the light faded.

Blanche Sawyer was screaming hysterically as well and the men from the pub rushed forward to pull Tarn away from Bonnie. The shrill pipe of a watchmen sounded down the street. He was still kicking and swearing as one of the men flung him back against the boardwalk of the pub. "Aye stop man, you'll kill the babe and the woman. Stop."

Tarn rubbed a hand across his face, the rage still churning inside him. "The bitch got what she asked for, didn't she. Listen at 'em, all screaming like banshees."

Ignoring the men, he pushed, kicking a leg out between them.

Claire who had rushed to her friend's side, fell back a step, still screaming HELP, HELP, over Bonnie's slack body.

"Run you fool, or you'll hang. You kick her again, and we'll do for you," one of the men warned as he raised his fists.

Tarn backed away, his eyes wide in disbelief. These were his friends, men he bent an elbow with each evening in the pub. All were men of temper like himself. He knew each had mistreated at least one woman in his life.

Swearing he looked from them to the woman he'd spent the weekend with, happily bringing her squeals of delight. Now Blanche was summoning the law to stretch his neck with even louder screams. What had she told him just before Bonnie stepped across the bridge? They were through, she never wanted to see him again. It was all Bonnie's fault.

The men had now formed a half-circle between him and his wife. One man pulled out a black-jack, another drew a knife. When he heard a lawman yell, "Hey, you men, hold him." Tarn bolted.

Two men linked arms and Bonnie's bloodied body was lifted with care and cradled over their joined hands. Tearful but determined, Claire led the cavalcade toward Bonnie's home. Shawn, the third oldest Magee was playing knucklebones in the alley, calling numbers with his friends as they tossed the carved pair of pig bones against the house.

As soon as she spied him, Claire held a hand out to keep him back, "One of you boys, run get the doctor. Shawn, go tell your Mum and Da." Two of Bonnie's little sisters, Meara and Reagan, appeared at the door at the commotion and they both began crying. At their feet clung a sobbing toddler. She watched both girls bend to sweep him up between them.

"They just left for the store," the third boy whispered as Shawn stood silently with his hands over his mouth in horror.

Instantly Claire made up her mind and directed the men, "Turn here, we'll take her on to my house, mother's there. Shawn, Shawn," she shook the boy whose eyes were white with terror. "We'll take care of her, do you hear me, we're going to take care of her. Send your parents and the doctor there, to the Wimberley's," she shouted, "as quickly as they get home."

She slapped her gloved hand smartly against the back of the hand he held over his mouth. He blinked and dropped both hands. "Nod if you understand." Slowly he nodded and she gave a quick kiss to his reddened face. "Bring them."

Claire rushed after her friend, then her foot slid and she stopped in horror. There was a trail of red blood leading up to her front door. Fighting panic, she raced after them and around the men onto the porch screaming for her mother and the maid.

Her mother had been setting the table. The men stood with the bleeding girl on the porch as Mother Wimberley grabbed the silverware and shoved it back in the drawer as she ordered the maid to remove the rest. Running at Claire's desperate call she opened the door and directed the men to carry the girl into the dining room and carefully lay her on the still white covered table. Frantically the maid jerked the crocheted lace mantle away leaving the thick linen cloth for Claire to smooth.

Like the experienced field nurse she had been during the recent Civil War, her mother calmly set the other woman to boiling water and ordered Claire to run and grab the dishpan. The men she thanked and ordered to leave. When they hesitated she barked. "Out, let only the doctor through when he arrives. Go on, guard the door."

Already neighbors were drawn to the commotion and Mother Wimberley jerked the curtains closed in the dining room before turning back to the girl on her dinner table. Impatiently she grabbed a snowy napkin and dipped it into the boiling water the maid held as she looked to her frightened daughter. Wrapping an arm around the girl she whispered fiercely, "Can you hold the pan dear Claire?" At the firm embrace and calm of her mother, Claire stopped crying and nodded. At the girl's determined nod she turned to the maid. "Bess, help me get her ready."

"Blessedly, the child is unconscious," she reassured the others as she lifted the dirty skirt and removed Bonnie's underclothes. Claire moved forward, firmly holding the pan as directed. She shuddered as the tiny infant rushed into the world with only a single violent kick before floating dead in a sea of blood.

By the time Dr. Krantz arrived and scrubbed up most of the horror was over. The three women had cleared away the abomination of the dead baby to the kitchen, they had washed and inspected Bonnie's terribly bruised body, replacing the blood stained tablecloth with a clean one. Claire had brought her own feather pillow down to place under her friend's head, her mother's old flannel gown to clothe her. In the soft clean gown with its baby rosebuds, her friend's face alone shown with its new red marks among the fading bruises of her last assault. Claire leaned to kiss the ivory whiteness of her forehead, held her own breath as the old doctor prodded and probed, bringing passing grimaces of pain to the silent woman and the three who watched.

When he finished his inspection, Mother Wimberley directed the two men outside to admit the Magees. She expected just the parents, but all nine rushed in the door and hovered about the girl. Only Bonnie's Mum walked out to the kitchen to keen over the poor dead baby. The Magee men rushed out to find the magistrate and press charges. Bonnie's Mum pushed the bawling younger children home.

After the assortment of family were escorted out, the men on the porch were summoned to carry the tall woman upstairs to the spare room. The girl led them to her room instead. Claire rolled back the ruffled spread and top sheet and held aside the flowing canopy as the men gently placed the girl in the bed.

"Is she dead?" one asked.

"Of course not, the doctor thinks with care she will recover." At his next question about the baby, she shook her head. The men swore and she thanked them and rushed them out of the room. At last she had her friend to herself. Kneeling beside her, holding Bonnie's hand, she prayed the doctor was right about her recovery, wrong about her never having another child.

CHAPTER FIVE

It was a miserable week for all in the house. Bonnie remained unconscious until noon the next day. When awake, Bonnie cried noisily over the lost baby or moaned in pain. Her mother and sisters came each day to check on her. They were grateful to find her cossetted in Claire's room, but were unable to comfort the girl. Although Bonnie insisted she could walk and go home, no one would let her leave. Instead, the women forced her to take the laudanum as prescribed and only allowed her up to attend to her bodily needs.

No one mentioned Tarn, at least in the haunted-eyed girl's presence. Bonnie's father and brothers stayed away. Bonnie wondered if they were trying to shield her from their rages, or were afraid to see her battered state. Along with the healing bruise around her eye there were the enormous new ones on her chest, shoulder, neck and of course stomach. The doctor had pointed out to the girl that she was lucky. If her shoulder hadn't taken most of the blow, Tarn's fist would have broken her neck.

Bonnie heard the Wimberleys talking. All over town, there was talk of a lynching. But Tarn wasn't found.

Claire kept fluttering about. Through the haze of her pain and misery, Bonnie was aware of her friend's constant presence. Nothing provided her any solace or comfort except the mind-numbing drugs.

Dimly she heard the Wimberleys arguing. "The child just brought a message from your foreman. "If you're not back at work today, you needn't return, either of you." Bonnie tried to see them, wished they would both leave. Claire picked up her hand and Bonnie pulled it away to curl into a ball.

Claire's mother's voice was insistent. "Claire, you have to return to work. Only time will help Bonnie. You're sitting in here, looking as wounded as our patient. It does neither of you any good."

As the two women bustled out of the room, Bonnie sighed and surrendered to the comforting dark shadows.

Friday morning when Claire saw the figure waiting, she ran the remaining steps happier than all week.

"Oh, Lynne, it's terrible news, all of it." She raised a green gloved hand to brush at her eyes. "I've wished and wished you were here to tell me what to do and to make sense of it all. It's as though our whole world has turned upside down and everyone has spilled down helter-skelter."

"Well, it is bad at home too, but at least mother is better. I've been doing the laundry this week and it's made me appreciate how hard she works for us. But now I'm afraid the children are falling ill." Lynne saw the little blonde's lips tremble and knew if she didn't make a joke or say something quickly, Claire would be bawling. Then she would never learn what all the terrible changes were.

"Nonsense. It can't be all that bad. Why just this morning I was sprinkled with fairy dust so I get to wish any real trouble away. Just tell me slowly, one thing at a time. First, where is Bonnie?"

In their circle of light she watched her friends face flicker through several transformations, the somber look, a twinkling smile, and then the pouty lips again. "Well, you remember she left Tarn Sunday night."

"Yes, she told us Monday. I was worried because she had a bruise."

"A royal shiner. It's iridescent green now, or at least it would be if you could see it for all the others."

"Others?"

"Oh, it was a terrible fight. All because she learned he was tom-catting on her, and her so big with his child."

Lynne nodded encouragement, but stood back toward the edge of the light, making sure even the cloud of her breath wouldn't land on her friend.

"She was so magnificent on the factory floor. You should have seen and heard her. Lynne, you would have been so proud." There was such a sad, wishful sound to her voice that her friend gasped and leaned forward to hear every word.

"The foreman kept us late, you know more tales about cut-backs." At the alarm in her friend's eyes, Claire picked up her courage and cleared her throat. "Well, Tarn was waiting for us when we finished work Monday. Blanche was yelling at him. We learned later that she told him to get lost. His friends were hooting and jeering and he saw Bonnie. She was like some warrior woman as she ran across the bridge to face him."

Claire covered her face, then Lynne insisted quietly. "Go on, tell it all."

"She turned back and grinned at me because he had turned away. Then he hit her and she spun around. He grabbed Bonnie and she struck out at him. He was mad about Blanche and about the money. When she kicked out at him he grabbed her by the hair, than knocked her down in the muddy street. I was so angry. I called him such names as my mother would whip me for … for so much as thinking. All that hateful lot that stand around the pub just laughed and egged him on. We were screaming so loud for help, but no one would come."

Lynne clenched her fists. "If only I'd been there, I would have taken a board to the thick-headed devil, not hollered for help."

"With that brute, you never could have hit him hard enough. Even his friends had trouble pulling him away."

Tensely Lynne watched as Claire finished her animated tale. "But just when I thought I might faint from terror, Bonnie kind of wilted like a little flower curling up around to protect her baby ... but oh Lynne ... he kicked her. Kicked her and called her the most awful names."

Tears stood in Claire's eyes now, making them opaque like blue marbles in the morning light. Lynne noticed that some of the women were stopping and listening, then walking around the two girls shaking their heads. The street worker cleared his throat before extending his iron pole up to snuff their light. Somehow, the light seemed unchanged. "Poor Bonnie, poor kind, quiet girl. A sin that she had to love such a worthless terror as Tarn Micheals." Lynne said, her voice harsh with her heavy breathing. "Is she all right?"

Claire sniffed delicately into one of her embroidered handkerchiefs. "Well, even the worthless men wouldn't stand for that and pulled him off. They were going to hold him for the police, but he broke free and ran away. Lynne... our poor Bonnie ... there was a trail of blood in the snow when two men helped carry her home. Her parents weren't home and there was no time. I had them take her to my house. My mother is the soul of charity."

Lynne tried to interrupt, then gasped.

"We'd sent for the doctor, but the baby died."

They stood in silence as both thought of all the times Bonnie had talked about her future and her precious baby. Lynne interrupted the sad thoughts.

"A blessing that. If he were like his father, he would have broken her heart. Now she can heal and get over him. Ooh, if I were just a man, I would kill that worthless devil," Lynne whispered.

"That's what Bonnie's da wanted. Called Tarn a devil and worse. He went after the magistrate and tried to file a warrant for murder against the black Irishman for the death of his own unborn child and attempted murder of his wife. They told him there was no law to protect children until they were born. If he'd been trying to kill the girl, than she would be dead. They agreed they could probably charge him with disorderly conduct, for beating Bonnie in the streets."

"I guess it would be all right if he had beat her at home like before. The law is always for men, it never protects women," Lynne added.

"That's what her mum said." They shared a brief grimace, then Claire continued. "When the law went to question him, he had fled. His friends said he had been talking about going west. Everyone figures he did."

"And Bonnie?"

Claire shook her head and the hood fell back enough to reveal her bouncy curls. "Well, you know our Bonnie. For months now she has known her marriage was a mistake, but she couldn't stop loving that big hulking Irishman. She was hurt and ashamed, of everything being so public, and she's cried and cried for the lost baby."

Claire finally paused for a breath. "But this morning she stopped crying and seemed her old self. She hasn't said anything, but it's clear she's accepted all that has happened, probably sees that it's for the best. When I went to check on her she was sitting up for breakfast and ready to go back to work. Mother and I were able to persuade her to rest until next week. The poor darling, I haven't had the heart to tell her about the job."

Lynne looked sad. "I wish I could rush over to the Magee's to hold her. But would that be a kindness, to give her the fever, and perhaps her brothers and sisters as well. It sounds like you've been the good friend she's needed."

"I've tried, but she is so sad." Claire stared at Lynne, wished they could hug each other. "No, she's not at the Magee's. Mother wouldn't let her leave, she's been at our house ever since it happened."

"I'll pray for her, send her my love and explain about the fever keeping me from her in a note as soon as I get home." For a minute, Lynne wished she didn't have to ask, but somehow she had to find the rent money. "Wish I could send something to help her out, but things are pretty shaky at home."

"Don't worry. I used last week's earnings for the doctor. Who needs a silly corset anyway? And I plan to send my purse over to Bonnie's clan after I collect today. You know I would only buy a new bonnet or something foolish anyway."

Lynne bit her lip, disappointed by the news. "At least both you girls are safe for the moment. What did you mean that you couldn't bear to tell her about work?"

The trail of workers had thinned and Claire looked around in the gray light. "Goodness, look at the time, walk with me dear Lynne."

Lynne followed, still keeping her distance as the girl fled light footed down the snowy path. Together they melted into the gray fog that always surrounded the mill stream, cautiously staring down at their boots as they hurried forward. On her side of the bridge, Lynne heard rather than saw Claire stop just outside the factory doors.

"It's the mill. The foreman laid off Bonnie. Oh, and Lynne, you too. But don't get angry. It's nothing personal. He laid off everyone on the sewing room floor. The rumors we've been hearing about the mill are true. They have decided to close it. Seems they've built newer ones down south. Land is so cheap there after the war. We heard they don't have to pay hardly anything, a penny on the dime for what they pay us. Everyone is frantic. Several people are talking about going west together. Even Mother and Father."

She held the door open so that the harsh light from kerosene lanterns inside set her small figure in dark relief. "I guess we three won't be factory girls anymore, but we'll always be friends. Come at the end of the day if you can, to walk me home. There's so much to talk about. I found another dream man in the advertisements. One for each of us."

CHAPTER SIX

Bonnie lay in the soft bed, the feathers cushioning her aching head and body. Claire was such a goose. In her lucid moments, Bonnie offered to go home and give her back the bed but the girl would hear none of it. Instead she brought broth and cool water and sat to talk until Bonnie drifted back into the dark dream world of muffled pain.

Nearly a week, and she had no more strength than a kitten. At times she would hear Mum and her sisters clattering up the stairs to Claire's bedroom. They would stand timidly in a circle around the bed and Bonnie would struggle to open her eyes and talk. Once she asked if Tarn knew about the baby and Mum had turned the air blue with her oaths. The bigger girls had covered the little ones ears, as though they had never heard a swear word before. They heard plenty from their Da and some from Tarn, but even she had not heard so many from Mum before.

At times after they gave her the bitter red medicine, she would see Tarn as before, striding along like a handsome hero. Then he would turn into a terrifying villain and she would twist and gasp in pain to avoid his blows. Worse was the half-awake time when the drugs wore off and no one came to the room. She would test her legs, double up in pain, then walk wearily down to the indoor bathroom. These were the worst times for she feared Tarn might be lurking about the house, waiting for an opportunity to break in and find her. She could still see his face, hear his words. He had wanted to kill her and she had no doubt if he found her, he would do it.

The times of total awareness were the worst. There was the full force of the pain, the crippling ache as she stood and walked. Once she had dared to raise the gown and look at her stomach in Claire's full-length mirror. It was tender to the touch and horribly bruised but then she turned sideways and saw its flatness. The pain now was in her heart, as though someone were squeezing the life blood from it. She had broken then, sobbing as she struggled over to the bed. Mother Wimberley and the cook had come, trying to comfort her. She had been unable to stop crying. Claire's mother had given her another dose of the laudanum and she finally blacked out.

In the evenings, Claire would sit beside the bed and talk about the happenings at the mill that day. Even in the twilight dream world Bonnie understood that the mill was changing. Every day more and more workers were let go.

On Friday morning, Bonnie pushed aside the medicine. When Claire brought her breakfast, Bonnie refused to stay in bed but insisted on dressing. Claire gave up arguing since she was hurrying to get ready for work. Downstairs, she asked her mother to take charge and rushed off with a quick kiss on her cheek.

Determinedly Bonnie rose and dressed. She needed to go to work, the job was at risk she knew. Maybe if she showed up, she could save it. Mother Wimberley walked into the room just as Bonnie started to slip her bare feet into her shoes.

"Where do you think you're going?" Mother Wimberley asked.

Bonnie weaved a little as she stood. "Work."

Mother Wimberley walked forward and backed the girl toward the bed where she sat down abruptly. "You're too late to go, the mill whistle blew twenty minutes ago. Besides the doctor wants you to wait and rest this week. Time enough to start back on Monday."

Bonnie looked around in confusion, stared up at Mother Wimberley. "I can't take Claire's bed any more. Let me help get it cleaned and I'll leave."

"Leave, nonsense. If it will make you feel better, I will let you trade rooms. It will be easier if Claire is back in here with all her things." Again, Bonnie weaved a little as she stood. "I need to help you clean."

Mother Wimberley and Bess, the maid argued, but finally agreed to let her trade rooms with Claire. They refused to let Bonnie help with the work. With the maid's assistance, Bonnie descended the stairs barefoot with her few possessions in a tote and took a seat at the big dining room table. Weary from just those few steps, she agreed to rest a minute and take a cup of tea.

While the two women worked upstairs, Bonnie brushed and neatened her own hair, made sure her dress was fully buttoned, and worried her feet into her shoes. Exhausted from the effort, her hands trembled as she cradled the warm teacup and sipped at the tea.

Mother Wimberley smiled at her as she passed through the dining room with dirty linen, the maid at her heels. A minute later she settled at the table and poured herself a cup of tea and added more to Bonnie's cup.

"You look lovely dear. Really though, you should be in bed."

Bonnie shook her head, "No, I'm sick of being a burden. I need to go home now. I should have been back at work, but Claire told me I must wait until Monday, Doctor's orders."

"She is right, quite right. Dr. Krantz said you needed bed rest and he left medicine to help you sleep so you can heal."

"That old quack. He took all Claire's money, but you said the baby had already been born dead before he arrived. I heard you both talking."

Mother Wimberley stared at her, her brow puckered as she tried to remember when they had had the conversation. "I thought you were asleep."

Bonnie shook her head again, pressed her fingers to her forehead to make the woman in front of her stop reeling. "Drugged. I'll not take it anymore. I don't intend to be a shadow woman or one of the doxies at the tavern. Don't give it to me again, no matter if I plead for it. Promise me."

Mother Wimberley stared at the pale girl, whose whole body trembled with determination. She held out her hand and took the shaking one. "I promise, no more. But you must rest. If not Claire's room, the spare room."

Bonnie shook her head. "No, no more bed," then her voice faded. "I canna manage the stairs anyway."

"Fine, then come into the parlor. You can sit up on the fainting couch and just rest until Bess and I finish the upstairs room. Then we'll help you back up to bed."

"I don't want to be drugged again."

"No, I promise. It will be hard for you, but we can all help. You're quite right. I've seen the women you've talked about. I don't think you've had enough of the drug to do you harm, but we'll manage from now on without it. But you did need it, you've been through a lot, more than you realize."

Mother Wimberley rose, pulled her arm to get Bonnie to stand, then let the tall girl lean against her. When she herself swayed, Bonnie stiffened. With her lip caught between her teeth, she let her host lead her into the unused parlor. Exhausted, she sagged back against the high head of the couch, draped her arm against the sofa back.

Smiling, Mother Wimberley raised her feet, noticed the unlaced shoes on the stockingless feet and gently removed them. She spread a lacy shawl over the sleeping girl and rushed to help Bess so they would have time to finish both rooms before starting supper.

On the way home Claire felt the weight of her final payment and the knowledge that there would be no further ones in the near future. Hadn't she told Lynne she was going to give the money to the Magees. It seemed the right thing to do, but she wasn't sure whether to hand it to Bonnie first or to her parents. Her father might take the money. According to Bonnie he would drink it all up given the chance. Yet if she waited and offered it to Bonnie, the proud girl might feel ashamed and refuse. What if the money came between the way they felt for each other?

To delay, she walked across to the Back Bay streets and walked in and out of the small boutiques on Newberry. At the third shop, Lambtons, she was captured by a lovely mint-green day dress that was still on the wire frame of a headless mannequin. The silhouette was so different than the dresses her mother wore, instead of a full bell shaped skirt, the dress was narrow in the front, at the waist and sides.

Claire was surprised to see a very sour-looking woman step forward and a much taller man join her. Fascinated she watched the pair argue and struggle to control the mannequin. When the woman turned the figure to the side, Claire clapped her hands in surprise and the woman gave her husband a smug shake of her head. The man looked flustered and blushed as the woman fluffed the full folds of the garment caught at the rear of the dress.

It was a bustle. Claire had read about the new fashion but this was the first time she had seen it in a garment. The money she had worked so hard for this week pressed within her pocket. No one would fault her if she kept what she had earned. She knew the fabric and color would suit her complexion and hair to perfection. Somehow she had to have this dress.

Claire knocked and was greeted by the two older of Bonnie's sisters, Brigid and Darcey. Bonnie had told her during one of their talks about Brigid's eagerness to go to work already. The girl would not wait as they had to earn her graduation certificate. In their plain little frocks the sisters all looked alike to her unless they were lined up like stair steps. Like Bonnie, their hair usually looked dark brown, but in the sunlight red highlights would make it glow like chestnuts. Brunette, the fashion magazines called it. Unfortunately the younger Magees didn't work to keep it clean or combed like Bonnie did her own.

Claire smiled, raising her scented handkerchief to her nose from habit. It hid the smell of mutton stew and cabbage. The large room had been well swept and there were no animals crowding about as she had seen in many of these small places. But then, where would they sit. There seemed to be a box, broken stool or rickety chair at every turn as the girls happily arranged them around the big boards they used for a table. Bonnie's Mum rushed forward to take Claire's gloved hand in her own. "Come in, come in and sit. Stew's not ready, but you're welcome to stay and wait."

Claire smiled and took the offered seat, not even examining too closely before settling. She held on to the woman's hand, noticing how flustered she looked, probably at having nothing to offer to drink or eat.

"Did you see Bonnie today? How is she doing?" Bonnie's mother didn't have a chance to answer as Claire continued to babble. "This morning I had all I could do to keep her from coming back to work with me. She is doing so much better."

"Aye, she was up, wanting to help your mother scrub your room and iron the sheets. She said she was ready to come back home, but she's not you know. The boyos have taken the porch bedroom but there's room enough for her back with my girls. I'm afeard it hurts her heart a little, you know, to be here so soon."

"I feel the same. Mother and I want her to stay with us. Lord knows there is plenty of room in that big house. I've been in the sewing room and Mother and I have it cleaned and fixed up a treat. We want Bonnie to stay there if you can spare her."

"Aye, it would be for the best, I'm thinking. Her Da and brothers are some hurt for not protecting her, you see. It makes a strain at the table."

"Where is Mr. Magee, Ian and Shawn?"

The woman laughed and Claire saw a brown tooth and wondered if it hurt. "Working, can you believe, all working."

Claire laughed as well. "That's wonderful, they all found jobs."

"Aye, the men are working toting wood and such where they're raising new tenements. They be finally replacing the burnt ones for the fired area nearer town."

Claire tried to remember what she had read about the Boston fire. Not as big or bad as the Chicago fire, but it happened in winter of '72 and had left a nasty scar on the city one could still see today. Acres of businesses in the financial and industrial district had burned.

Thousands were left homeless but only thirty or so died. The fire department claimed their horses caused the disaster. She remembered the funny headlines, horse flue epizootic to blame. Four years later, and only now were the farther, poorer regions being rebuilt.

"Wool-gathering, Bonnie told me you're apt to do that."

Claire blushed, leaned forward even though the girls seemed distracted enough with their little brother. "I wanted to give you this."

She held out the small purse, watched the woman's eyes light up for a moment before closing the girl's hands around it again. "No need, did ya not hear? They've work and we're fine. Besides, I thought Bonnie said there was less work at the factory these days."

Claire didn't fight, just closed her hands around the tiny treasure and slipped it into her pocket. "It's closed. We three need to find new work. I was just worrying how to explain it to Bonnie but I think I may have seen another opportunity. We have an interview Monday. Isn't the grace of God wonderful?"

"Aye, sometimes you wonder if he's listening. You know, when things seem dire, like for my poor Bonnie or your friend Lynne. More bad has happened there. A neighbor of hers came out to bring Bonnie word and I sent her on to your mother."

"Then I really must hurry, Lynne was worried about the children, I hope it's none of them."

"I didna know. The woman looked unwell herself so I didn't dare invite her into the house. There's death in the tenements this winter and I have too many here to let it in the door. I told her how to find Bonnie and sent her on her way."

Even worrying about the angel of death Mum Magee had sent from her door could not distract Claire from the thrill of closing her hand around the money in her pocket.

CHAPTER SEVEN

Bonnie woke in a cold sweat, completely disoriented. She looked about the dimly lighted room, finally figured out where she was. Shivering, she hastily jammed her bare feet into her shoes once again and struggled to stand. As always when she straightened, the muscles of her stomach screamed in protest. Weaving, she worked from the back of the couch, to the doily covered table and onto the Bible table in the corner, almost upsetting it as she put all her weight against it.

Coming upright she listened but could hear no voices. Terrified, she continued to struggle, emerging from the parlor and using the balustrades of the stairs to make her way to the front door. When she got the door open she stood in the cold air and swayed. She needed to get home, rush into her Mum's arms and safety. But as she took a step forward fear swept through her. What if Tarn were there at the house? What if he were only waiting for her to emerge from this sanctuary. He had sworn he would kill her.

In terror, she fumbled for the door behind her and managed to creep back into the house and slam the door shut. Her hand tangled in the lacy curtain over the stained glass window in the door and she sobbed as she fought to turn the knob despite her hand slipping with the curtain in the way.

"Here now, leave go," Bess's sharp voice surprised her. "Stop before you tear the lace."

Bewildered, Bonnie pulled her hand back and swayed as she tried to focus on the stout form of the maid. "Who are you?"

"Who do you think? Bess, Miss, the same who's tended you this long week. Come away from the door now I say. You're not well enough to be about, 'specially without your petticoat and a cloak about you."

Bonnie stood, shivering, her eyes wide with fear. When Mother Wimberley stepped forward, drying her hands, Bonnie let the women take hold of her and lead her to the stairs. Shakily she walked between them all the way up. This time they turned her to the smaller room near the front of the house. Instead of the thick feather mattress, there was a thinner, cotton stuffed, blue ticked pad.

"Hold her Bess, let me spread out the sheets."

Bonnie felt the need to explain to the woman gripping her tightly. Mother Wimberley returned and shook out the sheets and plumped the pillow before adding a knotted quilt to the top. "I have a cloak somewhere, it's a yellow and purple tartan. Not as hideous as it sounds."

"I'm sure 'tis lovely, Miss," Bess said. Mother Wimberley took over supporting the girl as the maid knelt to remove her shoes and quickly removed the brown dress before slipping her flannel gown back on.

Even when she was back in bed, Bonnie kept talking. "I didn't mean to be so much trouble. I know I should go home, that's where I was headed." She reached out to clutch the arm of the woman busy tucking the sheet snug on one side while Mother Wimberley did the same on the other. Bonnie's voice quivered as she added, "I thought I saw him out there, my husband, Tarn. I thought I saw him waiting." Lowering her voice to a whisper she added, "He means to kill me."

"He's gone now," Mother Wimberley reassured her. "You're safe and snug here with us. Now hush and go to sleep, you darling girl."

"Should I fetch her medicine?" Bess asked.

Bonnie rolled her eyes in terror and shook her head. Just as calmly Mother Wimberley answered. "No need for that any more. No need at all." She bent down and kissed the sweat-dampened forehead. "When Claire comes I'll send her right up. I'm going to stay here beside you until she comes home, okay Bonnie. Someone will be with you, don't worry. You're safe."

Bonnie gave a tremulous sigh and relaxed. "Safe."

Claire raced from the Magee's toward her own home, afraid she would miss the messenger who had come with news of Lynne. Instead she arrived just as the front door opened and the maid asked a woman with a mop of carrot red hair what she wanted.

Cautiously remembering Mum Magee's warning, she slipped around the large woman onto the porch and pushed the maid back inside. "Call Mother," Claire whispered.

Bess snorted. "Reckon dinner will be later still, seeing's how I have to replace her upstairs. Hold your horses, I'm fetching her."

Claire felt resentful of the woman's rudeness, but the woman on the porch didn't seem to notice.

"I've no time. I'm Mrs. Garretty, live below the McKinney's. Girl would want you to know, seeing as how you three are always together. Her mother killed herself today."

"She what?" Claire asked in disbelief.

"Well, same as, she did. Went off her head ripping out of her clothes and screaming to roll in the snow. She'd had the fever, the typhoid, like half of 'em have, including some of my own. But it wasn't the fever that killed her."

◇◇◇

Claire's mother pressed forward, securing the door behind her as she stepped out to wrap an arm around her daughter. "What are you yelling about out here? Don't you know we have a sick girl inside?"

"Yeah, heard about the tall one, they told me tales about her along the street as I asked directions to all of you. Now, I've no time for this, I've children sick of my own. They be burying her in the Potter's Field at sundown. Reckon it's fittin', way she died and all. Neighbors are claiming the landlord raped her, but I live below. Raped her the first of the month, every month, if you know what I mean. She wasn't so high and mighty like she pretended. Reckon that's something for that snooty daughter of hers to deal with too."

"Shame on you, gossiping about the dead," Mother Wimberley snapped.

The red-faced woman stood still and crossed herself. "I helped to dress her when we carried her upstairs. She took the lung fever during the night. I listened to her confession, bathed and helped dress the body. Maybe you didn't want to know, but I wasn't telling tales."

"If she died of pneumonia, then she didn't commit suicide. I can't understand why you would want to spread rumors and lies at a time like this. What's wrong with you?" Claire's eyes had filled with tears and she'd turned into her mother's arms to cry.

As the mountainous woman thundered down the stairs she turned back to look at them. "Be you believers?"

"Of course we are," Mother Wimberley snapped.

"In the pillow, I found a crown of feathers. You know what that means, don't cha?"

Claire wiped at her cheeks and stepped away from her mother's embrace. "It means God will hear your lies and judge you for he has welcomed her soul to heaven. It's a terrible sin to speak ill of the dead."

The woman's red face paled as she crossed herself and then turned to run heavily back down the lane.

Claire didn't turn away when her mother swept her into her embrace again. Later the two women entered the house arm in arm and Mother Wimberley led her into the parlor to talk. For several minutes she explained about Bonnie's improvement.

"I've treated many people who have tried to overcome addictions to opiates. Dr. Krantz was right in prescribing laudanum. It was necessary to keep the girl sedated until her body could recover. As I told you, I was a nurse during the war. It was all we had to ease their agony. Like most who are grievously wounded, they don't understand their limitations and can cause even more harm if allowed to move about too soon. Later, I saw a lot of men who suffered more from the effects of the treatment than from their wounds."

"You're saying our Bonnie is a drug addict now?"

"No. She was lucid this morning and told me she didn't want to take any more of the medicine. It made her feel strange, lost in dark dreams. She is a very smart woman, our Bonnie. She would rather feel a little pain now than suffer the depravities addicts all suffer later. It means she will moan and cry even more without the deadening effect of the drug. At her insistence we moved her to the spare room today. Bess and I just finished ironing your sheets and when we go up, you and I can make your bed."

"I don't understand, if she's not addicted, than what is the problem?"

"One of the effects of the medicine is fear, often irrational fear and visions. She thought she saw Tarn when she tried to leave and walk home today. She came back inside terrified that he was here, wanting to kill her."

"He's not. The men at the tavern, the police, they all say he ran away. He's gone west to escape arrest."

"I didn't say he was really there. She thought he was and she was frightened. I promised her we would not leave her alone. I've been sitting beside her while she slept. Now Bess is in the room with her. But after we get your room ready, if you could sit with her, so she's not afraid."

"Of course, I want to."

"She will struggle with chills, fever, retching, and may well scream out or try to attack you if she imagines you are trying to harm her. I just wanted to prepare you to deal with her sensibly but to be cautious. I didn't want to have to explain everything when we were in the room."

Claire stared at her mother as together they went upstairs. With each step, her dread grew. How could the world go from being wonderful to horrible so quickly? As they walked up the stairs, she began to mumble the Lord's Prayer for comfort. Her mother joined in and as they turned into her room she felt an answering peace drop around her shoulders.

CHAPTER EIGHT

Claire sat beside the bed and tried to put all she had heard today into some order in her mind. Instead, she felt tumbled into chaos.

Bonnie shivered and Claire listened to her teeth chatter. Quickly she ran and opened the hope chest in her own room. She returned to spread out the maple leaf quilt atop the simpler one with its pale squares fastened with knotted bows. She moved the corner, smoothed a hand over the diamond with its bright gold leaf. Each square had been pieced cattycorner, the bright leaves, orange, gold and red were appliqued with delicate stitches. Her favorite was the central square with its whimsical little bear. Her mother had helped her design it, teased her about the bear.

She looked up and saw Bonnie staring at her, her own mouth turning up at the corners. Claire leaned forward with a bounce and hugged her. Bonnie groaned and Claire sat back with a repentant glance. "I'm sorry, I didn't mean to hurt you."

This time Bonnie gave her a real smile, swallowed dryly. Claire lifted the glass of apple cider that her mother had sent up and Bonnie took a thirsty gulp, then slowly drank more. She abruptly leaned her head back and Claire set the glass down.

"What made you smile, goose?"

Claire blushed at the teasing name. She had been goose, Bonnie willow, and Lynne 'Miss sensible.' Obviously Lynne was the smart one, Bonnie the tall flexible one, and Claire the silly one. "I hate that name."

Bonnie's eyes grew sad. "I'm sorry." A second later she smiled, "go on, and tell me what you were smiling about."

Claire explained about the quilt and her memories. "Mother teased me about the center square, 'What if your husband doesn't want to sleep under a bear?'"

"Then I'll let one of my boys sleep under it." Claire shook her head at her foolishness. "But then, girls of twelve are often foolish."

Bonnie grunted and squirmed a minute, trying to see the pattern. Groaning she leaned back. "I can't move?"

Claire sat very still, remembering all of her mother's warnings. Yet Bonnie seemed herself for the first time in days. What harm could there be in allowing her room to sit up and move about?

"I guess Mother has you tucked in a little too snuggly. She's been very worried about you, you know."

Bonnie thrashed her head back and forth on the pillow. "Please, I need to use … I need to go."

Claire rose, pulling the tucked sheet and quilts free along one side and moving out of the way. Bonnie flung the covers back further as she rose, moaning as she struggled to stand. Claire stood ready to support her but Bonnie teetered a moment before straightening up and gulping air. Weaving, she touched the short foot board of the bed as she walked from the room.

Claire stood wrapped in confusion. By the time Bonnie returned, she was wringing her hands. Bonnie walked up so softly it startled her. The tall woman stood with her arms braced above her head on the door frame. "Show me, I want to see the bear."

Claire smoothed back the covers, smiled nervously as she looked to see her friend's reaction to her first quilt. Bonnie shuddered and

shook her head. "No, take it off. The bear makes me think of Tarn."
She shuddered again.

Confused, Claire looked at the black rearing bear, a childish
outline at best, amid the squares of bright leaves. Quickly she folded
the quilt back up and moved to the far side of the bed with it in her
arms. "Come on, lie down, and I'll put it away again."

Bonnie seemed to sag, sliding against the upright frame of the
door into the room until she again could grip the footboard. Claire
darted past her to return the quilt to her room.

But when she returned, Bonnie was still standing. Grimacing, the
girl swung one long leg forward and back. Claire desperately wanted
to call her mother but knew how busy she was. Her father expected
dinner to be waiting when he arrived home and today there had been a
half-dozen disruptions to delay it. Calming and tending to Bonnie,
cleaning the rooms and laundering bedding for both, talking with the
frightening Mrs. Garretty, and then the long talk they had shared in the
parlor about Bonnie. Claire knew her mother would be working in a
frenzy to get it finished on time.

"Aren't you tired?" Claire asked.

"Only of lying about so much," Bonnie said, then groaned as she
changed to the other leg, swinging it but now facing her friend. "As
much as I hurt, you'd think the big gorilla broke all my bones," she
said with a grunt of a laugh. "My chest hurts so I can't get a deep
breath. Maybe he broke my ribs and the doctor missed it."

Now she stood, still clutching at the short foot board with one
hand, the other pressed against her chest. Straightening, she raised one
leg after another, knees bent as though she were marching.

Claire couldn't resist humming "When the Saints Go Marching
In," and joining in. They did the high knee march until Bonnie was
panting heavily and perspiration dotted her cheeks and forehead.
Claire pretended to be worn out as well and slipped past Bonnie to

collapse in the bedside chair. Bonnie sagged back onto the bed, her long arms behind her to keep from falling backward.

Claire listened to her ragged breathing and wondered if Bonnie was right. She knew there were many things a doctor couldn't see. Unless a bone was broken so it pressed against the skin or poked through, they would probably not know to treat it. "Whew, I don't see how soldiers march for miles. That few minutes was brutal."

Bonnie smiled and Claire noticed her breathing was less labored. Bonnie moved her arms from behind her and sagged deeper into the bed, the bedding caught beneath her.

"If I'm staying, I might as well have my gown again."

Claire felt her breath catch as she whispered. "You're already wearing it."

Bonnie's eyes grew round in fear as she lifted the flowered skirt and then closed her eyes.

It was ten minutes before Claire had helped her friend to settle back to sleep under the covers.

Bess entered the room with the usual tray of broth and pitcher of cold water. Claire raised a finger to her lips before slipping past and down to dinner.

Her father and mother were talking, heads bent together under the brass table lamp. Claire remained on the stairs out of sight, merely enjoying watching them together. She heard her mother describing the frightening Mrs. Garretty, whispering how terrible it was that Lynne's mother was dead. "Poor orphan." Her father's response shocked her.

It was true. All the young McKinneys were now on their own. What would Lynne do? For just a second she imagined the table below with her parents gone. How could she cope? She shuddered and pushed the fear away. Her father was holding her mother's hand, smiling at her. Even as Claire entered the room he leaned closer and kissed her.

Claire bounced the rest of the way, making a tsking sound at them. Both blushed as they drew apart and she slipped to place an arm around their necks before kissing each in turn.

"Smells wonderful. I'm starved."

"Good thing you came down, thought you and your friend were happy slurping broth. I was going to finish this chicken off by myself," her father teased.

Claire bowed her head for a moment, then took the plate her mother had quickly filled for her.

"How is the girl doing?" she asked.

Claire described Bonnie's exercise and their marching, even the bit of confusion for them both. "She's asleep but I need to hurry back. Bess is grumpier than usual and I'm not sure she and Bonnie get along."

"Well enough so you don't have to bolt your food. You know eating fast like a pig can make you look like one," her mother chided.

Claire slowed down, chewing the beans in her mouth as she cut the boiled chicken into tiny bites.

"Tell us about work," her father said as he took a sip of wine.

"Finished. We packed the last sewing machine, needle, thread and fabric today. Next month when the crates are unboxed in Georgia, some southern belle will be running my machine," Claire couldn't hide the disappointment in her voice.

"Sorry to hear about Lynne's mother," her father said and Claire forced her own problems away.

"Poor darling. The last time she talked she was anxious to get back to work. Now with her mother gone she'll need the job more than ever and it's gone," Claire said, pushing the food around on her plate, no longer hungry. "I offered my pay to Mrs. Magee but she refused to take it, said the men were all working."

"Men, you mean that worthless husband of hers has a job. Those little boys, what's their names?" Father asked.

"Ian is nearly sixteen, Shawn thirteen. Not so little now. They found work on the new tenements being built on the last of the burnt acres." At his nod, she added, "Maybe I can give my last pay to Lynne."

Her father smiled, looked at his wife and winked. "No new bonnets or fripperies this week? That doesn't sound like you. Besides, you can't help the whole world you know."

"Yes, but it's my money you said. I want to help my friends. Lynne said the little ones were getting sick too when we talked."

"That was a day ago. Probably all fit as fiddles by now," he said.

"I'll see when we go to the funeral?"

"Funeral. She can afford to have a funeral?"

"Burial in Potter's Field," her mother answered.

"Hmm," her father added.

Claire put her fork down beside her plate. "Why are some people so poor while others have so much? Why do some have to suffer while others make merry?"

"God must have his reasons. Not sure how merry you are tonight if you're counting yourself rich. Remember we'll be selling this house, the foundry and packing just the minimum to take to Oregon. Any misfortunes along the trail, you could be the poor needy friend someday." He stared from Claire's worried face to his wife's. "Mayhap we can help them, your mother and I will think about what is possible."

Claire smiled at her father, drank more of her tea as her mother scolded her to finish her food if she wanted dessert. Once again she ate, trying to alternate between hurrying up and chewing every bite one hundred times.

Dessert was individual egg custards, a favorite for both girls. When she asked about letting Bonnie move around, they both thought it made sense.

CHAPTER NINE

Claire had eaten and bathed. Dressed in her gown, robe and slippers she finally entered Bonnie's room to replace Bess. She set down the lit candle, her small book and the cold dish of custard on the little round table near the bed. The maid was drowsing beside her patient but woke instantly when Claire touched her shoulder. Bonnie twisted in bed, moaning and mumbling in her sleep. As the women watched, her legs and feet moved beneath the covers as though she were kicking someone.

Bess touched Claire's hand and both women stepped outside the room, easing the door closed behind them. "I don't see why your mother refuses to dose her, least ways she could sleep."

Claire's mouth turned down at the corners. "Mother knows best, besides it's what Bonnie wants as well. Go on now, I'll be here with her."

"What can you do if she wants to fight you?"

Claire nodded but walked the maid toward the stairs. "Father and Mother will be up soon. I can yell out if I need help. Go on down now. Your dinner's on the stove but it'll get cold. You don't want to waste that delicious chicken."

Bess curtsied to her and hurried down the backstairs to the kitchen. Her little room beside the pantry butted up against the stove. In the winter, it was the warmest room in the house. In the summer, the maid always made sure to cook early and bank the fire long before night so she wouldn't roast to death.

Claire slipped back into the room, stood at the table a minute running her tongue around the corner of her mouth as she looked at the golden custard in the candle's glow. Sighing, she took up the book instead and sank into the empty chair beside the bed.

Later, Bonnie's ragged breathing made her look across at the girl. Holding the candle nearer the bed, she saw the sweat drenched hair and gown. She rushed to dampen the washcloth in the basin under a stream of cold water from the pitcher. She squeezed it dry then rushed to the bedside. When she wiped her face and neck, Bonnie gasped. As she lifted back the covers, Bonnie's hand came up and grasped her wrist, squeezing fiercely. Claire squealed, dropping the cloth, and Bonnie sat up, her eyes wild in fright.

"Ouch. I was only trying to wipe your face, to cool you off."

Bonnie released her and muttered, "Sorry. Sorry. What's going on?"

Claire spoke softly, cheerful now to have company. "You asked to move to the spare room today, so that's where you're at. You also told mother you didn't want any more laudanum. Your body seems to be having trouble. When I first came in, I think you were reliving your fight with Tarn."

Bonnie stared at her owl eyed, then fumbled for and lifted the wet cloth from her lap. Roughly she wiped her face, pushing her hair back with it. "Thanks."

Claire traded her the glass of water for the sweaty cloth and went back to rinse it in the basin. She handed Bonnie the clean cloth and watched the girl unbutton her gown and run the cloth over her chest and throat before sagging back against the pillow.

This time Claire returned with another glass of water and the dessert. "Not sure if you feel like eating, but Mother made custard tonight..." Bonnie reached to snatch the treasure and squirmed backward to sit up against the head of the bed. Claire watched the girl take the first spoonful and savor it in her mouth. When she gave a dry cough Claire held the glass for her.

"I have some terrible news to tell you, about Lynne."

Bonnie shuddered as she let the spoon rattle in the empty thin china cup. "I'm cold." She shivered again for emphasis and Claire removed her own robe and slipped it around her shoulders. Bonnie mumbled, "Thanks. I heard that horrible woman shouting in the street."

"Mrs. Garretty? She came to tell us Lynne's mother is dead. I don't think the rest she had to say is important."

Bonnie stared at her, pulling the covers up over her chest, still shuddering. "Could be. You can't blame her for doing whatever it took to keep her family safe."

Claire sat down in the chair beside the bed, tucking her gown around her legs and wrapping her arms around her body. "You believed her?"

Bonnie shrugged, pulling the covers up over her lower face. "I want to go to the funeral with you."

Claire looked ready to argue but Bonnie gave her a stubborn look. "We'll see. Mother and Father already agreed that we should let you up to move around more. We'll ask in the morning."

"No, we'll both go to be with her. Poor Lynne. I can't imagine life without parents, can you?"

Carrie shook her head. "No, mine are so wonderful. They were talking about going West again after dinner. It's so frightening but I'm not afraid of the adventure as long as they are there with me."

Bonnie's face looked so sad. "I think it's time for me to leave Mum and Da, if I'm to amount to anything in life. I think things are too different now ..."

Her voice trailed off and Claire studied her friend in the flickering light. Carefully so as not to squeeze too hard she leaned forward to touch her face to Bonnie's. There were no promises she could make, no words to make all the hurt go away. She needed to tell her about the job at the mill, but how could she tell her more sad news when her heart was already breaking? Tomorrow, after she had rested. Maybe they could talk about it all in the morning.

Claire woke to Bonnie screaming. Rushing she struck the flint to light the candle and held it out to look at Bonnie. Bonnie was tossing back and forth, running her fingers across her skin, pulling at her hair, and moaning.

"Shh, shh, hush now Bonnie. What's wrong?"

Bonnie's eyes opened and she stared around in the shadowed room. "My skin, my skin is on fire. Oh God, help me Claire, help me." Then Claire watched in horror as the girl raked her nails down her arms, raised her gown to scratch red streaks up and down her legs.

Claire's mother appeared at the door, a shawl thrown haphazardly over her nightclothes. Together, they were able to haul the tall girl to her feet and lead her down the stairs to the washroom. While Bonnie sat on the wooden box, her mother turned a wrench and warm water began to fill the hip-sized marble tub. At the sound of the running water, Bonnie frantically tugged up her gown while Claire raised the lid on the inside toilet.

"How, how does all this work?"

"Father, replaced the iron pipes at the Tremont. Wouldn't hush until he installed the same system for us. There's a spiral shaped pipe that runs from the cistern in the attic. The water gets heated as it flows down through the warm fireplace. I'm afraid with the fire banked, it won't be that warm right now."

"The toilet?" Bonnie asked as she let Claire pull the gown off. She tiptoed over and sank into the small tub, shivering at the delicious feel of the tepid water. Claire's mother turned the wrench when the water stopped feeling warm and Bonnie took the cloth and bathed her legs while Claire closed the seat and took her place on the box.

"It has a handle." Claire gripped the lever on the side and pushed it down. "Gravity moves the contents on out to the end of the yard through some large iron pipes. It works pretty well, although it can smell a little in the summer."

"Then we use the waste water from the tub to flush out the pan in the bottom and wash everything out a little faster," Mother added.

"Do all these houses have indoor privies?"

"No indeed," Mother Wimberley said. "My husband is what you'd call a Progressive. Believe it or not I argued when he wanted to put this in the house. Everyone claimed it was unhealthy, especially taking baths so frequently, but my goodness, it is convenient."

Claire tried, but could not help looking at all the bruises covering Bonnie. Now with the red streaks along her arms and legs, she looked like some poisonous plant. Bonnie blushed and held the small washcloth over her chest, self-conscious as she felt their eyes on her.

"Don't be shy, darling. We're both grown women. You've nothing we don't have, although God was a little more generous to you." Mother Wimberley said and passed the soap over to her. "I'm going to put some water on the stove, so you can have a cup of tea when you've finished. If you want, I can heat enough for you to wash your hair."

Bonnie nodded shyly, leaned forward to shield her body from view.

"Claire, why don't you carry those dirty clothes in and we'll get them rinsed out and hung up to start drying. Then run up and get Bonnie's things for her to put on when she finishes."

Finally alone, Bonnie ran the soapy cloth thoroughly over every inch, then scooted so she could wet her hair. Using the same bar of soap she quickly worked a lather into the sweaty mop. By the time she finished, her arms were quivering. The weakness, her fear, her sore body all left her sitting there, damp-eyed and shivering. There was a tap at the door and Claire whispered, "It's me, with your clothes."

Bonnie called hoarsely, "Come in."

Claire stepped through and put her brown dress and underthings on the closed lid of the toilet. Then whispered, "Just a minute." She returned with the kettle of heated water. "If you're through soaping, lean forward and I'll rinse it."

Bonnie leaned forward as Claire poured the warm stream of water over her head and worked her fingers through to rinse it. Bonnie muttered, "Sorry, my arms got tired."

"No problem," Claire sang. "I'll just suds it again, here let me get more water." She poured the last into the tub and closed the door again.

Alone, Bonnie sat and silently cried. Claire entered without knocking and Bonnie sucked in a breath to stop. Claire must have known, but said nothing. She merely dipped her hands under water to work the bar until her hands were covered in lather. Then she sat on the rim of the tub to work the soap through the tangled brown hair.

Strong fingers massaged her scalp and in moments Bonnie's eyes closed in bliss. This time it was Claire's mother who tapped on the door and held the kettle to pour while Claire rinsed it through her hair.

Like a sleepy toddler, Bonnie tolerated the women toweling her dry, helping her to dress and even brushing out the tangles in her long hair.

Later, seated at the table with a warm cup of tea in her hands she found herself crying again. "I'm sorry, I don't know why I'm crying."

Claire's mother reached out to hug her. "Because you need to, Dear. Go ahead and let some of the sadness drip out and you'll feel better."

Claire concluded her description of the past week at work. "I hadn't the heart to tell you earlier, but the mill closed. Yesterday was the last day ever."

Bonnie tilted her head to face her eye to eye. Instead of more tears, Bonnie laughed instead. "Perfect, my life is even more perfect." Bonnie sat forward, her fingers laced to support her heavy head.

"No, it's not that bad. I already found a place that we may get a job starting next week."

Excitedly she described the little dress shop and how perfect it would be to work there. Someone as tall and strong as Bonnie would have no trouble helping to stock the shelves. Claire knew she could get hired to help shoppers find the perfect thing to wear. Bonnie stared at her friend, hearing the bubbling enthusiasm that made Claire such an optimist. She didn't have the heart to say no.

Instead she grinned and wiped her eyes. "Alright, alright. I surrender. Not sure how strong I am right now, but I'm still tall."

"You are regaining your strength every day, you know you are," Claire's mother said. "I know you have suffered an incredible trauma, but Claire isn't the only one who wants to help you. My husband and I both want you to stay with us as long as you like, at least until we take our wagons to Oregon."

"No," Claire shouted. "I want you to go west with us." She turned to her Mother, "Please Mother, please."

Bonnie straightened in her chair and shook her head. "No, I can't take charity. I'll stay until you leave Boston. Whatever I earn, at this store or somewhere else, I will pay you for my keep."

"Nonsense," Mother Wimberley stood as though just insulted. "You are welcome here. If you want to pay, you can do it by working and helping us get ready for our trip. I'll even let you buy food from time to time, but I will not take your money. If that's the only way you are willing to stay, than you'll have to go home."

For a minute Bonnie looked stricken. "I can't go home." She trembled, then shook her head. "But you will let me earn my way?"

"Of course," Mother Wimberley still stood, her hands on her hips like a little hen whose feathers had been ruffled. "We all want you to stay."

Bonnie made the mistake of standing too quickly and swayed a little on her feet. "Maybe I can rest a little until you're ready to go, Claire."

"You know the way to the parlor. No sense making the trek back upstairs," her mother said. "It's too nearly dawn to go back to bed anyway."

Bonnie nodded and used the chair backs and table to walk from the dining room, then brushed the brocade papered wall as she made her way over to the stair rails and used them as before to navigate her path back into the dark parlor and over to the horsehair stuffed lounging sofa. Behind her she could hear Claire and her mother whispering frantically. Wearily she collapsed onto the seat, letting her hair cascade down the outside of the arm as she let her neck rest on the high end.

A minute later Claire appeared. Silently she lifted the dropped throw from the floor and covered Bonnie's legs. No matter what her Mother thought was going to happen. She was not going to abandon her friend in Boston, no matter how many rich and eligible bachelors were waiting for her out west.

CHAPTER TEN

Claire wore her best dress beneath her green cloak and tugged nervously at her bottle-green gloves while they waited outside for the store to open. Bonnie wore her best dress, the mended brown one beneath her truly horrible plaid cloak. At least her hair was braided and the braids neatly coiled at the back of her head thanks to Claire's nimble fingers. Claire had also used her Mother's powder and the barest dab of rouge on her cheeks to make the fading bruises nearly inconspicuous.

Bonnie knew she was still so pale she looked lifeless. This was pointless. She had argued with Claire on the long walk over to the Back Bay shops but her silly friend wouldn't listen. What if they took one look at Bonnie and turned both girls down? Claire was the one who was thrilled at the prospect of working in a clothing store, not Bonnie. If she never had to handle another fancy garment she couldn't afford to wear she would be happy. At least there would be no sweltering starch vats, large mechanical mangles, or huge pressing machines. No chance blisters, bruised fingers, or blackened nails if you didn't move your fingers fast enough.

Twenty minutes before the posted opening time, they were certainly not late for the interview. Claire was still talking, the sound as happy as a bird chirping good morning. "At least these people will be so much easier to work with. Did I tell you how the foreman tried to grope and back me into a corner yesterday?" Bonnie listened to all the details, enjoyed hearing how Claire had escaped the obnoxious man's advances and avoided him until after closing. As she talked and the details became more numerous her voice rose in volume. Bonnie nodded and kept an eye on the empty street.

"The store owners, the Lambtons, seem a lovely couple. Well actually she was a little stern and dowdy and he, all that's charming and elegant, but…"

"Shh," Bonnie whispered. "I think I heard something."

Claire spun, reassured that the street was still empty. But as she turned back around she saw a smiling face at the open door and raised a hand to cover her mouth.

"Good morning, ladies, won't you come in," a warm baritone voice said. Blushing, Claire gathered her skirts and curtsied in greeting. As she walked forward, Bonnie reached out to give her waist a pinch.

Claire cocked her head and gave Bonnie an eye roll as she tugged the shy girl in behind her.

Bonnie followed against her better judgment. It was clear from the handsome man's smile that he had heard everything. From the back of the store they heard a slam and his wife, as sour faced and thunderous a woman as Bonnie had ever seen came rushing toward the front of the store. She held a trap with a dead rat in one hand, her broom in the other.

"See, what did I tell you? Look at the belly will you, six, no eight babies. Lord knows how many more are here, running about at night, nibbling on hat boxes, leaving their stench in the stockroom."

The man cleared his throat but she was on a roll, stomping down the main aisle to wave the disgusting trophy in his face. "Bella," he barked. She stopped and looked up as Claire shrieked and ducked behind him. Bonnie calmly reached out her hand. "Here, I'll pitch it in the rubbage bin for you before the customers arrive. Maybe we'll have time to sniff out her babies too."

The girls giggled as soon as they left the shadow of the store. Both now had new jobs, to officially begin on Monday. Bonnie had been able to find the damaged hat box and the nest of babies, thus securing her a job in the stock room. What had really impressed the woman was how easily the girl dispatched the babies as though dealing with rats was an everyday occurrence. Of course, in the tenements it was.

The clincher was when Mrs. Lambton was preparing to dispose of the hat. Bonnie had convinced her it could be cleaned and reblocked, No one need know. All it would need was a new box. Together they had set out three more traps, moved boxes to uncover the entrance hole and plugged it. Bonnie was smart enough to leave the hat project until Monday when she reported to work officially.

In the meantime, Claire had welcomed two older women into the shop and convinced them that a four dollar wine colored brocade looked far prettier with their navy skirts than the three dollar green satin.

Mr. Lambton was just hiring Claire when his wife came out to announce Miss Magee was just the kind of girl they were looking for. While the couple argued, Bonnie leaned calmly against the counter as Claire pointed out the perfectly lovely mint green dress she planned to buy on the installment plan with her pay. At her announcement the couple stopped arguing and both girls were hired.

On the way home, they walked along the river, watching the city spring to life all around them. "Just think, for lunch we can step out of the shop and sit on the dock to eat."

"And have a lot of dock workers whistling and asking us if we need a jolly time," Bonnie said.

Claire laughed, "Well maybe. But won't it be fun to work in such a posh establishment, compared to that sweaty, smelly old mill. I would have started today when they asked, but I know you still need more time to recuperate."

Suddenly Bonnie gasped and crouched down behind a post. Claire stopped her happy chatter. "What's wrong, are you in pain?"

"On the barge… on the opposite shore … don't you see him?"

Claire raised a hand over her eyes and stared but all she saw was a burly, red-headed sailor and a tall, stringy stevedore.

"No, one man is built like Tarn but has red hair and is too short. The tall man with dark hair is far too thin. Did you see a third one?"

"The man in the gray sweater?"

"Tall but too skinny." Claire stepped up and took her arm to help Bonnie stand. "See, neither is Tarn."

Bonnie stared and trembled. "I guess I'm still seeing things. Do you mind if we stop off to visit Mum? I'd like to tell her my good news and let her know she can stop praying so hard for me."

Claire linked arms and together they walked homeward, Bonnie matching her pace to match the shorter girl.

Claire was still chattering, sharing all the same details they had told her Mum minutes before. The morning had looked to be clearing, but by the time they reached home, clouds had scudded in creating a dark gloomy day. The burial would be after four according to Mrs.

Garretty. At the insistence of Mother Wimberley and Bess, Bonnie begged off and went upstairs to nap. Really her head was pounding and her whole body ached. Again she wondered if she would be able to earn her pay at the Lambton's.

As Bonnie closed her eyes she remembered Claire's description of Bella Lambton. The woman did not seem that different than herself. Bitterly she wondered if that was how her best friend saw her, as sour and dowdy. Certainly her clothes were dull and ugly, at least Mrs. Lambton was dressed in new, conservative clothes and shoes. Bonnie would be happy to be dressed even half as well.

Maybe she could do what Claire had suggested, purchase something decent to wear by making weekly payments from her salary. Startled, she sat upright. She hadn't asked Mrs. Lambton about the salary. Sighing, she relaxed, Claire would know and she would certainly tell her all about it several times before the day was through. At least Mum had insisted again that she needed to save her money, use it for herself now they were doing okay. Smiling, she relaxed enough to sleep.

Claire stared at the sleeping girl and smiled. With her braids unpinned, Bonnie looked very much like her younger sisters. Despite the abuse she had suffered and the horror of losing her son, she was still so young. Surely with Tarn gone, she could have another chance at a happy life. Saying a silent prayer, Claire reached out to shake her awake.

Bonnie looked up to see Claire haloed by the light coming through the bedroom window. She smiled, her heart feeling a moment of joy. "You look like an angel, my angel. I haven't stopped to thank you or your mother for all you've done for me…"

Claire laughed and tugged on her hand. "Don't be silly. I'm anything but an angel and you know it. Hurry down before dinner is cold. I've got a surprise for you."

Two mourners huddled inside the shelter to watch the slender girl lead the procession of the grave digger and two men toting the tightly shrouded body. The girls could hear their friend giving instructions.

Lynne spoke as she finally found the markers for her brothers and father. "Here, they left room between father and my brother Sean, the baby boys are buried at their feet. Please, can you dig a place between them for Mother?" She asked, but it was with a firmness of command.

She stared around the gray fogged cemetery, looking for the priest. A dark clad man walked from the small shed at the edge of the field and she was surprised as two cloaked figures joined him.

She listened to the minister intone the simple ceremony, wished it could have been her mother's priest. Thirty-five was so young to die, but three of her children already slept beside her. Softly Lynne repeated the oath she had made to her mother. "Nothing will happen to the three little ones who remain. No matter what it costs me, I will show courage, and do whatever it takes to ensure their safety."

When the soft words ended she looked up and smiled. The two witnesses were Claire and Bonnie. Silently they followed her from the cemetery, one trailing on either side. Lynne found her voice first.

"I'm surprised to see you here." She turned to search Bonnie's eyes for signs of her own loss, her own fears. The taller girl smiled faintly. "One of your neighbors sent word."

Lynne cleared her throat. "Mrs. Garretty?"

Claire nodded and moved closer. "We needed to talk to you anyway. We're making plans."

Bonnie chimed in. "The Wimberleys are going west in the spring, and Claire and her parents have invited me to go with them. We're going to the Oregon territory for free land and young husbands."

Lynne shook her head. "This sounds like one of your schemes Claire. I thought you were going to answer one of those ads for a bride."

Claire shook her head. "Bonnie made me realize how foolish that was. One might agree to marry a Tarn or a mad pincher like our floor foreman."

All three closed ranks. "The children are all three sick or I'd hug you dear hearts." Her voice thickened and she raised a hand to brush her hair back from her eyes. The ground all around the cemetery was still white and glistening, but the falling rain was rapidly forming a film of ice on the cleared, paved streets. "I don't know if you heard how mother died."

Claire extended an arm and leaned a hand forward to touch her damp shoulder. Bonnie instinctively reached a hand forward to squeeze her smaller one. "Men!"

It could have been an oath she spat it out so vehemently. Claire raised her head and all three laughed tearfully. "Don't lump them all together. We know they're not all bad. Our mothers found wonderful men to love and marry and we will do the same."

"How?" Lynne sighed. "Just when you think you couldn't meet a more wicked or despicable man than the likes of Mr. Huntmeister or Tarn, then you do."

Bonnie stepped in front of her, blocking her way. "Who? Has someone done something to harm you, Lynne? If they have, I swear," her brow puckered in concentration. "We'll help you get them."

Lynne stared at the somber light brown eyes in the plain, long face and smiled. Claire was trying to edge around on the slippery shoulder of the walkway so she could see Lynne's face as well. "It's not what he did, it's what he offered to do."

Again Lynne found it hard to speak, and she drew in a ragged, deep breath. "Dr. Stone's offered to hospitalize the sick children if I would agree to his setting me up in an apartment as his paramour." The angry words spewed out like steam against the cold wet night. In the dark she could barely see their faces but felt their sympathy. "This is ridiculous you know. We'll all three catch pneumonia standing about in this."

Claire pulled her forward and the three didn't stop until they had reached the awning over the corner grocer. The lamp was still on inside and the door unlocked. All three crowded in together. Once inside, Lynne moved over to one side of the corner stove, leaving her friends facing her on the other. Each shook rain from their cloaks and stared at the other. "I have to hurry on home, the children are all in torment with this blasted fever. The young wife from the first floor is watching over them."

Claire dipped around behind the counter to give the merchant a coin and came back with a small sack. Bonnie lifted the lid on the small metal skillet sitting on the stovetop and held it as Claire poured the contents into the oiled pan. "Now, you have to wait on the chestnuts. Tell us."

Lynne looked up. She should be crying for her mother, worrying about her brothers and sisters, instead the fear she felt in her chest was for herself. If she started, she was afraid she might give way to self-pitying tears. Bonnie reached across and jabbed her arm softly. "Tell!"

So she did. The horror of her mother's death. The comfort of the neighbors. The outrageous propositions by both men.

Claire listened to the emotional telling wide-eyed, her pretty face twisting into sympathetic or angry faces in turn. Bonnie merely listened. Toward the last, the chestnuts popped. When they smelled the first one scorching Bonnie reached out and opened the lid, shaking out a couple into each of their waiting hands. Claire held open the little crumpled sack for her to pour the rest into.

Each girl was lost for a minute in the fun of tossing hot little nuts from palm to palm, relishing their warmth and taste. Hovering round the stove, each prayed the owner would stay busy and not douse the lamps to signal them to leave.

"What are you going to do?" Claire whispered.

Lynne gave a twisted smile and shrugged. "I don't know. I just know I promised my mother on her death bed that I would do everything in my power to protect the little McKinneys. It's knowing what such a sacrifice cost her that makes me afraid."

For something to do, she reached for the tiny bag of nuts. Bonnie was the first to speak. "Sometimes you have to do what you have to do. No one could blame you."

Claire swore, the unlady-like expression far more expressive than the single epithet 'men'. "Here, it's not much. I put money down on a new dress today. I tried to give the rest to Bonnie's family but her Mum refused to take it now the men are working."

Lynne held out her hand, took the eighty cents. Far less than what she needed. Claire was still talking.

"Father is selling everything, trying to raise the money we'll need to outfit for the trip west. They say it's terribly expensive."

Bonnie nodded. "You know if I had anything, it would be yours. Claire and I are supposed to go to work at Lampton's Monday. It only pays fifty cents a day, but Mum and Da have promised I can save it up for the trip. I plan to travel with Claire. Maybe you and the little ones can come along too."

The last ended weakly and Lynne shook her head. "No, first I will sell the furniture and anything else of value for the hospital. Perhaps I can ..." but her voice trailed off. Each girl knew she had little to sell but herself.

The owner doused a lamp but as the girls backed toward the door he called. "Miss McKinney, my wife has been wanting a new bedroom suit. Would you mind if I come up to look at your furniture in the morning?"

Lynne blushed all the way to her ears, realizing the man had been listening.

"With my wife of course," he added.

She nodded, of course he had been listening but that didn't mean his intentions were dishonorable ones. "Yes, yes, that would be fine."

She followed the others outside, tried to figure out why even a kind gesture was so hard to accept. What had her mother told her about pride? What matter all the telling, Lynne knew what it had cost her. She would be glad to accept the owner's help, but could it possibly be enough. Claire and Bonnie waited and she stomped over to the edge of the lamplight where they stood.

Suddenly, a crazy notion came to her. "Claire, one thing before you go. If you aren't going to be needing those ads of yours for husbands, would you mind letting me have them."

Claire pulled her cape high over her blonde curls. The night was cold, but at least the rain had stopped. She tugged at the gathering on her handbag until the drawstring pulled free and she could retrieve the two yellow papers.

"It's obvious like Bonnie said, a person has to do what a person has to do. But I might as well check to see who is willing to make the highest offer. Perhaps one of those rich, lonely westerners would pay a bonus to get an innocent young bride. Perhaps not, but then what else do I have to lose?"

Lynne took the yellow pages and held them in the lamplight, smiling gaily. But her hand shook and her voice quavered.

Claire started to grab the sheets back, but Bonnie held her hand. "Well, it makes sense to me. Perhaps you should go by the newspaper office and make inquiries. It seems to me if Horace Greeley can say 'Go West, young man, go West!' no one can fault us for going west after the good ones."

The three laughed and for just a moment Lynne felt the faint stirrings of hope. It was so much like the afternoon in the school yard when they had planned to go to work in the mills.

She held out her pinkies and the other two laughed and linked theirs. They raised their arms and cheered. "To Life and Adventure."

Bonnie stared sadly after Lynne as she reached down to link arms with Claire. But into the dark alley and empty yard of the tenements she hoped Lynn knew her friend's hearts went with her.

As the pair trudged home in the damp air, it was Bonnie who had to talk. "I know it was your idea and I don't know what you told them to get them to say yes, but I am so glad that I'll be going West with you."

Claire bent her head forward, tugging the cloak even closer. Emotionally she felt connected to the woman beside her and leaned even nearer so that she was covered by Bonnie's cloak as well. "I'm so glad too, but without Lynne, it still doesn't feel right. Did you see how tired and sad she looked? I can't remember her looking so weary before."

Bonnie stumbled for the first time and Claire caught her. Bonnie was relieved they were so near home. "Oh, I am being selfish. How can I be happy when Lynne is so miserable?"

"No, that's not what Lynne wants or what we need. Guilt doesn't help anyone. Together we'll pray. Maybe Mother and Father will find we have even more room in the wagon than they thought."

CHAPTER ELEVEN

Sunday they rested after morning mass. Bonnie confided in Claire about her worries about her clothes. "I know I have two dresses, but neither seems nice enough for Lambton's shop."

"You know I would gladly share anything I have, but there is such a difference between our shapes. Let's ask Mother."

Bonnie smiled down at the top of Claire's mop of curls. "I'm afraid she's only a slightly rounder version of you." Claire stopped in the doorway and motioned for her to follow.

Her parents were settled in the warm parlor. Her father was napping under an open edition of the Globe, a scattered stack of papers on the floor beside his couch. Her mother sat in her rocker beside the fireplace, an embroidery project abandoned in her lap.

Claire's mother was excited about the project. Upstairs in the attic she found a black skirt that had belonged to their first maid, a woman nearly as tall as Bonnie. Of course it wrapped around Bonnie's flatter waist almost as far as the brown dress now did. As the two women happily poked about in chests and rummaged through the barrel of clothes they had planned to donate to the church, Bonnie held the skirt, feeling the stiff cotton fabric. Confused, she felt delighted to have something else to wear, but ashamed to be like a poor beggar.

Back in the spare room, all three went to work. Bonnie cut an eight inch width from the skirt's waist to the hem, then rejoined the split in the skirt and gathered it.

Using the extra cloth Bonnie removed from the skirt, Claire was able to make a narrow ruffle. She added four more inches below the ruffle and tacked both onto the hem of the garment.

While Claire repaired the skirt, Bonnie took apart the brown dress and removed a narrower section from the neck down the center back to the hem. She handed the brown wool piece to Mother Wimberley, then sat down to reseam and repair the dress.

For a blouse, Claire's mother constructed a pattern starting with the maid's uniform and measuring it against Bonnie's narrower frame. "There, but I'm afraid I need to rest. It will take me a few days to get it made."

It was decided that Bonnie would wear the skirt and sash overtop one of her day dresses. With luck, no one would notice it wasn't a separate blouse and the dress's skirt underneath could serve her as a second petticoat.

Claire was disappointed but Bonnie was thrilled. The new skirt hid her ugly shoes and she felt less intimidated about going to work in the store.

As always, Claire was talkative. First she suggested that they should consider helping all the orphaned McKinney children. What would happen to them without a mother or father now Lynne had no job? She sawed on that topic before, during, and after supper until her parents exchanged a look and promised to discuss it.

Happy once again, already anticipating they would say yes, Claire talked about the store. Finally her mother suggested the girls find something quiet to do for a while so Father could enjoy his paper and digest his meal in peace.

◇◇◇

After supper, they looked through the stereopticon at some of the double images. On the stiff cards, the albumen pictures looked identical, but when held in the device, the images looked three dimensional. It was something the three younger friends had always liked to do when visiting after school. On this cold, gloomy day it made them worry about poor Lynne.

Now, neither Claire nor Bonnie wanted to look again at the slides of Europe or the National Peace Jubilee in her mother's collection. Once had been enough to stare at the images from the last war, or the troubling slides of slaves on the block or runaways that made up most of her father's collection. But both were happy to settle down to view the wonders of California, the new railways under construction, and especially the series on western expansion and the Indians of the plains.

With each stereograph, Bonnie felt the knot squeezing her heart grow bigger. She couldn't help imagining her brothers and sisters excitement if they were to see the cards. Even Mum and Da would be thrilled to look through the Wimberley's gadget. The biggest hurt was knowing if she went out the door and took the alley across two streets she would be back home. If she were this homesick when living so near, how would she feel living across the whole country?

As Claire changed the cards and passed her the viewer, Bonnie tried to make the appropriate response each time. "Yes, it's beautiful, oh aren't they frightening, no I can't imagine sleeping under canvas."

Weary and sick at heart, she finally pushed the gadget back to Claire without looking. "Sorry, but I'm dead. I have to get some sleep. Excuse me."

Claire began to apologize and her Mother stood to begin fussing over the girl. Bonnie gave her excuses again and fled to her room. Only when the door was closed and she was in her gown under the covers did she let the fear expand. What had she done? Should she tell these wonderful people thanks, but she didn't want to go west. She wanted to go back home where she belonged. But did she? Could she squeeze back into her old life before Tarn?

What about Lynne? Was she lying sleepless in her bed tonight worrying about the children and trying to figure out a way to go west or to stay in Boston and the world they knew?

Bonnie folded her hands tightly under her chin and squeezed her eyes shut. She did the only thing she could. After the long prayer, she relaxed into fitful sleep.

She woke with the light tap on her door. Shaking, she shimmied into her dress as she wiggled the gown down her hips. Then she picked up the stiff black bombazine skirt and pulled it over her head. As she opened the door for Claire she fumbled to put the brown sash around her waist. Claire stared at her critically and Bonnie held out her arms and whirled.

"No, here sit on the bed." Claire commanded.

"What?"

Instead of answering, Claire turned her around and proceeded to smooth her hair and confine the braids in a crown on top of her head, securing it carefully with hairpins.

Bonnie stared at her questioningly and Claire gave her a tug over to her room. While Bonnie straightened the top of her dress which seemed much snugger, she twisted, trying to see if there were puckers now in the back. She worried that the new seam down the center was crooked, and the wide cloth belt was going to fold over.

Claire dusted her face and throat with powder. Bonnie sneezed and rubbed her nose and Bonnie dabbed powder on it again. Bonnie held her breath and tried not to sneeze. When she opened her good eye, Claire powdered the lid of the black one. Both girls laughed.

Primly Claire tied a silly little flat hat on top of her own head and picked up her purse. Bonnie smiled and together they descended to the kitchen and a warm, quick breakfast of ham and eggs. Biscuits of the same were packed for their lunch.

There was no shouting match this morning. Instead of entering from the front, the girls waited beside the back door for the owners to come down and let them in. Bonnie wondered if their home on the second floor took in as much room as the store below. If so, they would have more living space then even the Wimberley house provided.

Mr. Lambton had a smile for the girls. Although his wife didn't smile, Bonnie thought the woman seemed pleased. The woman was eager to help them get settled, holding the door and looking them over with approval, which Bonnie read as welcoming. Bella Lambton showed them both where to leave their belongings, and the small counter in the storeroom where they could eat their lunch. Claire would be a sales assistant for Mr. Lambton at the front of the store. Bonnie would be Mrs. Lambton's assistant in the stockroom.

Claire went up front with Henry Lambton to learn her duties. While Bonnie swept the entire floor-room as briskly as possible with a push broom, Bella followed along behind explaining what her duties would be. Bonnie was to keep the floors clean, the stock neatly folded and stacked, and to help unload and store new shipments in the storeroom. For most of the garments, she would also assist in pressing and hanging garments for display.

At lunch, she learned that Claire would share some of the same duties. She would dust all shelves and products as soon as she arrived each day. She would refold and properly stock any items that were improperly displayed. If she found a garment that was wrinkled or had any marks from customer handling, she was to take it to Bonnie for freshening up which might be brushing, or pressing. In worse cases, Bonnie might have to wash, starch and iron the item.

Although Claire might make the sale as she had Saturday morning, her duty would be to bring item and customer to Mr. Lambton to have the item rung up on the cash register and payment collected. If the store wasn't busy, she would remain to fold and box the purchased item. If there were other customers she would see to their needs and Henry would fold and box the purchases. At times, items might be purchased for later delivery.

In the past, they had used a delivery boy or the Lambtons themselves would make delivery in the evenings. Now with two shop girls, there would be times when one or both girls would be sent out to deliver items. If they had to take the horse drawn streetcar to a distant part of the city, the Lambtons would supply them with pennies for the fare. Any tips they might receive for delivery would be theirs to keep. The girls quickly decided to divide all tips evenly.

As excited as both girls were, they both agreed the Lamptons were excited too. You could hear it in the precise set of rules Bella Lambton kept making. Lunch would not be eaten outside on the dock.

Both young ladies were expected to observe the proprieties at all times. They must curtsy to customers, ask politely if they could be of service, and discretely serve any request from their customers or employers. In other words, they must behave as genteel young women at all times. At ten thirty, Bella found the girls whispering together in the empty store.

"You have not been hired to sit and titter." She tilted the tiny enameled watch pinned as a broach on her blouse to confirm the time. "This will be your time for lunch. Today you may dine together, but do not depend on it."

The girls curtsied and retreated to the storeroom. Bonnie sank exhausted onto the small wrought iron chair while Claire opened the one lunch box and set out the ham and egg biscuits onto the opened napkin. Primly she looked about, then walked to the small public loo in the back corner and returned with a cup of water from the sink.

Bonnie stared at the rust stained water and shook her head. "A short beer would be a lot safer. If you think Mrs. Lambton would approve, I could dodge out to the corner pub and fetch one for each of us."

Claire giggled and gave her a pinch as she pulled up the other chair. "Hush. Remember, decorous behavior at all times." Bonnie gave a snort and pressed her hand over her mouth just in time. Outside the room they heard a rustle and both girls became somber. It didn't need to be said. No matter how many rules Bella had, no matter how many tasks were added to their assigned duties, neither girl wanted to lose another job.

Bonnie was quickly exhausted. Bella had decided they needed to inspect every box in the storeroom for any more "infestation." Bonnie had pointed out that all the traps were still baited and unsprung. Her employer had scowled at her and insisted. Before, the lifting and stretching would have been nothing. But even with the week of bed rest, Bonnie still had not recovered her strength. Although the bruises were green and purple tinged along her shoulder and arm, around her stomach they were still vivid and dark.

Fortunately, most of the upper boxes were lingerie and delicate undergarments. She stood, leaning into the step ladder with one hand braced on the shelf and turned each box around for Bella's inspection, then returned it to the shelf. Top shelf taken care of she stepped down one rung to repeat the procedure with the next items. "No, go back up. I think we'd better open and inspect them."

Trying to stifle a groan, Bonnie did, handing down each box and waiting until Bella could lift the lid, push back the tissue and sniff and move the garments away from the corners.

As Bonnie accepted a third box to exchange with the next she had an inspired idea. "Aren't you glad you didn't find anything?"

Bella sputtered and stepped back. She cocked her head, pretending to hear something. "Was that the doorbell? I'd better go help Henry. I'll send his girl back to help you finish this. Do not stop. I want every item checked."

Bonnie nodded. As soon as Bella left she turned to step onto the counter to lift, inspect and shove each box back into place.

Claire stood beside her, putting a hand out to clutch the buttoned ankle of her shoe. "Wait, I want to see them too."

CHAPTER TWELVE

"Wasn't that fun? Isn't this the best job ever?" The girls were walking home. Bonnie felt her feet drag, and a strange trembling breathlessness. As soon as they turned the corner from the shop she indicated the empty wharf. "Please, remember we were going to rest here each day."

Claire stopped abruptly as Bonnie sank onto the crude bench beside the sea wall. The happy girl continued to chatter as she twisted and turned in front of her.

"Did you ever imagine there were so many wonderful 'unmentionables'?" she whispered.

Bonnie shook her head. "Puts me one petticoat and two stained drawers to shame, that it does."

"Shh," Claire hissed and Bonnie tried to raise her head enough to look at her. "What I can't believe is you knew the name of every blasted one of them, unmentionables. Do you own some of each?"

Claire sat down on the bench beside her, placing a hand on her friend's bowed back. "No, of course not. But someday I will."

As Claire raised her face to the breeze off the bay and Bonnie watched her friend's face pink and her eyes look heavenward in rapture she smiled.

"If their business doesn't pick up, I don't see how the job can last, at least not for the both of us. I can't believe they were hiring help."

Claire stood up. "Don't be negative. Mondays are always slow." She held out her hand, wiggled her gloved fingers. "They weren't really hiring. I stopped to shop on the way home Friday and asked them about a position. They didn't act as though they'd ever considered the possibility. I had to use a little persuasion. You know, the way I do with Mother and Father sometimes."

Bonnie sighed and reached up to grab her friends hand as she rose. "Explains a lot."

Claire was skimming along, in full babble once again. "But I wonder how they advertise? I've never seen a Lambton's ad in Godey's, the Globe, or the Herald. There's not even a window so you can look inside and see all the pretty clothes for sale. Other than the one sign with Lambton's Clothiers on the door, you'd never know the shop was inside. Tomorrow I'll ask Henry about how they generate customer interest."

"Henry, is it? Best be careful Mrs. Lambton doesn't hear you call him that."

"Oh, Bella is a bit of a scowl, isn't she? Did you ever see such opposites, sunshine and storm clouds? She needn't worry, I certainly am not interested in him and Mr. Lambton is the perfect gentleman."

Bonnie didn't comment but she could imagine Lynne's voice adding, "No one is perfect."

Her friend was in Bonnie's thoughts still as she turned down their lane and saw all her brothers and sisters. They were playing in the street with neighbors in the fading sunlight to enjoy the rare warm break in the weather.

Bonnie swept up Clyde and hugged Ian and then Shawn. Both shop girls were quickly surrounded by the bevy of little Magees, Brigid, Darcey, Meara and Reagan.

Reagan grinned up with a chocolate smeared face. "Brigid brought home chocolates. You should of come sooner. Meara gobbled the last up."

Bonnie surrendered the toddler to nine year old Darcey and turned to hug Brigid. "First day on the job. So now there are five of us with jobs." Ian and Shawn grinned at her, but Shawn spoke. "Four. We was told there'd be more work for us on this and the next building too, but not for Da."

Bonnie looked around as her Mum opened the door to call them in for supper. Bonnie walked forward last with her arm around her oldest sister and both leaned together to plant kisses on their mum's cheeks. Mum raised her apron to hide her blushing face. "Come in, come in. There's always room at the table."

Claire declined, saying she had to hurry home. Bonnie called out she would be home soon. She kissed the young girl beside her, feeling the weariness in her slender frame. "Now you're a working woman, too." Brigid's eyes glistened with proud tears as she ran inside. Bonnie stepped into the room and into her mother's arms.

The small flat was as crowded and noisy as ever and Mum seated Bonnie and served her a cup of stew first. Bonnie looked around for Da and Ian mumbled, "Stopped at the pub."

As soon as everyone was served, Mum sat down beside her oldest child, happy tears in her eyes. Bonnie noticed there wasn't a dish in front of her.

"Ate enough tasting it. Reckon to set some aside for the old man, when he comes home," Mum volunteered.

Bonnie moved the cup over to her mother. "This tastes wonderful, Mum, but the Wimberleys will have a place set for me. You finish it for me."

She sat, happy for the first time all day as she looked at the faces she loved. When she turned back to her, Mum was finishing the last of the broth, letting the spoon clatter in the empty mug.

"This job doesn't pay as good as the last, but I should have fifty cents a day to bring home," Bonnie said.

"Aye, that's all you make. Shawn and I each earn sixty a day, and that's just for toting. The carpenter told me if I keep showing him something, he might apprentice me on. Then it'll be a dollar a day, just for me."

She smiled, surprised to feel jealous of her own brother. But then, why would she be surprised. Ian was nearly as tall as she and a sight brawnier. Men made more, that was the way of it. "What about Shawn?"

The younger boy blushed. "Told me to wait until I started shaving, then he'd think about it."

Everyone laughed and Clyde reached up to feel of Shawn's face and Ian's cheek. He shook his head at Shawn. "Nope, no prickles."

Everyone laughed. "What about you sis?" Meara asked.

Brigid raised her head, looked about a little confused until Ian repeated the question. "Thirty-five for now, but if I work hard and pay attention, I can get to be a dipper. That pays fifty a day, the same as Bonnie."

The boys finished and Bonnie watched them walk to the back room and look back at their Mum. "Don't go smoking again, and burn down the place," she called. Ian waved a hand at her and made a face. Both women knew the words that weren't said. "Oh shut up."

Clyde was bawling at being locked away from his brothers and the younger girls teased and tried to get him to play with them. Darcey was already washing up the things from supper while Brigid sat asleep with her head on her arms at the table.

"Mum, you know the Wimberleys asked me to go west with them, but I was thinking there be no need now Tarn is gone."

Her mother walked with her out of the crowded flat into the night air and closed the door behind her. She clutched at Bonnie's hand.

"I know you and Da told me to keep the money I make, but I was thinking if you need it, I can help."

"Go with them. You can see what you'll have if you stay. I'll have all Brigid's pay. Ian and Shawn gave me nearly all of theirs this week."

"And Da?" Bonnie looked at the tired woman before her, wanted to say more.

"I asked, but you know your Da. First time he'd a dollar of his own in months. Drank too much Friday night, still fluttered on Monday. Why he got the sack so soon. Went out for a wee bit of the hair of the dog tonight," she shook her head.

Suddenly she grabbed and squeezed Bonnie's arms. "Listen to me darling. You see what I have, what you'll have, if you stay. Go West. If you do well there, you can send for the little ones. There's nothing for ye here."

Bonnie bit her lip then turned away. Her Mum called after her and Bonnie turned back. "Don't you want your thunking stick? Pretty dark out there."

Grinning, Bonnie walked back for the discarded two by four and swung it in her hand all the way to her new home.

◇◇◇

She left the thick board on the porch as she entered the warm house and turned toward the dining room with its glowing chandelier. All eight candles were lit and the family sat enjoying the meal as the maid bustled in with dessert.

Claire leaped from her seat and raced to grab Bonnie, almost crashing into Bess. "They said yes. Mother and Father want Lynne and the children to go West with us. Isn't it grand?"

Bonnie sank into her chair in shock and Bess came back with a plate of food. "Person ought to have the decency to show up for meals on time, especially if they're guests in a home."

"Hush, Bess," Mother Wimberley scolded.

Bonnie bowed her head in shame. "Sorry, I stopped to visit my family."

The maid was already storming back to the kitchen, angry at being reprimanded for saying what was true. "Inviting in people like stray cats, never mind who has to do the work of waiting on and cleaning up after them. Bleaching linens and washing out bedding like it's no extra work. Not a word to me about it, just orders to make up the attic and move things about to have room for the new ones. Sick people, dying of disease. No thought about bringing their epizootics into the home for decent, clean people to catch."

"Bess, I said hush now," Mother Wimberley ordered.

All heard the loud clank of dishes dropped into the sink on top of the ones already there.

Mother Wimberley twisted and threw her napkin onto the table as she stormed out to the kitchen. Her husband half rose, "now Mother." She ignored him, slamming the kitchen door shut behind her. All heard her raised voice, "Anything you break will come out of your pay."

They all sat in strained silence, listening to the volatile exchange in the kitchen. "There are plenty of women wanting a job as good as this if you don't want to do it anymore. I'll be happy to accept your notice."

"Notice, there be no notice. I'm not staying to take the typhoid fever and die. You can do your own work from now on, you and that spoiled princess of yours and that filthy gutter rat she done brung home."

"Get out!" they heard Mother Wimberley scream and Claire's father reached out a strong hand to clutch the arm of each girl to keep them seated. Mother yelled again. "Out now and take nothing you did not bring with you into this house."

"Stealing, now you're accusing me of stealing. I've never taken a thing that wasn't given me, never in my whole life."

"Leave the uniform, please. I will have Father Wimberley settle your pay after I take out for any damage to my kitchen."

They heard the maid scream and swear and all remained seated, staring at their plates.

"There might have been an appeasement, but not after that. You girls stay put, we'll be back in moments. Go ahead, Bonnie, eat your supper darling. You look tired." With that Father Wimberley walked out to the kitchen and his angry wife.

CHAPTER THIRTEEN

Bonnie sat at the long table, staring at her friend. The glow of the candles gave her the same golden halo she had first seen around Claire after Tarn beat her. "Your maid's right," she said, then carved off a bite of ham. Fork loaded with potatoes and peas, she savored it. "You Wimberleys are big hearted and full of charity, but there are costs you're not thinking about."

Claire's eyes squinted then opened wide. "I can't believe you agree with Bess."

"Aye, I do," Bonnie said.

"Fine, I suppose you want to leave, move back home and live in that crowded little flat." Claire said throwing her head up in anger.

"Aye, I would like it. But I'm no longer welcome, me Mum told me, just before she said goodnight."

"Oh Bonnie, I'm so sorry."

Bonnie shrugged, tried to sound confident. "I'm a grown woman, time to go out on my own. She didn't slam the door, just reminded me it's time I make a life. I plan to stay here, then go west whenever you leave. Mum told me once I get set up, she hopes I can help me brothers and sisters."

Claire settled, her chin lowered. "We really do want you to come west with us, you know we do."

"Aye, I will. Now I'm well, I'll come as the maid. I've never been one to stay in the house or stand at the stove. But I can clean and will gladly, and do even more next week than this one. When and if I'm ever fully healed, I can lift and load as well as anyone, you know that I can."

Claire's parents stood framed in the kitchen door clapping. Bonnie smiled at them.

"What about your job at Lambtons?" Claire asked.

"I was hoping to keep it too. Save a little money toward my future. Do most of the work by getting up a little earlier, working a little later in the evening, if that's all right with all of you."

Claire's father remained standing with his big arm around her dainty little mother. Both nodded and the man escorted his wife back to the table. "Now let's have a nice bite of cake and a little cup of coffee to celebrate."

Later, the whole time the girls worked at clearing the table, Bonnie talked. "There's no need to clear the attic for the McKinney's. They can have the room I'm using and I'll move into the maids. Be easier for me to get my chores done if I'm in her room. It's enough that your mother will take on most of the actual cooking."

"Bonnie, you know that's not how I want things. You're my friend."

"Aye, and I always will be, and so will Lynne. But your mother promised I could work and earn my keep. I intend to. No need to hire another when I'll be here and wanting to do the work anyway."

Bonnie lifted the remaining dishes and carried them toward the kitchen. As they entered, the maid shrieked at the sight of her and fled into the night.

She carefully set the dirty dishes on the counter next to the broken plate and chipped saucer already resting there. Together the girls stood and laughed.

◇◇◇

Next morning, Bonnie managed to cook bacon only a little too done, eggs only a little too runny, and toast way too singed. The best part was she was dressed and had the meal ready on time when Father Wimberley rose. He insisted she eat her own food in order to learn how to improve it. When his wife came down the stairs she was surprised and pleased to see them seated at the table eating and talking.

Bonnie shoved the last bite of toast and egg into her mouth and rose hastily to curtsy at the missus. She lifted her cup to swallow a gulp of hot coffee to wash the terrible food down before speaking. "Your mister showed me how to make coffee the way he liked. Now, may I serve you something, Mother Wimberley?"

"Call me Elizabeth, and this is Robert."

Bonnie shook her head, "I think of you as Mother and Father Wimberley if that's all right with you."

"Of course, Bonnie, that is even better. Mother Wimberley followed her in and showed her how to test the egg white on the fried egg and to remember to smell the toast rather than repeatedly open the oven. Together they checked the inventory for the kitchen and Claire's mother explained that she would take care of cooking lunch and supper, unless Bonnie were already home to cook.

They agreed the marketing could be a problem. The maid had visited the farmer's market and the grocers daily. Bonnie proposed twice weekly trips to the market and a larger order to the grocers with home delivery from him or she could pick it up at the end of the day. They decided on delivery.

Rushing with the first grocery order to drop off, the two girls excitedly ran through the street. "Is my hat okay?" Claire called.

Bonnie smiled at her friend. No need to talk about how great the job was this morning. Claire was in heaven working at a place where she could have a reason to primp and dress up every day instead of only Sundays. "Lovely."

The Grocers was open. Impatiently, Bonnie tapped the counter, looking around for the familiar bald head. The man came from the back with an oath, tugging at his bloody apron. "What can't wait?"

Bonnie swallowed hard and lowered her head, then at Claire's elbow, she raised her head and extended the list. "I need this order filled and delivered to the address on the back."

"Right now?" Mr. Sanders thundered.

"No, anytime today, as long as the meat arrives by two this afternoon. Is there a big charge for delivery?"

The man stared at her in irritation. "No charge for delivery, most people do tip though." Suddenly he stopped talking and studied the girl before him, then looked down at Claire. "I know you, you three girls' came in Saturday evening."

Bonnie stood mute, wondering what would come next. Claire finally spoke up. "We bought chestnuts to roast, you spoke to Lynne about her furniture."

"Right, he slapped the counter."

Bonnie backed up tugging at Claire. "We have to go, we don't want to be late for work."

"No, wait," he rushed to raise the section of counter barring customers from the back of the store, "It's about your friend."

Bonnie forgot her reticence with strangers and boldly stood to look him in the eye.

"My wife and I, we bought her furniture. Terrible, her mother dying and everything, the little ones so sick. Later, my wife tried to make me go ask for my money back, but there is nothing to fear with the typhoid being spread by objects. The paper says it's from fevered secretions of victims and possibly polluted water."

"I know, Lynne told us that."

"Have you talked to her recently, since the little girl had the seizure? How is she doing?"

"Mary Anne is sick?" Claire asked.

"Oh yes, it was horrible. My wife and I left but we saw her rush down with the child and the couple in the front apartment, the man rode them in his cab somewhere. You could ask them to find out. I keep seeing that poor child and praying for all of them. Your friend was so desperate."

At the tenement the building was marked as quarantined. The girls looked fearfully around. Claire saw a man harnessing a team of horses in the stable yard behind the building. Bonnie clutched her hand as they ran up to him just as he was climbing aboard.

"Hey, you."

"Heya Missy, you need a cab?"

Bonnie shook her head. "No, our friend, someone gave her and her little sister a ride yesterday morning. We thought it might have been you."

The black man shook his head. "No Missy that be Mr. Sommers. He's already left."

Claire looked dejected, looked about as someone walked past on the street. "Bonnie we have to hurry."

"Do you know where he took her and the little girl?"

"Yes Miss, I talked to the pretty lady. She rushed that poor child to the hospital 'fore she croaked like her mother."

At the horrified expression on the girls' faces he continued. "I reckon she be smart to do that with them little boys too. This here disease ain't nothing to take a chance on. Saw her later when she was walking back down the street from the newspaper office, a big smile on her face."

Bonnie waved and hollered thanks as the two ran down the street toward the Back Bay shops.

Bonnie had always been the fastest runner at school. Tall and lean, as a girl she liked to imagine she was an Indian princess named Willow, running like the wind. Now Claire began to pull ahead, calling over her shoulder to urge Bonnie on. By the second street Bonnie was wheezing, face scarlet, her heart thumping loudly and painfully in her chest. Before they turned the corner onto the wharf to head down Newberry she bent down from the stitch in her side and tossed up the runny egg mess.

Chest heaving, hobbling her way across, she once again collapsed on the bench beside the pier. Claire stopped and looked back to her friend. She started to turn toward her and Bonnie made a waving motion, to move her on. Gasping for breath she sat, hands gripping knees, and tried to breathe in the tight, tight clothes. She felt like her flesh were being squeezed and burning bright beneath the snug wool dress she still wore beneath the black skirt and white cotton blouse of the maid. Worse, sweat was now pouring down her face and body. She could feel it soaking the fabric beneath her arms and the middle of her back. It felt like when she was working in the mill over the starch vats in July. Lord only knew what she looked like.

Claire stopped, breathing deeply as she stared across where Bonnie sat heaving. She tried to decide what to do, which was more important. Going back for her friend or being punctual for work. She felt relieved when Bonnie motioned her forward. Maybe she was right. Claire needed this job, had been the one to find the position. At the amount of trade the place had, it was unlikely the Lambtons could afford to keep both on as shop girls. Now, Bonnie had a position as maid at their house, wouldn't she be better off not having to work two jobs. If she couldn't keep up, was that any reason for Claire to lose this wonderful job?

Claire kept walking, turned the corner and rushed until she stood at the back entrance and knocked on the employee door. She had wiped her brow, fluffed her sleeves and made sure her hair and hat were in position before knocking again. It was still a couple of minutes before she heard feet on the stairs and the door swung open.

Henry Lambton stood at the door, his shirt open at the throat, his face a little flushed. Claire blinked, surprised at how affected she was by the sight of his collar-less, coatless appearance. She blushed and looked down and gasped to see he was in his stocking feet.

He moved to push the door closed so he was hidden behind it. "My apologies, we were just getting ready."

Claire began to apologize at the same time. "I'm sorry, I wasn't sure what time you expected us to arrive and we were afraid to be late." As her words ran over his he seemed to recover his dignity a little.

"Eight o'clock should be sufficient, I think," he said. "The shop doesn't open officially until nine. I would think an hour would be adequate preparation time. My wife hasn't told me what she thinks about the matter, but since she's not ready yet, well seven … or whatever time this is, is absurdly early. So come back at eight." He began to close the door and Claire caught it and managed to catch his attention.

"Wonderful, we really were in such a rush. May I, may I slip into the back for a moment, just to get a cup of water. Just for a second, please."

"Of course." He swung the door wide, managing to stay hidden at the same time.

A minute later Claire emerged from the customer's loo, her little collapsible cup dripping water as she stepped slowly forward trying to keep it from sloshing. She looked up and smiled, again struck by the intimacy of seeing her employer embarrassed at being caught 'unpolished.'

The man ran a hand through his uncombed hair in response and grinned. Both blushed again as she scooted past and out into the air where she could breathe.

From the top of the stairs she heard the strident voice of Bella demanding what was taking so long and Claire was relieved to hear the door slam closed behind her.

She walked back around, concentrating on the water in the cup until the smile on her face was squashed. Even with care, there was one less circle of the precious liquid by the time she reached her friend.

Bonnie looked up, surprised as Claire extended the cup carefully. "We're way too early, can you believe it," Claire said happily.

Bonnie's hand shook as she reached for the brownish water and swallowed most of it in one long gulp. "Thank you," she whispered. "I thought …"

Claire was glad she didn't finish the thought, wondered what kind of honest answer she could give. "Eight, they think eight will be early enough and give us plenty of preparation time. I'm amazed that they opened the store at seven for us yesterday."

Bonnie leaned back and worked at breathing more normally so she could talk. "Aye, thought they were as excited about having employees as we were eager to be shop girls."

Claire seemed to finally see her as she gasped out the last. "Oh Bonnie, look at you."

Bonnie tilted her head to look up at her, aware only of the horror in her friends face. "As bad as all that. I was afraid …"

Claire took the cup, dampened her handkerchief in the remaining moisture and passed it to her friend. What had their maid complained of, endless linen that would never wash clean because of the gutter rat? As she watched Bonnie wipe her face the ugly thoughts continued. This would be her second ruined handkerchief, and her robe seemed to have a permanent smell. Ashamed of herself, embarrassed that Bonnie might read her mind, she stood and looked about.

"Luckily we still have plenty of time. Let's go back behind the store, and we'll get you put straight enough."

Bonnie shuddered but pushed heavily to her feet. Slowly, trying to relax enough to get her breath, she was grateful for the grayness of the morning and the crisp clean air blowing from the bay to cool her skin. She carried her cloak over her arm, instantly felt chilled by the sea air. Claire noticed and scolded her, demanded she put it back on. Surprised, Bonnie heard her teeth chatter as she struggled back into it.

As her breathing slowed, she confided to Claire. "It's my fault, I still have my brown dress beneath. Thought it was better than my thin petticoat. Running, I've sweated it through."

In the alley with the door closed and no windows looking down at them, Claire and Bonnie backed behind the ledge of the loading dock and Claire held onto the cloak as Bonnie worked the buttons loose on the underneath dress, then somehow managed to wiggle like a side-show contortionist to drop the brown dress to the street beneath her black skirt.

Cautiously she stepped clear of the dress and picked it up to fold into a tight bundle. Surprised, she sneezed at the strong smell of it. She held it out toward Claire. "Ooh, do you smell that."

Claire recognized the bitter odor instantly. She stared in pain at her shivering friend. "Yes, it smells like the laudanum."

"Do I still smell of it?" Bonnie whispered. Claire leaned forward and shook her head. "I can't tell, I think you smell like cloves and moth balls." She answered as she covered her nose.

Irritated, Bonnie put the damp brown bundle on the edge of the dock and looked around. "Turn around Claire," she whispered fiercely.

Claire turned and faced the street while Bonnie squatted. Claire almost turned back around as she heard ripping cloth. Minutes later, Bonnie stood and moved around her. Determined, Bonnie walked around and whispered. "Just when you think things can't get worse."

Claire looked confused and Bonnie leaned closer to whisper. "The bleeding started again."

"Oh," Claire looked shocked and Bonnie fought the urge to laugh at her friend. What had the girls' mother claimed, 'we are all women here.' Bonnie rolled her eyes. "Well, you know it happens sometimes."

Claire blushed prettily and Bonnie pushed at her heavy damp hair. "There's probably no hope, but do you have a comb in your bag.

At least if I get my hair neatened, there might be a chance of saving this job."

CHAPTER FOURTEEN

As Claire worked her magic, using her fingers and comb to work the tangles out of the damp hair both girls relaxed. Claire braided and restored it to a neat stylish appearance and the distance between them seemed to vanish.

"I'm sorry Bonnie. I forget you're still sick. You never complain and I was in such a panic about this job. I should have asked about starting time. Bella gave us so many rules yesterday."

Bonnie turned around where she stood in front of the seated Claire and leaned forward to hug her. "Hush, angel, I didn't think about it either. We're still used to the Mill hours."

The Mill reminded them and together they said, "Lynne."

"Oh Bonnie, I put her misery out of my mind. What if she loses her little sister or even her brothers? Poor Lynne."

"Shh," Bonnie shushed her, leaning inward until their foreheads touched. "You heard what the coachman said. She left the newspaper office smiling. Mr. Sanders bought her furniture so she had enough to take Mary Anne to the hospital. She's at the hospital, so you know she will be safe now."

Claire looked uncertain. Bonnie said, "After work, I'll need to go straight home to get supper on the table. But maybe you can go by Lynne's place and see if she's back or the neighbor in the front…"

"Sommers…"

They heard the door open behind them. Bonnie glanced toward the brown bundle now wedged tightly under the bricks against the corner of the dock and decided to leave it there. Smiling she turned to mount the large steps onto the dock, whispering to her friend as she passed, "You can check with the Sommers."

Claire shoved the comb into her bag and drew it closed as she followed, annoyed that Bonnie seemed to be giving the orders.

Both dropped a curtsy to Mrs. Lambton and Claire watched as she seemed to sniff as Bonnie stepped past. "Sorry, the damp makes the wool smell," Claire explained.

The woman nodded wisely as both stepped past her to store their belongings in the workroom.

The second day at Lambton's went better than the first. Bonnie finally had a chance to clean and block the hat, much to Bella's sincere approval. When a shipment of clothes arrived and the workmen moved the large crates inside, it was Bonnie who assisted Bella in opening each box so she could inspect and inventory every item. Then Bonnie carried them to the workroom. Before the new items were placed on the shelves, each box of the old ones of that type of garment had to be taken down and inspected as well. The new items went on the bottom, the older ones on top, unless the new ones were kept out to be carried up front to be displayed.

Bonnie had a stack of dresses to press and hang to fill her afternoon. Her stomach was growling noisily by the time Bella relented and told her to eat her lunch. Bonnie had just returned from washing up when Claire came back to join her.

◇◇◇

"Oh lucky you. You get to see all the new things when they first arrive."

Bonnie smiled and shook her head. "You goose. I guess it's lucky if you don't have to climb up and move every box we moved twice yesterday yet again."

Bonnie watched Claire lay out the napkin and put the lunch out on it, waiting to see the same little smile she had shown yesterday. Of course the food was leftover from what Bess had cooked, but Bonnie had selected and packed it. Her own mouth was already watering at the thought of eating the thick ham sandwiches with their brown mustard and thick slices of bread. She'd also packed them both a slice of cake.

Bonnie relaxed as she saw Claire's satisfied smile and took a moment to pray before reaching for her sandwich. Claire joined her and the girls again whispered "Lynne," together. Minutes later Claire returned from her own quick wash up with the cup of water.

Bonnie chewed a bite of the thick sandwich staring at the little tin cup. Claire seemed to read her mind, "I know it's awfully brown."

"I was thinking how sweet it tasted when you carried it to me this morning. You know the color is just from the rust in the pipes."

Claire took a dainty bite of the big sandwich and nodded. "Our pipes do the same." She stared at the cake and smiled at her friend. Bonnie swallowed another bite, already feeling full. "Maybe I should pack a little less tomorrow."

Claire grinned and they ate quietly for another ten minutes. Then Claire began to talk, whispering but just as happy. "There were three customers already this morning, and all bought something."

"Good," Bonnie said. "We got in more than enough to replace it."

Claire looked displeased and slowly wrapped her sandwich. Bonnie wrapped the last half of her own and restored them to the box along with the salt shaker. "Do you want to share one slice now, save the other for later?"

Claire nodded and took the small one close to her to open first. Bonnie tried not to look disappointed.

"It's a new business," Bonnie whispered. "Her father gave it to Bella and Henry for a wedding present."

"Oh," Claire looked shocked.

Bonnie and Claire separated at Lynne's tenement building and Bonnie walked on to the Wimberley's. Once home, she crept into the kitchen and was relieved to see Mother Wimberley opening the oven. She noticed Claire's mother was flustered looking and she wondered how this could really work. Obviously she was used to having someone else take care of the house and kitchen duties.

"Hello, Bonnie, where's Claire?"

At the snap in her question, Bonnie suddenly felt tongue-tied. She set the loaded lunch sack down on the kitchen table. Instead of answering, she pointed to the bathroom and disappeared. When she emerged, she sighed with relief to find the kitchen empty. Stealthily she stepped to the stove and opened the oven. Inside she found a simmering pot roast and pan of bread. As the kitchen door swung open she jumped. Bonnie looked guilty.

"Smells wonderful," she muttered.

"Good, now you've washed up, can you set the table, please?"

Bonnie looked around nervously, took down the plates she had washed that morning and bumped the door open by backing into it. Staring at the bare table, she hugged the plates to her. Mother Wimberley pointed to the china cabinet. "Middle drawer."

Bonnie set the plates down on the sideboard, careful not to bump into the silver bowl already there. Heart pounding, afraid she might break something like the last maid, she opened the first drawer and saw lace covers and cautiously closed it to open the one below. She put her hand on a white cloth and Mother Wimberley shook her head. Bonnie touched a yellow one next and was rewarded with a nod.

She shook the cloth out over the clean table, and at the woman's slight frown looked down to see what she had done wrong this time. Carefully she evened and smoothed the cloth and then smiled hopefully.

Mother Wimberley smiled. "You know, you need to be able to talk to me or Robert, even when Claire isn't here."

Bonnie nodded, then said, "Claire stopped by to see Lynne."

She didn't miss the panicked expression on her mother's face. "I thought her tenement was under quarantine."

"Aye, she was going to ask a neighbor to fetch Lynne or tell her how things were going. We learned from the grocer this morning, Mr. Sanders, that she had rushed the little girl to the hospital."

"Oh no."

"Aye, and maybe the twins. Claire was going to find out more, but not take any chance of exposure."

When Claire's mother raised her hand to her throat Bonnie felt the same fear in her chest. When the woman stared out the window, Bonnie felt the same concern as the sky darkened. Even with the big two by four, she had been afraid to walk the streets after dark alone.

"Here, I'll run meet her as soon as I set the table, don't worry ma'am." Bonnie dealt the plates around the table like cards from a deck and then raised her hands. "The silverware?"

"Left, side drawer."

Five minutes later Bonnie pulled her cloak back on and grabbed the two-by-four to head out.

Bonnie walked briskly in the cooling air, her right hand swinging her big stick. She didn't want to run again, the pain this morning had been disabling and that was the last thing she needed. In the distance she could hear a dog barking and a child crying. Closer to hand, she heard the scrabble of tiny feet and was glad not to have a lantern to reveal the rat. Some she knew were large enough to attack a person, not a healthy adult, but a little baby, old person, or ailing child.

She was nearly to the towering tenements when she heard quick footsteps running her way. Instinctively she raised the club and when a voice squealed in fright, she lowered it and opened her arms.

She wrapped the short woman in her embrace. "Thank goodness, Claire, I was starting to worry."

"Bonnie, oh Bonnie. Tell me not to do this again. I was coming out from the apartment the coachman told me about. They told me Lynne and the children were all at the hospital. I was in such a hurry to get home, I almost tripped over a body lying in the entry way. I thought it was a dead person. Mrs. Sommers told me it was just someone who had been evicted from their apartment and had snuck inside to sleep and stay a little warmer."

"Shh," Bonnie wrapped her arm close, tugging her along as she whispered, "I promise. Your mother looked so panicked and I realized what a big mistake I made. I just wanted to be home to get the food on the table, but she had everything done but setting the table. I know she could have done it faster and better without my help."

"I just want to know Lynne is safe. It seems wrong that we're not able to help her," Claire yelled.

A voice in the dark hollered. "Quiet, we're sick in here."

Trembling, the girls rushed to exit the shadowed alleys and emerge into the open lane that lead to the nice homes where the Wimberley's lived.

Only when they saw the brightly lighted windows and the welcoming porch did the girls slow down. Like a miracle, they saw a hooded figure emerge from the porch swing.

"Oh Lynne," they rushed forward and Lynne didn't raise her hands to stop them from hugging and kissing her. "Don't worry, the nurses have assured me you can't pass it on unless you're feverish or sick."

"I know it's late, and I shouldn't be here, but so much has happened."

"Mr. Sanders told us about buying the furniture and Mary Anne's seizure and how you took her to the hospital."

"I barely got her there in time. Oh girls, I nearly lost her."

"Sit," Bonnie urged, "I'll bring you some food."

Bonnie burst into the house, stopped at the sight of the Wimberleys standing huddled together in front of the table, wringing their hands. "It's Lynne, she's outside. I need warm food, something for her to drink."

"If you know it's safe, bring her inside."

"As soon as they had Mary Anne bathed, her fever dropped and she began breathing normally. I knew I had to bring the boys as well. But I didn't have another twenty dollars and the need was urgent. I knew my options, and decided a stranger in the yellow sheets was better than the men who had already made offers. At least the ads all promised marriage. So I went into the office of the Globe and agreed to accept the offer of Mr. Phillip Gant if he would wire the additional money I needed."

Everyone had to make a comment, whether oh no, or poor darling, or you didn't. Lynne used the time to finish cleaning her plate. It was Father Wimberley who passed her a cup of black coffee, Mother Wimberley added cream and sugar. "Go on, finish the story."

"I finally convinced the newspaper man to send a telegram. I used some of the laundry money and the funds you shared Claire to pay for the wire. Which reminds me." She passed the dirty plate to Bonnie and stood to unpin her purse to hand the contents to Claire. She drained the last of the coffee and handed the cup to Bonnie as well. Bonnie slipped into the kitchen with the dirty dishes and put them into the sudsy water in the dish pan before coming back out with another cup of coffee and a slice of cake.

Lynne was exacting a promise from Claire and Bonnie decided she would just ask Claire later. "So you took the boys to the hospital."

"Certainly. I emptied the coal barrow and loaded them into it wrapped in a quilt. I bumped the boys down all three flights of stairs and pushed them to the hospital. You should have heard the nurses complain when I unloaded the sooty darlings."

Everyone laughed and ate a little too as they stared at their brave friend.

"What are you wearing under your cloak?" Claire asked.

Lynne leaned back to let it fall open to reveal the white ruffled cap and smock. "They are so strict about visitors and I couldn't leave them alone. One of the nuns helped me to sneak into the hospital as an aide. I've done whatever I could to be near the darlings the last two days." For a moment her face became shadowed and they all tried to imagine what she had endured.

She shrugged and smiled, "Tonight I will finish packing up the few books and special things from our parents. I wondered if I could bring them here to store until I send for the children."

Claire burst out in tears. "Of course, Miss Silly. I thought you were the sensible one. We were going to take you all on the wagon train with us when we go West in the spring. Now you'll have to wire your stranger and tell him you can't come."

They all heard the rattle of the cup in its saucer and Bonnie leaned over to brace her hand. "Don't cry Lynne. They've asked me to come too. There'll be two wagons and plenty of room. Father Wimberley's going to move a second wagon full of his foundry equipment."

Lynne's voice was clear and calm and everyone grew quiet as she spoke. "God has numbered every hair on our heads. All this is meant to be. According to the newspaper man I am legally betrothed and if I am not on the train tomorrow morning I will be arrested for fraud."

"Nonsense, we can get a lawyer. No jury would …" Mother Wimberley said, but her husband said, "Hush."

"Well, let us bring the children in the spring when we make the trip. You won't have to worry about them with all of us to keep them safe," Bonnie said.

"Of course, Mother and Father want the children," Claire added.

"The boys are hardy, stout little men and hard workers. Mary Anne's hands are so nimble and she is the best little dish-washer and laundry folder you've ever seen. Hopefully, once I'm in Montana, Mr. Gant will supply additional money to send for them." Her voice filled with uncertainty at the last.

"Nonsense, if they are such good workers I can use the boys in the foundry, only where it's safe of course, and Mary Anne can help Elizabeth around the house. We'll be glad to have them and let them earn their keep."

"After we've fattened them up and got them back on their feet. We'll make sure they rest first. Yes, we will be happy to keep them forever," Mother Wimberley insisted.

Lynne rose. Bonnie recognized the proud stance.

"I am learning to be grateful for the kindness of others. I will trust them to your care until you reach Oregon. Somehow I will be there to meet you and take them home with me. I cannot give them up forever. But I trust you dear hearts," she reached out to Claire and Bonnie, "to keep them safe as we move into our next adventure."

She stepped past them to the porch steps.

"Now, forgive me but I've got to go home to finish packing, then back to the hospital. Is there anywhere special you want me to put things when I drop them off?"

"Set them on the porch. We'll store them," Bonnie and Father Wimberley said in unison.

"Good. I guess I'll bring the children back with me in the coal barrow in the morning. The hospital plans to release them tomorrow at noon but it would be better if I see them settled before I leave. The trains at eight and I've got a lot to do before then."

They were still trying to persuade or say goodbye when Lynne was only a shadow.

CHAPTER FIFTEEN

Bonnie had meant to stay awake. After she finished clearing up the dining room, sweeping the downstairs rooms, and washing dishes, she put a washtub of her own clothes to soaking and laid down for a moment's rest. It was the smell of coffee and the loud rattle of a pan that woke her the next morning. Embarrassed she rushed into the kitchen still dressed and took over the skillet. This morning she flipped and only broke one yolk.

The kitchen smelled of the brown dress and other clothes in the tub and Bonnie prayed she hadn't ruined anything by leaving them to soak. As soon as Father Wimberley was in the dining room she got to work, rubbing the garments on the washboard, rinsing and wringing them out. Even though it was still dark, she managed to hang the garments on the line outside and clear out the smelly water.

On the way back inside she opened the gate and stepped through to inspect the front porch. Lynne had already been back. Bonnie carried in two bags of clothing and bedding which she set in the entryway on the hall tree before going out for the large box full of books and other items.

Father Wimberley walked out to look. Bonnie already felt flustered and exhausted and dawn hadn't even broken. "You think the clothes are clean?" he asked.

Bonnie opened each bag and sniffed. "I'll take the clean up to the room I was in. Guess I have time to rinse out and hang the rest of these things before work," she said it as though she expected him to argue but he merely nodded and walked over to carry the box back to the table.

Bonnie sank onto her knees to run more water into the tub and add soap to the many children's clothes and dirty sheets that tumbled out. Sniffing, she sprinkled some of the bleach crystals over top. Later, she was ready to take them out to hang when she heard voices in the kitchen.

Smiling, she vacated the bathroom to Claire and smiled as a sleepy Mother Wimberley said. "I don't think there are enough eggs. Do you know how to make porridge or pancakes?"

Numbly Bonnie nodded as she stepped forward to put water on the stove top to boil. "I've washed the dirty clothes Lynne brought, if you can watch the pot, I'll go on out to hang these."

"Of course. Remember you need to eat and get tidied up for work yourself. And Father Wimberley wants to know if you've made the lunches yet?"

Claire exited the bathroom, a sunny smile on her face, and asked, "What's for breakfast?"

Bonnie had to bite her tongue. No sense acting the martyred cinder girl. She had agreed to be the maid. "Porridge will be ready in minutes or I can fry you ladies a couple of eggs."

She opened the small icebox and removed the ham while she talked. Quickly she sliced two thick slabs of bread, reached up for the mustard pot and slathered both pieces before carving thin ham and layering it in between.

"Ham and eggs sounds nice," both said, looking at each other.

"Ham and eggs then."

As the water hissed on the stove she added the oats, stirred and covered the pot as she moved it to a back-eye.

Somehow she managed to pack the Mister's lunch and one for them as well. This time she made only one sandwich and split it into two halves.

She served the ladies of the house and then toted the clothes out into the cold yard to hang. Hooking the empty basket beside the back door where she'd found it she turned just in time to see Lynne trundling the barrow slowly up the street. Without hesitation she ran to help, taking one handle and hugging Lynne at the same time. Together they pushed the old wooden cart with its big wheel up to the kitchen door.

In minutes she had the sleepy children and Lynne to herself. They were seated around the small table in the warm room with a bowl of porridge for each of them. She fried a little of the ham and put it in the middle of the table.

Bonnie stared from one hollow eyed child to another and across to her friend who looked little bigger or better than Mary herself.

"It's lovely, but I don't know if we can eat very much," Lynne whispered.

Bonnie laughed and hugged her again. "I never realized why Mum was so tired until I volunteered to be the maid. Whew, I hate housework."

Lynne smiled. "If I ever get rich enough, I will never do laundry again."

At their laughter and voices, the Wimberley's poured into the kitchen. In minutes, the sleepy children had been kissed by each and swept upstairs by one or the other of the Wimberleys.

Lynne and Bonnie remained at the table, eating the porridge and then Bonnie packed her a lunch for the train. When they heard the mantle clock chime seven they both rose and rushed upstairs. The twins were half-asleep in the bed Bonnie had used for a while. Lynne was happy to see each held one of their wooden guns. She smiled her thanks at Father Wimberley and then kissed the boys goodbye once more.

Claire and her mother were in the other room sitting on either side on the big canopy bed. "I want Mary Anne to sleep in here. I've always wanted a little sister."

Lynne put a hand on her heart when the child held up her doll and opened her arms for another bye kiss.

Bonnie knew she had no time left but she stood on the porch and held Lynne beside her a little longer.

"I asked Claire to take the money by to pay Mr. Huntmeister, the landlord. I warned her not to go alone."

"I'll go along and protect her."

"I'll write. Once you get my letter, write me too. I could not go and leave them if I did not know you girls would love and care for the children like your own."

"We will, and the Wimberley's are everything that is kind."

Lynne stood on tiptoe to kiss her cheek and then darted away.

Claire came running down the stairs calling her name and waving to Lynne. Down the street they heard a dog barking. "It's so far to the train station," Claire said.

"She's going to the newspaper office. They are sending her there by cab."

"Oh. Goodness, we're going to be late. Are you ready Bonnie?"

"A minute, just a minute."

With her only other dress on beneath her cloak, Bonnie had no intention of running today. Claire seemed anxious and frustrated with their pace so Bonnie kept her distracted with talk.

"That was truly generous of you, putting Mary Anne in your own bed." Bonnie looked sideways to watch her answer and was rewarded by Claire's bright smile.

"They are all three so little. What is Mary Anne, seven or eight? And the twins, not much older?"

"Mary is seven, same as my sister Meara. The twins are eleven, two months younger than Brigid and she's already working. Their young, though they are big-footed boys that will probably grow as tall and brawny as their father and dead brother Sean. Aye, you remember Sean, you were sweet on him as I recall."

Claire blushed and giggled. "He was handsome, two years and a bit older then all three of us. He made you look googley-eyed a couple of times, too."

Bonnie laughed, as she looked around. On the left were the barges and ships in the bay and on the right the narrow little street with all its shops. "See we're here already, with time to spare, and I didn't break a sweat or toss my breakfast on the pavers this time. How are you doing?"

Claire's face was glowing. "Warm, because I have to take two steps to one of your long strides." As they walked around to the back-door to wait, Claire pointed to the shop beside theirs. "See the blue banner across the door. Brighton is having a sale."

Bonnie hoisted Claire to her perch from yesterday. "How about me? Am I as red-faced as you?"

Flustered, Claire opened her bag to search for a mirror as Bonnie set the lunch bag on the dock beside her. Satisfied, Claire passed the mirror to Bonnie.

"You're not going to make a fuss of me mop this morning?"

Claire frowned as she pulled out her rolled magazine. "A bit blowsy, but I think you look pretty. Too bad you got the white blouse and black skirt so dirty. That dress is all wrong for the shop."

Bonnie wanted to complain but held her breath. "It's washed and hanging on the line. Should be ready tomorrow." She reached up to straighten her own hair and secured the braided bun.

"Can you believe how brave Lynne is, traveling to Montana alone to marry a handsome stranger?" Claire turned the magazine around to where the Brighton ad was listed but held it still on her lap.

"She's always been the wise and brave one." Bonnie stared at her own hands, remembered when she had been young enough to believe love and marriage were the answer. "She picked the rancher to wed, right? I don't think I'll ever be that brave again. Marriage doesn't guarantee happiness."

Claire studied her friend, taking in the paleness of her skin and how much thinner she looked. "Don't say that. The man of our dreams is somewhere waiting for us." At the sound of the door opening behind them, she accepted Bonnie's steadying hand as she dropped down.

"Here, look at the ad before we go inside," Claire said but Bonnie shrugged.

It was Mr. Lambton who held the door as the girls climbed up the steps together. "Just a minute, I'd like to see that."

Mrs. Lambton stood just outside the workroom and Bonnie smiled at the intense look of impatience on the woman's face. "Hurry, hurry both of you. I have a surprise. Your pinafores are ready."

Claire stopped talking to Mr. Lambton and left the magazine in his hands as she sailed into the room in excitement.

"I decided to go with the maroon. Oh, I just can't wait to see if they fit," Mrs. Lambton said.

"Bella, come look at this," her husband called impatiently.

Claire made a face and mouthed 'maroon,' but Bonnie shed her cloak and quickly lifted the longer dark cotton apron from the hanger and pulled it on. She straightened the big ruffled sleeve caps, shook it so the larger ruffle at the end of the apron unfurled and turned her back for Claire to tie a large bow.

She swished from side to side and smiled. "This be a life saver, since my dress is so drab today."

Claire fussed with the shorter apron and turned with a shake. "Hurry, make sure to cup your hand so the bow sits right."

Nervously, Bonnie bent her knees so she could concentrate on making a full, even bow. Claire was ten times fussier than all of her sisters put together and she had never satisfied any one of them.

Claire was busy hunting her mirror again and trying to hold the small circle so she could see how she looked. Impatiently she tugged her friends' hand and pulled her toward the front of the store where the big tri-fold mirror stood. "Oh, Lord, I look like a fat cranberry."

Bonnie stood behind her, tilting her head so she could admire her own garment. As she'd expected, Claire had tied a perfect bow and the streamers reached down enough to hide most of her worn gray dress beneath. Not surprisingly, she watched Claire fussing with her own bow and retying it.

As Bonnie now stood closer she was surprised to see how large her eyes looked, muddy brown her brothers called them. Claire had told her they were hazel. But then the girl claimed her hair color was brunette, not mud brown. Was it only two weeks ago when she had thought herself enormous and fat. Now in the mirror she looked gaunt, her collar bones pressed into view at her throat. Making sure no one else saw, she pushed the open neck of her dress and the square yoked apron aside to see her left shoulder. The twirl of colors were now tinged with yellow and were definitely fading.

As the sound of the quarreling store owners grew louder, Bonnie moved aside and studied Claire in the mirror. The apron was not the best color for her, but it framed her lovely gingham dress to perfection. The ruffles and bow made her look like a child's doll with her head of blonde curls and big blue eyes. "You look like a Christmas angel."

Bella turned and clapped her hands in delight. "Look, look at them Henry. Our Lambton's girls."

"Very pretty," he said, then looked back at the ad. "I don't know Bella, it seems bad form to mark down our merchandise and hawk it on the street."

Claire had brightened at the attention and the word pretty, then frowned when they went back to arguing. Annoyed she stepped away from admiring herself and reached for the magazine. "You don't sell everything at a discount. You just mark down the winter gowns that didn't sell and a few of the staples that are out-of-style and put them on a special rack or sit them out in their boxes on the counter. I probably wouldn't go to a sale at Brighton, they're only giving ten percent off."

"How much would you mark things down?" he asked.

"At least twenty percent off. Of course I never find anything in my size left at a sale, but at twenty percent off I enjoy looking."

Bella stared at her husband. "Are you thinking what I'm thinking? The girls could help with the tags and I have the new sandwich board too. After we open the door, they could take turns walking up and down the street to get customers to come into our business, not the Brighton's."

◇◇◇

Bonnie walked down the street, hidden by the big wooden sign boards. The air was nippy and she waited at the corner to stare at the bay before turning to walk back toward the store.

Claire came to the door, squeezing past two customers as they entered. She ran up to the end of the street to turn Bonnie around. "Can you believe these two have been in business over a year and this is their first sale, and they've never advertised?"

"No-oh. It's a good thing they have you to tell them all about it."

"Yes, it is. My goodness the way Bella protested when I picked out those hideous dresses to mark down. And the squeal when I told her no one buys ruffled pantaloons or hoop petticoats anymore. I told her she should mark those fifty percent off but she refused. The woman has no idea about fashion."

Bonnie rolled her eyes at the girl. "I've seen several customers leaving with purchases."

"Of course, she's not the only woman stuck in the past. Come in, Bella agreed you could have your lunch break now. Can you believe she tried to get me to walk carrying the sign?"

Bonnie lifted it over her head and Claire helped her stand it open in front of the store. "What was she thinking?"

Claire giggled but as Bonnie slipped through the crowded store, the vivacious blonde remained behind to help customers and make a few more sales.

CHAPTER SIXTEEN

At the end of the day, it was Claire who paused at the bench beside the pier. Bonnie handed her the sack lunch and smiled as her friend devoured her half of the sandwich. There would be nothing to feed the gulls today. It had taken all Bonnie's will-power to leave half for her friend.

"You and your bright ideas. Guess we have to stand out in this again tomorrow." Bonnie leaned over to raise her friend's hood against the wind. Her own cheeks were chapped pink from the afternoon wind and she adjusted the hood on her own cloak all the way forward.

Claire finished the last bite and shivered. "Well, I didn't expect they would want to do it so quickly. It's a good thing we were already familiar with their inventory."

Bonnie wanted to complain. Her third day of work and she had spent the first hour climbing the ladder again to reach down items she had lifted and moved each of the first two days. Her hope was that they would all sell so she didn't have to put them back on Saturday. Claire's idea, but she had been the one to have to move all the garments so that the ones for sale could hang together on one rack.

"Actually, my favorite part was walking outside on the sidewalk, at least until this blasted cold wind started," Bonnie said.

"Well, at least you don't have black marks on your nails from writing sales prices as quickly as Henry calculated them out."

Suddenly she smiled. "But they were both so happy. I'm sure this is the first of many sales for the Lambton's."

Bonnie laughed and tugged her friend to her feet. "Don't forget your mother has been alone with three sick children all day. We'd better hurry so I can get food on the table for your father."

It was worse than she feared. Not only was there no food cooked, the kitchen was cold which meant the stove had gone out. Bonnie worked quickly to look for something to cook. In minutes she had chopped up the remaining pot roast and vegetables and added water to heat it for a thick soup. She didn't know how to make bread but found the box full of hand written recipes and after lighting the oil lamp, tried her hand at spoon bread. While it was in the oven she ran out to carry in clothes.

The sharp wind had dried the garments stiff and cold. She brought in the first load of the children's clothes and threw them on her bed. On the way out she sniffed and smelled the bread starting to burn. After adjusting the wood in the stove and moving the pan, she ran out to get her own clothes.

Claire came down smiling as Bonnie forced the kitchen door closed behind her. "Mother and the boys were all asleep with Mary Anne in my bed. Who knows what kind of day she's had, I didn't dare wake her."

Claire folded her arms around herself. "Ooh, it's cold."

Bonnie set the full basket on the floor and walked through the house with Claire. Together they managed to get a fire going in the living room and the parlor fireplaces. Claire showed her how to light the chandelier as Bonnie covered and set the table.

When Father Wimberley entered the front door at six, the meal was on the table. He smiled at the weary girls and darted up the stairs to fetch the others.

Father Wimberley carried the twin boys down, while his wife brought down Mary Anne. After a trip to the bathroom and a chance to wash up before eating, the children sat at the table, all hungry and curious.

Bonnie served everyone soup and passed around the bread. They were surprised when Mary Anne started a conversation. "We had a long nap in your bed Aunt Claire."

"Did you all, even Mother?"

Mother blushed and took a spoonful of soup. Bonnie poured tea for everyone and served Father Wimberley his wine.

Tom nodded. "Our Mother is in heaven now with Father and Sean, and Danny and Nan."

"Danny and Nan?" Claire asked.

"Our baby brother and sister who died of cholera," Jim answered

Mary Anne said, "They're all in heaven, but we're not going there yet."

Tom said, "We're going to move out west to live with our sister Lynne."

"Lynne is going to Montana to marry a cowboy and make a home for us. We're going to ride west with you, aren't we?" Jim asked every one, looking hopefully from one adult to another.

"You certainly are. All you children and your Aunt Bonnie and Aunt Claire. If you want you can call us Mother and Father."

"Just for the trip?" Jim asked.

"For the trip and as long as you want," Mother Wimberley said.

After dinner, Bonnie led the children into the warm parlor where she and Claire had looked at the stereopticon and set them down with the pictures and the adults to talk. Then she went to work clearing the floors and dining room and cleaning dishes. Afterward, she set up two irons on the stove top and stood the ironing board up in the warm kitchen. Before bed she made sure each child had a clean pressed outfit for tomorrow and she had the black skirt and white blouse starched and ironed for work. The rest of the clothes she rolled and left in the basket to iron tomorrow.

In the morning despite the colder weather, she needed to rush to the farmer's market and back before the others were awake. Although these were still a little sapped, growing children needed milk and fresh vegetables. She checked with Mother Wimberley before they went up and had her check the list and put out money.

Bonnie started the fire in the stove and put two kettles of water on before she left the house. She raced through the sleepy streets intent on arriving early and getting back before even Father Wimberley awakened. The trip seemed a waste to her at first, there were only two vendors when she arrived. She bought a full gallon tin of milk, three dozen eggs and a fifty pound bag of potatoes. All things if she'd purchased from Mr. Sanders, the grocer would have delivered, but at a much greater cost. The only green vegetable available was turnips, and those because the fat globes still had their leaves on top. She couldn't remember if there were still carrots and onions enough and they weren't on the list but she bought both since she still had plenty of money. She was leaving when a third stall opened, a fishmonger. She had only eaten them once, but was thrilled to see he had oysters. She used the last of the money up on fish and oysters.

In thirty minutes she made the entire trip, pushing the food in the coal barrow Lynne had left behind. She left the seafood on the porch and stored the rest of the food in the pantry. Next she put tea in the kettle and made up lunches. This time she sliced thinner bread but made each of them a sandwich. On another sheet of paper, she made a second list for the Grocers. Tea, coffee, bread, flour and apples, she pondered about the meat but decided to let Mother Wimberley finish this list as well. She hoped they could afford to feed them all.

She put the irons on the stove and managed to iron up all the McKinney's sheets before the Wimberleys came down together. Mother Wimberley showed her how to make pancakes and Bonnie worked on those as the woman praised her hard work and carried up the warm sheets and the children's clothes.

As Claire walked past to the bathroom, Bonnie smiled. Today instead of resentment, she felt proud that she was already well enough to do so much more than her friend. Besides she had enjoyed the market trip and felt strangely alive and happy. She could do this, and she knew she would more than earn her keep.

When she served breakfast, she was shocked when the children swarmed under her full arms to hug her. "Thank you, Aunt Bonnie."

Beaming, she urged them to be careful but wondered how her life could have changed so much for the better with just the loss of one sorry man.

Bonnie continued to iron at work, pressing blouses and skirts from the stockroom to hang and quickly fill in the racks that had been picked over the day before. Then Claire came back with a dozen garments that had wilted and needed freshening for the sales racks.

There was so much energy this morning as all rushed to get ready. Bonnie smiled as she watched Bella dust shelves and Henry frantically push the broom around. Claire folded and neatened the remaining unmentionables on display on the counter.

No one had to say it, yesterday had obviously been their best day of sales yet. Just before the doors opened, Bonnie and Claire donned their fresh pressed pinafores. They posed in front of each other, admiring their hand-embroidered names above the store name that Bella had added the night before. The day was sunny but bitter cold and Bonnie was relieved when Henry Lambton carried out and leaned the store boards open on the sidewalk in front of the store.

Bella disappeared upstairs and came back with a kettle of water and tray of tea cups. She put the kettle on top of the pot-bellied stove in the back and stood anxiously watching the door.

While everyone waited nervously for the frantic rush of customers, Bella poured a cup of tea for all of them. "Do you think there are enough things left to sell?"

Claire looked at the nearly empty boxes on the counter. "Bonnie and I can get down some more lingerie if you can handle the customers."

"Yes, that would be good. Maybe we should pull some more of the dresses for the sales rack?"

Claire raised her eyebrows and looked at Bonnie. "There are a few more, if you think we have time to change the tags." Henry nodded and Bella took Claire's cup as she went to look at the thinner racks of clothes. She took her cup back as she handed Bella two more dresses. "That's really about all, you don't want to mark them down if they will sell at full price. These others are too nice for that."

Henry took the dresses and went to his tablet to figure prices and mark the sales numbers on himself. Bonnie collected all the dirty cups and took them back to rinse out on the way to the workroom. Nine fifteen, and still the doorbell hadn't rung.

The women worked in the storeroom, Bonnie handing down the older boxes and Claire and Bella deciding which they should discount. By the time they worked through the second shelf all were beginning to worry. Claire rushed to the front of the storeroom with her arms full and Bella followed.

Curious, Bonnie patted her hair and looked out to see a single customer, one she recognized from earlier in the week, looking through the sales rack. Claire left Bella and Henry pricing the unmentionables to curtsy and offer to assist the woman, calling her by name.

The woman gave her a frosty smile. "Is this the huge sale my friend Edith told me about?"

"Yes, it's our End of Winter Sale," Claire improvised. "So our customers can look their best for the spring Holidays."

"I see, that's very sensible of you. I think everyone on Newberry Street has the same idea. I've never seen so many shops with banners before. Of course, yours is the only shop without one, but my friend told me I had to come here today."

Bella's eyes widened with alarm.

"Well we have the big wooden sign outside, so we didn't think we needed a banner too," Claire said.

"Really, I didn't see a sign of any kind. I worried at first that you might have closed for the day."

Henry darted from behind the counter and stepped outside. His color would have risen even without the biting wind. In a minute he was back inside. "Someone took our sign," he said in shock.

Bonnie grabbed her cloak and pulled the hood up before stepping out to look for the giant sandwich board she had worn all morning the day before. She saw where it lay across the street near the edge of the dock. Running, she managed to snag it but had to struggle a minute to keep the wind from whipping it away from her.

Henry in an overcoat with his bowler hat pulled down came out to help her wrestle it back across to the store. "I think the wind is our thief," she said gaily.

"Here, let's wedge it in against the bricks." In minutes, they had the folded sign wedged so that it couldn't be budged by wind or man.

Back inside, Bella was offering their first customer a cup of hot tea. "I'm sorry, but I forgot there's nowhere for you to sit," she looked about and called, "Henry."

"Yes, darling." He was removing his coat and hat as he and Bonnie walked toward the back door. In minutes he carried down a small round table while Bonnie held the door to their apartment open. While he was gone, Bonnie rushed to peek through the huge space. It was as large as downstairs, but two of the rooms were completely empty. As she heard his steps on the stairs she looked about frantically. Spying a round doily on the back of a chair she lifted it and looked around for anything else useful.

"Grab the cookie tin," he snapped, "and if you could carry a chair too." Bonnie smiled and both hands full, led the way down the narrow stairs, her elbow on the rail. He followed with two chairs and pulled the door firmly closed behind him.

Despite the cold, the girls laughed all the way to the corner. "Lord, what a day."

"You and your End of Winter sale. I never knew Bella could smile so much."

Claire rubbed her fingers together, "Money, money, money. Could you believe her asking what else they could mark down? Honestly, I thought I would die."

"My favorite moment was when Henry thought someone had stolen his sign."

"No, Bella serving us tea. The customers really loved that little table to sit at and nibble on tinned biscuits."

They cut through the alleys and the wind and their laughter stopped. "They're proud, but they're not as well off as they'd like us to think."

"What do you mean? Come on, tell me all that you saw."

Bonnie talked as they worked their way closer to Sanders' grocery. "Well, everything they own is very nice. The space upstairs is just as big as the store is downstairs."

"Yes, yes," Claire's eyes were bright as she waited for details.

"Two rooms were furnished, well three, if you count a table in the kitchen where we stole the chairs for downstairs. The setting room was modest with a little black Franklin stove instead of a fireplace. Bella had doilies on everything, the back of the sofa, arms of chairs, table, I mean everywhere. I think she made them. There was a small bag full of thread and a tatting bobbin."

Bonnie watched Claire's face change with each fact. For some reason, she seemed to resent the fact that Bella could do needlework. Of course Claire could sew as well as anyone in Boston now Lynne was gone. None of the three girls had mastered needlework since none went to finishing school. Claire should have gone, but they had all chosen to become factory girls instead.

◇◇◇

They stopped at the grocer and stood with their hands over the stove as Mr. Sanders got their order. Since they would be having fish, there had been no need for delivery and wasting money on a tip.

"Go on. What else did you see?"

"Well, there wasn't a lot of time to look about. I think Henry knew I'd been snooping because he snapped at me. You know, today he was short tempered the way Bella usually is, and she was warm and friendly, the way he normally is. Did you notice that?"

Mr. Sanders raised a hand and the girls approached the counter to pay. "Well ladies, did you find news of your friend?"

Claire smiled. "She sold or gave away most of the rest of their things and she is on her way to Montana as a mail-order bride."

"Really, how extraordinary. Well, I must say I am shocked."

Bonnie bristled. "When you don't have a choice, you do what you have to do."

He coughed and read the amount of the order. Bonnie paid, still glowering at him.

"All three children were hospitalized, and because of that were saved. They are living with us until we travel west in the spring," Claire said.

He held up his hand. "Wait." In a second he put three candy sticks into a small paper sack and stuck it in the top of the groceries. "God bless her for having the courage. I'm glad to hear the children are well. Forgive what I said before."

Bonnie bent her head and thanked him.

CHAPTER SEVENTEEN

On Saturday, Claire was still laughing about the children and their oyster shells. Mr. Wimberley solved the problem of them wanting to keep them upstairs by asking them to put them in the flower garden. That way they would have their own oyster bed. Since no one found a pearl they reluctantly surrendered all of them.

As they passed the sausage shop, Claire stopped and stared at the window. "That's what Lambton Clothiers needs, a big window. If people could see inside, it would lure them in to buy something."

Bonnie shook her head. "Let's just survive the last day of your big sales idea first. None of the other stores have windows. Bella would never go for it."

"Henry would."

Bonnie was busy arguing all the reasons a business wouldn't want a wall of glass and why Claire should stop giving advice unless they asked for it. If anything went wrong, both would blame her.

Bella opened the back door and both girls grew silent and entered.

◇◇◇

"The pay is so much smaller," Bonnie complained. "I can't believe they held out money for our aprons. What about our employee discounts?"

Claire frowned as well. "I can't believe they won't let me have my dress until it's all paid for. That will be ten weeks. We'll be on our way to Utah by then."

"I thought we were going to Oregon?"

"No, I think Father wants to go all the way to California but Mother thinks Utah is best. Anyway, we have to go through there to meet Lynne and deliver the children to her."

"I need another dress, the brown one I cut down is too tight around my shoulders. I'm afraid the old fabric will split every time I reach for something on the shelves." She leaned closer to whisper "And I need new drawers."

"Maybe you can buy a pair of pantaloons, I think Henry had marked them down to twenty cents by the end of the day."

"I restocked all six pairs on the shelf. Maybe I could buy a pair, use all that extra leg fabric and ruffles to make one or two more drawers."

They were whispering and laughing as they turned the corner beside the dock and a couple of sailors whistled and called to them. Blushing, both girls rushed toward home.

"You know she should be there." Bonnie whispered, no need to say Lynne's name aloud.

Claire turned to stare at her breathless companion. "She may be married."

Both raised a hand to their throats at the romantic thought. "I would love to have been there for her," Claire finally said.

"Aye, but I wouldn't have had anything to wear."

"There's still the church barrel in the attic. We'll need to go through it anyway in case there's a dress small enough for Mary Anne."

Bonnie looked at her, wished she had the nerve to ask for dresses for her sisters. Well maybe she could hint while they were working through them and the Wimberley's would donate them to the poor little Magee girls. The thought shamed her and she entered through the kitchen door instead of following Claire up the front steps.

Bonnie left the Wimberley's right after breakfast but they all arrived at church at the same time. The Wimberleys led their charges toward the front and Bonnie joined her family at the back of the chapel. Even in her drab gray dress, she had to smile as each of the girls walked proudly past her.

After dinner the night before, the women had returned to the attic. Using oil lamps to see by they sorted through the church barrel. Mother Wimberley handed her the uniforms from past maids. "Although I don't see how you'll be able to remake them to fit you, especially Bess's skirts." Bonnie didn't see much promise either, but she couldn't show up at Lambton's every day without at least one more dress, two would be best. "I can try," she had answered.

Claire and her Mother had picked everything out that was nice enough for Mary Anne. Bonnie had put her hands on the rest. She had felt the bile rise in her throat but she forced the words out. "Could I have these for my sisters?"

Mother Wimberley and Claire had both stared at her and then started talking at the same time. "Of course Bonnie, take anything that you like. If they can use them so much the better." Mother said.

"Charity begins at home, of course take them," Claire added.

Bonnie had struggled but managed to smile and say thank you.

The next morning she left after making breakfast, carrying her big bundle. Her sisters had been thrilled. Brigid and Darcey fit right into the clothes although they didn't have bosoms or hips. Even as tiny as Claire was, the waists of the dresses were loose. Bonnie and Mum had been able to baste the side seams and then tell them. "You look adorable." Brigid's hem was ankle high and Darcey's brushed the floor, but at least they fit.

The two danced around the small flat like princesses and Meara and Reagan had jumped up and down in excitement. But Meara disappeared inside the smallest dress and Mum had looked at Bonnie and sighed. Reagan had stopped jumping and said, "Oh dear." At five she was even tinier.

Brigid had argued, rightly, that now she had a job, she needed the dresses more than the others. Mum had allowed she could wear all but two. She should pick out the two for the little ones.

Of course they were ones that Claire had worn to the factory. No ruffles or frills, simple and plain. To Brigid's credit, she didn't pick the ones with the worse stains. She handed Mum a pink for Meara and a yellow for Reagan. Mum insisted they remake them without cutting away any fabric, so she could let them out as they grew.

Their dresses looked bunched and tucked. They still hung a little loose on them, but both girls were so thrilled that Bonnie and Mum pronounced it a good job and all had set off for services. Of course Da refused to attend. Ian and Shawn had grumbled and complained they needed to sleep, it was their only day off. To their credit they left their beds long enough for the girls to give them a fashion show. More importantly, each knew how to hand out compliments and the girls left feeling pretty.

◇◇◇

After services the Wimberleys surprised Bonnie again. "Don't you ladies look pretty this morning? Would you like to come over for a cup of tea?" Mother Wimberley addressed the girls.

Mary Anne and Meara smiled at each other, already friends from school. Reagan piped up, "Don't you like our pretty dresses?" Like gentlemen, Tom and Jim bowed and said gallantly, "Beautiful."

Mum apologized, but told the Wimberleys she had to get home to make supper for the men. The girls looked so disappointed she nodded to Bonnie. "Guess your sister can take you and bring you home in time for your meal."

The McKinney three were still pale and all were warned they couldn't play outside or too roughly indoors. Mr. Wimberley took charge of all seven children and led them into the parlor. He read them the front page news about the new gold rush in South Dakota and scattered attacks by hostile Indians. All were excited by that and the twins were happy to show the girls the stereographs of Indians and trains again. As Bonnie had imagined, her sisters were thrilled.

It was decided tea would be more manageable at the dining table. Bonnie kept the kitchen door open so she could watch her little sisters, all as shy as herself except for little Reagan. While she prepared lunch, Claire and her mother poured tea and delighted each child with a small slice of cake and a white cookie.

Bonnie peeled and added vegetables to the nice pork roast in the oven. Then she stood and beamed as her sisters tried to copy Claire as she sipped tea at the table with them and nibbled daintily at her cookie. The twins shook their heads, gobbled their treats and asked to be excused. Mother Wimberley and Bonnie took their places at the table and made small talk about the weather and how lovely each girl's new frock looked.

When Mother Wimberley asked if Bonnie had put bread in the oven yet, Bonnie realized the ball was over.

She asked permission to eat with her family when she took the girls home. As usual when she asked for anything, the answer was 'of course.'

As soon as they were outside, Bonnie looked at the girls and their smiling faces. She nudged her sister Darcey. "So which of the McKinney boyos do you fancy?"

Innocently the girl shook her head and blushed, "I don't know, I like them both." Her sisters cooed at her and Bonnie laughed. All walked home singing, "Coming through the Rye."

The minute the door opened on the flat, the song died.

Her Mum sat cowered at the table, her hands above her head while her Da slapped her. Her two brothers sat at the table watching silently while Clyde sat on the floor crying.

Furious, Bonnie rushed inside and pulled her father back, shoving him so hard he sat on the floor.

"Leave Mum alone."

He started to get up, swearing he would beat her too and Bonnie made two fists and stared him down.

Ian yelled, "Hey, back from church and already forgot 'Honor your Father and your Mother.'"

Bonnie turned and slapped at both of them. "What's wrong with you two?" She looked at them and the crying children. Numbly she stepped past to raise Mum's head and lift a rag to wipe the blood streaming from her nose.

"Canna you protect your own mother? She washes, cooks, and cleans for you. Never takes anything but the scraps for herself. How can you sit there like big lumps and let him beat Mum?"

Shawn stood up, raised a fist himself. "It's your fault. Begging from them high and mighty folks, then bringing their cast-offs to dress the girls up." His voice broke, "Then you parade them off to church. Shaming us all."

"I did not beg. I brought home a gift for them. I made them happy. What's wrong with letting them be happy?"

Ian spoke, pointing at the crying girls, "Did you now?"

Mum tried to stand up, "Stop, stop fighting. I'm all right."

"No you're not. There is shame here, but it's not mine. The shame is a house with three grown men who can't provide for their Mum and sisters. When did any of these girls have a new dress? New shoes? Act like men and provide for them. Protect your Mum and sisters." She looked back at Da as he managed to rise. "Don't act like a selfish, sorry dosser like Tarn," her throat raw she added, "or our Da."

Her father swore a blue-streak and stumbled past her. She fought the urge to grab his arm and beg his forgiveness. To say how much she loved him, but he couldn't act this way to Mum. Instead she let her head hang as she hugged her mother and held her from doing it.

The crying and shouting stopped as the door slammed.

Bonnie sighed and looked at her brothers. "You know I had to say it. When he's drunk he's ne'er himself." She waited until one, then the other nodded. "If he's not working, where did Da get the money to get soused?"

Ian looked down at his plate, then mumbled. "We felt sorry for him, I let him have mine. Shawn gave most of his to Mum and the little ones."

"You know how he is with the drink. Don't let him bully you or wheedle it out of you next time. Give him enough for a pint, no more."

She held out her arms for her brothers. "You're both strong, and brave, and hard working. You have to be the men in the family now."

Ian moved into her embrace first, then Shawn. But her younger brother couldn't help but jab. "Aye, reckon we be, now you're not here no more."

CHAPTER EIGHTEEN

Bonnie stayed to tend Mum and finish the meal. She kept a cool damp cloth on her mother's face, hoping it wouldn't swell too much. No one talked.

The beans had scorched, but she was able to scrape the good into a bowl. She had served them with onions and bread and everyone seemed not to mind the smell. As soon as the meal was finished, Ian and Shawn had gone out. The pot cleaned easily after she filled it with water to soak, the burned peeling out with her fingers.

Although the girls had taken off the new clothes and hung them up carefully, she could see their joy and pride in them was gone. Nevertheless, she carried the remaining two dresses to the deserted table and took them in at the waist as well.

Bonnie had wanted to ask her brothers to find her Da. Her heart hurt from the pain she'd caused him. But he wasn't Da when he was drunk, he was possessed by the devil. She didn't want to leave until she saw he was all right. What did their priest call it? "The curse of the Irish." It was more than the drink, it was the blue megrims. Hadn't she had them herself after Tarn's betrayal? A sadness that wrapped one's soul in sorrow and made life feel hopeless. Maybe the drink was the only thing that helped. She shook her head. No, giving up was for cowards.

Her father wasn't a bad man. He just felt useless and unable to find a decent job. The economy was still troubled, and Grant and his do-nothing congress had not even tried to help. With the drought in the southwest, there was an influx of farmers now, as well as immigrants and former slaves who would work for almost nothing. Jobs were scarce. It didn't help that most of the north wanted to keep the south bankrupt and poor. Many Southerners who had an education or money had moved north. Wasn't it the southern owned foundry that was pushing Claire's family business into the red?

The only hope seemed to be the west. As the government fought the Indians and pushed them off their lands and onto reservations, thousands of acres were free to anyone who wanted to homestead them. With the Union-Pacific railroad running from coast to coast, going west didn't mean staying there forever. Someday Bonnie could return to Boston to help her family. If she found the rich husband Claire was sure was waiting for them at the end of their trek. She swore.

Bitterly, Bonnie bit the thread and handed the garments to Brigid to hang up. "It's late. I have to go cook the evening meal for the Wimberley's and see to the little McKinneys." She looked at the sad children and sighed. "Can you girls take care of the house and Mum for a few days?"

As expected all said yes and she gathered them into her arms for hugs and bye kisses. "Remember, things are always darkest before the dawn. Things will get better. I know I spoke harsh to the lot, but the boys need reminded that they have a duty."

She leaned down to kiss her Mum. "Give Da my love. Tell him I'm sorry, but I cannot abide his hurting you. Every blow to you hurts all of us. He has to see that."

But if her mother heard, she didn't answer.

◇◇◇

Bonnie shoved her hands in her pockets and rushed through the shadows to her new home. She laughed at the word home, choking on the tears at the back of her throat. How could the same distance grow twice as long with the fading light?

Ian had been right. She had begged for the dresses, taken their charity. Wasn't her living with the Wimberleys taking their charity? Quickly she wiped her eyes, swallowed and spit into the shadows. The splat made her look down and she saw the beautiful pearly linings of the discarded oyster shells. The lowliest creatures in the ocean, yet God had filled their gnarly shells with pink and purple beauty. Straightening her shoulders, Bonnie forced a smile on her face.

She wasn't taking charity, she worked to pay her way.

Once the meal was served, she joined the family at the table. Claire had asked her how the visit went. She smiled and told them how happy the girls were, how much they had enjoyed the day. It was hard to keep the rest inside, how horribly things went wrong at home. But at least what she did say wasn't a lie.

The Wimberley's all smiled at her and Bonnie listened to Mary Anne talk about Meara, bragging to everyone that they were best friends, just like Claire, Bonnie and Lynne. The mention of her sister's name suddenly brought tears to her eyes and to the boys as well.

Bonnie looked at Claire and she took over. "Just imagine, she has made the trip all across the country by now. She's probably already married."

"By train and stagecoach and everything," Jim said.

Tom said sharply, "I don't want her married."

"Marriage is wonderful. Why, I gave her the notice myself. I can remember it word for word. 'Tall well-formed veteran without vices. Needs bride willing to settle in Montana on 640 acre horse ranch.'"

Bonnie could also remember Lynne's reaction to the ad, word for word. "It doesn't give his age or anything. And what type of description is that? He's probably an old goat with one leg or one eye. Probably tried his hand at mining, failed, and stayed behind to try ranching on a Federal land grant."

But Claire had argued with her. "No, I don't think maimed men can be called well-formed, and if it isn't the truth, it wouldn't be in the paper."

"What are vices?" Jim asked and Bonnie turned to see what Claire would answer, when she didn't, Bonnie spoke up.

"It means he doesn't drink or gamble or chase other women. He works hard and will be good to her, not beat her or call her names," the last she said wistfully.

"No, he's good like Daddy was, Lynne told us," Mary Anne piped up.

"She knew because when we three were sick and ready to die like Mother, he sent money for the hospital, so we could get well again," Tom said.

"There," Claire said with a laugh. "And now she is in Montana getting a place ready for you to live when we travel west in the spring."

"To live with a real cowboy," Tom yelled.

"Maybe he can teach us how to shoot Indians," Jim added, suddenly too excited to sit still.

"And ride a bronco," Tom shouted, "Rope and brand some cows."

"I want to learn to milk one," Mary Anne giggled.

Father Wimberley's voice calmed them down. "Well to get there, you have to get strong enough to help with the chores here and on the wagon train. That means eating all your supper, not talking."

"It's the only way to get any dessert. What do we have, Bonnie?" Mother Wimberley asked.

"Stewed apples with cinnamon. Think it's time I whipped some cream." Bonnie rose, carrying her own untouched plate of food to the kitchen. If she didn't peel them first, just sliced them thin, it would only take ten minutes for the apples to cook. Plenty of time to eat and whip the cream.

Later after the meal was served and the floors all swept, she went upstairs to check that the beds were clean and made-up for the night. She gathered the dirty clothes and bundled them all back downstairs. If she got up early enough, she could wash and hang at least one load before breakfast.

As she sorted the clothes she hummed, then caught the music inside and stopped as the words came unbidden. "If a lassie meet a laddie," the words left her cold. Hopefully her dear friend had been wrong. Bonnie took a moment to pray. Let Phillip Gant be a loving, handsome man with money, land, and a beautiful house. Let sweet, sensible Lynne be happy.

But the memory of Lynne's last words about the bride want-ads came back. "What kind of man would ever place an ad for a bride?"

Well, Lynne had done what she had to do. Hopefully she would write them soon so they could all stop worrying.

News didn't come that week or the next. The children were now strong and lively. Bonnie always compared them to her own brothers and sisters. Of course, the McKinneys now had all the meat and milk they could eat, the Magees just enough. Although Da had seemed to sober up and the lads were still working, the money only went so far. Brigid had new shoes that fit, ones she paid for herself. She would pass them down the way Bonnie had passed down shoes and dresses before. The little one's made do with hand-me-downs.

Her sisters seemed to light up when she came by to see them. Which was good, for without the girl's hugs, visiting home would be dreary indeed. She often scolded herself that she had gone too far that Sunday. Da seemed as though he would never forgive her, always slipping outside whenever she came in. He would glance at her furtively, never making eye contact. It hurt.

For that matter, neither had Mum or the boys forgiven her. Ian had accused her of being a Temperance beetle. She had never heard the term. When she asked Claire if she'd heard of it, Mother Wimberley explained they were wives and mothers against the sale of liquor in New York. They sounded smart to Bonnie. She had tried to tell each one she had hurt that she was sorry, but was she? Weren't they better off now Da had sobered up?

Both boys were giving money to the family, not letting Da swill himself into an early grave. Mum wasn't being beaten and sworn at on a daily basis. That had to be better for all of them.

Her thoughts came, dark and bitter. If Mum hadn't always accepted what Da did, if she'd fought back. If Bonnie had that image maybe she would never have tolerated Tarn's abuse. It wasn't the way it should be between people who loved each other. She didn't want her little sisters to accept that kind of treatment when they grew up. Nor her brothers to ever think it was all right to hit their wives. She'd had to stop Da, even if it shamed them both.

But home wasn't the same. Her Mum hung her head when Bonnie came in and never had any interest in talking. Bonnie tried, telling them about work, about how the twins were helping at the foundry. Meara loved to hear how Mary helped with the laundry, peeling the vegetables, and making desserts for supper. Meara insisted Bonnie teach her how to do each thing Mary Anne learned and she did.

A third week passed, then a fourth. It was terrible not knowing about Lynne but work at the shop and home went on. All the time Father Wimberley was building his fleet of prairie wagons. He had decided to sell his foundry to his largest competitor. In turn, the company had agreed that he could take some basic tools and specifications with him so he could create another business where ever they ended up. Light-weight, canvas covered, the new wagons would carry his equipment and all their belongings across the Great Plains. The boys of course wondered why they couldn't just take the trans-continental train like Lynne had.

Bonnie had stopped work to listen as Father Wimberley explained that the cost was too great. His plan was to take at least four of the marvelous wagons to Independence Missouri, selling two of them there. Then they would use the other two to make the journey to Salt Lake City, turning north above the Platte River and traveling on toward Utah. They might get on the wicked Mormon trail where it began at the funny sounding town of Nauvoo, Illinois. They laughed about the bigamist and the upcoming trial of their leader with his twenty-six wives. But even Bonnie was anxious for the adventure to begin.

It was the second week of April when the letter came. Father Wimberley had already decided they were leaving as soon as school was out. Lynne advised they should wait until summer to begin because the Sioux were on the war path. It led to endless debate. If they were going to spend four to six months traveling and Grant had just sent more troops west to contain the Indians, by the time they reached the western half of the journey at Independence, Missouri the trail should be safe. If they waited too long, they might end up traveling during winter. The date the school let out was May 15th. He wanted to leave Boston on May 16th. That way they should be in Missouri by July.

They wrote a letter to Lynne. Bonnie took special delight in telling her that Herr Huntmeister was dead. Apparently he had caught typhoid fever while collecting rent. He had suffered greatly before he died. His widow had accepted the payment of the back rent and written a receipt for payment in full which Bonnie inserted into the letter.

Father Wimberley wrote to tell her they expected to be in Utah by the end of-September. Three weeks later they received another packet full of her daily letters promising to meet them in Ogden, Utah. The children were so happy at the news they danced around the parlor. Claire and Bonnie joined hands and did their own dance. Soon they would see their friend again.

Everyone began to prepare. Claire's parents started to worry full-time. Father Wimberley came home with his books with their detailed instructions and maps. One was called *Western Trail Blazers*, the second one was a guide by Jim Bridger, *Wagon Roads West*. He and the boys poured over them and seemingly every other day he gave a new list to the women to prepare. Between their mornings at school and their afternoons helping one of Claire's parents, the children were once again tired and ready for bed after dinner.

Bonnie used the extra time to help Mother Wimberley calculate what they would take and listen to her sigh and complain about leaving behind so much. Then the next day they would pare down the list some more. Bonnie was so busy, she didn't know if she was happy, but she felt alive with excitement about the change.

CHAPTER NINETEEN

On the way to the shop, Claire noticed a tall soldier in a fancy blue uniform. His doublet was adorned with a double row of brass buttons and he wore a big hat and yellow scarf. He was fastening flyers to the walls of every business. Claire giggled and nudged her. "My, my, doesn't he look handsome, just like a toy soldier?"

The officer stood to admire the passing girls. He doffed his hat to them in a low bow and said "Ladies," before straightening with a smile. Bonnie turned to look at the man, noticing despite herself that he was as tall or taller than Tarn Micheals and even more handsome. Just the thought of her husband's name made her shudder.

Lieutenant Calum Douglas tucked the remaining flyers under his arm and frowned, looking down to make certain his uniform was straight and neat. He usually got the opposite reaction from pretty girls. The little blonde's response was normal. But it was the tall attractive woman beside her he had wanted to smile at him. Well, maybe like southern girls, she recognized a Galvanized Yankee when she saw one.

Even after a dozen years wearing the Union blue, he still remembered the pain of swearing allegiance to the enemy. But then he was just a fifteen year old boy who had held his father's head while he coughed up blood on the field in Spotsylvania, Virginia. All three had been pinned down at the Bloody Angle in a sea of blood and death and dying. The next week he listened to his brother scream in agony until he died from the infection in his remaining leg. Taking an oath to get out of Andersonville prison seemed an easy choice.

Hell, half their neighbors had enlisted with the Union at the start of the war. His father just didn't want to fight beside people he feuded with at home. They had never had a commitment to a cause. The Scott's blood in them all just roared with the need to fight.

Fighting on the western frontier against Indians, he had learned to forget how he became a soldier and an officer, just like he'd forgotten how to drawl out 'yes ma'am' to all the ladies.

He crossed the street to catch the horse-drawn car to the other side of town. He'd shake a few hands, hand out leaflets to the men working rather than those loitering on the street. If he hustled, he could be out of this snooty town and home with his hundred recruits in tow by the end of the month. Still, he glanced up the street to see if the tall girl had paused to look back.

Lambton's Clothiers was deserted except for the girls and the Lambtons. Bonnie hated walking about with the broom, trying to look busy. The work was nothing to complain about, far less demanding than the mill. The pay was comparable to anything else she could find. Still from the time she arrived until they left, she wanted to leave.

The longer the economy floundered the more business at the store became slower and slower. Bella seemed agitated, assigning Bonnie useless tasks since there was little work to do with no shipments coming in.

As much as Bonnie hated to enter the shop, Claire loved it. She was happiest there. Even though Bonnie had warned her not to, she was always discussing ways to sell more and had even mentioned her idea about a store window. Bella had been aghast, pointing out they couldn't afford it right now. Henry seemed to consider it. The couple quarreled whenever the topic came up.

Bonnie hated everything lately. Knowing they were going on a huge adventure made coming into the clothing shop harder and harder. Reading Lynne's letters made her desperate to see a new world. Although she'd no plans to ever marry again, she was intrigued by the listings for free land along the railroad lines out west. Now she had her strength back, she could see no reason why she couldn't claim and work her own land. Then she could send for her whole family and they could help her and have room to grow and have a house of their own. Aye she had her dreams.

Since her parents wouldn't take her pay, Bonnie purchased her own trail shoes. The price for a custom boot as described in the western trail blazer book was exorbitant. Instead she spent most of what she had earned on a pair of man's brogans that fit perfectly. The rest of her money she added to Mother Wimberley's purchase of some fine brown linsey-woolsey that the guidebook recommended for suitable apparel for their journey.

It suggested two outfits per person, and advised women to wear sensible pantaloons or split skirts so they could ride in a traditional saddle. It was the *Trail Blazers* opinion that side-saddles were suicidal.

Bonnie had never been on a horse and could not imagine ever riding, but the use of separates and split skirts appealed to her and Mother Wimberley had relented. From Lynne's description in her second letter, riding wasn't that difficult and was actually fun. Maybe she could learn.

Claire bought a wool dress from the Lambtons. A purple wool with some tiny blue flowers. Like her new green cotton, it had a modified-bustle. Bonnie thought it looked uncomfortable, but Claire insisted that if she had to wear wool every day, it would never be plain brown. She ordered the custom boots and even purchased a large parasol like the guidebook suggested.

Five weeks to go and so much to do. Just when she felt she had everything under control, it began to unravel. When she visited her family, she found Ian and Shawn looking at flyers. She had taken one and looked at them in horror. They were looking at recruitment ads for the western army. When she asked her parents if they knew what they were reading, her Da had walked toward the door and her Mum had turned to her cooking.

"No, you have to stop them. Don't let them enlist to play soldier, please Da. Mum say something."

"What difference to you, Bonnie dear?" For a minute she didn't recognize the voice until she heard the strangled choking last words. Flying across the room she reached out, wanting to wrap her father in her arms.

"Oh, Da, you know I love you," she looked about the room, "I love all of you."

"Nay, you've a new family now."

Bonnie shook her head, her eyes filling with tears. "You are my family, my only family. I work for the Wimberleys, sleep in the maid's room, clean and cook for them to earn my keep. They are kind to me, but they are not my blood. You are my family."

"But you be leaving with them to go West," Da said.

"You know why, both of you. When I get there, get a home, I'll send for all of you to live with me. You know there's nothing for me here."

"There's nothing for us here either," Ian said.

"Nonsense. You've jobs, good jobs, both of you, and the family is depending on you."

Shawn shook his head, "Nay, not for long. The second building will be done in another week, then there's no more work the man said, for anyone."

She tried to pull the words up, but they sounded false to her own ears, "You'll find other jobs, you're good workers." Her father stood, shaking his head.

"I'm going to be a dipper, starting Monday. I think they may take Darcey for me old job," Brigid whispered.

Bonnie smiled at her sisters, no longer children. Would they be as worn and cynical as she was in four years?

Bonnie forced a smile and patted their shoulders in approval. "Good, then there will be enough money coming in. I bought shoes for my trip, when you wouldn't take my money Mum, but I can take them back."

Her mother turned from the small cook stove and swept her into her arms. It was the first time they had hugged since she had stopped Da from beating her. "No, we all understand, you have to go."

Bonnie raised her head to keep from strangling on the tears she was swallowing but when her Da walked over and touched her shoulder the tears came in deep sobs. It was minutes before she stopped.

Smiling, aching, she forced herself to leave. There was dinner to cook and serve at the Wimberleys. She made sure to grab and hug and kiss each Magee she could reach. At the door, she snagged Ian and

Shawn. When they tried to push her away she pulled them into a tight three-way hug.

"Besides," she laughed, "you babies are too young for the army."

Clyde wrapped his arms around her knees. "No, they both have prickles."

Bonnie pressed a kiss to Ian's cheek, then one to Shawn's. The boy was right. Both stood as tall, or almost as tall as her. Although Ian's face had a fuzzy soft red beard, now Shawn's had its own red down.

"You're too young, it says you have to be eighteen."

"Aye, that's what it says," Ian answered. But there was a sad faraway look in his green eyes.

She had wanted to scream, 'no, don't go,' but had bit her tongue. They would do what they had to do. She had seen the signing bonus on the flyer and the rate of pay.

All the way home, she kept her arms wrapped around herself. Well, they had finally spoken to her. She had that at least. Every day until she left she would make time to see them. Maybe she could store up enough hugs and kisses.

The conversation as they walked to work was always the same. Claire felt they should get a raise in pay. "We've worked here for nearly two months, and Henry and Bella both seem satisfied with our work."

"With business the way it is, what will they have to pay us with? It's been a month since any shipments have arrived. For the amount of actual work, I think we're overpaid."

When Claire started to repeat her arguments Bonnie stopped her in the street. "If you mention that stupid idea about a store window again or our demanding a pay raise, I'll scream. It's plain they don't have the money."

"Don't be ridiculous, I told you Bella's father bought them the store as a wedding present. They can always ask him for help? Besides, if you look at how much they charge for their clothes, you know they make a lot on each one."

"No, because you don't know what they paid for each garment, or what they paid to have it shipped to the store, or what it costs for the expenses for the building. All we know is what they are paying us. I know you don't understand about money, but trust me it is a lot."

"I understand far more about business than you ever will. Get ready to scream, because I'm going to ask them," Claire said as she stalked past.

Bonnie stood and screamed as loud as she could. Two sailors on one of the boats tying up looked ready to run to her rescue. She waived a hand at them and followed her friend who had merely covered her ears.

They were standing, ignoring each other, as they waited for the back door to open. "We will be leaving in a month. You're supposed to only take two outfits. What on earth do you need more money for?" Bonnie asked, teeth gritted.

Claire turned toward her friend, tears in her eyes. "I heard Mother and Father talking last night when they were in bed. They were fighting about where all the money could come from for our trip. She was telling him it was hard now, keeping to the budget with four more mouths to feed. That Colonel Black is offering very little for the foundry and Father is spending so much to equip the wagons. If you and I earned more money, we could give our families more."

"What about the sale of your house?"

"There have been no buyers. They plan to lease it out until the realtor finds a buyer. I'm not even sure what that means, but they plan to leave most of the furniture. Mother is heart sick, but Father is determined that we're going and going to depart on schedule."

"I'm begging you. Don't ask. I'll use my pay for groceries."

"You already do," Claire hissed as the door opened.

Inside the store, Bonnie stopped and tied on her pinafore. Looking angrily at her friend she mouthed the words, 'Please don't ask.' Claire stuck out her chin and Bonnie bit her tongue.

Somehow Claire had tied her own apron with its usual perfect bow. As they exited the workroom, broom and duster in hand, they heard a loud siren like sound.

Claire gasped, "What is that?"

Bonnie stood frozen, listening, and then smiled. "It sounds like a child throwing a tantrum."

Henry was walking back and forth at the front of the store anxiously. Even as they watched, the hem of Bella's black skirt appeared on the stairs. Bonnie and Claire stood and watched her descend. She held an angry child in her arms, squirming and screaming the whole time.

CHAPTER TWENTY

The girls stepped back into the doorway, shocked as they heard Henry yell. "Damn it, Bella, what are you doing bringing him downstairs?"

Bella's face grew contorted and the girls watched in amazement as tears ran down her face. "I need help, I'm at the end of my rope. Nothing I do helps and I can't take his crying anymore?"

"He's your brat, you have to tend to him without bringing him onto the floor of the store."

"If you would let the girls go, we would have the money to pay the asylum bill. I can't take care of him, I never could."

"You're the one who wanted the damn girls. You thought our customers would be impressed if we had clerks. You even made those silly smocks."

"Pinafores." At her shout, the child howled louder and twisted more. Frantically Bella grabbed one leg and the opposite arm before the boy slipped from her grasp.

Bonnie calmly removed her uniform and folded the embroidered apron. Walking backward she mouthed at Claire, 'and you wanted to ask for a raise.' As soon as she reached them she gently but firmly took the little boy and curved him against her shoulder, gently rubbing his back. He took a deep gasp of air, clamped onto Bonnie, and stopped crying. As he rubbed his snotty nose against her gray dress, Bella gasped. Not reacting at all, Bonnie crooned softly to the boy as she twisted side to side to rock him and looked across at the store owners.

Bella used her handkerchief to wipe her own eyes and nose. "Good, follow me and I'll show you everything you'll need to care for him."

Claire stared in amazement as Bonnie and Bella walked past, then she hurried forward. Tucking the handle of the duster under the bib of the pinafore at her waist, she slowly pushed the broom to sweep the already clean floor.

As they left the shop, Bonnie walked tall and cocky, swinging her arms. Claire had to hurry to keep up with her. "Alright, slow down Miss Know-it-all, you were right, I was wrong."

Bonnie stopped, looked around smiling and sank down onto the bench beside her. "Barney, the little boy is three years old. His name is Bernard but she calls him Barney. I thought you told me they married a little over a year ago?"

"They did. The child is a moron. Her first husband's."

Bonnie shook her head, "I don't think so. He understands everything that's going on around him. There is something wrong with him, a disease some Jewish boys have that makes their muscles waste away. He probably won't live to grow up. I think it's very sad. He was a beautiful, normal little boy when he was born."

Claire shuddered. "I think he's gross. He looks so wobbly and twitchy," she shuddered. "Her first husband divorced her when the boy began to have problems."

Bonnie stared at her and shook her head. "He's a helpless little boy whose mother doesn't want him and whose father abandoned him. It's not his fault he's sick."

"Henry can't stand him either. When they married, her father was very rich. He paid for the boy's hospitalization as well as the store. Since the big bank collapse, he's anything but rich. Apparently, her parents were expecting Bella to pay them back from the store profits."

"Henry told you all that?" Bonnie asked.

Claire rose, fluffing her hair and rolling her eyes. "You're right, they are struggling. They have been living on the money from last month's sale, but their credit isn't good enough to order more merchandise. Luckily the store is paid for and spring is here so their costs are lower. It's a shame about the boy."

Bonnie strolled slower beside her, lost in thought. If her son had lived, he could have been deformed or handicapped because of her beating. "Have you noticed there are no handicapped children in the tenements?" she asked as she looked at Claire.

Claire stared at her, then her eyes widened with horror.

Bonnie nodded and they walked without talking until they reached Bonnie's home. With so many hungry mouths to feed and survival so tenuous, was it just understood that a weak, needy child would be too much of a burden. Did the doctors take care of destroying the feeble, or did the parents? The thought made her quake. The rich could afford a flawed child, and even then, most of them shunted them out of sight to asylums. Perhaps the more loving parents, kept them in some secret room in their own home.

"I told him we're going west in less than a month," Claire blurted out. "I had to after he told me so many confidences."

There was no need to remind her that Claire had decided they would say nothing until the week before they left. Bonnie shook her head. "I think it's a mistake. They'll probably fire one or both of us soon."

Claire shook her head. "Nonsense, Henry would never fire me. I make almost all the sales. Now Bella knows your good with Barney, your job is safe too."

◇◇◇

As she stepped inside the smoky room, Bonnie propped the door open behind her. She prayed Claire was right. Only Meara and Reagan were there to greet her. She hugged both, swung Reagan up into her arms and walked up to where Mum was just adding chopped cabbage to a boiling pot. Bonnie kissed her and felt overwhelming joy as her mother leaned back into her. Reluctantly she let Reagan down. "Where's Darcey?" she asked as she looked for the lovely nine year old.

Bonnie turned to stare as Meara answered, "She didn't come on after school. I bet she got a job."

"I want a job," Reagan said.

Bonnie laughed and bent down to the child. "No, I want you to stay little for now. Can you do that for me?"

"I'm not little, I'm five and big for my age."

Bonnie held her in a tight hug. "Yes, you certainly are." Then she turned to hunt the baby.

"Where's your brother?" she asked the girls.

"Ian and Shawn took him for a ride on their shoulders. He was fussing and staying underfoot. But they better ride him right back."

Bonnie laughed. Brigid, then Darcey, had been the mother hen for the younger ones, now it was Meara's turn. At least she didn't have seven to keep up with.

"Jump up Reagan and we'll go for a walk around and find them. Then I've got to go home."

"Me first," whined Meara and Bonnie laughingly waited for her sister to step up on a chair, then lean forward to link her fingers tight around her neck. Reagan skipped along beside them as they went to hunt the others.

She found the boys in the next alley. Clyde was wrapped around Ian's back the same as Meara was on her own. Her brothers were sharing a brown cigarillo between them and Clyde was leaning forward to draw in the smoke as each would blow it out. She walked up and swatted Clyde's bottom and he yelled then laughed to turn and hug her.

"I should swat your bums, teaching the baby to smoke."

Shawn grinned. "Hast to learn to be a man, sis, and that means doing manly things."

"I'm not a baby," Clyde said and Bonnie looked closely at him. Almost three, he was tall and strong hanging from his brother's back. She couldn't help but compare him to the sickly little Lambton boy. God might not have blessed the Magees with money, but there was a lot to be thankful for.

"No, you're a real big boy and a brawny one for sure. Now give me a kiss, I've got to go."

Clyde grinned and leaned back to kiss her cheek.

"No, you promised me a pony ride next," Reagan pleaded.

Meara clung to her, pulling her hair as she clutched tighter. Bonnie felt her smaller cheek against her own as she hummed a hug to her.

"Love you too girl, but I did promise Reagan." Meara released her grip and Shawn lifted the much lighter little one to replace her. "Don't fret beauty, I'll be your horse on the ride back." He stubbed out the brown smoke for later and squatted to swing Meara on his broad shoulders.

"Now, let's see who has the fastest horse," Ian shouted, already in motion.

Laughing, they all ran back toward the flat, each rider yelling and kicking their feet to speed them on and all the horses grabbing and tugging at the others to slow them down. Mum stopped and grinned at the ruckus as all three tried to enter the door together.

Breathless, Bonnie stood by a chair for Reagan to dismount. "Tell Da and the girls I'm sorry to miss them, but I've got to go to work."

Mum nodded, "They'll understand." Bonnie was glad when each made the effort to hug or give her a buss goodbye. Were they all as blue as she was at the thought of parting, yet it was weeks away.

CHAPTER TWENTY-ONE

Despite mother Wimberley's protest, father Wimberley started a fifth wagon. At dinner over lamb stew, he tried to explain it to her. "I'm clearing the rest of the timber on the factory grounds. No sense giving all that to those rebel thieves. Its good oak and ash, perfect for tool handles and oxen bows. I'll use the wider planks to finish this, and maybe one more wagon."

As his wife shook her head he continued his argument. "I can't move the heavy gear, furnaces and pour buckets. No sense dismantling the frames or forms – that's a big part of what he's buying. But he's got all those darkies working for him, why or how he does it I can't say. I thought we just fought a costly war to free them and they follow their slave owners up here. Only one I hired was always sneaking away to loaf somewhere, never got any work out of the man. Anyway, his labor costs are half mine so I haven't been able to compete. But I sold him the business, not the iron and coal that's left, or the timber on the land."

"You said we couldn't take everything with us, if you fill the wagons up with that sort of thing, we won't be able to load what you've promised. I must be allowed to take some of my things."

"And I don't want to leave all my nice clothes. It's just not fair," Claire added.

"I'm not changing any of that, I'm telling you what I've figured out. With my new assistants," he looked toward Tom and Jim and

Bonnie smiled as the boys puffed their chests out. "I'm casting shovels, picks, harness rings and buckles, things people need on these wagon trains. There are a hundred men a day headed to prospect in the Dakotas. Each one needs a pick, shovel, and a gold pan. That's the sort of thing I'm making now. We'll sell the wagons, tools, yokes, and all that sort of thing when we reach Independence."

"Isn't that what you've always done?" Claire asked.

"No, I've sold the metal parts and other men have added the wood. There's been shipping the metal to them and them shipping the tools to a store, here or farther west. Shipping costs damn near the same as the tool."

"Don't swear in front of the children," Mother scolded automatically.

Just as automatically he apologized and continued. "Don't you see, we'll be going there anyway? We won't have to pay shipping."

"Don't you have other orders still to fill?" Claire asked.

Father Wimberley smiled at his daughter, "You shouldn't fill that pretty head of yours with business matters, although you seem to follow it very well. I've only two, one left after tomorrow. That rebel snake wrote into the sales agreement that I can't accept any more work orders. Guess he figured I'd have to leave the unused materials behind when he did it."

"Didn't you read the contract before you signed it?" Claire asked innocently.

"Of course I did, I read it all, but it was there in the fine print somewhere."

Claire looked over at her mother and Mother Wimberley frowned to shush her.

"Anyway, now I've figured out how to build the damn wagons, I can make more and use up those resources, not leave it for the damn carpet-bagger."

Mother Wimberley dropped her spoon with a clang against her plate and he apologized again.

Claire, in her softest voice asked, "I thought carpet-baggers were Yankees who traveled south to take advantage of the poor southerners."

Father Wimberley slammed his fist against the table. "Well, whatever the scalawag is called, he won't beat me out of all that's mine. That's what I'm doing, and why, and don't any of you ask me anymore questions."

He stood, and stomped off toward the parlor and his brandy and cigar box.

"Claire dear, why do you do that? You know when he swears he's already upset. You don't need to agitate him further with your silly questions."

Claire looked up innocently, blinking her long lashes at her. "I'm sorry Mother, I just wanted to understand."

"Yes, dear. You children finish. Bonnie, when you serve dessert, you may take Father's into the parlor, and don't forget to add cream to his coffee."

"Yes ma'am." Bonnie spoke for the first time all evening.

Mary Anne stared across at her brothers and dared to ask. "What do you get to do at the factory, do you pour the metal?"

Tom looked at Jim before answering. "No, but we get to grease the molds and take out the finished tools."

"We get to shove the hot tools into the sand," Jim said and Tom finished, "the sands wet and it helps to clean and cool them. We get to wear the thick fire gloves when we do it."

"It makes a sizzle sound and smoke rises up," Jim talked over him.

"Wow," Mary Anne sighed.

Again, Bonnie watched the little boys straighten up. What had Shawn said, they had to learn manly ways. This pair were well on their way.

◇◇◇

The next day at the Lambtons began much smoother. Bonnie automatically went upstairs to tend the child and Claire went about cleaning up and straightening the stock. Without asking she moved the form with one of the bustled dresses to the front of the store, then asked Henry to help her move the sales rack to the back. Satisfied, she moved clothes around until their arrangement on the racks suited her better.

All the time she worked, Henry asked her questions about the wagon train, including the ones the boys had first asked, why they weren't going by train, how long the trip would take, the exact day they were leaving.

◇◇◇

Upstairs, Bonnie again sat down with Barney and while cajoling him, managed to get him to eat a bowl of warm porridge with molasses in it. Mum had always taught her a full stomach solved most of the problems in this world, especially for children.

Bella sat at the table with her, watching in fascination as Bonnie asked for the little birdie to open wide and Barney would smile and then open his mouth to take the next bite.

"You're good with children."

Bonnie smiled. "I'm the oldest of eight, reckon I have to be."

"Eight children, my goodness. One seems a lot to manage to me."

"You're doing better. He wasn't crying this morning."

"No, he wasn't." She looked so sad and wistful.

Bonnie wanted to ask what she was thinking, but she knew it wasn't her place to pry. Instead she studied the neat apartment. "Looks really nice today."

"That's partly because you gave it such a thorough cleaning yesterday. Thank you."

"It's what I do for the Wimberleys. I'm getting pretty good at it. Took me awhile to catch on but Mother Wimberley is a good and patient teacher. My cooking still can't match hers, but it's a lot better too."

"You work for Claire's mother. I thought you girls were friends."

"Dear friends, since we were little sprouts at school. Lynne McKinney, she's our other friend. They're both as dear to me as my own sisters. When we go west, we'll get to see Lynne again."

While Barney finished eating, Bonnie described each member of her family, starting with Clyde. Finally, Bonnie set him down carefully on the floor and Bella moved closer to the boy. She looked apprehensively at him and Bonnie placed a comforting hand on her shoulder as she cleared the table. "He's fine, he can sit up without any problem for a while. Later, when he begins to tire, I'll take him back into his room."

"Won't he cry when you do?"

"No, I'll sing to him before I go, hand him a toy, and he'll lie quietly playing with it. I hum and sing as I work and as long as he hears me, he's happy."

"Oh," she said, and Bonnie felt some of the stiffness leave her shoulders.

"I don't know though, there's not so much to do this morning. I can't hardly stand to be idle." Bonnie tied on an apron and stood washing the few breakfast things at the sink while Bella sat staring strangely at the little boy. Bonnie wiped down the table then dried her hands on her apron. She looked around, then took the tablecloth and spread it over the beautiful surface. The lace hung down all around and the dark wood shown through making the pattern look even more beautiful and intricate.

"You are so gifted, this is beautiful work."

"Thank you, you told me that before. This one is crocheted, the doilies are mainly tatted work."

"I wish I knew how to do it. I'd love to make a piece of lace for my Mum."

"Then sit down while Barney is so happy and I'll show you how. It will give you something to do while you stay with him today. Then I'll go down and help Henry run the shop, so your dear friend doesn't have to keep him occupied by herself."

CHAPTER TWENTY-TWO

As soon as dinner was cleared and the rooms swept and left ready for breakfast, Bonnie asked permission to go to visit her family and stay for an hour or more.

"Of course you may, but it's awfully late," Mother Wimberley said. Bonnie looked at the children surrounding Claire and Father Wimberley. All were half asleep, clearly another hard day. Mary Anne had the bread made and rising for Bonnie, as well as potatoes and onions peeled. When Bonnie came home, the girl and Mother Wimberley were going through the recipe box to pick a card out for dessert.

Bonnie clapped her hands. "Bedtime, tend to your needs and then it's up you go."

Mary Anne was the first to rise and visit the bathroom. Bonnie hugged her as she walked by. On the way back, the little girl stood with her back to Bonnie waiting for her to work her hair into one long braid. The boys rose to go together. "Wouldn't hurt you boyos to do a little wash-up. You know, you won't have time in the morning before school." Bonnie smiled and pretended to be shocked as she checked Tom's neck and peeked into Jim's ear. They were too tired to laugh but she knew they would do as asked.

Claire reached out to take the sleepy girl up to her room. Bonnie knew how Claire loved to chatter and play dress-up, but she doubted if Mary Anne would stay awake tonight.

Bonnie turned to Mother Wimberley. "I know ma'am, but I didn't get to see Brigid or Darcey the last couple of days. They're both working late and with my new position as nanny and maid for the Lambtons, I have to get a jump on to get home in time for my work here."

"Goodness, they're awfully young to have a full-time job. I know we have the Wimberley children working, but they go to school first each day."

"Aye, Brigid is eleven and Darcey but nine. I told Mum they were too young and they should stay in school, but she just said they could read and write so it was up to them to decide. I've worried a lot about both, but especially the little one."

"Of course, go on, but be careful in the dark."

"Aye, I'll take my new cudgel Father Wimberley made me. Should be good enough to knock the devil out of anyone still awake enough to bother me."

Bonnie also took her bag with the surprise for Mum and the girls. Claire might complain about Bella, but Bonnie found her to be wonderful. She had gladly let Bonnie shift from the stockroom to tending her little boy and cooking and cleaning for them. Bonnie had protested that she would rather work downstairs since she needed the money so badly. "The pay will be the same, of course," Bella had promised, "I need you upstairs more."

Street lights had been lit in front of the Wimberleys, but in a minute she was in a dark alley and holding her breath. Although she had claimed to be unafraid, she really wasn't. Up ahead she heard a woman giggle and sigh. So the night birds were working already, pulling the gents into the alley for a quick flip of their skirts for a coin or two.

Bonnie swallowed hard and tried not to make any noise as she rushed toward the flat. She heard a male voice whisper harshly, "hush," and she ran the rest of the way.

Still shaking, Bonnie rapped on the door. She heard a voice and called. "It's me Bonnie."

She expected it to be her Mum or Da to raise the bar and admit her, but it was little Reagan who stood there hopping from foot to foot.

Bonnie rushed forward, scooping the little girl up into her arms and into the room. Only when the door was barred again did she put her down.

"Who is it?" a voice called from behind the curtain at the back of the room.

"It's just me Da, I wanted to check on the girls to find out how the job at the candy factory is working out. I hadn't been able to wait to see them the last two visits."

She wasn't surprised when her parents came out from behind the curtain, both still dressed. It was Da who lit the lamp and soon the girls who were awake joined them. Bonnie smiled as chairs, stools and boxes were drawn out around the circle of the lamp. It took Bonnie mere seconds to kneel onto the rolled bedding and look at the little girls who were curled together. She pressed back the tangled hair to kiss Brigid, then grunting, reached far enough to kiss Darcey as well. She sighed, when both remained asleep.

"They're beat, and that's true," Mum whispered.

Da grunted, "It's too late for a decent girl to be about."

Bonnie nodded and her mother got up to pour a cup of tea which she passed to her daughter. Neither commented about it being barely warm. The strong brew tasted bitter from the old kettle and helped

Bonnie to become more alert. "I didn't realize how late it was. I'll not come so late again."

"Aye, it's all right," Da said. "I've been going over to walk the wee cailins home in the evening. There are a lot of bad sorts about these days."

"I can remember when you walked us three home from the mill, it made us feel so safe and special," Bonnie said.

Her Da coughed and bowed his head and suddenly Bonnie sprang forward and gave him a tight hug and wet kiss on the cheek.

She coughed as well, blinking to clear her eyes.

"What's in the tote?" Meara asked.

Bonnie laughed and pulled out the little collar she had tatted for her mother and passed it over to her. "The shop owner's wife showed me how to tat lace. I made it for you."

"Ooh," her Mum said, leaning forward to take the lacy little scrap, "It's lovely."

Bonnie blushed but couldn't hide her pride at the praise. "Well, her work is so much better. But she gave me the bobbin and this big hank of thread. I thought if you and the little ones want, I can stop for a lesson every chance I get, then you could make your own."

"Show me," Mum said and the little girls leaned forward.

Bonnie's hands shook at first. The first two loops were too tight and she had to unravel the string a few times to restart it, explaining what she was doing to her attentive audience, then when she finally had the first loop right, she quickly began to draw the loops around the initial circle, noticing Reagan had moved so she was between her arms with her little nose between her and the work.

"Back little silly," Meara said.

Reagan crawled out of the circle of her arms and Bonnie continued tatting, letting the thread flow through with the movement of her hand and pointed finger as she added a big loop again and continued with an outer series of smaller loops, connecting to the side of the first outlined circle. "And it's like that, but you can vary whether there are big circles or small and once you get a pattern you like you just keep going. Who wants to try first?"

The little girls both scooted back and her Mum leaned forward. "I had a granny who could make lace, but she used a wool board and a lot of pins."

"Did she show you how?"

Mum laughed as she reached out to touch the little loops. "No, I was wee like Clyde. When I got too close, she would prick me with one of the pins she carried in her mouth."

The little girls giggled.

"Tis late girls." Da said, "Time for bed."

Mum sat back and her small sisters gave her quick hugs before clambering back to bed. Bonnie dropped the little piece and bobbin back into the bag. "I'll stop tomorrow and show you again Mum." For the second time in one day, she gave her mother a quick kiss.

Bonnie stood up from the stool and her Da moved the furniture back against the wall. Her Mum carried the lamp back toward the bed in the corner before blowing it out. In the dark, all Bonnie could hear were the shallow breaths of all her family. She held her breath for one delicious minute as she listened. Carefully she felt around for the latch on the door and lifted it, then fumbled against the wall for her cudgel.

"Steady, there dear girl, I'll be walking you home," her Da said.

Bonnie stepped out into the crisp night air, wrapping her arms around herself. When her father reached for her elbow, he felt the heavy stick she carried. "Aye, what's this? You're armed."

"It's a cudgel Mr. Wimberley made for me to carry, so you don't have to walk me back."

"Be still now, I'll carry the weapon."

Bonnie surrendered it as she gave her father her elbow. She leaned toward him and he tucked her closer. "I'm glad you offered. I heard voices on the way over."

"Aye, MacPherson's lasses. He once told me I should put my women on the street to support me, since I have so many."

"Oh no," Bonnie gasped.

"Aye. Never trust a Scott, they're all a bad lot. Care only about money."

They moved quickly down the long alley to the connecting side street. In the distance they saw a woman walking in the lamplight.

"I didn't think your boss lady was so nice."

"She can be difficult, but she has a son, he's sickly."

He listened, not commenting and Bonnie speeded up the words. "She has me look after him and their apartment upstairs instead of working in the shop. When I asked about the lace she makes, she showed me how."

"Must be some trouble, this boyo."

"Yes, he has tremors and weak muscles, and he's so helpless you know. I cannot help but love him and treat him tender. I think she was afraid she would make him worse, but she's learning how to deal with him and it's better for the both of them."

"Aye, working your magic are you Bonnie, dear?" He stopped beside her, looked up at the dark windows of the big house.

"My magic?"

"Aye, you always see what's true and you're ne'er afraid to say it. You care for everyone, my big strong girl, even your old Da."

Bonnie choked on her tears, turning into his arms. Up the street one of the girls called. "Take him into the dark dearie, the coppers will nab you if you do it out here."

Da swore at the woman, patted his daughter's shoulders and then watched until she let herself in the garden gate and slipped safely inside the house.

CHAPTER TWENTY-THREE

The family were back from church and finished with dinner. The children were in the parlor, the guide books and maps spread around them. Mary Anne dutifully read the tiny print on the stereographs trying to find the name on images that the boys were locating on maps. After one or two, she complained. "No, no. I'll name the place in the picture, you look for it on the map."

Bonnie was washing up in the kitchen and Mother was spreading out a fresh tablecloth, so Claire was the one to run and open the door. If she was surprised, she didn't show it. Instead she ushered her employers inside.

As Bonnie heard the introductions she dried her hands. Nervously she patted her hair but didn't remove her apron. It had been over a week since Claire told the Lambtons about the trip west. If she was going to be fired, she didn't need the humiliation of being caught in her worse dress, the sad brown one with its crooked seams and patched pocket. Slinking, she moved from the kitchen to silently join the crowded parlor. A high squeal made her stop and clap her hands in joy. Moving past the startled Wimberleys, she rushed to welcome Barney Lambton and his parents.

Bella gave her a tight smile and Bonnie beamed. "You brought Barney to visit the children. Thank you." She held out her arms and Bella blushed in delight at the warm welcome and reluctantly surrendered her son. In the past two weeks, she had grown strangely fond of the boy, to the point that if her parents suddenly came to take him back to the asylum, she wasn't sure she could let him go.

While Claire continued with the introductions, Bella stood holding her breath, watching as Bonnie carefully sat down on the parlor floor with Barney in her arms. The boy grinned, wildly excited, making his head and arms wobble crazily. Mary Anne leaned forward to softly pat his head. Tom and Jim made furtive glances, keeping their heads down but missing nothing.

"Sorry to intrude, the girls each invited us. You look surprised so if it's inconvenient, we could..." Henry trailed off.

"Nonsense, we're delighted. Excuse the mess, we were all just relaxing in the parlor," Mother Wimberley said. She looked around and saw only Claire. "Darling, could you make the tea and bring it into the parlor. I'll get a couple of chairs for our guests."

Henry politely took them from her and carried them carefully into the room, lifting them over the sprawled children. He noticed all three of the Wimberley children had moved closer and were fussing over Bella's son. Sniffing in disbelief, he put the chairs down where she pointed.

He smiled as Mrs. Wimberley pinched her snoring husband and he sat up sputtering with the Sunday paper spilling onto the floor. Still complaining she stooped to pick up the tightly printed pages, half-heartedly trying to fold them. Her husband seemed to awaken at the crumpling of his papers and took over folding and smoothing them back into neat order.

Claire entered the crowded room with the full tea tray. Her mother pointed to the cleared low table in front of the sofa and she set it down. While her mother poured, she watched in amazement as

Bonnie and the children fussed over Bella's son. The twins were taking turns explaining the stereopticon to him while Mary Anne kept saying "just let him see it."

Tom looked up at Bella. "Is it alright Mrs. Lambton if we let him look?"

Henry answered for her. "He has a lot of physical limitations. He's a very sickly child. I told Bella she should stay home with him."

Bella blushed, making her black shiny hair and eyes look even darker. With her beak like nose she looked like a bird for a minute as she seemed to fluff up in size. "He's not sickly, he has developmental issues. The sunshine is good for him, besides, we were the ones invited, not you."

"Not true, Claire invited me to come talk to her father about their plans to travel west."

"Can we," Jim asked.

Bella stared angrily at Henry and at Claire, and then turned back at the boys' question. "Certainly, but don't be disappointed by his reaction."

Bonnie moved so that the boy was sitting upright in her lap, his head just below her chin to hold it steady. "Stay still, Barney. They want you to see the picture," she whispered.

Mary Anne raised up on her knees, her dress scrunching around her to reveal her white stockings and bare feet. "It's a picture of the wagon-trains circling up for night. They do that to protect the animals and people from Indians or dangerous animals."

"We're all going west soon and we'll be in a wagon train like this one," Tom said, his own voice excited as he looked directly in Barney's face. The child seemed aware of all the attention and remained still but his eyes grew brighter.

Bonnie took the device from Jim and gently held a hand across both Barney's arms so he didn't strike or accidentally break it. He grunted in annoyance but remained still. Slowly she moved it closer and everyone in the room waited for the little boy's reaction.

When there was none, Bonnie carefully lowered the viewer to hand to Jim. Barney gave a squeal and tried to reach for it. "There," Mary said, "I told you to let him see it."

As soon as Bonnie returned it to his forehead the child grew quiet. Bella raised her folded hands to her heart and sighed.

Suddenly the tension was broken. Although the children continued to talk to Barney and show him more stereoscopic images, the adult conversation began and continued as though they were not in the room.

Henry asked a great many questions and Bonnie was not surprised when he and Father Wimberley took their conversation and the western travel guides and maps out to the dining room. Bella stayed behind with Bonnie and the children, fascinated to watch Barney interact and seem to respond to whoever was talking. The noise he made was mainly gibberish, but he definitely turned his head and his focus to whoever was talking.

"Would you like to hold him?" Bonnie asked. "I wanted the children to meet Barney, because they've heard me talk about him so much. But I'd love to run home and get my Mum and sisters. They want to meet you so badly, to thank you for the bobbin and thread.

"The shuttle and cord. Do you think you could bring Clyde too? You said they were nearly the same age." Bella didn't hesitate but held out her arms for her son.

As Bonnie transferred him to her arms she dabbed the drool from the corner of his mouth with her apron.

"Mary Anne, could you bring some milk, warmed with a drop of tea and sugar. He's probably hungry and tired by now. Don't worry Mrs. Lambton, if he fusses I'll take him to my room when I get back. I'll hurry."

Handing the apron to Bella and stepping around the three children, she rushed out the door.

When Barney started to fuss, Mary Anne shot up and raced to the kitchen as the boys crowded forward to whisper baby talk and hold out their hands. Barney immediately extended his hands to clutch each boy.

Breathlessly, Bonnie returned with her whole family. The men stood outside on the porch, each managing to take turns peeking in the windows. Mum carried Clyde into the parlor. Bonnie beamed at her sisters, as they stood in the entry, each of the four carrying some lace that they had made. She felt real pride when she noticed her mother wore the collar over her faded dress that Bonnie had made.

Mary Anne scooted forward with the warm milk and everyone waited quietly while Bella managed to feed her son without any major accident. It was Tom who lifted the discarded apron to dab the little boy's mouth.

Clyde wormed his way between the McKinney twins and everyone gasped in delight when Barney offered him some milk. Clyde took the cup and drained it. Mum scolded but Mary Anne ran to make a refill.

Barney stared about but his head began to wobble. Bonnie stepped around the trio of boys on the floor to sit on the sofa beside Bella. Without asking she took the weary boy from his mother's lap and curved him against her body so his wobbly head rested on her shoulder.

"Mrs. Lambton, I want to introduce you to my family. Each wanted a chance to thank you in person." Turning to the twins, she asked them to move by motioning her hand. Quickly they scooted toward the arched door of the dining room, but none left. Mary Anne noticed Barney was asleep and handed the warm milk to Clyde. Cautiously she moved up among the girls, leaning forward to look at the lace each held.

Mum curtsied and found her tongue first. She spoke slowly and carefully, her face growing redder with each word. "You're as beautiful as Bonnie said, and so is your wee lad. I thank you for the work you've paid our girl for and for your gift of teaching her to make lace." She touched her collar, suddenly out of breath and words.

Bella straightened and extended her hand like a queen at court. "I thank you as well. I believe I recognize that beautiful piece you're wearing," she turned sideways and included Bonnie in her praise.

Mum gasped and touched the woman's hand before curtsying and backing away. She moved behind her daughters and pushed Brigid forward next.

"You have five beautiful daughters?" Bella asked.

"Aye, and three brawny sons. That little one tussling with the McKinneys is my baby Clyde." The boys stopped wrestling and Bonnie watched the twins escort Clyde out to the porch with the other men.

Brigid was shaking like a leaf. For the first time Bonnie noticed her budding bosom beneath the pretty print of Claire's discarded dress.

"This is the next oldest girl, my sister Brigid, who is eleven. She works at the chocolate factory off Derry lane." Brigid raised her head, stared at Bonnie and held out her small diamond shaped piece. "She and Darcey work each day, so they've had the least time to learn tatting, but look how well they're doing."

Brigid blushed, stumbled a little as she curtsied and held the lace forward. Bella took the girl's hand and gave it a squeeze, then lifted and turned the tightly knotted work each direction. "A very good first effort. I'll send you more cord and another shuttle. Bonnie can bring it after work."

Bonnie fought the urge to stand and catch the girl who looked like she might faint. Instead Brigid folded into a beautiful, graceful curtsy and whispered, "Thank you, ma'am."

"Darcey, nine, she also works," Bonnie said.

Darcey moved forward without a nudge and held out her work without a tremble. She looked across toward Barney and Bonnie rolled the now sleeping boy so that the girls could see him clearly. "Oh, isn't he precious?" Darcey said. The girls behind her cooed and Bella used the dirty apron to wipe at her eyes. She studied the lace, blinking.

"Lovely, just like you my dear," Bella said.

"Meara, seven, she's in class with Mary Anne." Meara hung back, wrapped an arm around her friend. Together they stepped forward.

This time Bella didn't have to feign a compliment. "This is exquisite. Have you really only been doing this two weeks?"

Meara beamed and remembered to drop a knee. Mary Anne made a curtsy at the same time. "Yes, ma'am," Meara said.

"I wish someone would show me how?" Mary Anne protested peevishly.

"I'll have plenty of time to show you on the trail," Bonnie answered. "This darling is Mary Anne McKinney, also seven."

Already bouncing from foot to foot, Bonnie held out a hand toward her impatient youngest sister. "Our little Reagan, five." She turned and whispered to the excited little girl, "Make your bow and show your work."

Reagan extended the largest piece of lace. "I'm the littlest but the best, aren't I Mum?"

Mum looked mortified. Bonnie laughed, "None of your boasting Reagan Magee. I said it was the largest piece of lace, not the best."

Reagan stuck out her chin. "Well, I'm the littlest."

Bella smiled, unable to resist the lovely girl. "It is beautiful work, especially for someone so young." Reagan gave a smug look to her sisters and made her little curtsy. "But I think the best lace was made by Meara Magee," Bella said.

She smiled and turned to find the winner. She smiled wider at discovering the girl bunched beside her friend at the tea tray, each sticking sugar cubes in the other's mouth.

Meara pulled out her cube and looked at Mary Anne to squeal in delight.

Barney startled in her arms and Bonnie stood up with the boy to rock him. Half awake, he turned to stare fascinated at all the little girls, then he grinned. It really was a rakish male grin. Each of the girls rushed forward to make a fuss over him.

CHAPTER TWENTY-FOUR

Two hours after arriving, the couple headed home. The Magees were long gone, but only after Bonnie carried the boy to the door and introduced Barney and Bella to her father and other brothers. Clyde had walked up and gently held Barney's foot while they all talked. That contact made Barney stay still and calm, just watching as each of the men stepped forward to meet and thank Bella. It was almost her favorite moment of the visit.

◇◇◇

Henry had been too busy talking about the wagon trip with the Wimberleys in the other room to meet any of them. Bella held her sleeping child, aware of his warm weight in the shadowed light of the tenements. She felt annoyed that Henry made no offer to carry the boy but he was still distracted. "Are you glad we came?" she asked.

Henry stared down at her, as though surprised to see her there. "Of course. They are actually doing it, leaving this claustrophobic world of hurry, hurry and bill collectors. For months they will sleep under the stars, wake with the sun, and travel miles through exciting new places."

Bella stared at him. "The boy is heavy."

Henry shook his head. "You're the one who wanted to bring him." He stared down into her pleading eyes and shuddered. "Fine, but wipe his face and don't give him to me if he's wet."

After the transfer, Bella sighed. "They were so kind to him, especially the children. I never expected that."

"I want to go with them," Henry blurted out.

Bella almost stumbled she stopped so abruptly. "You, sleeping under the stars, riding in a wagon for months on end? You want to do what?"

"Claire's father is building extra wagons. We can buy one all equipped for the trip for $300, if we add a second wagon, it would be only $200 more. He will select the oxen and prepare all the supplies we need for the trip. They're leaving in two weeks."

"Five hundred, or even three hundred. We don't have any money. We owe Papa and we have the store to run. We must earn money to pay Papa back."

"When? How? You know we're trying. If we wait, the collectors will come in and take the stock. They'll close the shop, and put it on the block to auction. How will we pay him back then?"

At his raised voice, the boy woke and started his high whine. They had emerged near the water and as Henry's eyes grew wilder she felt a clutch of fear for her son. Beside the dock was a rough bench. Reaching out for the boy she said. "Let me have him, he may need to pee."

He almost dropped him, he passed the boy off so quickly. Bella grasped her son, gently stood him up and unfastened the front of his pants. She scanned the street, but the boy was already fidgeting. She tugged the pants lower and a stream of water hit the edge of the pier. A minute later, they were all three walking home. No one spoke.

"You are being ridiculous. Barney cannot make the trip."

Henry shrugged. "Why not? He can sleep and drool and cry all the way to Utah, or on to California. Bonnie will be there, and the McKinney children, to help look after him. You were just talking about how kind they all were to him." The little boy suddenly stopped and squatted down in the street. There was a bad smell and he reached for what looked like dog droppings.

Bella quickly moved him back into her arms, brushing at his hands. "Don't talk crazy. We have no money."

"I know the Brighton's are interested in our shop. They have the Haberdashery and would like to add a second shop for women. We could sell them our store, use the money to buy the wagons. We can take almost all the stock and load it in one wagon. Just leave the things that don't move and the racks, etc., whatever we don't want to sell in the new store."

"New store?"

"You didn't read the books. I'll ask Claire to bring them so you can see. When we get there, we can set up in a temporary shop on the street with the canvas from our tent and wagon cover. Lots of people do it. Then as we sell merchandise and get money, we rent a place. Finally when we are rich enough, we build our own fancy new store. A year after we arrive, we send your papa back all his money."

"What if we can't sell anything there either?"

Henry walked backward so he could hold her attention. "Nonsense, the women will go mad for the latest Eastern fashions. Out west they have nothing nice to wear, only drab clothes made out of tents and flour sacks. The men are digging gold and silver out of the ground and have nothing nice to spend it on. They order wives from back East like that McKinney girl and those women want decent clothing. If you don't like Utah or the Dakota Territory, then we'll go on to California or south to Texas. When they buy all our stock, we will order nicer things. We can have them made by Chinese slave labor in San Francisco from your patterns based on the latest styles from back east. We'll sell it for more than we can here in Boston, and we'll have twice the mark-up."

"I'll never see Mama or Papa again."

He unlocked the door and Bella rushed through the empty store toward the stairs, desperate to wash and clean the little boy before he went into one of his fits. "Later. We'll talk about it later."

Henry latched the door and paced back and forth thinking. Before he could change his mind, he unlocked the door and walked down the street toward Brighton's Haberdashery.

Next morning as the girls arrived, the couple split up with their favorite girl. Bella took Bonnie upstairs and lifted each different type of doily from the back and arms of the furniture, then handed her a large bag of thread and dropped the lace on top.

Bonnie shook her head, bent down to pick up the boy who was grunting and waving his hands and rolling his head.

"Bella, I can't take all this. Clumsily she removed her purse with last week's pay. "If this isn't enough, please take it out of this week's pay."

She expected her to refuse the money but Bella pocketed it all. "This should cover it, but I am only loaning you the lace for them to see some finished pieces. I've seen work like mine sell for a dollar or more a piece, so your sisters can see how lucrative a business it can be."

Bonnie lifted one of the starched doilies, stared at it in amazement. "Where, how would they sell it?"

"They can visit the shops, when they find one that sells similar work, they can offer it on consignment. Do you know what that means?"

It was opening time before they descended the stairs, Bella carrying the bag of thread and lace and Bonnie carrying Barney and a bed-roll she had made up to let him lie down in the workroom. Today she had to press all the stock that needed freshened according to Bella.

As they arrived downstairs, they both saw the gleam of the wooden floors and Bonnie noticed the precise way the clothes were all arranged on hangers. Claire had been busy. Through the storeroom door she was not surprised to discover more than a dozen garments piled on the counter, waiting to be pressed.

As they listened, they heard Claire's bubbling voice full of enthusiasm. "I'll bring the books tomorrow, of course, Father will want them back right away."

Bella's face darkened as she heard Henry's warm baritone voice reply just as enthusiastically. "The very next morning, I promise. Bella and I have decided we want to travel west as well. As a matter of fact, I already have a buyer for the store and stock that we can't move."

Angrily, the little woman dropped the bag and stormed toward the front of the store. Bonnie knelt to pick it up but watched. She noticed as Bella must have noticed, the couple moving apart a little guiltily.

"What do you mean we decided? When was that? And how can you have a buyer for MY store?"

At her raised voice, Claire backed away from the counter and moved to circle the furious woman. "I'm going back to help Bonnie," she muttered. At Bella's furious glare she raced toward the backroom.

The girls entered the storeroom and closed the door. Claire took the bedroll from Bonnie and at her explanation, rolled it out. Through the thin walls they could clearly hear every word of the argument. Bonnie set the listening boy on the small mattress and motioned toward the cupboard door where the irons and ironing board were stored.

Claire set up the board, then lifted both irons and carried them out to the small stove. She returned with them to the storeroom. "It's cold."

"Then start the fire," Bonnie said.

Claire shook her head, "I don't know how."

"Fine, watch the boy."

Claire rolled her eyes, "I know nothing about babies, especially ones like him."

Bonnie rose, irritated. "Don't you think it's time you learned both of these things before you travel into the wilderness to marry and have a brood of your own?"

"No, I don't. You, father, and the twins will be there to start the fire. If and when I have children, I will have a maid or nanny to take care of them for me. And believe me, I will not have a brood."

Bonnie blushed. Did she think of Lynne and her as inferior because they were part of large families? Lynne was one of seven children, Bonnie one of eight. Claire was right, so many children meant all would grow up with less – less attention, food, clothes – if they survived to grow up. But there were blessings with a large brood – more noise, love, helping hands, and workers. Da always said his wealth was in his children.

From outside they heard a shout. "But it is my store, dear wife. Don't you remember it was the dowry your papa offered to entice me to marry you, a divorced woman with your half-wit child?"

The girls gasped in shock, waited for her answer. When it came they would never have heard it if Claire hadn't opened the door.

"He is not a half-wit, he is physically limited, not mentally. Yes, my dowry, my property that I brought into our marriage." She answered, trying not to cry. "I know why you're doing this. It's not for adventure or sleeping under the stars. You are following that shop girl out there, aren't you?"

"Don't be silly," he yelled.

Claire looked shocked. At the next scream, the boy seemed to hear Bella's fury and terror in it for he started to scream as well. Firmly Bonnie lifted him, then handed him to Claire.

Quickly she walked out and set the irons on the cold stove with a clang. Making as much noise as possible she started the fire to heat them and then walked to the front ignoring the fighting couple. At least when she looked their way, there were no signs that the fight was physical.

Bonnie opened the front door to the warming air, then used the sandwich board sign to prop it open. She gave them both a scolding glance but said nothing before walking back to check to see if the irons were hot.

Bella stormed back after her, stopping in shock when she saw Claire holding her son. Furious, she stepped inside and jerked the boy from Claire's arms so quickly he started squalling. Then she pounded up the stairs to their apartment.

Bonnie clutched the bag of treasures, eager to reach the tenements. At least there would be people talking in the crowded flat and she wouldn't have to walk on egg shells. Claire had not spoken a word to her or any of them since Bella's accusation. But she had managed to smile and talk to the customers. As quickly as Claire walked up front, she sold a nightgown to an older woman who entered the invitingly open door.

Bonnie had to admire her poise since no one could tell she was upset. Later, after lunch, she charmed a mother and daughter into buying an expensive dress. Bonnie couldn't remember another time when Claire had been quiet for so long so she knew she was angry.

At least the couple seemed reconciled when they left. Earlier, Bella came down the stairs as soon as Henry went up for lunch. Bonnie had finished her ironing and carried the garments to hang on the racks. To her amazement the two women stood together at the counter accepting payment from their customers, smiling cheerfully. The contrast between the two, both petite, slender women was remarkable. Claire was blonde, blue eyed and vivacious and Bella, was dark, quiet and aloof.

Bonnie turned to see Henry standing holding Barney. Perfectly tailored and groomed, the man was undeniably handsome with his blonde hair and neatly trimmed mustache. The small boy in his arms was strikingly vivid, his hair and eyes black against his white skin. His lips looked rouged they were so red against the fragile face. The customers stopped and fussed about the boy, delighted with his beauty. Bella stood, her face paling to match her sons.

Henry thanked the ladies, then carried the boy forward and handed him to Bella. She looked at him, as though unable to speak. He bent down and kissed her forehead and whispered something. Bella blushed and turned to carry the child back upstairs.

Bonnie stopped at the bench on the pier, even though she was anything but tired. Claire stepped past her, then stopped.

"I want to talk," Bonnie said.

Claire looked annoyed but finally flounced down beside her.

Bonnie extended her arm around the girl's shoulder and embraced her. "Tell me what you're feeling. If the Lambtons can make peace after such a terrible row, surely you can forgive me for handing you the boy."

Claire shook her head. "It's not you, not really. Although you could be considerate of my sensibilities, handing him to me after I just told you I didn't know what to do with babies."

Bonnie laughed. "I had no choice. I didn't want my bosses to get into a donnybrook in the front of the store. Who would pay us then?"

Claire finally smiled, "They were having a terrible fight, weren't they?"

"Aye, besides I knew you worked wonders with children, I've seen you many times with my own and with Lynne's. Barney's small, but he's not a baby."

"I'm just upset. If they want to argue about traveling west, why do it when we're present? They had all night and morning without us."

"It sounds like he was telling you their plans before he'd talked them over with her. It would make any woman mad, even you."

"Those things she said about me, about Henry wanting to follow me. It's not true, there's nothing between us. He has never shown any interest in me by word or action."

"You sound unsure if that's good or bad? Have you taken a fancy to her husband?"

Claire stood up and stomped off without an answer. Worried, Bonnie quickly caught up with her but neither spoke. If Claire couldn't give her a denial, maybe Bella was right to be jealous.

CHAPTER TWENTY-FIVE

As soon as they parted, Bonnie's spirits rose. She entered the tenement flat, spreading out the lace work and calling to her sisters. Only the youngest two came running.

"Ooh, aren't they pretty," Meara said. For several minutes Bonnie explained how to tat the last ruffled rows. Then she rolled her neck to ease her tension. "Where's Mum and Clyde?

"With the boys."

"Where with the boys? Do you mean with Ian and Shawn? I thought they were still at work," Bonnie said.

"We can't say," Reagan blurted at the same time as Meara spoke. "Ian and Shawn have no job. Their last paid day was Friday."

"Where's Da?" Bonnie asked, her voice full of suspicion.

"Waiting to walk our sisters home safe," Reagan said.

Bonnie looked outside, then turned back. "Here, set the table up and I'll start supper."

She shook down the ashes and added coal to the small round stove, then put on a pot of beans and salted pork. When she turned back around the girls had positioned the lace pieces up and down the table.

"Aren't they lovely?" Meara asked.

"Aye, and worth a mint. I spent all last week's pay on the sack of cord and a second shuttle." Meara started to interrupt but Bonnie continued, "Just the round reel of thread in the center is the bobbin. Mrs. Lambton tells me each piece of lace is worth a dollar or more."

"Oh," Meara gasped and sank down onto the broken- back chair beside her.

"Oh my goodness," Reagan echoed.

"Aye, and I have to bring them back in the morning. Have you paper so we can copy the patterns?"

Meara shook her head. "My slate and chalk are at school."

"Where's Da's pencil?" Bonnie asked.

In minutes she was hunched busily over the unpainted boards, carefully drawing inside each loop of the lace. She did the simplest one and it took half an hour. She moved the next doily over just a little so there was no overlap.

"I'm late, so I cannot wait to see Mum and my brothers. I'll be back in the morning to pick this lot up. Make sure they stay clean. Put them in the sack when it's time to eat. Don't wipe off the patterns you've drawn, but wipe the table before you lay them on it." She looked down at the black outline on the dirty board. "Guess it'll do. When you run out of room on this side, flip both boards over."

Meara was already busy drawing the next piece of lace. "We know, we can do it, go on."

Roughly she hugged and kissed each in turn. "Add water to the beans and keep them stirred. Whatever mischief they're about, they'll be hungry tonight." She turned back and opened the door to yell, "Bar the door until they're back."

As she ran through the gathering shadows, her heart pounding like a drum, she feared she knew the only place where Mum could be with the boys.

◇◇◇

The perfectly horrible day continued as she ran in the kitchen door. Mother Wimberley was wringing her hands. "Father will be here any minute and there's nothing cooked and the grocery order never came. Where have you been?"

"Didn't Claire tell you, I had to stop by to show the girls the lace Mrs. Lambton made?" Shaking Bonnie managed to grab her apron from the hook and tie it on as she knelt to look in the icebox. It was then she touched the list in her apron pocket. She took out the slab of bacon, tossing onions and potatoes to a waiting Mary Anne. Both started to work, Bonnie slicing and dicing the meat.

"No, she didn't tell me anything, just ran up to her room in tears. Did you girls have a fight?"

Bonnie started her fourth fire of the day and threw the bacon into a cold skillet. Claire was right, as long as she was there, she would be starting the fires. At least everyone had the new sulfurs to strike so it only took a minute.

"Nay ma'am, but the Lambtons did."

She diced onions and potatoes as quickly as Mary Anne peeled them. Mother Wimberley stood in the way until Bonnie continued the explanation. "Henry wants to go west and has arranged to sell the store," Bonnie said as she stepped around her with the cutting board and dumped the diced vegetables in, then stepped back around her to finish the rest.

"Anyone could tell that if they listened to the young man last night." Mother Wimberley said, hands on her hips.

"That's enough dear Mary, now wash up and go set the table if you please. I think I hear the men."

Bonnie added the last vegetables, stirred them and sprinkled them with a grind of pepper and pinch of salt. "I'll bake later, ma'am, just have to use this baked loaf up tonight."

"Yes, but why was Claire so upset?"

Bonnie cut and put seven thin slices of bread on the plate and sliced down their middle. She took down the jam just as Mary Anne ran in to say everyone was here and took the bread and jam. Bonnie took out the cold butter and milk and handed them to her next, then frantically pumped the kettle full of water for tea.

As she diced the heel of bread and put it into a small pan she answered the frustrated woman. "Bella overheard him telling the news to Claire. It was new to her and since her papa bought the store, not Henry, they got into an ugly fight." She cracked an egg and added cream to beat it a second before pouring it over to smother the bread. She slammed the knob of brown sugar a couple of times against the table, then sprinkled what broke off and a dust of cinnamon over the bread.

"That's all I know, ma'am. Claire made two sales today but it was awfully tense at work. Henry wants her to bring the books on the wagon trains tomorrow, if Mr. Wimberley doesn't mind. Just for a day or so, he said."

She held the pudding in mid-air. "That's all I know Mother Wimberley."

The woman looked unconvinced but stepped aside so Bonnie could shove the bread pudding in the oven. A minute later Bonnie carried out the platter of hash and a bowl of pickled beets.

"Smells wonderful," Father Wimberley said with a smile. Bonnie leaned over to hug her assistant.

Bonnie looked at the twins then shook her head. "Pumps waiting, you know no dirty hands at this table." They shot out of their seats and she gave each a swat as they zipped past.

By the time they returned, Bonnie had filled all the glasses and was ready to sit down to eat.

Claire called down the stairs. Bonnie heard her sniff at the food and then ask in a choked voice. "I'm sorry, may I be excused from dinner. I'm not feeling well."

"Of course, Darling. I'll send Bonnie up with a hot-bottle immediately."

Bonnie smiled, "Of course ma'am." But she didn't move, just stood with her head bowed and her hands gripping the back of the chair as she waited. Only when Father Wimberley's deep voice finished the prayer did she return to the kitchen to prepare the princess a towel wrapped hot-water bottle.

While she stood at the table making Claire a plate of food, she whispered to Mary Anne. "Peaches are open and the pudding is almost done." She tapped a finger to the child's nose, "Keep a watch."

Mary Anne giggled and nodded.

On the way up the stairs Bonnie's stomach rumbled in complaint. Stealthily she took a bite of the fried dish and swallowed. Pretty good for ten minutes and an empty ice box. She backed cautiously into the room and turned around to the sound of Claire crying.

Instantly she felt pangs of regret. She and Claire had fought, but with mean words. Sometimes those left the deepest scars. Hadn't she learned that from her marriage to Tarn or her fight with Da?

Bonnie set the tray and milk down quietly, then sat on the edge of the bed to pat the lump. "Be still, your Mother sent me up with a hot water bottle, in case you're having cramps."

"Go away," Claire said.

"No," Bonnie said firmly and leaned over to embrace her friend. "I'm sorry, but you know you made me mad first."

"Get off," after a minute Claire groaned, "Please."

Bonnie sat up and waited a minute. "Fine, here's your friend and a plate of food. If you eat it while it's hot, I'll send the dessert up with Mary Anne."

Claire turned around and sat up in bed, taking the hot water bottle to put its warmth in her lap, then grabbed the dish. "Mm, this tastes as good as it smells." She stopped to take a bite of pickled beet and the tears started again. She set the plate back down and used the sleeve of her gown to wipe her eyes.

Bonnie rose to open the wardrobe to find a handkerchief. When she came back, Claire was washing the tears down while swallowing her milk.

"My question was mean, I'm sorry. Aren't you going to forgive me?"

Claire started bawling and Bonnie knelt to wrap her in her strong embrace. "There, there, cry it out."

Carefully she eased back into sitting on the bed. It was a couple of minutes before the sobs died down but her shoulder was soaked by the time Claire stopped crying enough to talk.

"I do, you were right. I hadn't realized it until you asked me the question. But I think I love him. Oh Bonnie, what can I do?"

"Have you told him or done anything? Either of you?"

"No," she howled the word.

Bonnie held her and shook her firmly. "Stop this, stop it right now. He has a wife and child. It would be a terrible sin. You will say or do nothing, do you hear me?"

Claire brought her hands to her chest as though Bonnie had stabbed her. Ruthlessly Bonnie covered Claire's mouth and tilted her head so she could look into her eyes.

"You are not in love with him, you goose. You will never be in love with him. From now on you will not smile and chat about fashion, or traveling west, or what he is interested in doing. No more standing beside him behind the counter, or holding up garments and telling him how much you like this one or that. No more flirting with danger. Think of Bella his wife. Think of poor little Barney."

She moved Claire's head up and down like a puppet. Finally she saw reason appear in the blue eyes and released her.

"I promise," Claire whispered.

"Aye, well wipe your eyes and blow your nose before your mother or our little Mary Anne sees. Put it out of your mind. It was a whimsy, a passing dream. No more of this nonsense, ever. Now eat."

Claire took up the plate but ate slowly. Bonnie heard her own stomach growl and Claire ate a little faster. Finally she handed her the empty plate and glass. Bonnie was almost to the door when her friend called.

"Wait, you said I made you mad first. How, what did I say?"

"It was that superior tone you used. You don't need to know how to make a fire. You won't have a brood of children – like people who do are sows or mongrel dogs." Bonnie said with a swish of her hips and a snap. "I hate your precious princess attitude," she finished with a jut of her chin.

Claire stared at her friend, saw her anger but felt her hurt. Claire nodded, her lower lip trembling. "I'm sorry."

"Aye, well think a little before you say things. We've not all been as blessed or spoiled as you. I don't know but I would feel the same if I had been, but no one likes a snob." Bonnie added, feeling better for saying it. "Watch what you say."

Claire nodded, her trembling lips and tears proof that she understood. Groaning Bonnie crossed to her. "Nay, don't cry my sweet. I love you goose," Bonnie said and bent to kiss her hot cheek before hurrying off.

◇◇◇

When Bonnie came down she passed Mary Anne carrying up a tray with a hot cup of tea and bowl of bread pudding and peaches. She smiled at the wee lass and rushed to the dining room.

But all that remained of the hasty meal was the lingering smell, empty dishes, and a single pickled beet.

Bonnie started bread to rise as she cleared up in the kitchen. She dug the crust stuck in the pan loose to nibble and drank the last peach juice in the empty jar.

After she put the clean dishes away she sat at the kitchen table and gnawed at the little, half-peeled raw potato. Later when she put the bread in the oven, she found her dried- out plate of food and laughed at herself as she ate it.

CHAPTER TWENTY-SIX

The corporal knocked on the door, waited to hear the officer say come in.

Calum Douglas lay on the bunk, the top five buttons opened so the uniform front was folded over. He didn't move, waiting to hear why he was needed again so soon.

"It's another Irish mother trying to sell the kids."

Grunting, Calum rose, buttoning the hot doublet. A week in this town and he could not wait to get out, but they had only recruited forty-two men. Corporal Carter might sneer, but Grant had charged him personally with getting men for the western front.

Calum took the time to dust his boots so the bright polish showed and brushed his hair back, donned his cap, then removed it and tucked it under his arm.

He stepped through the door, snapping a sharp salute to the Corporal who returned it throwing in a little heel click. The sergeant by the door gave a scowl and half salute. Scowling Calum walked up to the small desk and stared at the three figures before him. It was the same boys who had tried to enlist at dawn. Then they had come with their father and been turned away because they needed proof of age. Clearly they were determined.

The thinner but perhaps older one spoke. "Sir, we've brung our Mum, she can tell you our ages better than anyone."

Well, at least this parent looked sober. He saw the boy on her right give her hand a little squeeze. "Aye, sir, I be their Mum. Birthed them both. Ian be nineteen, Shawn will be eighteen tomorrow. They're both working men, bringing home steady money."

He squinted at the trio, tempted to tell her to come back tomorrow. But he didn't have the heart to torture her further. She looked as though she would faint on the floor if he said boo to her. He cast a glance to the sergeant by the door, caught his nod and grinned. Bates had been his wet nurse when he donned his first blue uniform at about the age of these lads. At least they were both tall and sturdy lads.

"All right. Sergeant give these boys a go over," he looked back at their mother, "Ma'am, let's get the paperwork filled out, shall we?"

He read every word, paused and looked up at her with each paragraph. Not surprisingly, her eyes were anxiously following each move the sergeant made with her boys. He lingered on the closing remarks, about the death benefits. He watched her face pale but she did not flinch. The sergeant released the boys and they walked up to stand firmly beside her. When he turned the sheet around, she signed each form.

He took the papers from her, checked the signature and the boy's names, turned behind him and held his hand out. The Corporal dropped in four double eagles. "All right men, here are your enlistment bonuses." The lads didn't even let the coins warm in their palms before they turned them over to their mother.

He watched her tremble as she pocketed the money. Obviously it was more money than she had ever touched before in her life. At least his mother had been dead, and he had enlisted to be with his only family, his father and brother. Disgusted, he put his cap on and turned to the sergeant.

"Take these men and show them to their quarters."

The woman finally showed a reaction, gasping as though struck. "No."

"You signed the forms, they're in the army now."

The boys looked as alarmed as their mother but recovered quicker. The older one took her arm and turned her toward the door and led her through, the younger one trailing after them. Calum motioned the sergeant back to his seat. Quietly he stepped to the door, standing out of sight.

"It's all right Mum. We'll be fine," Shawn said.

"Oh God, what have I done. I'll be mugged before I reach the flat. If I don't, your Da will take the money and drink himself to death. My dear boys, I'm a Judas. If anything happens to you, your blood will be on me head."

"Shh, quiet Mum."

"The little ones will never get to kiss you bye. It's not right," she wailed.

"Shh, shh." Ian whispered. "You can carry our goodbyes to them. Here." He leaned in and kissed his mother on the lips. "For Brigid." He looked over her shoulder and motioned to Shawn. The boy leaned forward and kissed her as well. "Love to Brigid." They repeated the steps for three more names.

"What about Clyde?"

Together they leaned in to kiss her cheeks and gave her clumsy punches on the shoulder. "There's for the little man."

"For Da?"

Each pumped her hands in a firm shake and kissed her cheeks roughly.

"For Bonnie?"

Calum sighed, no wonder she had let these two enlist, how many children did she have?

"Best give her the same," Shawn said to Ian.

Calum stepped through the door as though just leaving. All three stood pink cheeked but determined to complete the ritual. He smiled as he saw the boys kiss their Mum and shake her hands at the same time.

"I've thought of a solution for you Mrs. Magee. Follow me please."

Next door to the room they were using for recruitment hung a blue and white sign labeled 'Western Union Telegraph and Cable Office'. They stood behind while a man payed for a telegram. Then Calum stepped up to the counter. "This woman needs to open an account. These young men will be signatory to the account."

The teller smiled, handed a form through the window. Mother Magee stood there, not reaching for the form. The boys looked just as hesitant.

"There are telegraph offices now at all the major stops along the train line. We can set their pay up so half is automatically wired to your account each month. It's as safe as any bank."

"'Tis far from where we live."

"Show her the map," he ordered.

The teller stood and pointed to the map. "We have four branches here in Boston. Here, and one at each of the train lines. You present your pass book," he held it up, "and you can deposit or take out any or all of the money. We've been doing the money transfers since 1871 and never had a lost transaction."

Finally she took the form. Calum watched Ian fill it out for her and she signed, then she took out her purse and the four gold coins.

"We require a hundred dollars to open an account," the young man said.

She turned the purse upside down and two dollars and thirty three cents in change poured out. The boys dug in their pockets and now there were three dollars and forty cents on the counter. Calum swore, pulled out his own purse and laid the missing money down. The teller took it and filled out the small black book with the amount of one hundred dollars.

"We'll pay you back sir," Ian said.

"Damn right. I'll collect eight and thirty from each of you on your first pay day. Count on it."

Bonnie woke before dawn and dressed in the cool room. Rushing, she started the fire in the stove and made biscuits, fried the last of the smoked ham, and made gravy. She used ashes to damp the fire and left breakfast on the back of the warm stove after packing the lunches and leaving a note for whoever woke first.

Jumping at every noise in the dark, she raced over to the farmer's market. Relieved to find three wagons pulling in, she bought quickly and ran back to put away food, then raced through the sleeping tenements to see her Mum and pick up the lace.

Her knock was too loud and she heard a muttered "Who is it?"

"It's Bonnie, I've come for the lace."

It wasn't one of the girls who opened the door but her Mum shushing all back to bed. No screaming or crying scene. Quietly she slipped inside to give her a hug. Mum nodded at her, made a face. Carefully they made it through the sleeping figures on the floor toward the little round stove.

Bonnie watched her Mum shovel out the ashes with care. She knew she would use them with the accumulated lard she stored in a jar to make the families soap on the next good day. Both the bucket and the jar were full. She had not seen Mother Wimberley make anything like the harsh lye soap. Their soap came from Sanders' Grocery and smelled of roses or lavender.

"You had the wee lasses working by candle light to finish, you know. Look see what all they did."

Bonnie took the lit candle and stared at the table, for the first time noticing it was still up in the crowded space. She smiled with the same pride as she heard in her mother's voice.

"Were they able to finish it all?"

"Aye, it's in the tote by the door."

"You kept out the cord and shuttle?"

"Course I did. Meara said you paid dear for it."

"Aye, but Mrs. Lambton says the lace will bring a good price, if you find a store that will take it on consignment. That means you agree on a price, they keep half and give you half when it sells."

"Steal it more than likely."

"Leave only one or two pieces to begin. When you check back if it's gone, ask for your money and if they give it to you, leave two or three more. That way you won't lose too much. If I get a chance, I'll try to find a shop for you before we leave."

Mum had put water in a pot to boil and set the kettle on the now blazing fire. Bonnie knew the oatmeal would be ready when the first Magees tumbled out. That would be Da and the working girls no doubt.

"Reagan wouldn't tell me where you were with the boys last night. Do you think it would be all right to slip in and give them a morning kiss?"

"Nay, they not be there."

Bonnie sank with a crash on the nearest seat and the crate broke beneath her.

CHAPTER TWENTY-SEVEN

They were all awake, sitting rubbing eyes and yawning like a flock of owls. Bonnie finally found her voice. "I was afraid it was something terrible like that."

"Nothing terrible about it. It's what the lads wanted. They're old enough to know their own minds," Da said.

"They're not old enough to enlist. Didn't the recruiter refuse to take them?"

"Aye, he did when I was there with the lads in the morning. Man said they'd need to see their birth certificate or read the record from our Bible to believe they were of age. Since we didn't have nary proof, have none for any of you, we left. But Ian and Shawn got to talking on the way home…"

"So that's why Mum went?"

"Aye, well if you don't want to hear me tell it," he rose, filling his pipe as he paced back and forth.

"They figured if they brought their mother, she would be proof enough," Bonnie said, her voice dead.

In horror she stared at the couple who suddenly were standing close, arms around each other's waists. "It was what they wanted," they both said together.

"Twas because of what you said," her Da added.

"What I said? I told them it was a crazy idea and to throw the papers away."

"Aye, but you told them they should act like men and work to provide for and protect their women folk. There's no other work, they looked hard."

"I'll go to the camp. I'll tell the recruiter the truth."

Mum gasped, "And make your parents liars?"

Bonnie stared at them, shaking her head as she walked to the corner to retrieve the bag of lace. "I won't be the one doing that."

"Aye, well you be leaving and the wee ones can't earn enough between them. The only work I've been offered in the past two years was watching the factory at night for less pay even than Darcey earns."

"So take the job. With the girl's pay and the sale of the lace, you'll have enough to get by."

Her parents shook their heads. "You were right, just enough to eat isn't enough. Look around. There's not a thing a body needs that we have. You've no idea what the bounty for enlisting was," Da said.

"I saw, twenty-two a month pay plus a forty dollar signing bonus for each."

"We're putting the money in the bank. When there's enough, we're going to buy a small house where we can garden and raise the girls without so much to fear around them," Mum said.

"I don't have to go west. I can stay and work too."

"I thought your bosses were selling out and going west. Didn't you say you and the Wimberley girl were the only shop girls in the Back Bay shops?" Da said.

Bonnie thought about it, could she find work or would she be just another mouth to feed.

Mum walked up and Bonnie opened her arms. Her sisters crowded in against her and Da walked around to put his arms around them all. Suddenly she felt the staggering impact of a little body against her legs. She leaned down to pull the boy into her arms.

Coughing to clear the tears in her throat she patted the little bare bottom and Clyde curved tighter into her arms, crying as though it had been a swat instead.

Mum took him, nodding toward the girls. "Serve the mush. Sister's hungry."

"Sweetheart hush, I was just giving you a love pat," Bonnie said.

"Nay, it's not the pat. He's been crying since your Mum left the lads at the camp. You should have seen the pair when we come home. Crying like somebody had beat them. Enough to make you tear up."

"Which direction is the camp? I won't say anything about their age unless the boys have changed their minds and want to come home."

"Wouldn't help. The whole camp is loading on the train this morning heading west. That's why the lads didn't come home to sleep and say goodbye last night."

"When, when is it leaving?"

Mum and Da exchanged soft looks but Reagan blurted out. "They said the eight o'clock express. I heard them whispering last night when everyone was crying."

Bonnie sprang up, grabbed the tote full of lace and ran toward the Wimberley house. In the dark a strange man yelled out at her, but on she ran. Inside, she pounded up the stairs and burst into Claire's room without knocking.

"Oh Claire, wake-up, wake-up."

Claire and Mary Anne both sat up. Claire's blue eyes looked out of focus but Mary Anne's clear gray ones were instantly alert.

"Leave me alone. I'm not going to work today. Tell the Lambtons, tell Bella," she cupped her hand and hissed at Bonnie, "it's my flow."

"No," Bonnie swatted her bottom and the blonde woman sat up in shock. "We promised each other when we went to work at the factory that we would never miss work for that, and we never did. I know why you don't want to go and it has nothing to do with your monthly."

She looked past Claire to Mary Anne's curious face. "Get up monkey, run get this goose some hot coffee. It's made on the stove."

"Add cream and sugar," Claire said. She rubbed her rear as she pulled up the frilly comforter. "I'm not going, I'm never going back there again."

For the first time, Bonnie noticed her puffy face, the shadows like dark smudges under her eyes. Quickly she moved to the basin and dampened the washcloth draped on the rim and squeezed it almost dry. She walked over and knelt beside the bed, folding the cloth to press against Claire's pink face.

Claire gasped and tried to push it aside but Bonnie held it against her hot cheeks. "Keep it there. It will take down the swelling." When Claire obeyed, Bonnie continued, whispering in case Mary Anne was faster than she expected.

"Even if I could be there this morning to tell them, you cannot stay home. If you do Bella and Henry will know you heard them. It will not only cost us our jobs, but your father the money from the sale of the wagons. You know he is counting on that."

Claire snuffled and took the cloth into her own hand and pressed it closer.

"You don't know how I feel. You've never had your heart broken," suddenly she dropped the cloth and stared across at Bonnie. "Oh Bonnie, I'm sorry. Of course you have."

Bonnie felt the familiar ache but forced it away. "My brothers have enlisted. The train is leaving this morning. I have to run to the station to tell them goodbye. Here," she thrust the tote onto Claire's lap. "Return the lace to Bella and don't forget the books on the wagon trains you promised to bring Henry. Hand them both to Bella."

On the way out, she stood to hold the door as Mary Anne carefully squeezed past with a cup of pale coffee and a plate with breakfast for the princess.

"I packed the lunches, don't forget them. Tell Henry and Bella why I'm going to be late. Maybe they'll understand. But even if I lose this job, I have to see my little brothers off."

CHAPTER TWENTY-EIGHT

Bonnie clutched her side as she ran into the train station. She had gone to the wrong one first by mistake but the clerk inside was glad to direct her to the one a mile away where she could catch the express train west. Miraculously, she was there before the soldiers.

She leaned forward and fought the urge to throw up. As though she had anything inside to throw up. A tempting smell reached her and she spotted a little boy hawking pasties.

She unfastened and pulled her thin purse from beneath her skirt waist and found a dime to purchase three of the warm meat sandwiches. Holding back two, she looked around and found a narrow bench underneath the window where she could devour one.

In the distance she heard the sound of drums and men marching. Relaxing she let her mind drift to anything but the coming farewells. More potatoes and onions then meat, the pie was still well-seasoned and tasty. Maybe she could fry some herself at suppertime. Mother Wimberley probably wouldn't want them for supper, but they would make a better lunch then the usual.

Bonnie turned to watch the troops led by two officers on horseback. All wore Union blue, and seemed to march in step. She shot to her feet, suddenly eager to see Ian and Shawn, wondering if they would look like the others when dressed in blue.

Hastily she wiped at her mouth, brushed at the front of her dress. Turning to the side, she ran her tongue over her teeth as she raised her empty hand to her hair. Blushing, she tried to repin the escaping bundle.

There was a long whistle and Bonnie turned toward the offending sound.

"Corporal, discipline your men," the leader said.

As both dismounted, he handed the reins to the corporal who passed them to the drummer boy. "Yes sir."

The officer tipped his hat to Bonnie and said, "Apologies, ma'am," as he disappeared into the station.

Bonnie nodded, but was aware of his thorough appraisal, every bit as rude as his soldiers.

"Attention men," the corporal barked. "You are in the United States Army now. Soldiers do not whistle or make ungentlemanly remarks to ladies. Do you understand me, men?"

"Sir, yes sir," two of the soldiers answered. Bonnie noticed that these men, like the officers were much older than most of the recruits. Bonnie stepped down from the platform and walked up to stand beside the corporal.

"Sir, I'm looking for my brothers, Ian and Shawn Magee."

The man finally turned around to look at her.

"I came to tell them goodbye," she said.

He stuck out his chin and then nodded. "Back row. At ease men."

Bonnie waited breathlessly as the two men moved from the back of the group of sixty plus men. "Step over there ma'am, they'll join you," the Corporal said.

"Thank you, can you tell me where these men are going, so we can write to them."

He stared at her as though she had grown an extra head. Finally deciding that there was nothing prohibiting it, he answered. "Basic training is at Columbus Barracks near Columbus, Ohio. Then they'll be sent to join the western army. No one can tell you where they will be stationed there, lots of territory and only a few men to do a lot of jobs."

The boys had finally reached her and Bonnie curtsied to the man then opened her arms to hug the two soldiers beside them. Tearfully she tried to talk. Ian reached out for the meat pies. "You plan for us to eat these, or that hound over there."

"Oh, they're for you. I didn't know if you would have had breakfast."

Ian tucked his in a pouch at his waist and Shawn reluctantly did the same. Bonnie stared at them, taking in every detail. They looked more afraid of her than they had been of the man giving orders. Laughing and crying at the same time she pulled in one then the other to kiss and hug.

She cupped their faces and held them both close to her to whisper. "I can get you out, if you've changed your minds."

Ian swore and Shawn stepped back and it was answer enough. "By gawd, sister, what do you think we are?"

She stared at them, tears threatening despite her attempt to be brave. She pulled them back in close to her, rubbing her face between theirs and whispering, "I love you. Please don't take any chances. I couldn't bear to know something bad happened to you because of me, of anything I've said."

"Giving yourself too much credit. We're not a couple of pudding heads. We've been planning to enlist since we saw the flyers. Only waiting on an excuse," Ian said.

The boys stepped away from her, with each word, letting them grow gruffer and gruffer. Bonnie heard the wetness underneath the words. "Don't worry, we've got each other's back," Shawn said.

"Back in line, men," the officer stepping out of the station said.

She watched the boys raise their hands in salute and smiled. She would tell the girls everything about how they stood, how they looked in their stiff blue uniforms and brass buttons. Smiling gaily, she mounted the steps of the platform and waved to them.

"Don't worry, sis, if we see Tarn Micheals, we'll give him a message for you," Ian called.

"Right enough we will," Shawn added.

Suddenly in the hard chins and cold eyes she saw the men in the uniforms and let her hand drop. They would do.

"Don't worry, ma'am, we'll take care of shearing the lambs before they face the worst."

Bonnie turned to stare up at the handsome Lieutenant. There was something in the teasing blue of his eyes that called to her. Suddenly she remembered seeing him with Claire when he was posting flyers.

Glancing discretely past to where her brothers were lining up she dared to examine the officer more closely. His shoulders looked too broad and his uniform seemed molded to his muscular frame. His black boots gleamed in the sun. He really was as perfect as a toy soldier, just as Claire had said.

"Load up men, horses first," he pointed to the cattle car that now had open doors and a ramp, "you jacks enter last."

Calum tilted his hat to her one more time then followed the men into the car. In the shadow of the doorway, he looked back at the platform. Smiling in satisfaction he noticed the girl still stood there with her hand shading her eyes. Hopefully she was still looking at him. He waited as all the new men settled and then looked back to notice her gone. For a moment he felt foolish.

Only when he was sure that the horses were roped securely in the back and all weapons were safely stowed in a corner, did Calum and the corporal leave the new recruits to their loving sergeants for the long ride to Ohio.

◇◇◇

Bonnie slowed to walk to work. She didn't think the Lambton's would be angry at her. Although neither had mentioned any brothers or sisters, they probably had them and would understand. It was her only time to be late in two months. Unless like her brothers, they had decided and were only waiting for the excuse to do what they wanted all along.

For some reason she couldn't make herself worry. She realized for the first time that everything seemed all right for all of them. She crossed herself and stood a moment to pray.

On the way to the shop, she left the delivery list with Sanders, then stopped and quickly walked through each store as she passed, checking for lace for sale.

She entered Lambton's Clothiers through the front door, astonished to find them busy. Bella was helping a customer and Henry was ringing up the purchase for another. Bonnie walked up to Bella who surprised her by gripping her hand. "Did you get to see them off?"

"Yes, thank you. I only cried a little. They looked so handsome in their new uniforms. So proud and brave."

Bella shuddered, "I cannot imagine how I would feel if it were my Bernard."

Bonnie was amazed by the sentence. Had the prognosis for the boy changed and she hadn't been told? No, his mother had changed. Bonnie squeezed her hand as well.

A plump matron opened the curtain to emerge before the three way mirror. "What do you think? Where is the other girl, the one who knows so much about fashion?"

"Claire is taking care of something important upstairs. But I can tell you, you look lovely."

Bonnie chimed in, "It's not often the latest fashion is so perfect, but you have just the figure to make the little flounces look good."

The customer stared at the tall girl, then beamed. "I do have a little extra there that needs adorned, don't I?"

All three women laughed and the customer bought the dress.

On the walk home, Claire blushed when Bonnie complimented her on her courage. "I know it wasn't easy for you."

"No, Bella helped though, trusting me with Barney to watch so I could lay down instead of having to wait on the customers like usual. I thought I would have to stand and look at Henry all morning and was afraid I would break down and cry."

Bonnie wrapped an arm around her friend for a quick hug. "Aye, it's hard to play the stoic when you feel all hot and mushy inside. I dare say I gave me brothers a load of trouble by hugging and kissing them in public. But I couldn't bear the thought of their leaving, and I might never get another chance?" Bonnie drew in a ragged breath and bit her lip but the tears still appeared.

Claire felt the same. If only she dared to chance it, then she would have something to console herself with. "I don't know if I'll be able to manage the rest of the time before we leave or on such a long trip, but thanks for reminding me how much it meant to my father. My feelings don't matter that much."

Bonnie reached out to touch her hand as she heard the girl's voice break. "Courage, girl. You're a brave lass and I know you can do it." But even as she clutched her hand, she wondered if she would be able to. Could Bonnie function if she had to see Tarn each day or maybe work with him? She looked at the little blonde beside her and said a prayer.

CHAPTER TWENTY-NINE

Two weeks had flown past, full of sorting, packing, and paring down. It was their last day in Boston. A week before the move, the realtor had brought a buyer to the house. Father Wimberley had sworn beneath his breath but taken the offer. It was two hundred less than he was asking, but he needed the money. It galled him that it went to the same scoundrel who bought the foundry, this time for less than his first offer. Nothing was said about the furniture.

Bonnie felt blessed that the Wimberley's had suggested she help find someone who could use the things they would have to leave behind. Now the Magee's flat was crowded with a real table and chairs and three bedframes waiting for mattresses. The second best china now glowed on a sideboard made from the drawn doily decorated boards of the old table. When she had taken the old housekeepers clothes to her Mum, the garments were as welcome as Claire's old clothes had been to her sisters. Gone was her threadbare dress and for the first time Bonnie could remember, her Mum looked pretty.

This time there had been no beating for taking a hand-out. Da was sober and kindness itself now that he had work. Bonnie prayed the change would last.

She felt restless, glad that the day was so nice, the air sweet and clean and welcoming. They had eaten early, then gone to early mass. Now everyone stood around waiting for Father Wimberley to return with the Lambtons and their loaded wagons. Sunday had been chosen since the streets would be empty and moving the wagon and ox team might be easier. Bonnie watched one of the animals hitch its tail and another smelly mess hit the pavements in front of the house.

Her sisters were giddy with excitement. All five little girls kept running around like pretty butterflies around the wagons and animals. Mum had warned her to keep an eye out that none of them tried to smuggle on board, especially Meara who couldn't bear letting Mary Anne go.

Meara and Reagan had gone with Mum to the store to collect money for their tatting on Friday and they couldn't have been prouder. Bonnie wondered if it was the first money her Mum had ever earned, she knew it was the first for the little girls.

Bonnie rubbed her hands up her arms, wished there were some work to do to keep her busy. Mother Wimberley insisted on leaving the house clean, despite Father Wimberley's arguments. Bonnie had cleaned and waxed the floors and woodwork as the mattresses were carried out to the wagons and placed on top of the carefully loaded supplies in the wagon beds. Everyone had dutifully filed out after supper to sleep under canvas for the first time.

Bonnie was glad to have enough work left to tire her out. By the time she climbed into the wagon with the McKinney children she was exhausted enough to sleep in the strange setting. It had actually been pleasant, listening to the lowing of the grazing cattle in the yard, feeling the press of the sleeping children beside her.

This morning the roses were gone and all of Mother Wimberley's flowers. She had been scandalized. Father Wimberley actually looked pleased with the muddy, cropped, and spotted yard and decimated shrubs.

He surely was imagining what the sharp trader would think of his big deal when he saw the empty house and ruined lawn. At least someone was thrilled that the time for the trip was at hand.

Bonnie couldn't help worrying that her family would need her and she would be miles away from home. But would they, now three worked instead of just her. Mum and Clyde walked the girls to and from work now. Her brother's would be sending money every month. With the flat wall-to-wall with all their new treasures, Mum and Da were actually looking for a small house to rent on the outskirts of town. They wanted a place where they could keep chickens and raise a garden. They all were getting along fine without her. The real question was would she be able to survive without them?

Bonnie looked around and was surprised to find Da and the little boy standing beside the massive animals feeding them some pulled grass. Da tried to get the little boy to pet one of the beasts, but Clyde was too smart to get his small hand near their wet noses.

Bonnie jumped as the girls squealed in delight. Finally the Lampton's wagons were here.

She watched the boys tumble down from the second wagon, run up to look around at the harnessed oxen. "Aw, you should have waited on us, we could have yoked up the teams," Jim complained.

"I know you could, but Da and the girl's wanted something to do so they helped me do it."

"Did you remember to make the picnic lunch?" Tom asked.

Bonnie smiled, eleven but always hungry just like her own brothers. "I packed it, and all the other food in the house. We're all ready to leave."

At the words, Bonnie suddenly found herself surrounded. Barney Lambton was abandoned by her sisters as they crowded against her. Bonnie felt tears in her eyes, knew her throat would sound hoarse if she tried to talk. Mum and Da held her the longest, their voices as watery as her own.

"You'll be careful. You'll write, like your friend Lynne did?" Mum asked.

"I'll be fine," Bonnie said, knowing full well she wouldn't be. "I'll check on the boys when we reach Ohio. Father Wimberley thinks we'll be there before they ship out. I'll send mail back from there and remind them to write you too." She raised a hand to her throat, watched Mary Anne and Meara embrace beside her. "If you move, how will my letters reach you?"

"Send them to Father Patrick at the rectory. He'll get them to us," Da said.

Bonnie began the long walk, lost in her own thoughts. When her own stomach started growling, she handed out food. At the pace the oxen moved, if someone needed to get down to find a bush or just walk or run around, they could do it without the short train stopping. According to Father Wimberley, there would be no stopping until nightfall. He was determined to make his daily twenty miles.

The road was the wonderful macadam surface made of finely crushed rock heavily compacted and they only encountered four buggies before they reached the outskirts of Boston. In the country, the few wagons and buggies they met were annoyed but easily able to work around them.

Finally the light was fading. As they passed a farm house and empty fields, Father Wimberley walked out to the house and asked if they knew a safe place they could stop and camp for the night.

When he came back he was red-faced and wouldn't answer any of their questions except to nod. A bearded man soon walked down and smiled at them. "I haven't seen this big an outfit in years."

"Oh," Father Wimberley said. At the man's smile he answered. "It's just my family and friends. We plan to join a bigger outfit when we reach Missouri."

The farmer led them over a hill and off the road onto a grassy area. He helped them make the first awkward circle of the wagons in the field of high grass. "First ones through this month, got some good food for your animals, right beside the river here with plenty of sweet water." He walked them down and while the men led the oxen to drink, the women started a fire and began to cook. When they returned, they led the oxen into the circle and used the oxen yokes between the spread out wagons to make the circle large enough to contain all the animals.

"Where are your horses?" the farmer asked.

"Decided we didn't need them," Father said. "The women don't ride."

"Oh, that's a mistake. You need at least two good ones. Save you money in the long run. That way one of you can ride ahead, locate a campsite and water hole before dark. You just lucked out making it this far before having to stop."

"How far out of Boston are we?"

"About twelve miles. Now, that will be $1.50 for the night."

Father Wimberley stiffened and Bonnie understood why he looked so angry. "There are only two families here, the spare wagons in tandem are to carry goods we plan to sell in Independence. I thought you said .25 per family."

"I can let you stay, for .75, but that's the best I can do. You've got eighteen oxen, that's a lot."

"For water and grass growing along the river?" Bonnie asked.

The farmer stood there, his thumbs tucked in the sides of his overalls, staring at the tall woman in disgust. "You be in charge?"

Bonnie shook her head, rested her hands on her hips. "If we're paying that much to feed our animals, you ought to at least provide them with corn."

"I'm not hauling corn back here for you."

Father Wimberley spoke, "The boys and I'll get it, just show us where to find it." At the farmer's nod, he ordered the twins. "Grab your coal barrow boys."

The boys raced back with the first barrow and Bonnie smiled at them as they started to share it among the animals. "Go on, go get a couple more before it's too dark, we girls can take care of that."

"Can they eat that much?" Tom asked as the big oxen happily crunched the hard corn. Jim turned back with the empty wheelbarrow.

"We'll throw it on top in the wagon with the tools. No sense letting that farmer skin us. Hurry, but stay together," Bonnie warned.

It was very dark as the third round ended and the women strained to hear the voices of the men and boys as they plodded back to camp. The twins had remembered some trick they used on buying coal but didn't take the time to explain it to Bonnie. Now she saw the two men carried burlap totes full of corn while the boys pushed the last overloaded barrelful.

Men and boys were all grateful for the river water Claire had carried up for them to wash the chaff and dust from their hands and faces. The warm food was wonderful, even if it was just beans, cornbread and pork. Bonnie smiled as she collected the tin plates to clean as she chased the weary pilgrims off to bed. All would sleep tonight.

CHAPTER THIRTY

Father protested and the argument continued between the two men throughout the next day, but finally he agreed to buy a pair of saddle horses and gear at the first opportunity.

Day three started with hot coffee and mush with some fried bacon. Bonnie realized the daunting task she had to feed everyone. Mary Anne was a blessing, but the child was as weary as the rest by the time they stopped each day.

Today, under her big toes and heels, there were blisters the size of silver dollars. At least the shoes hadn't worn a sore on the back of her heel the way her shoes for the mill had done. Bonnie was pleased when Father Wimberley pulled off the road beside a spring. The water splashing down from a crack in a big limestone outcropping was sweet and cold. Bonnie used the brief time to remove her shoes and socks and soak her feet in the cold water.

She laughed when the twins took a spot on either side of her to do the same for their feet. For a minute they were busy comparing blisters. Then Father Wimberley and Henry Lambton stood over them. "Don't we get a turn?"

◇◇◇

The routine was the same now. Father Wimberley drove the lead team. Mother Wimberley rode on the wagon seat, helping to guide the oxen. Each team of six were pulling two connected wagons

Bella Lambton sat on the seat of the second wagon while her husband walked at the head of the oxen to drive them. Propped in the wagon box at her feet rode Barney, happy at the gentle rocking motion and the voice of his mother calling to the animals or her husband. She spent a lot of time talking to the boy, describing what she saw. Talking to him of New York and of her own parents, he talked back to her. The sound was sweet and melodic and more and more like words.

Once in motion the dumb animals seemed content to follow the team and wagons in front of them. Bonnie walked beside and drove the last team while Claire Wimberley sat at the front of the third wagon, shaded by the canopy and her wide-brimmed bonnet. She made no pretense of guiding them, ignoring the smelly rumps of the animals by reading old copies of her magazines.

At times each of the women would abandon their perch to walk about, gathering wood for the evening fire whenever they spotted fallen timber or picking something edible to add to the meal. The boys ran about between wagons, pelting the teams whenever they slowed, replacing the drover whenever someone wanted a break.

Mary Anne took turns riding in the front wagon of each. She flitted about, climbing down to run and pick wild flowers or to chase butterflies at every opportunity. Tom and Jim climbed up in the tandem wagons to talk and play, then ran when called to manage the off-side of the lumbering beasts. When they found it, all would fill their pockets with gravel. It was easier to get the animals to obey a stinging rock then the flick of the short whips.

After the third day, Bella lured Mary Anne to ride with her so she could rest her voice and let the child entertain Barney. Soon she was showing her how to tat. Mary Anne learned quickly. When she changed wagons, she took the needlework along, teaching the tricks to Mother Wimberley, trying to teach Claire.

Twelve days later they stopped in New Rochelle to visit Bella's parents.

Her parents were furious that Bella sold the store without letting them know. They could have bought it back. She knew her father was struggling now that the bank had failed. Bella couldn't defend herself. Henry took over.

"It was just a matter of time before we lost the business. You don't understand how difficult it is to run a store when the city's commerce is shrinking all around you. We've most of our stock in the wagons, and when we get out West, I expect we will be able to sell it all for a large profit. Then we can repay you."

Later after dinner, Bella was able to get her mother to look at her grandson. Barney sat listening and watching Mary Anne sing him a lullaby. When Mary would stop he would make little crooning sounds back to her. His eyes were shining with love and there was always a smile on his face these days. The women watching stood speechless until Bella's mother reached out to touch him for the first time. Smiling through their tears, the women hugged.

◇◇◇

As soon as Bella joined Henry in their bedroom, their argument began in fierce, deadly whispers. "I just learned you didn't do what you promised. You didn't send my father part of the money we owe them. I insist we at least pay back half. That will leave each of us with the same amount of money, and our debt will be cut in half."

Henry argued they needed the money. Bella argued if they were robbed, than they wouldn't have the money and would still owe all the debt. "What will you say then?"

He didn't answer, just snuffed out the lamp. From the corner of the room, they heard Barney whine. Both went to bed angry. When the crying boy woke her later, Bella changed him, then slipped out of the room into the night.

In the morning, while Henry and Father Wimberley prepared the animals to leave before dawn, Bella knocked on a bedroom door and entered on the hastily murmured words, "Come in?"

Bella breezed into the dark room and rushed to kneel by the white gowned figures. "We're leaving in the next few minutes." She extended the wad of money and folded her father's hand around it. "It's the first half, we can repay the rest when we get settled, hopefully this year."

"Bless you child, wait and I'll give you a couple of books to read about the new western territories."

Bella started to protest, but her mother reached out to grip her hand tightly and shook it. "I'm sorry, about the boy. I was just trying to do the best to protect you both."

A younger Bella would have yelled and screamed about how unfair it had been, about how much she had missed because of it. Now she just leaned down and kissed her mother's smooth, dark cheek. "I forgive you, I know you did it out of love."

Bella could not see her father but heard him cough as he worked the dial on his safe. Her mother found and handed her two books and Bella heard the hidden safe lock. Shaking, he stood to write a note at the bedside table. He walked over and kissed his daughter on the mouth as he handed her a piece of paper. Just as silently, Bella left them.

Later, she carried Barney out to join the Wimberley children standing on the manicured lawn of the big house. While the men carefully backed the big oxen to hitch to the wagon she hid the receipt in the secret box in the wagon bed.

They crossed the bridge over the Hudson at dawn Saturday morning and camped at Fort Lee in New Jersey that night. It was fewer miles than he wanted, but Father Wimberley has come to realize that the oxen would only move at their own pace, about two miles an hour. Now they would leave the ocean behind and travel inland across country to Columbus, Ohio.

Pasture was abundant and lush. People seemed amazed and delighted by the small wagon train. They were able to get fresh eggs and milk every day and to hear each person say no one had traveled past in a covered wagon for years. The old timers talked about the rush of wagons through in the 1840's, younger ones remembered the land rushes from the late 50's up until the war.

One night Henry Lambton started complaining about Father Wimberley's leadership.

Father explained, "I realize it will take time, but we are saving the expense of all traveling by train, three to five hundred per person, to reach Utah. We are both saving a fortune in shipping costs since we're each hauling a wagon full of goods to sell. Finally, I've put a lot of work and money into building these wagons. This is the most economical way to transport them west."

He stared at the young man, while all the faces around the fire stared at his own glowing face. "Henry, I explained all of this to you back in Boston. You don't like it, go your own way. Otherwise, shut your yap and don't bring it up again. I don't care if we're the only ones on the road, it makes it safer and faster for us to travel."

Without another word, the young man rose and rushed Bella and the sleeping boy off to their wagon. Not until the next morning when he pulled his wagons into line was Bonnie sure what he would decide. She was not surprised to see him walking along without speaking to anyone, even his wife. A day later she walked back from the woods to the wagon train and saw his blonde head bent over the blonde curls of Claire. Of course that silly goose would still listen to his complaints.

Looking away, she was shocked to see Bella standing frozen, apparently walking back from a similar errand. Her eyes were dark, bright, and hard and made Bonnie think of a hungry raven.

Not until they reached Harrisburg, Pennsylvania did they find and buy two horses, saddles and all. Both were good, solid animals, well trained with gentle temperament. The gelding and mare were named Bob and Sue. Bays, they had rich brown coats, black legs and muzzles, and long black manes and tails. Bonnie loved them.

It was the day Henry found the receipt in their wagon box. The ensuing argument was loud enough for all to hear.

"I told you we need that money, you stole from me."

"My parents desperately needed the money, money we owed them. We still owe them. I left us half. If it's as easy to sell the clothes out west as you think, we'll have plenty of money."

"You think it's that simple. We have the wagons and now there are no more expenses. What about camping fees, fresh food, or this horse? Don't you trust that I know what is best for my family?"

"I think you would never have paid them anything. I did what I thought was right. What you should have done. What you told me you had done before we left Boston?"

Bonnie waited to hear a slap or blow to put a physical end to the argument. She expected to at least hear some swearing. The silence was unnerving. It made shivers run up and down her spine. She could remember Tarn turning silently away from her, then turning back to explode in violence and profanity.

The night became eerily quiet. Even the animals seemed to be holding their breaths and waiting.

CHAPTER THIRTY-ONE

The horses changed everything. The men now posted up and down along the wagons, talking to everyone, making sure the oxen moved along by flicking them with new, longer whips. Now each of the boys took care of walking beside the lead bullock of the two lead wagons. At night, everyone still slept inside under the canopies, the tents neatly stored at the foot of tailgates.

Bonnie took every opportunity to ride the horses. Usually she rode with Father Wimberley or Henry Lambton, leaving the train behind to scout ahead. Once or twice, she talked Claire into riding along. She gladly traded her position beside the oxen of the third pair of wagons to ride. For an hour she would feel free, cantering the horse ahead looking for the evening camp site with water and grass. She also searched for fuel, or possible food that they could gather. She often saw game along the trail - turkey, squirrels, rabbits, or deer. Neither of the men hunted and Father Wimberley refused to teach her how to handle the rifle. It was her only frustration.

◇◇◇

They reached Columbus, Ohio five weeks and a day after leaving Boston. It was mid-June and so-far they had traveled in good weather making good time. Bonnie wanted to leave the main road and travel to Columbus Barracks to see her brothers. Henry Lambton thought it was a foolish waste of time. The skies were threatening and Father Wimberley agreed they couldn't spare the time. They needed to keep moving while the roads were good. If they turned off on the road to the fort they might get mired in mud and lose an entire day.

Bonnie had already changed into her split skirt and carefully combed and coiled her hair into a tight bun for the ride. She didn't argue, just donned a yellow rain slicker and took her place beside the nervous oxen.

As soon as they started the wagons, the rains began. The road was amazing, brick and macadam alternating in sections. There was clearly no danger of getting mired down if they stayed on the main road. Bonnie wasn't sure she could bear it the farther they plodded away from the arsenal and training center. For the first time in a couple of days, they encountered a large cargo wagon headed the opposite direction on the road. When the men rode up beside the wagon to talk, Bonnie moved up closer as well.

"A fine day for traveling. That's a big load you're carrying."

The man nodded, looked at the oxen and series of wagons and shook his head. "You folks lost?"

Father Wimberley smiled though he was clearly no longer amused by all the barbed questions. "On our way to Independence, Missouri."

"Well, this road will get you there. Not near so pretty once you pass Vandalia, Illinois. Up 'til then, she's a peach to travel. Especially on a day like this one."

"Where are you headed?" Henry asked.

"Just up another six miles. Taking supplies for the Columbus Barracks. They been ordering a lot, feeding and training a bunch of troops again, getting 'em ready to fight the Indians. Hadn't been so busy since the Civil War ended."

"Is there a short-cut from here?" asked Bonnie.

The man looked at the tall woman and grinned. "Well, I might could give you a ride, but the road changes up ahead. Still pretty good. We could talk awhile if these mules get mired."

Bonnie blushed and looked off to the right. "I meant riding from here."

"About three miles, if you can fly due North. But they ain't no road that way. It's all farm country. You can't get this bunch through though, no way."

Bonnie turned and walked ahead to the Wimberley's wagon. She climbed up into the back of the wagon, took out a sandwich she'd made up for lunch and one of the apples she and the boys had picked yesterday. She shoved one into each pocket. She pulled a canteen from under the end of the oilcloth and shook it. She was filling it from the half-empty barrel on the side of the wagon when Mother Wimberley walked up beside her.

"What's going on?"

"Mother Wimberley, the man says the Columbus Arsenal is three miles across country due north. I've got to go see my brothers."

"Walking alone?"

"I'd rather ride Sue. But walking if I have to."

"Robert!"

Father Wimberley stared down at her, then dismounted and handed her the reins. "Henry, you'll need to escort her."

"Nonsense. I'm not riding to hell and back on a whim."

"Get down then," Father Wimberley said through gritted teeth. "Boys," he bellowed. Tom and Jim came running and Bonnie turned back to grab a rucksack and add two more sandwiches, then removed the one from her pocket and put two apples in its place. She crossed it over her chest, the strap of the canteen in the opposite direction.

"I don't think you've thought this through," Father Wimberley said.

"I'd feel better if you'd let me take a gun along, or at least your knife with its compass," Bonnie argued.

"And have you shoot yourself or one of the lads. Never," he said as he removed the belt with his special knife from his waist. Bonnie waited until Tom was in the saddle then adjusted his right stirrup. The angry man adjusted the other.

"Claire," he yelled. Claire leaned forward to stare at them. "Get down, you'll have to manage Bonnie's team until she and the boys return."

"It's raining," but Bonnie and the boys were turning off the road into the high grass toward the distant hill.

Bonnie was used to feeling she knew her direction each day. They rose with the sun and kept it over their shoulder all morning so they were headed west. At noon it would be overhead and in the evening they would walk toward the setting sun. But north, the man had pointed toward a distant hill and that was the way she led the boys.

When they reached the hill, Bonnie looked about, trying to decide what to do next. Tom seemed to understand. "Here, I can show you how to read it."

Bonnie smiled and backed the mare to stand beside the boys. "See the needle?" Tom said.

"It has to point to the red N," Jim added.

Tom glared at his brother. "He showed me too, you know. How come you get to ride in front?"

"I'm the oldest," Tom answered.

"You can ride in the saddle on the way back. Hold on now, we'll let the horses figure out this part. When we're off the hill maybe we can let them run. Clamp on with your knees and be ready?"

Bonnie clucked at Sue and gave her a thump in the ribs with her heels and the mare cautiously climbed up the hill. She kicked the mare and held the reins loosely as she walked just as carefully down the long mound of the other side. Ahead were open fields with an occasional fence.

The gelding followed then nudged past her, his ears flicking forward and his big head shaking. She heard Tom's whoa but suddenly she and the boys were all busy just hanging on as the horses stretched out into a gallop until they approached the first fence. As though it weren't there, they gathered and jumped it and Jim started to slide. Bonnie reached out to grasp his arm and push him back into position. Instantly the horses slowed, as though aware of their owners inexperience. They shook their bridles and Bonnie pulled the reins back more firmly into her hand, showing the boys what to do.

Calmly as though on parade the big horses walked in the direction Bonnie steered the mare. This time they saw the rail fence far ahead. "This time hold onto the reins but lean forward so Jim can grasp the pommel. Ready," she asked as the boys both shook their heads but Bonnie was kicking the mare into action again and as though born to run and fly the mare ran and leaped across the fence. She heard the boys excited shouts as they followed.

She noticed a farmer on a wagon staring at the yellow coated riders. He pointed toward the corner of the field and Bonnie and the boys rode toward it. When they arrived he had the gate open.

"Nice day for a ride," he said.

Bonnie had the grace to blush and apologize. "We're new riders, just wanted to see if we could do that."

"Yeah, lucky you didn't spill and hurt the horse or yourselves. It's raining, makes the grass slippery." He pointed at a narrow dirt road with weeds growing high along each side. "Best to take the road."

"We're riding to the Columbus Barracks, there's a fort or arsenal? She waved as she talked, "north this way?"

"Yes, at the end of this road."

"But the freighter told us there was no road, we should go due North across country to find it."

"He's a dummkopf. Stay on the road. You'll be there alive in about an hour. Walk these pretty horses." He ran a hand down one, then used a big hand to scoot Jim up closer so his butt was on the saddle pad.

He slapped Bob and the gelding took off at a nice prancing walk and Sue moved out beside him. It had stopped raining by the time they saw the tower of the main brick building and Bonnie had opened her coat and lowered her hood. The boys did the same.

Lieutenant Calum Douglas stood on the steps of the arsenal looking across the soggy parade grounds when a smile parted his lips. The smile grew bigger as the woman unfastened her yellow slicker and let it fall back and catch on her saddle. He sighed as he recognized Bonnie from the station in Boston. She looked like the figure head on a ship riding tall in the saddle with her marvelous breasts pointed forward and her hair rolling in coils down her back.

She turned her head, looking from left to right, searching. When she saw the handsome officer from the station in Boston she grinned. Kicking Sue into a jog she pulled up as he extended a hand to catch the mare's halter.

"Hello, I remember you" Bonnie called, swinging her leg over to dismount as soon as the horse stopped. "So I am here in time to see them."

"Awe, the lovely Miss Bonnie Magee. He reached out to snag the halter of the horse with the two little boys on it, smiling as they scrambled down without the grace or pleasure of the woman. "If you mean those scoundrels Ian and Shawn Magee, aye, you're in time."

He watched the smile fade from her eyes and felt sorry for his choice of language. "I'm afraid they're in the infirmary. If you'll follow me." He waved an arm and started into the building. "Who are your body guards, more of your older brothers come to enlist?"

Bonnie stopped and the twins stepped up beside her, each taking an arm at her gasp. "Tom and Jim McKinney," one of the identical boys answered. They stared at him sternly and then gazed up at her pale face in alarm. Calum surrendered to the bizarre urge to apologize to the lads.

Calum looked at her, amazed to see her golden glow had disappeared so rapidly. "Sorry, gentlemen, I'll take over." He reached out but the boys refused to move. Ignoring them, he reached between one boy and her body to slip an arm behind her and one beneath her legs to lift and sweep her up and into the building.

The lads actually growled but ran to keep up with him. He pointed to the door and one opened it and he told the other, "Go secure your mounts." The other looked confused, then ran back to slip the reins of the horses over the rail. The second lad ran and was soon ahead of him to open the door for them at the end of the hall. Behind them he heard the other lad clattering after them, oversized slicker dropping to the tile behind him.

CHAPTER THIRTY-TWO

"Where can I put her down?" Calum asked.

The Corporal looked up in confusion, then pointed to an empty cot. "It's that woman."

The Lieutenant nodded as he gently laid her on the bed. "She came to see the cubs. I made the mistake of telling her they're in the infirmary. I think she fainted. Do you have smelling salts?"

He stared at the startled man who looked from the boys to the woman and then back to the lieutenant. "Sir?"

Calum snarled, again wished they had a doctor, before turning to look in the one cabinet in the so-called infirmary. Tending to new recruits mainly involved lancing boils and soaking sprains. The rest were like the three now here, banged up after a fight or an accident. He found the smelling salts and turned back to see the corporal had taken the opportunity to begin unbuttoning the woman's shirt.

"Here now, stand back from there," he barked.

"I was just going to look and loosen her corset. I heard that was why most women faint." The man stuttered.

"That's not Claire. Bonnie don't wear a corset," Tom blurted and the other boy nodded.

The Lieutenant straightened and stared at the two lads, revising his estimate of their age. "And how would you two boys know that?" They at least had the decency to blush and back up as he approached the bed. He sat carefully on the edge of it, opened the foul bottle and waved it under her nose.

Bonnie sat up and coughed, pushing his hand away. For a moment Calum could not move. The shirt opened enough to reveal a glimpse of the bounty barely contained by a thin chemise. He capped the smelling salts and reached out to rebutton her.

Bonnie grabbed his hand and for a few seconds held it against her chest so he could not get away. Calum found he could not breathe.

"I was going to…" he finally said.

Bonnie looked around frantically, saw the young lads then recognized the two officers and he saw her panic leave. Angrily she shoved him away and quickly secured her dress.

A man moaned behind a curtain and she swung her legs over and stood quickly, swaying. Calum moved closer to support her and she shot a firm elbow into his ribs. He backed away and she walked to move the temporary curtain.

Ian lay moaning on the bed, his face damp with sweat. Bonnie quickly knelt to examine his face, smelled whiskey and vomit and stood up. "What's wrong with him?"

"He and Shawn decided they weren't cubs and got into a fight with a bear," the Lieutenant answered.

"They were drinking," she heard another cough and pulled the next barrier aside so she was standing between the two bunks, staring in disgust at her two brothers. "Do you have any hot coffee?" She asked, looking from him to the corporal.

"I can get some."

"Do, please. And you lads go with him, bring me back a pitcher of warm water."

She knelt to look at Shawn, then turned back to Ian's cot. When she heard him wheeze when he breathed she looked toward the lieutenant in alarm. "Has a doctor been called to tend them?"

"I'm sorry, this base has no doctor. We're only temporary, the entire garrison should move out next week."

"For where?"

But she wasn't looking toward him for an answer. Bonnie moved Ian's head from side to side, satisfied that his face was only bruised. Like the corporal before, she quickly unbuttoned her brothers' shirt. The boys ran back in with the pitcher and she pointed to the basin hanging on the wall. "Find the gauze or winding bandages," she said clearly. Using the small towel Tom handed her, she soaked and wrung it out, then wiped and sponged off Ian's face and neck. Roughly she pulled on the tail of his undershirt and heard his ragged groan.

"Sir, if you could help me get him up and over to that desk?" she looked beseechingly at Calum and he was instantly there, lifting the boy who weighed no more than she had and carried him to sit up on the desk. At her nod, he helped her tug off the boy's undershirt. An angry blue mark high along his abdomen showed where the pain was coming from.

Unblinking, Bonnie rinsed the rag and washed his chest and belly, ignoring his shudders and grimace. The corporal entered with the pot of coffee and two mugs. Bonnie smiled at him and asked sweetly. "Pour two and add a drop of whiskey please. My Da swears by the hair-of-the-dog to treat a hangover."

She took a cup and held it to Ian's lips and ordered him to drink. The corporal stood holding the second one. "Give it to Shawn, if you please, while it's hot."

Ian sputtered on the first sip, quickly took the cup and swallowed noisily. When empty, she passed it to the lads. "Another."

By the end of the second cup his eyes were open, although blood shot, and he was clearly aware it was Bonnie tending to him.

"Hey, Sis, for a minute I thought I was dreaming."

"Tis no dream. Now for your cracked rib. Do you think you can stand?"

"Aye," but he swayed and his knees started to buckle. Calum held him, moved so the lad's hips were braced against the edge of the desk. The lieutenant shook his head at her.

"Aye, lad, I need you to make a muscle pose. You remember the way you used to do for me when you had that card of the strongman?"

Ian looked up at her, for a moment wondering if she was making fun of him. It was something he liked to do when he was five. She took the roll of bandages from the Corporal and smiled at her brother in encouragement. Swallowing he stood, raised both arms bent above his head; made two fists, and puffed out his chest as he grunted.

Before the snickers of the others could distract him, Bonnie carefully stretched the binding around from one shoulder over the hurt rib and passed the end to Calum who pulled it tight. She wound it around the bulging rib twice and when Ian relaxed his breath she wrapped it across the other shoulder and back again, all the time pulling it tightly as she wound it. Finally she split the end and made a knot over his shoulder.

"How does that feel?" she asked.

"Aye, better." He took a deeper breath, let it out again. "Much better. How did you know how to do that?"

"A trick Dr. Krantz taught me." At her darkening face, Ian almost said Tarn. Bonnie nodded. She didn't add that she used the trick with a roll of gauze now to make a binding to keep her heavy breasts from bouncing and aching as she stomped along the road each day.

Angrily, hands on hips, she turned to face the Lieutenant. "I trusted you to take care of my brothers."

Calum's face darkened. "I told you we'd shear the lambs before we put them into battle."

"Didn't you even assign someone to take them under their wing, protect and advise them?"

"Aye, and that's the man in the third bunk, the one they started a fight with."

Ian looked at her in protest but it was Shawn who started talking. "He was kidding us about kissing our sister."

"Which was all right, 'till he started talking about wanting to kiss you, and other things," Ian said.

Furious, Bonnie turned to move the curtain from the last bunk. Unbelievably, the man was still sleeping. He was so large, he barely fit onto the bunk, and his booted feet stuck over the rail at the end. He was snoring and reeked of whiskey. Outraged that such a brute would attack two innocent boys, she looked around for a weapon.

"Wake up you big brute," she screamed. "I'll teach you to pick on a Magee." With that she used the only weapon she had been able to find. She lifted an overflowing bedpan over the sleeping giant.

All the men in the room yelled "No, don't," but it was too late as she dumped the contents over his head and then slammed the empty pan against it for good measure.

Choking, gasping, the man awoke with a roar, looked about for someone to strike. When he saw the woman in front of him he stood there shaking and roared in outrage, then turned and ran out of the room. The younger boys raced to the window and looked out and shouted back to everyone. "He jumped in the horse trough." Tom yelled.

The Magees were both shaking their heads as Bonnie walked back and used the last of the warm water and a bar of soap to wash her hands.

"You shouldn't have done that, Bonnie. Wasn't all his fault."

She looked at the bedpan with its foul contents near Ian's bunk and both boys raised their hands and said, "Oh, no."

"Back here, both of you. The rest of you get out." Bonnie roared.

In seconds the only ones left in the room were the shaking soldiers.

CHAPTER THIRTY-THREE

Bonnie stared at the boys, tears filling her eyes. They were little changed since she'd last seen them. Ian had a ragged red mustache that was too big for his thin face. Shawn had the outline of a fuzzy beard along his jaw extending from where he was still trying to grow sideburns. It made his bruised cheek more obvious.

Bonnie opened her arms and beckoned them. They both came without question. She held them close, kissed one, then the other then shook them and squeezed them closer still. "I cannot believe you want to be dossers after you saw what it's done to your own Da. I'm ashamed of you both."

Shawn sobbed and shook his head. "Nay, we're not. That's the first time we tried it, ain't it Ian?"

Ian just clung to her, pressed against his sister as though he wanted to hold onto her forever. "Aye, well, other than a nip Da gave us a time or two. Makes you feel like shit. I want nothing to do with it again. Clarence, he's the one you doused in piss, he dared us to take a drink."

"He called us babies. Sis, we're no babies."

"You are if you let his like taunt you into doing what you know is wrong. Drinking your pay, when Mum and Da and your sisters are counting on it for food."

"Nay, we set it up to send half back before we ever touch it. They wrote they already used the first one. Where's the letter Shawn, show Bonnie what they wrote."

Bonnie released them, stood to pace about the smelly room. Shawn pulled the letter from his pocket and handed it to her. "They rented a house," Shawn said.

Bonnie scanned the paper hungrily, confused as the writing changed along the way. "We think it's mainly Meara's writing, but maybe some of the others too," Ian answered her unspoken question.

Bonnie skimmed along, only reading out loud when Shawn asked her to.

Finally moved everything, house full already. Clyde didn't want to leave. Da had to put him on his shoulders and carry him the whole way for when he put him down, he kept screaming and running back to the tenements.

The house is closer to where the girls and Da work. We have a well and an outhouse of our own. Two rooms just for the beds and a kitchen to eat in and a room to sit beside the fire. We have chickens and pigs. Da says we'll never be hungry again. Mum complains she knows nothing of gardening.

My teacher sent me home with a book on growing flowers. Not sure what use it will be but Brigid and Darcey are studying it of the evenings and think it will work on vegetables too.

We all made this, even Mum, and tatted hair through from everybody's head. You're to wear it close to your heart like a ~~talix~~, ~~like a tablie~~, like a charm to keep you safe. Even found a few of Bonnie's hairs in the brush on the porch, maybe a few of your own. Never take it off or leave it behind.

Be brave, be obedient, and be true. Pray God keeps you safe.

Love,

And all the names were written in a list to fill the last page along with lots of love spelled in various ways. There was even Clyde's name in wobbly letters with a heart drawn beside it.

"Did you write them back, tell them how you're doing?"

After their promise that they would, Bonnie wiped her eyes and handed the cherished letter back to Shawn. "Aye, so show your talismans to me."

Ian groaned as he reached for his shirt. Shawn stood and unbuttoned his own. Neatly sewn along the opening placket beneath their single row of brass buttons, each lad had a piece of lace, the pattern changing as it stretched from the collar to the hem of the shirt.

"Aye, and who did all this neat sewing?" she asked as she watched both boys carefully get dressed.

"Twas Clarence. He's the only one we dared show them to."

"Clarence?" Bonnie rolled her eyes at the thought of the big giant she had soaked.

"He'll probably never speak to us again. Wasn't bad enough we beat him up, then you had to do that to him and bean him with the pan," Shawn said.

Bonnie leaned forward and kissed one, then the other. "Well, let's go try to apologize. The lads and I have to get back."

All the way down the hall, she described their trek from Boston to Ohio. As Shawn held the door open she was saying, "I love it, fresh air and exercise every day and there is so much to see along the way. I don't think Claire likes it very much at all, but strangely Bella Lambton and little Barney seem to love it, although they both ride in the wagons all day, like Claire and Mother Wimberley. You can ask the twins how they feel," she looked past their blue shoulders to see the grounds full of men looking their way.

Clarence was toweling off and Bonnie was amazed to see the massive shoulders and stomach of the giant were marked with red and blue bruises. There were several marks on his face, including a small knob rising on his forehead where she had struck him with the bedpan. The lads had told the truth. They had attacked the man. What idiots?

She blushed and one of the other soldiers quickly passed the bear his shirt. Unwilling to back down, Bonnie walked out to the top step then descended with as much grace as she could muster. Her brothers followed timidly beside her. She stopped a foot before the giant, aware of the Lieutenant and his men raptly watching. Sweeping a deep curtsy, Bonnie slowly raised her eyes, up and up.

"Please forgive me, Clarence, forgive us," she said in a voice that carried across the parade ground.

The man raised a hand to push back his wet hair from his face, ran a hand down across his full beard and studied her. The boys stood nervously beside her, ready to run or save her, whichever looked wiser.

Slowly the big man smiled and extended a hand. Bonnie put hers in his and let him hold it as she stood upright. Amazingly, she still had to look up to watch him give her a gap-toothed grin. "Yes, ma'am."

Impulsively she leaned in to give him a hug, and stood on tiptoe to kiss the first part not covered with hair, his nose. "That's for being so good to my brothers. But remember, don't let them drink."

The man laughed and so did everyone watching.

Jim was sitting in the saddle this time, with Tom behind him. Bob looked more ready than the boys.

Bonnie accepted a boost up by Shawn. This time, no more embarrassing kisses. She merely clutched her brother's hands and told them to look for her along the trail. She expected to be in Utah in mid-September if everything continued to go well.

"Stay sober, and save all your fighting for the Indians," she whispered before releasing them.

As she clucked to get her horse started she realized a rider in uniform had joined them. Miffed, she turned to stare at the lieutenant. "We know the way back," she said.

"All right. But I thought you might want to try to cut-off the caravan so you don't have to ride so far. Perhaps I was wrong." He turned his horses head as though ready to ride off and Bonnie called after him.

"Thank you. We would be grateful, Lieutenant ...?"

"Calum Douglas, Miss Magee."

Bonnie pulled up her own horse and Sue snickered in annoyance. "I'm Mrs. Tarn Micheals. Didn't my brothers tell you I'm married?"

If the lieutenant was disappointed he managed to not show it. "No, my pardon Mrs. Micheals. Let's get you and your bodyguards safely back to your husband."

Tom started to say something but Jim nudged him to be silent. "Thank you, but Tarn is already out west. Now, which way is this shortcut?"

He pointed to the left side of the grounds and they rode away from the tall building. As they rode, he explained to the boys that they were looking at the famous Shot Tower, where most of the ammunition for the Union army was made during the Civil War. As he continued to give them details Bonnie was glad not to have to answer more questions about her husband. The less she thought about Tarn Micheals the happier she felt.

But it was good to remind herself as well as others that she was still a married woman. According to the Catholic Church, there was no such thing as divorce. A rogue and a villain he might be, but Tarn

Micheals was still her husband. That meant she had no business being attracted to handsome lieutenants.

She was aware the lads were telling the officer about their traveling companions and their mad dash across the fields and jumping the fences until the farmer scolded them. Both lads had put their slickers back on and the oversized gear made them look younger. She had thought of them as almost grown, the way they walked beside their oxen, managing the teams as well or better than the men in their party did. Were they even twelve, Lynne's sturdy little brothers? Mary Anne was only seven, the same as Meara, both closing in on eight. All were so serious, so wise for their ages. But then, you couldn't grow up poor and Irish and stay a child.

Look at her brothers. Shawn just fourteen, Ian not quiet sixteen. Men in uniform, getting drunk, brawling with giants.

When the conversation lagged, Bonnie rode up beside the tall soldier. "I'm sorry Lieutenant, I said many things which I regret. You've been so kind to us and such a gentlemen. I'm sure you had other duties that are more pressing."

"Douglas, Calum Douglas, Mrs. Micheals. You're welcome. The army expects its officers to be gentlemen. The only thing left on the schedule today was yet more target practice. We spend half of every day marching, the other half on target practice."

"I envy your men. I would love to learn to shoot, so would the boys. We could shoot game and add more fresh meat to our diets."

"Don't the men in your group hunt?"

She heard Tom's stomach growl and realized there was a way to get the frost out of this man's voice. "No, Father Wimberley is convinced more western travelers are killed by shooting themselves or others in their parties than any other way. Would you mind if we stop to eat our lunches? We've plenty to share."

Up ahead there was another mound shaped hill and she started for it. Calum extended a hand to catch her reins. "Not there. That's an Indian mound. A sort of graveyard for their whole village."

Bonnie shivered. "We rode over one today, how horrible."

"Best not to disturb enemy spirits," he said.

Bonnie looked around as though they might see an Indian Ghost emerge from the ground. Only when they were settled beside a small brook with a nice shade tree did she relax. They let the horses drink, then left them dragging reins to graze while she pulled out the sandwiches, handing Calum her own and asking permission before taking a bite of each of the twins before handing them over.

Calum held his sandwich out, insisted she take a bite or he wouldn't eat any of it. Bonnie blushed, felt strangely excited to take a bite of the food he held in his capable hands. She caught Tom nudging Jim. Suddenly she couldn't raise her eyes from her lap.

Calum knew he was being foolish, fawning over a married woman, but he couldn't take his eyes off her. One minute she was facing down men right and left, next she was as unsure and timid as a child. Quickly he swallowed the last bite of sandwich and dusted his hands.

"Looks like you get the first shooting lesson. Do you have any weapons other than that large Bowie knife?"

She touched the big knife at her waist, shook her head in answer.

"Have you ever fired a weapon?"

Again, she shook in reply.

"What kind of weapons do the men have in your party?"

"They've each got a revolver, rifle, and double-barreled shotgun." Tom answered. "They were the ones recommended in the manual on wagon train travel."

"I see, and plenty of ammunition."

"A bag full for each," Jim replied.

"Okay, then our first task is to pick a target. What do you want to shoot, one of those daisies or the hole in the trunk of that tree?"

"I want to shoot something we can eat. A squirrel, rabbit, deer or even a turkey. I see game every evening when I'm looking for a campsite, but Father Wimberley won't share his guns or go hunting himself. It is very frustrating."

Calum smiled, delighted to see her move from shy to fierce yet again. He lowered his voice to a husky whisper, "Then we have to stay quiet and walk over the hill and look for a target that's interested in being shot."

"Boys, tie the horses to the tree, follow, but stay quiet and behind us. I've got limited ammo, but I think enough for three shots each. Bonnie can go first, then if she misses you all realize we're going to shoot at something static. We can't expect game to be that obliging."

He held the rifle up as the boys stepped back from tying the mounts. He knelt down and motioned for all three to watch. "I think Wimberley is too cautious. If there's trouble you need to know how to use your weapons, not try to figure it out then. This is a Winchester rifle, it uses the same ammo as my colt revolver. Use a revolver if it's a wolf or a man coming in close to you. Use a rifle for anything at a distance."

"When do we use a shotgun?" Jim whispered.

"When you're shooting birds that you've flushed nearby, or when you're fighting for your life up close. It sends a lot of small shot out in a cloud around where you aim so you usually hit something. But anything big you're not going to stop and the gun's kick will knock you on your ass. Today, we'll use the rifle."

"Tomorrow?" Bonnie asked, then looked shyly at the ground.

Calum swallowed, waited until she raised her eyes to stare back into his own. "Darling, I wish there could be a lesson tomorrow, but I'll tell Wimberley to take out the weapons and let you all practice.

The Indians this side of the Missouri may be scarce and peaceful, but there are marauders to watch out for. Desperate men have been known to attack wagon trains to rob pilgrims. You've been lucky so far, but you need to be ready."

Chilled by the warning and strangely excited by this man's voice and eyes, Bonnie and the boys watched while he demonstrated how to load the gun, how to keep the safety on when they were walking, take it off before raising the gun to aim. He made each one hold the rifle, emphasizing setting it tight against their shoulder and demonstrating how to sight an object through the notched guide along the barrel.

When he thought they were ready, he moved forward and they crept over the hill. Excited, Bonnie almost screamed but instead she grabbed his arm and pointed. On the other side of the field stood a small deer half-rearing to eat blueberries from a bush. Calum motioned them all to get down. He knelt in front of her, rested the rifle along his shoulder and rolled his eyes back to signal her.

Ignoring him, Bonnie pushed the safety off and raised the rifle to her own shoulder the way he had shown them. Calum moved back, angry for a moment at her over confidence but Bonnie stood rock still, aimed and slowly squeezed the trigger.

In amazement the boys squealed as the deer seemed to leap and jump from the shot and then disappeared from sight back into the tall grass. He would have called them back but they were already half way across the field. Bonnie coolly ejected the shell then put the safety back on before passing the weapon over to him.

"You lied to me about never having fired a gun."

Bonnie shook her head, trembling with the excitement of the shot. "I've just imagined doing that a million times. Do you think I got him?"

"Her?" In the distance they heard the twins shouting. "Yes, I think so." He took the rifle and extended his elbow. For some reason he felt an inordinate amount of satisfaction as she grinned at him and slipped her arm through his.

One look at the boys holding up the head of the sweet looking deer was enough. She surrendered the long knife from her belt and turned away while they gutted it. She could hear the boy's excitement, seemingly undeterred by the blood or the horror of the moment.

She already intended to claim one of the rifles and to begin to use it, but for now she would leave dressing the animals to the men. Bonnie waved her arms and spun around. She had known she would be able to do it.

Not worrying whether the ghosts or the farmer might appear to chase her away, she stood and picked the ripe blue fruit from the bush to fill the little knapsack and started back to the horses with the boys following carrying the deer between them. As she started down the hill, a bee that followed her from the tree buzzed close beside her ear.

Frantically Bonnie brushed at it and the insect flew beneath her tangled hair and stung her neck. "Ouch," she swatted it, which only made it sting more.

Calum came quickly up behind her and caught her to him. "What's going on? What's wrong?

As soon as she answered, he lifted her hair to remove the dead bee. He used his thumb nail to scrape the stinger out then ordered her to remain still. Bonnie stood there, not wanting to cry but anxious. What if the superstition of the soldier was right and the ghosts of the Indians they rode over were now attacking her.

"I hate bees. I haven't been stung since I was as little as Clyde. My whole hand swelled up.

Instantly he released her. For a moment Bonnie felt lost.

Suddenly Calum was back, holding the hair away and daubing cool wet mud over the bite. "They're nothing to joke about. I've heard of people dying from a bee sting."

The boys suddenly stopped laughing, dropped the deer, and rushed over to look at the bite. "Be still Bonnie," one whispered. "Does it still hurt," Tom asked.

Feeling incredibly well cared for but foolish, Bonnie straightened up. Pretending to not be worried, she quickly twisted her hair back into intertwined loops and pinned it up on her head where it belonged.

Calum was walking back from washing his hands in the water and he stood there, dripping water onto his pants as he stared at her.

CHAPTER THIRTY-FOUR

Bonnie suddenly felt confused and light headed. For the second time today she felt woozy. Embarrassed, she tried to stand and was grateful when the Lieutenant stepped closer and held her arm to steady her.

"Lads sorry, but we're going to have to go now."

"Hey, I want to shoot," Jim said. "Me too," said Tom.

"You two. Shorten the stirrups on the mare. Each of you are going to ride on your own horse all the way back. Let me know when you're done."

"What about the shooting?"

"Let's do that when we catch up with the wagons." Not wanting to alarm them he walked Bonnie over to a rock beside the stream and sat her down. He dipped his neckerchief and used it to wipe the clammy sweat from her face and neck. Then he let her drink some of the cool water from his cupped hands.

He looked up in time to watch the boys trying to pull up into the saddles. "Bring all three horses over here boys. You can use this rock to mount up."

The horses stamped, communicating the nervousness of their young handlers. Calum stood up on the big rock and drew Bonnie up in front of him. Then he grinned at the twins. "Alright men, the next will be hard, but you can do it. I need you to hoist the deer up behind the saddle on Champ and tie him there using the straps on the saddle."

It took a couple of minutes, but finally they had it secured on the nervous horse.

"Is she all right?" Jim asked in a whisper.

"Of course she is," Tom answered, looking to Calum for reassurance.

"She will be. I just don't want to take a chance of her fainting or falling off. Relax, I've got her. Move Champ over beside the rock and hold his bridle."

Hoping she was unaware of what he was doing. Calum ran a hand along Bonnie's firm hip and down her thigh to swing her leg over the saddle, quickly vaulting up behind her. He took a second to get both boots in the stirrups, lifting her to sit in his lap.

Bonnie's head rolled back into the crook of his neck and he felt her hot, damp face against his cheek. "Okay, hand me my rifle, carefully." Jim carried it over reverently and as soon as possible Calum took it and shoved it in the holster on his saddle. We're ready lads."

This time they were able to use the rock and quickly scramble into the saddles. He reached out, moved the reins in Jim's hand until they would give him full control and held them up to show Tom. The other brother adjusted his own grip. Calum rode out of the woods until he found the dirt lane he needed.

Calmly he urged Champ into a quick walk and was pleased to see the two bays step along behind him. He wouldn't be surprised if the pair had once pulled a fancy carriage together, they were so well-trained and attuned to each other. God bless whatever sent them to market when these innocents had needed them.

Calum circled Bonnie's waist, letting her lean back far enough so he could see her face. Her breathing was heavy, her eyes half-lidded. He wet his own lips as he stared at her full pink ones. Then her lips were moving like she was talking. The rocking of the horse beneath them was arousing. He tilted his head in order to listen and caught her heavy sigh, then the words, "Careful, Tarn, go easy. Remember the baby."

Suddenly all he had been feeling was doused with cold water and he focused on getting the travelers back to their wagons safely.

It was an hour longer before they left the narrow lane for the broad hard-packed section of the road. He looked in both directions, then hissed to hush the boys who had been talking the whole way. He felt he knew everything about each person traveling with Bonnie, at least the boy's opinions of them. For the last mile he had tried to ignore them since they were arguing about the details of their earlier race with Bonnie and who would get to shoot first. When he heard the creak of a wagon wheel he yelled, "Up ahead, you can let 'em run the rest of the way. Hi-yah, Hi-yah."

As the horses sprinted ahead he watched the young jockeys lean closer to their mounts necks and grip the pommel and reins tightly. Instead of terror, he saw wide grins on their faces. Laughing, he shook his sleeping cargo.

"Bonnie, my sweet Bonnie, are you awake darling."

His reward was her half turning and pursing her mouth to press against his own. For a minute he couldn't breathe. No matter how wrong it was, all he could do was savor the hot sweetness of her kiss. When she sighed, he turned her back to brace against him and spurred his horse forward to catch up to the lads.

He rode up, his horse prancing as he raised his hat to a pretty blonde walking wearily beside an ox team. No doubt the spoiled and corseted Claire. Ahead, still astride their pretty horses, the boys were laughing.

A young man, his coat off to show damp circles under his arms was glaring after the happy duo. "About time you scamps came back. Where is Bonnie?"

So this was one of the men in their small cavalcade. From the boy's description, this would be Henry Lambton, the store owner. It was easy to see why two such lads would not take to the dapper gentlemen. Tom was already dismounting to hand his reins over to the man. Calum smothered his own laugh as the arrogant man tried to mount without adjusting the stirrups. It helped that Bob decided to spin while he was halfway up.

Calum rode up slowly to capture the animal and calm Bob so the storekeeper could correct his mistake before trying again. Beside him now was a young woman, half-dozing in the sun. With her dark hair and bitter downturned mouth, this would be Bella Lambton. He leaned over and saw the pale little boy in the floor of the wagon beside her and smiled. Again he tipped his hat and said "ma'am," startling her awake.

Now that her husband was seated, Calum rode up to the lead wagon. A tall, handsome man with a worn expression was working the lead team.

"Hello there, can you give me a hand, Mister Wimberley I presume."

"Yes. What's going on, what's happened to Bonnie?"

Calum smiled, at least there was one decent human being. "She was stung by a bee, seems to have had a bit of a bad reaction. Is there somewhere I can lay her down?"

Of course," he said as he yelled "whoa" to his team and the two McKinney boys moved to grab a horn of the leader on either side. He clambered into the center of the joined wagons and held out his arms as Calum reluctantly surrendered his burden. He stared into the shadowed stillness, not surprised when a little girl climbed over the bench of the wagon with a rag and a gourd of water in her hands.

"You must be their beautiful little sister, Mary Anne." The child looked at him shyly but nodded her head.

Again he tilted his hat to the woman looking back through the wagon at him. "Mrs. Wimberley?"

She nodded, confused that he knew her name and she didn't know his. "She'll be fine?" she asked.

He backed his horse then rode up beside her. "Make her some willow bark tea and give her the rest of the day to rest. She should be good as new by morning."

"Of course, but, who are you?"

Calum doffed his hat and bowed over the hand she offered. "Lieutenant Calum Douglas. I'm in charge of the company of new recruits that includes the Magee boys, Shawn and Ian. Bonnie came to visit them, but I guess you knew that."

"Yes, we've worried about her and the lads all day. We almost stopped at noon to wait on them but my husband argued she might come across to intercept our train and we would miss her and the boys. I've been angry at him, afraid he just didn't want to waste the day and not make his blasted miles. Are you sure she is all right?"

"You made the right choice. Yes, she'll be fine. I'm going to leave her in your good hands. I've got a lot of men to keep in line, so I can't stay much longer. I'll probably have to ride home in the dark."

He was relieved when he saw the pretty blonde looking over the tail of the wagon at her friend. "Are you sure she's all right?"

"With you three ladies to see to her chores and this little lady to nurse her, I'm sure she'll be fine." He stared into blue eyes in a flawless face and understood why the boys had described Claire as pretty as a China doll. Too bad they had added that she had about as much sense. He untied the deer and turned Champ and let him rear.

"She shot the deer before she got the bee sting collecting these." He unlooped the knapsack full of blueberries and handed them to Claire.

"Okay lads, your turn to shoot. Have you picked your target?"

Mr. Wimberley stood, his hand on the tailgate of the wagon. "Hey, I don't hold with shooting."

Calum sat with an elbow on the pommel of his saddle and stared at the solemn face. Quietly, pitching his voice so only this man could hear, he told him all he had been thinking as he carried a helpless Bonnie back. No reason he should be the only one losing sleep worrying about her.

"Then you should have stayed in Boston. As I told the lads, the Indians along this way won't be a problem, at least 'til you cross the Missouri. But you never know when vagabonds and robbers might attack a lone wagon train. With four helpless children, four beautiful white women, and only two men to defend them, you better start carrying your weapons and know how to use them."

He turned and saluted the twins as they raised their fingers in a smart salute to him. By the time they had fired their rounds, the men had circled the wagons for the night early and quartered the deer. With the women busy cooking the meal, Calum wasn't surprised to see the two men walk up carrying all their weapons.

CHAPTER THIRTY-FIVE

By the time he had shown all four how to load, clean and shoot all the weapons, the women had food ready. Calum knew he would be in trouble if he didn't head home, but he happily joined them for dinner. He stared in amazement as he saw Bonnie sitting on the edge of the bench in front of the campfire beside Barney Lambton and Mary Anne.

Not since leaving for war at fifteen, had he felt such a strong desire to have a home. There was a strong hunger to have a family, a wife and children of his own. On seeing him, Bonnie smiled and looked ready to rise. He sprinted over to her side before she could. He didn't respond when the twins giggled, but took the plates of food and ate without even tasting it.

Everyone talked, especially the men and the twins, everyone but Calum and Bonnie. The evening star was peeking above the pine trees as he rose and held a hand out to the woman beside him. Bonnie stood, then accepted his hand to steady herself.

"Which is your wagon?" he asked.

She looked around, clearly confused for a minute. Claire pointed to the wagon closest to the woods. They wandered past the fire and into the shadows beside the trees. He heard voices whispering as they walked past but nothing was going to make him miss this opportunity.

At the lowered tail-gate, he turned and whispered. "May I lift you?"

Bonnie felt strangely warm at the vibration of his voice. She raised a hand to his chest as he put both hands at her waist and set her up on the end of the wagon.

"I have to go," he said.

"I know. Thank you for all you did for us today."

"I noticed you didn't kiss your brothers good-bye today."

She tried to see him, but all she could see was the reflected light from his teeth as he smiled, and the shimmer of his eyes. "I didn't think it wise, if it's going to make them have to fight."

"No, probably not." He took a breath in case she had something more to say. "I can carry a message from you."

Suddenly Bonnie's heart began to race. Did she dare?

"You can trust me," he whispered as though reading her mind.

Trembling, she leaned forward. "My love, Ian," she leaned closer and kissed him softly.

Calum breathed, swallowing in her breath with the words and kiss. She drew back. He leaned in, waiting for the next kiss.

"Care and love, Shawn," the kiss was soft and quick.

"It will be dark and dangerous, the journey home," he whispered, hoping.

Bonnie pushed against his chest and he stepped back. The moon now illuminated the planes of his face but left his eyes in shadow. She shook her head, wrapping her arms around herself as though protecting her heart. "No, it wouldn't be right."

He felt the slow pain of her rejection. "Good night then." He stepped away but her voice called to him in the dark.

"Be safe, please. God go with you."

◇◇◇

Luckily there was a full moon to light the narrow lane. Still smiling in wonder at the woman he'd kissed, he rode back to the barracks. When a tree branch smacked him in the head he took it as a reminder from God. He rubbed his head and set his cap back straight. She was already someone else's wife and if he had heard her right, perhaps someone's mother.

Bonnie was up early, eager to pick up her duties. The deer meat hung over the ashes of the fire where it had smoked overnight. She stirred up the fire, made coffee and hoecakes and as the smell of the hot brew spread out, the sleeping campers began to wake up.

Claire came out of her wagon last, groaning as she sat on the tailgate, still in her wrapper. Bonnie smiled and then served her friend a stack of cakes drizzled with molasses. "Thank goodness you're back with us. Yesterday was a nightmare."

Mother Wimberley stepped up and finished frying cakes and serving. The men were soon yoking oxen and saddling horses for the boys to take down to the stream to water.

Claire came down from her wagon when the area was clear, stood in her gown and wrapper and whined. Bonnie washed the dirty dishes while Mother Wimberley walked over to fuss over Claire.

"Hurry darling, get dressed. The men will be moving the wagons out in a few minutes."

"No, I don't want to do this. I walked all day yesterday and my feet and legs are killing me," she looked past her mother to where Bonnie hummed and worked. "Why can't we just take one day and rest somewhere and let the animals rest? I'm not tough like some people, I wasn't built for walking along like a cow day in and day out."

Bonnie's eyes flashed and she finished and quickly turned to preparing the food for their lunch. Unless they encountered rich grazing for the animals, they usually ate while on the move. Father Wimberley had never stopped at noon to warm the meal. Today she wrapped some of the cooked venison inside some of the left over hoecakes, then stacked them all inside one metal plate and secured another overtop of it. She made a second package as Claire hobbled up to the cold fire pit.

"Can I see your big bite?"

Bonnie stared at her, wondered why Claire was complaining about her. She turned so the red, muddy spot on her neck was visible.

"Oh. Does it feel better, do you feel okay? The way your toy soldier was fussing over you, I expected it to be bigger."

Bonnie loaded the prepared food, stood the coffee pot in the corner and wedged everything in place with the bag of fruit.

"He's not my soldier, and he's certainly not a toy. He escorted us back for our safety. Why, didn't you like Lieutenant Douglas?"

"I don't know, for some reason he was so wrapped up in paying attention to you that he never even spoke to me. It was as though I was invisible."

Bonnie smiled and reached out to tweak the little blonde's chin and point to her thin robe. "You dear, are a little too visible."

Claire blushed and sprinted as fast as her sore feet would allow toward the Wimberley wagon. Bella held Barney's little hand as she walked him back from the bushes. She was just in time to watch the girls' argument and turned to see Henry ogling the little blonde. Angrily she bit her tongue as he straightened when Claire disappeared over the tailgate with one bare white leg exposed.

◇◇◇

Bonnie walked alongside the wagon as Mr. Wimberley and the twins led the first team out of the circle and moved his wagon down the road in position for the day. She could hear Claire getting dressed inside. "Don't worry, no need to be jealous. I told him I'm married and not interested. Today you just take it easy. This dumb ox is back on duty."

Then she walked over to help the boys connect the three pairs to their wagon. Mary Anne ran up to her and Bonnie caught the sweet girl. "I can drive today if you need me." Laughing, Bonnie swung the child up onto the wagon seat. "I certainly do."

Singing *Goodbye Liza Jane,* she led her team onto the road, smiling as the children joined in the song and the boys took their position beside each of the lead wagons.

The two men mounted their horses and rode past, exchanging a look between them as they listened to the pretty song. The big difference today was they wore pistols on their hips and carried their rifles in saddle scabbards beside them. Resting in the wagon boxes, ready to pull out if needed, were the loaded shotguns.

When Bonnie looked back to the camp site, the only sign that they had been there was the circle of ashes in the center of the trampled and eaten grass. She had almost expected to see the handsome lieutenant.

Dressed but still annoyed, Claire climbed out onto the wagon seat beside her mother. Mother Wimberley patted the pretty girl's knee and smiled. It was hard to stay angry when the day looked so beautiful. The trail climbed a little rise and they were surrounded by rolling fields on one side, a pine thicket on the other.

Bonnie's song changed to *In the Pines*, and the children's sweet voices filled in around it.

Suddenly Claire swore and twisted on the seat, trying to see the girl singing. "Switch sides Mother," she ordered and her Mother shook her head but obliged by sliding under her impatient daughter. Claire leaned out and stared back up the trail. At the top of the rise, Bonnie stood illuminated by the soft glow of morning. "I knew it," she stomped her foot and turned around, gripping the seat beneath her in anger.

"Darling, what is wrong with you today?"

"Don't you hear her, don't you know what it means?"

Claire's mother looked completely baffled. Claire made a fist and propped her chin on it. "Bonnie never sings. The last time she burst into song and was happy all the time, was when she was falling in love with that horrible Tarn Micheals."

"Oh no, you mean that nice young Lieutenant Douglas is another bastard like the last one."

"No, but he is handsome. Why would two handsome men fall in love with Bonnie?" She didn't add 'and why not me' but her mother heard the complaint beneath her words.

"Well, Bonnie is loving, sweet, patient, hard-working and smart."

"No, she barely had better marks then me. Lynne was the smart one. And how smart can she be, she married a bounder like Tarn?"

"I seem to remember you were pretty taken with him for a while yourself," her Mother said.

"But Bonnie is so tall and plain and her clothes are horrible. What do they see?"

As their wagon wound up the next hill, Mother Wimberley leaned out her side and saw Bonnie on the last rise, striding along in step with the team, her mouth open in laughter as she talked with the children. She was too long limbed and lean, but with those large high breasts, there was no denying that she was a striking woman. Where the sun blazing down would have destroyed her or Claire's complexion, it seemed to have polished Bonnie's into gold and her hair sparkled with copper highlights. For a minute, it looked as though she were going to step off the trail into the air like some winged goddess of old.

Mother Wimberley sat back in her seat and held her breath. That had been her imagination. With all the girl had been through, the poverty, abuse, her tragic marriage, she should slink along with bowed head and humility. Instead, Bonnie who had always been shy was now never afraid of offering her opinion, as though she thought it as good as anyone else's. It seemed that the more adversity heaped upon her, the stronger and brighter she emerged. Like the rough ore Robert smelted and turned into shiny steel. For the first time she looked at her cherished child and felt sorry for her.

"Well she is very tall and Tarn and the Lieutenant are both exceptionally tall men. Maybe that's why they like her."

Claire smiled, as suddenly happy as a blue sky when all the clouds were swept away. "I think you're right, Mother. And I don't want a tall man, they're too hard to kiss."

Her Mother stared forward at the unchanging view of oxen tails as she wondered if she dared ask how Claire knew that.

CHAPTER THIRTY SIX

During the six weeks it took to reach the Missouri, they encountered no marauders. Bonnie knew part of it had to be the fact that they kept guard at night. The rest had to be Tip and Tyler. At a farm in Indiana, the boys had fallen in love with a pair of black and white dogs. Low to the ground with lovely splashes of white on their faces and legs, the black, long haired animals were used by the farmer to herd cattle. Like the twins, the dogs, were almost identical.

Taken with the boys, the farmer was generous. After selling them a wagon full of bagged wheat and pumpkins, he threw the young dogs into the price. Father Wimberley protested at first, but when he saw what good herders they were he accepted. With two alert barkers in camp, they would keep any prowlers from sneaking in on them.

Barney Lambton was thrilled with the friendly dogs and would grab their fur and squeal whenever they came near. In turn they would lick him and run along to herd him whenever he got up to walk. It gave Bella a little time for herself and she made a point of slipping them treats to keep them nearby at night.

◇◇◇

It was the first week in August when they finished the first leg of their journey. Camped beside the big river, Bonnie smelled the raw wetness of it and studied the city lights. She wondered if her brothers or the handsome Lieutenant were already there somewhere. Tomorrow they would cross where the Missouri met the Mississippi over the new Eads Bridge into St. Louis. Father didn't trust it, especially since half of it was taken up by a railway span. He planned to move one tandem wagon across at a time.

At dinner the night before crossing, there was a lot of talk and argument about what to do next. At sunset, the boys had pointed out a big frame building with sunflowers painted on the roof and the word flour, laughing that someone didn't know how to spell flowers. Father Wimberley announced he would sell the wheat and pumpkins tomorrow. The bags had been piled in the second wagons for each team, on top of the tools and foundry supplies. Stuffed among them were the big orange pumpkins. The women had made pies and soup from them for three weeks but several had been bruised or spoiled and were fed to the oxen. All were glad at the idea they would be gone.

"I think it might be the place to sell the buckets and tools from the foundry too. I'm not sure what we'll find on the trail to come. We've freighted it this far, but I might have an easier time selling the wagons if they're empty," Father Wimberley said.

Bella argued that Henry should try to sell some of their goods as well. They had no idea what waited for them at the end of the trail. All the travelers had read the books with their tales of abandoned furniture and treasures along the difficult road. He told her he had made his plans and would stick to them.

The flour and pumpkins were an easy sale and he doubled his money. Father Wimberley was disappointed at his first three tries to sell equipment. He sold ten shovels and picks at one hardware, but still had a wagon full. Finally he was sent to find a man staying at the

Southern Hotel. He met the buyer in the restaurant in the grand, block long building. The man said he was wanting to buy equipment for his gold mine in the Black Hills. Mr. Wimberley convinced him he would be able to use or convert all of the equipment for that purpose and offered to make him a good price.

As soon as the man saw it, the deal was struck for the equipment. Then the man astonished them all by paying eight hundred for the tandem wagon and team. To celebrate, Father Wimberley collected his family and drove the remaining wagons to the tallest and largest building they had seen since leaving home.

Across from the Southern Hotel was a vast grassy area soon to become a town park. Without asking permission, they made a square of the remaining wagons and picketed the cattle and horses. Leaving the women and boys with the wagons, he and Henry checked into two rooms. After bathing and dressing in clean clothes they visited the barbers in the lobby for a shave, haircut, and shoe shine. Restored, the men took over the duty of watching the remaining wagons and the women and children went up to the hotel rooms.

Later, Bella, Mary Anne, and Barney stayed upstairs to sleep in the soft feather beds. Claire and Bonnie came down with the twins. The boys didn't want to sleep in the hotel since their dogs weren't welcome and ran back to the wagons. The young women were both giddy with being clean and well-groomed for the first time in weeks. They promenaded up and down in the hotel lobby and received many curious and admiring glances.

At the barber shop, the men had been told St. Louis was now listed as the fourth largest city in the country. Father Wimberley finally talked Henry into trying to sell his merchandise. By the time the girls arrived, Henry already had a single team of oxen harnessed to the wagon full of clothes. It was agreed the three of them would go. Bonnie would stay with the wagon while Claire and Henry talked to the store manager. Claire was confident if a man came down to see the stock, he would buy it.

The manager at the first store refused to even look. The manager at the second came down and laughed at what he saw. He complained that he couldn't tell what they had with everything stacked and piled the way it was.

Henry was ready to give up when Bonnie spoke up. "It's in the same shape as any other merchandise you get arrives in. You can't expect it to be shipped across country on hangers or racks, can you?"

"What did you say?" the man demanded.

Bonnie stuck her brogan up on the box frame. "You heard me. If you want to loan me an iron, we'll press any or all of it, and Claire can model it. Then you can decide."

The man stared at the tall woman with her flashing amber eyes and directed them to drive the wagon on into the warehouse. An hour later, after hard-haggling, they had sold two-thirds of the stock, all at a substantial profit. On the way back to the hotel, Claire smiled and squeezed Bonnie's hand. "What happened to my shy friend?"

"I think she died with her baby," she answered quietly. But as she drove back, she didn't miss observing Claire's other hand was firmly clasped in Henry's.

To celebrate their successful day, the Wimberleys and Lambtons dressed for dinner, the men folding most of their money into secret cloth belts at their waists. The women all were bathed, perfumed and powdered, each dressed in their finest. Bonnie put on her best dress, the black and white one made from the maid's old uniform. She sat to let Claire fuss with her hair, pinning it up in big loops and braids.

Mary Anne's hair was brushed to a fine luster and held back with a blue ribbon to fall loose to her waist. She wore a blue dress with white stockings and Bonnie knew she realized how pretty she was by the way her gray eyes glimmered in her tanned face. Barney was dressed in a little black suit with a red tie and the children both looked impressed with each other.

On the way down to the restaurant, Barney began to wail. Bella and Henry were quickly distraught.

Bonnie took the crying boy and talked to him all the way to the restaurant. "Do you want to go out to the wagons with the boys, Tom and Jim?" He shook his head, but stopped crying. "Do you want to go see the big oxen or the horses, Bob and Sue?" He put his fingers in his mouth but finally shook his head. "Oh, so you want to go see Tip and Tyler, you want to go see your doggies?"

"Doggies," he shouted. People already seated inside turned to see the pretty child and smiled. Bonnie wasn't surprised when the protests were brief and half-hearted that she and Barney stay. Mr. Wimberley promised to order dinner for the four and have it delivered out to the wagon train.

Bonnie sauntered through the long main lobby, aware of appreciative glances. When a man doffed his hat and spoke to her, she bustled past as though insulted. Outside, the air was still warm and she took her time walking out and across to the park. Near to the hotel was a church. She noted its stained glass and bell tower and asked one of the young men waiting to take the carriages of people arriving for dinner what it was. Delighted to learn it was Catholic she planned to ask Father Wimberley to wait until after morning mass before leaving.

As she approached, she noted that most of the people getting out of the carriages at the hotel were pointing to the wagons. She saw the boys had managed to start a campfire in the center of the wagons, which made the white canopies stand out prettily against the night sky. The boys had also managed to bell the cattle and hobble the horses to allow them to grace on the lush lawn surrounded by its thick hedge.

As she squeezed through between two tall trees, she was surprised to see a crowd of sorts had gathered at the gate of the park. As she walked closer the dogs charged out of the circle, barking excitedly. Barney screamed in delight. Two policemen entered the gated park while one remained outside, telling people to "move along, nothing to see here." The dogs slowed her passage so the policemen arrived before she did.

"Aye, what kind of mischief is this? Do you not know a public park when you see one?" The first officer demanded.

The boys stood up, moving closer together. "Aye, indeed we do officer," Tom said.

"Aye, sir, sure we do. We have them in Boston, you know," Jim added.

"And you be?" the second officer asked.

"Tom McKinney, and me brother," and the second boy spoke, "Jim McKinney, sir."

Bonnie smiled as she heard Jim's voice crack on his name. At least the boys were sharp enough to lay on the brogue. She heard the officers' chuckle. "Aye, you sound like you've a bit of Irish in you both, Mister McKinneys."

Bonnie stepped into the light and set down Barney to be slobbered on by his dogs. "We all be," she said with a deep curtsy, "I'm their guardian, Bonnie Magee. And if I'm not mistaken, that's a wee bit of a brogue you've got yourself?"

The policeman cleared his throat and thumped his baton on his hand for emphasis. "We don't allow camping nor campfires, nor grazing cattle and horses in our parks, ma'am."

Bonnie stepped closer to the light, placing an arm around the shoulders of the two frightened boys. "We're right sorry for trespassing, sir, but you see we've rooms in the hotel next door and the oxen and horses were weary from their long trek from Massachusetts. We thought this was the area for travelers to picket their animals placed here by the hotel. We'd no notion it was a public park. I didna' see any sign."

The second man looked displeased. "None have been posted because it's not officially opened. The area where you're standing will be a fountain, once it's in place with its statues and oil lamps, they will hold an official grand opening."

"I see, then we not be trespassing in a park, is that what you be saying? And it be all right if we leave after early mass in the morning, rather than try to hook up and travel in the dark?"

"Technically, ma'am, but on the other hand…"

Bonnie laughed, as she heard one of the dogs yip in pain. "Aye, let me rescue Barney from the dogs or the dogs from the boyo. Then come sit and share a cup of coffee with us and we'll sing an Irish ditty together on this warm summer night."

"We didn't make any coffee," Tom whispered.

"It'll only take a second if you please, the lads can fetch an oil cloth so you can sit without damaging your handsome uniforms." Bonnie smiled as one boy ran to get the oilcloth and the other to fetch the pot with leftover coffee from the morning to set on the fire.

Before they could argue again, Bonnie began to sing "*Annie Laurie*," and the boys ran up and joined in as they set things right for their company.

When they finished, their small audience at the gates clapped and the police officers bowed. "Would that we could. It does a man's heart good to see such a bonnie lass so well named, but we have our duty to perform. Go on with your singing and we'll disperse the rabble for you."

Bonnie curtsied and the boys bowed. Just as the men reached the fence, the hotel bell boys appeared on the portico of the hotel and Bonnie whispered a prayer. As though God were still listening, the men squeezed through the trees where she had entered minutes ago. Bonnie began to sing *"Glory, glory, hallelujah,"* and heard the song picked up and sung by people walking away from the gate.

CHAPTER THIRTY-SEVEN

She woke in the middle of the night to the sound of bells ringing. Instantly she was on her feet, grabbing the shotgun stored under the wagon seat. The bells were getting faster and she pointed in the direction of the sound and fired the shotgun.

There was a surprised shout and the bells stopped. One of the cows bellowed and the dogs were suddenly awake and yipping in the direction where the herd had drifted. Afraid that she had shot one of the oxen by mistake, she ignored Barney's startled wail and looked toward the campfire where the twins had been on guard. As expected she saw them startling awake and she leaped down from the wagon on the run, pumping the gun to be ready to fire again.

She found all twelve animals bunched in the corner of the natural corral. Panicked she looked around and called for the horses. A nicker from the far corner of the park was followed by a whinny and the slow movement of the horses back toward the fire.

Jim arrived first, then Tom. "Oh Bonnie," he gasped. She pulled the lad in close to her. Tom arrived next. "What was it? What did you fire at?"

Impatiently she was turning the lead animals out of the tight corner. "Here, help me lead them into the wagon circle. I may have shot one of them."

Minutes later the boys had moved the oxbows strung between the wagon tongue and next wagon tail to herd the animals inside.

Carefully as each was inspected, she released them back outside, untying the ropes that had been used to tie them all together. Finally she found a blood spotted hide on one of the oxen. "Here's another one," Tom said.

Bonnie sighed. "Go unhobble the horses and bring them in to check too. I don't know why they didn't make any noise."

Jim ran to bring them and Tom swallowed. He petted the broad face of the bullock beside him and lifted the heavy head. "Poor Shadrach."

Bonnie smiled and looked at the placid ox grazing beside her, "Who's this guy, Meshach or Abednego?"

"Meshach," said Jim.

"You've given them all names?"

Tom stared at her and shrugged. Carefully Bonnie ran a hand over the firm bodies and up and down the legs of the two horses. Jim held the halter on Bob while she checked Sue, then reversed it while she checked the gelding.

"Do you think it was Indians?" Tom asked.

"Rustlers," Jim asked.

"I didn't get to see them clearly, but the profanity sounded like rustlers. Why they didn't make noise sooner is what bothers me? I thought you put bells around the necks on all of them."

Tom shook his head. "All but these two. Their necks are too big." He lifted the animal's long tail and Bonnie smiled as she saw the bell tied near the end.

"Lucky for us. They took them off of the ones they saw as they roped them. If they hadn't missed them on these last two they would have stolen the whole herd."

"I bet Bob and Sue were sleeping. They've been eating since we got here. The grass is so green compared to what they usually find. They might have been Indians, the thieves were so silent," Tom said.

"Or half-breeds," Jim whispered in awe. "They're always the villains."

Bonnie gave Tom a chuff on the shoulder. "Could be, is that why you two fell asleep, the grass is so green."

"It was all that fancy food from the hotel. We're just not used to it," protested Jim.

The dogs stood attentively beside the lads and she shook a finger at them as well. "Bad dogs. What is your excuse for sleeping on the job?" She looked across the animals who were now hanging their heads to stare at the alert boys beside her. "They didn't eat too much grass, did they?"

"We kind of shared our dinner with them, there was so much. The fire was warm and it feels so safe here, kind of like you're in a secret garden."

She listened, but it was all calm and quiet and the oxen without their bells were moving around silently in the dark. Even the little boy had stopped crying.

"Well, when you're through helping me with these guys you best get to bed for real. Tomorrow will be a long day for all of us."

"What are you going to do? Are they hurt badly?"

"No, I hope not. Their hides are pretty tough and the blast was from pretty far away. We just need to scrape the shot out so it doesn't become a runny sore for them. Then once we get the pellets, we'll dab it with salve to keep the flies away."

While one boy held the animal's head, the other held the lantern and Bonnie patiently scraped across the hide, removing four pellets from the white spotted ox and six more from the dark brown one. She let the boys apply the smelly salve, releasing one, then the other animal.

Swatting each lad while giving them a hug, she sent them to bed to sleep in the Lambton's wagon with the little boy. Sitting down beside the fire, she felt the same heavy languor that had stolen over the lads and the animals. To fight it, she picked up the lantern and spent her time on watch, walking about to recover the bells the thieves had cut and left behind.

With each one she recovered, the little tinkle that it made signaled another delusion dropping away. Thieves could have attacked them at any point along the trail before. They had been lucky. But now, they were setting out across a harsher environment that was less settled and with less grazing and water at hand. There would be many desperate men and Indians at hand to take advantage if they ever dropped their guard again. Somewhere in the west, maybe in this very city, Tarn Micheals now lived.

Bonnie had a fresh pot of coffee brewed when the travelers came down the path from the hotel. Claire whined all the way. "Why do we have to leave in the dark? Can't we stay another day, there is so much more of the city to explore. Henry and Bella still have merchandise they need to sell."

Bella brushed past her and raced to the wagons, calling her son's name as she ran. Barney sat happily wedged between the twins on the oilcloth with the dogs stretched out beside them. "Hi, Momma," he called and Bella's face changed as she smiled and said good morning to her beloved child. The boys sprang up, excited to talk about the cattle rustlers who had visited in the night. While they jumped around and talked, Mother Wimberley shook out the clean clothes she had picked for them.

"Hurry and change. We're going to Mass and then we're headed West," she added the word hurry as she handed each one clothes.

Bonnie offered the sausage and camp fire biscuits and was pleased when all were accepted. "I thought you would be eating fancy again this morning. I'll need to stir up some more for our lunch."

"No, the restaurant wasn't open and Father wouldn't wait. Oh, Bonnie, aren't you tired to the bone with all this. We must have walked a thousand miles already, but Father says we're only now getting started. Isn't it horrible?"

Bonnie smiled and turned to pour the batter into a long pan to shove into the campside stove, a metal box that Father Wimberley had made. "It's not been all that bad. When I get tired, I just climb up on one of the oxen and ride a few miles, just like the boys."

Claire rolled her eyes. "Gawd, you don't have to always be so contented do you?"

Bonnie's eyes flashed and Claire immediately looked repentant. Bonnie donned her bonnet and gloves, then extended a hand to the now silent Claire.

The little blonde raised her head to her tall friend and together they walked to the huge cathedral, leaving the three Lambtons behind to finish the breakfast and guard the wagons.

Inside, the sanctuary was dark and cool. They walked forward to kneel before taking their seats in the nearly empty pews. As the morning sun rose, color flooded the marble floors from the large stained glass windows. Bonnie's head was bent in prayer as the priest in his white robes began the service. Behind her she heard marching feet and turned to stare as several soldiers filtered into the pews behind them.

Irreverent as it was, she searched for a familiar face. Finally disappointed, she turned back to face forward. None were her brothers or Calum, even though she knew none could be. They would have passed through here over a month ago. For just a moment, she felt disappointment on her tongue, then she looked up at the streaming light. As she prayed, she felt comforted with the reassurance that they were all safe. Noticing the small pencil and pad of paper for prayer requests in a pocket on the back of the pew, she took it out and began to write.

As they left the church, Claire was now awake and as sunny as ever. She seemed to glow as soldier after soldier doffed a hat in her direction. All felt revived. Boldly Bonnie stepped up to the nearest soldier and asked where they were bound.

"I don't have an envelope, but I have two brothers stationed somewhere along the trail at one of the forts. I wondered if I gave you a letter, if you could pass it on. I would love for them to know they are in my thoughts each day. We should reach Fort McPherson by the end of the month."

"It's used, but I have the envelope from a letter from home, if you don't mind reusing it."

Eagerly Bonnie took the crumpled and stained envelope as he removed it from his breast pocket and took his letter out. She hurriedly shoved the pages inside. Along with using all the paper, she had taken the pencil. Hurriedly she wrote Ian and Shawn Magee on the flap of the envelope and tucked it in before handing it to the soldier. When he smiled at her, she blushed and smiled as well. But this time she wouldn't be sending a kiss back to them.

She handed the pencil to Tom and asked him to run it back inside. She could only pray that the letter would be as important to her brothers as his was to this young soldier.

◇◇◇

In their absence, Henry had harnessed the oxen and Bella had made the lunches. He and Father Wimberley were locked in debate about how to run the wagons. They decided to leave them in tandem for another day. In minutes they were all on their way west. As they pulled out of the park gate a man ran up to them.

"Please mister, have you a wagon to sell." Father Wimberley looked over the man who was holding his arm close to his body. "We done had our outfit stolen during the night," the rough looking man added.

Curious, Bonnie walked up to stare at the man, then reached into the wagon for her shotgun. The man winced and stepped back.

"I might, but it wouldn't come cheap," Father Wimberley answered. Bonnie looked at the still loaded bed of the second wagon and shook her head. Cautiously she walked back to examine the back of the tandem bed of the Henry's. Bella leaned over to ask what it was about.

"A man claims his wagon was stolen during the night and needs to buy one today. The Wimberley's wagons are both full but the second might hold the remainder of your stock. I don't know if he's going to make a realistic offer, but it might be a chance to make a profit."

Bella called out to Henry and Bonnie watched the other members of the group beside the side of the road. There was something familiar about the dark eyed man who stared at her hard. Decided, Bonnie walked up to join the men.

The one holding his arm was arguing, "Three hundred is a might dear, we've just been robbed. We could pay you fifty, then at the end of the road, maybe pay another two hundred."

Bonnie used the wagon wheel to step up so her mouth was at ear level and hissed. Both mounted men turned to look at her. "Don't look, but the man behind the gate was at the department store yesterday. I'm pretty sure the one talking is the one I shot last night. Be careful."

She sat back against the wagon as Claire and her mother tried to follow the conversation.

"Hey, we'd like to see the wagon up close. Show us all its features, you know, any built-ins or secret boxes, that sort of thing."

"Well, Mr. Wimberley has some fine details. The benches fit into interior slots on each side and clamp during the day, but can be taken out and used for seats when you camp," Henry started to explain but the older man beside him put up his hand.

Mr. Wimberley stared at the buyer, angry now. He took a deep breath and held it. Slowly he moved the rifle from the sleeve of his saddle and angled it across his arm. "Sorry, we don't do business on credit. Good luck to you," Father Wimberley looked to the twins. "Move 'em out lads."

Bonnie dropped down from the wheel as Sue moved forward with her rider. She kept the shotgun cradled in her arms but looked straight ahead as she started on the new part of their journey. Even over the creak of the wagons and the plodding and lowing of oxen she heard the man whisper.

"You will be sorry, just you wait mister. You and them women will be real sorry."

CHAPTER THIRTY-EIGHT

At noon they paused beside a stream to water the stock and eat. Father Wimberley stared at Bonnie's gun. "You planning to shoot some birds?"

"Maybe, if those vultures we left in St. Louis show-up. His last words weren't loud enough for you to hear." Then she repeated the threat.

Father Wimberley stared at his wife and daughter. Henry stared at them too, then back to Bella and Mary Anne. Finally he turned to stare at Bonnie intently.

"You said he was there when we sold the clothes?"

"I'm sure of it. I don't think they were really after the oxen last night, they just couldn't get close enough to get the money without waking the dogs or boys."

"It doesn't make sense. How were they able to get past the three of you and two dogs to take the bells off the animals in the first place?" Henry asked.

Bella leaned forward from coaxing Barney to eat. "Maybe someone at the hotel, one of the bell boys or waiters, saw your wallets were thin and thought there was probably a lot more in the wagons. You both were talking about all the profit you made in town."

Claire grabbed Bonnie's hand. "Maybe they drugged you."

"Put something in our food? If they searched the wagons and didn't find what they were looking for, maybe then they tried to take the animals instead," Bonnie said. "It could be. I ate a little before dinner came and let the boys and dogs finish my meal.

"That's why they wanted us to show any secret places in the wagon," Henry said.

"If we had, they might have robbed us there and then," Father Wimberley said. He looked at the frightened women in front of him, but didn't need to voice what they were all thinking.

"I think our priority at this point is to keep moving, stay on guard. As soon as we get an opportunity we'll join up with other wagons," Father Wimberley said.

In St. Louis, Father Wimberley had been disappointed at the price he was offered for the tools and the other spare wagon. He had decided to wait until Independence to sell anything else. For the two weeks until they could reached it, they heard terrible stories from everyone who passed or they met along the trail. The few wagons they tried to join forces with were pulled by horses and mules. As good as their ox teams were, they couldn't keep up with the other wagons.

Most of the horrible stories were about the Indian raids and the atrocities they'd committed against whites. The Battle of Little Big Horn was discussed everywhere. No one could believe the daring Custer and every trooper and horse had been slaughtered by a united Indian force. The only thing that comforted Bonnie was the knowledge that Ian and Shawn had been safe in Columbus with Calum Douglas to protect them on that day in June.

Each morning, Bonnie and the boys were in charge of working the teams and moving down the trail while the men slept late in the wagons after their guard duty.

The thinner Bonnie became, the hungrier she felt. With all the walking each day, it seemed she had become taller and lankier with each mile. So each day she made an effort to find something to add to the food supplies. Many days it was berries or fruit, but now they traveled armed, most days there was fresh meat to cook at dinner and plenty of scraps to feed the dogs.

Bonnie tried to remember there were weeks still to go but she worked to enjoy each new experience as though today were the last trail day. She liked the freedom of riding ahead to examine the trail, the edge of fear and adrenaline that came with being armed and alone in a dangerous place. She loved to hunt. In Boston, she would never have ridden a horse or fired a gun. Now she felt ready to protect herself and others.

If the St. Louis thieves were trailing them, they had not caught up yet. Bella argued they had stayed in town where there were so many travelers passing through to prey on. That would be easier than struggling along the trail pursuing them. Still, Father Wimberley tried to pick spots not used by other travelers, especially if they provided cover for the wagons. So far, grazing and water had not been a problem. But interrupted sleep and shared watch duty were wearing on nerves. Most of the party seemed weary, and Barney was beginning to suffer from the hotter summer weather.

Independence was thronged with wagons, trappers, soldiers, and a bustling, hustling population. It seemed the whole world was running into this little spout before spewing out into the west. When a troop of Calvary soldiers came through, Bonnie hungrily searched for a familiar face but saw none. She was excited to learn the soldiers were headed to Fort McPherson and it was along their trail as well. Again she sent word to her brothers to tell them all were well.

Bonnie kept the children close to her while the adults focused on selling. When a handsome man waved at Mary Anne, the little girl spoke to him despite his threadbare uniform. When he moved, Barney screamed. The man was on a wheeled platform rolling along the boardwalk because he had no legs. For just an instant, Bonnie thought of Lynne and her well-formed veteran and crossed herself in prayer.

Henry sold the Lambton's second wagon, along with four of his oxen. After moving the left-over stock to empty the wagon, Henry and Bella didn't bother with the store owners. They just sold the merchandise from their remaining wagon in hopes that it would leave room for them to sleep. Father Wimberley tried every store, then also set up shop from his wagon bed to sell ox-bows, oak handled tools, and gold pans. A store owner came out and bought half the remaining lot at noon so he could get rid of the competition. Father Wimberley then sold his empty wagon without a team. Now with only one wagon each, he let Henry borrow a pair of cattle so they had four oxen apiece.

The big priority was to join a wagon train headed to Utah for safety against the Indians or any other marauders. Finally on their second morning in town, the team Henry had sold and nine other wagons joined them. As they left town, they felt safer with more rifles and men.

A mile out of town, the large troop of young soldiers rode with the wagons, flirting with the ladies and joking with the children among the train. Finally they moved out to survey the area and look for any Indians who might cause them a problem later. For the first time in weeks, all the travelers felt safe.

Bonnie saw no chance to shoot game, but the newly formed caravan met for a shared supper, enjoying dishes made by others. Then in the starlit night with the howl of wolves in the distance, the men brought out fiddles and jugs to play a tune. While Bonnie and Claire sang with two other young women on the train, the married couples moved out to dance hesitantly in the flickering flames of the campfire. The children danced around amid the older couples.

Bonnie was aware that several young men were looking over the serenading women. It made her feel annoyed and pleased at the same time. She smiled when she saw Claire shed her bonnet to reveal her golden curls. At the second tune, men came up and shyly asked the singers to dance. One short fellow asked Bonnie, but she shook her head, announcing she was married. As the others danced she sang a duet with a sad-eyed old man about the lost love of Barbara Allen.

Now as part of a train, the night watch for the men was only two hours long. Horses and oxen were kept securely in the larger circle. With only two wagon beds with mattresses remaining, it meant some would finally be sleeping in tents. Father Wimberley volunteered to sleep with the boys in the tent the first night, giving up his bed to Bonnie. Bonnie would have argued, but she looked forward to sharing the wagon with Claire.

As the camp settled down to sleep, Bonnie teased the pretty girl about dancing with so many handsome men tonight. Claire laughed and Mary Anne interrupted to announce she had danced with two good-looking boys herself.

"Tom and Jim?" Bonnie asked.

"Yes, but I wasn't counting them. The dark-haired boy with the long nose, you know the one that looks like a gypsy."

Bonnie smiled. She had noticed the little boy that looked closer to her sister Reagan's age than Mary Anne's.

"Was he a good dancer?" Claire asked.

"Very good, he was a little short but he could move to the music. I also danced with the boy from the last wagon. He was tall, but he wasn't any good at all."

"Why didn't you dance, Bonnie?" Mother asked from the other side of the little girl.

"Well, first, I am married. Second, they were all too, too short for me." The others laughed. "And third," she hid a deep yawn behind her hand but didn't reveal the third. She heard the other women yawn and sigh. In her mind's eye, she imagined swirling about the fire in the arms of a handsome Lieutenant while her brothers stood with the fiddler, singing the tune.

CHAPTER THIRTY-NINE

Grass was becoming scarcer but there had been plenty of water for the stock. The men took the time to top off the barrels first each day. Bonnie no longer had to drive a team and was trying to figure out what to do with the new freedom. Claire was delighted to have other women to talk with on the train, ones who listened to and shared her complaints about the endless trip.

Bonnie felt a little jealous, but realized the more she changed, the less in common she and Claire seemed to have. Never one to walk before, the blonde now would climb down from her wagon seat and walk along the train to visit her new friends. She also seemed to enjoy the attention of two of the single men. Of an evening, both usually called after supper to invite both girls to walk around the circled wagons with them. Claire always looked so pleadingly, that Bonnie made up the fourth.

As soon as they left the Wimberley's wagon, the men would move to flank the lively blonde and compete for her attention while Bonnie trailed along behind like a faithful hound. As the men returned her to her parents, one would step back to walk beside Bonnie.

Bonnie noticed she wasn't the only one who was jealous. Henry was arguing with Father Wimberley. "It's wrong for a sheltered young woman to be allowed to parade around in front of God and the rest of the train. It could be bad for her reputation."

Bonnie coughed, "She wasn't alone, or do I look like a bread pudding to you?"

"No, well I know she wasn't alone. But I just don't think it's seemly, that's all."

"Well, when you have your own daughter, you can train her up the way you like. If Claire is to find a suitable man to marry, she needs to have a chance to make her selection from the eligible men she meets. Then if she finds one she likes, her mother and I will make sure he is worthy." He rose blustery and stiff and moved his back as though it were hurting him.

"Robert, are you all right," Mother Wimberley asked.

"Just not used to sleeping on the ground yet," he answered.

"Then take your bed back. I can bunk with the boys. We've done it long enough now," Bonnie suggested.

"No, well, if you want to try. But don't be surprised if it's not as fun as it looks," he said.

"Do you have guard duty early or late tonight?" Mother Wimberley asked.

"Don't have it at all. Me or Henry. Best to bed, all of you. We'll be moving out at the crack of dawn tomorrow."

"Tomorrow and every day," Claire said.

Bonnie took the time to bank the fire and set a kettle of water ready to brew coffee in the morning beside the flat rock some other traveler had left behind. Tom came up and tugged at her hand. "We don't want you to be afraid."

She took his strong young hand and looked about for Jim. "Where are your dogs?"

Jim slipped up beside her and took her right hand in his. "We don't know. There was a lot of howling and they took off right after supper." He shivered and Bonnie raised her arms and tucked them both in close.

"Here pup, here," she called, bending to rub the kettle across the stone to make a sharper noise. "Tip, Tyler. Come here boys."

Through the strange quiet of the night she heard an answering yip and in a second a blur of black and white surrounded the trio, jumping up against them.

The boys laughed, cuddling their dogs while scolding them.

"Guess we better see if they like sleeping in the tent tonight. No sense letting them become a couple of wild coyotes." The dogs gave low, strange howls as though they were going to change at any minute.

Bonnie left the four and stepped up to the front of the wagon. Father Wimberley stared out at her in the dark. "What's going on?"

"Nothing to worry about. Just thought I'd like to have the gun in the tent with us, that's all."

"You think something is out there."

Bonnie felt it again, the eerie sense that danger was all around. "Don't know, just best to be ready in case."

It was Mary Anne's little piping voice that filled the silence. "But everyone knows Indians never attack during the night."

Bonnie checked the safety and whispered. "Aye. Goodnight cailin, sleep tight little love."

As she walked to the rear of the wagon she heard the older man fumbling around in the wagon. She knew he was searching for his guns. Feeling better, she followed the low white gleam of the tip of the dog's tails to the tent.

At dawn, the campsite looked ordinary. The dogs were scampering about, begging for scraps. The children were all beautiful and wide-eyed for the new day. Bella and Henry woke with an argument. It started as the usual one about Barney and what to do to help him feel better. Suddenly Henry was yelling, "Nothing will make him feel better, he is an accident of birth. Why don't you just accept there is nothing that will ever make him right?"

Those at the campfire tried to pretend they weren't hearing every word. The Wimberleys exchanged glances and looked back at their own wagon. Bonnie was glad Claire was still asleep for the fight quickly escalated into one of charges from Bella that he was making a fool of himself over the Wimberley girl. "If it were Bonnie, I could understand, but what is there about that silly little blonde to get you so stirred up?"

"Would you stop with your ridiculous, jealous rants? I'm married to you Bella, isn't that enough?"

Barney started to cry and for a blessed few moments the camp side became noisy.

Bonnie poured coffee and served biscuits smothered in gravy, but all the time she kept praying for the miserable couple. What was there about love? It was such a strong, inescapable pull but it didn't always take you in the right direction. Look at her own life. What a disaster it had been to fall in love with a demon like Tarn Micheals. Now older and wiser at eighteen, she still spent each night dreaming about another tall unattainable man, this one in uniform.

No matter how wrong and hopeless it was for Henry Lambton to care about Claire, she couldn't condemn him. At least her friend had shown real sense and maturity. She was looking elsewhere to find a man to marry, rather than coveting another woman's husband.

But when Bonnie looked up, she saw the blue-eyed girl looking as beautiful and perfect as any woman could. She was staring at the neighboring wagon with one hand over her heart and tears in her eyes. Aye, maybe she wasn't so smart after all.

◇◇◇

Even though neither man had been assigned guard duty, Bonnie could tell both were weary. Their party were all relieved that their wagons were not the drag ones on the train today. They had been rotated up to the lead spot with the Lambton's wagon in the lead. Poor Barney had coughed most of the night. It had to be all the dust. Unlike the rest of the party he was pretty much trapped behind all the lead animals and the cloud of dust they threw up.

Today, Father Wimberley and Henry Lambton rode point guard for the wagon train, scanning ahead, their guns ready. Tom prodded the big oxen in front and the animals moved forward as bravely as the biblical heroes they were named for. Bella guided the lead wagon, Mary Anne sat beside her to help Barney sit up to look around at the rolling hills and rocky cliffs.

Mother Wimberley and her daughter guided the second wagon, with Jim prodding the team when needed. Bonnie walked beside their wagon, keeping a nonsensical conversation going with Claire. They were pretending they were at the end of the journey, both happily married to rich, prominent men, and neighbors with Lynne McKinney Gant. The three would be pillars of the community. Claire would set fashion trends, Lynne would host the literary community, and Bonnie would lead women to fight for their rights.

Claire's mother laughed, especially when Bonnie talked about how women in the new western states would have all the same rights as men. They were already allowed to buy land, at least along the new railroads. She was sure someday they would have the right to vote. When both laughed at her, she blushed. "Well, it may be a small club, but I think there will be women interested."

"In being like men?" Claire asked. "Are they all going to wear bloomers in public like Amelia Bloomer did way back in the 50's?"

"I don't know anything about Amelia, but if she thought women should have the same freedoms, than yes," Bonnie answered.

It was an uneventful day. As usual, there was no stopping except to water and rest the stock while the travelers ate and took a brief rest break. Since today there were no bushes or hills to hide behind, the rule was established that men use the left side of the wagon, women the right. The children giggled, but everyone respected the privacy rule. Soon they were back on the dusty trail west.

CHAPTER FORTY

The day started the same way as all the others. This time the Wimberleys and Lambtons were in fifth and sixth position. Barney Lambton began to wheeze and cough. Bella got down from the wagon seat to carry the boy clear of the dust. When Henry noticed her, he dismounted and boosted his wife and her sick child into the saddle.

The way he looked at both of them with regret and sorrow was not lost on anyone as he led the horse along beside the wagons. Tenderly he touched the boy, whispered something to Bella. She placed her hand over his where it supported the child's back.

Claire raised her hand to her heart and gasped. Bonnie saw the stricken look on the girl's face as she climbed up onto the vacant wagon seat. Had the girl assumed this man didn't have love for his wife and child? Well for one, Bonnie was relieved to see him publicly display his feelings.

The twins looked at each other and mounted as they usually did when it was too dusty.

Bonnie noticed they had split the team of giant oxen so each had one now to ride in the lead pairs for each wagon. The big bullocks were so well padded, which helped when riding the stiff ridge of an oxen's back. If Shadrach and Meshach minded, they didn't show it. Heaven knew how everyone would deal when the trail became even dryer. As she looked down the train, she saw others copying the McKinney boys.

Bonnie knew there would be no hunting this morning so she didn't bother to take the shotgun or rifle. Instead she snagged the gunny sack and set out to find fuel for the fire. She waved at the lead riders as she approached, telling them what she planned to do. Even in the short week, everyone in this larger party had grown used to the tall woman's habits and waved her on. Bonnie veered to the right of the wagon train, noticing a few stunted trees ahead. Trees and bushes always meant water was present, even if it was underground. Anything edible would be nearby.

Unlike the trail they had followed before crossing the Missouri, this side of the big river had more traffic. That meant it was picked over. At least this year, the traffic had slowed for the last two months during the Indian raids. For just a second she recalled the fear of two nights ago, when their own dogs had howled.

Bonnie shook her head at the nonsense. The Indians they had seen in Independence looked anything but dangerous. The stories were probably as exaggerated as those of gunslingers and desperadoes. The western army was growing stronger every day with reinforcements like her brothers. Their presence meant settlers were once more on the move, headed to the Black Hills and the new gold and silver strikes, as well as to the lands in the newer states where the Indians had been swept off onto reservations. There was land to be had in the west, for free or almost. Ten dollars to file for 160 acres and all one had to do was stick to it five years working the land and building a home. She had nearly twice that saved and she knew she could work.

She was already at the brush line with all her musings. Well, if the papers could be believed, thousands of early settlers had abandoned their homes due to the bad weather, Indians, and disastrous economy. Some of them had probably already built homes and raised fences on their 160 acres. She intended to buy or reclaim one of these abandoned homesteads. Who needed a man if one had a home and land?

Suddenly her mind stopped wandering as her eyes focused on a dark piece of blue cloth and one shiny brass button.

Bonnie was running as fast as her long legs would carry her. Suddenly she felt a hard thud against her head and everything went dark.

Minutes later the lead riders pulled up, their conversation about the long-legged woman who had out- paced them forgotten. In the middle of the road an Indian wearing a feathered bonnet sat mounted on a pinto horse. He raised his feathered staff in one hand, his open palm in the other.

The men sat frozen until one nudged the other and both held their hands in the air to mimic the man's gesture. The long-haired man rode up to them and in surprisingly clear English announced. "I am Washakie, Chief of the Shoshoni, friend to white men, enemy of Sioux and Blackfeet. I am here to collect my toll."

When the three rode back to the wagon train, all there were excited and alarmed. The men riding beside him introduced the chief to the other members of the party as they moved in closer. The man talking stumbled over the Indians' name.

The chief repeated what he had told the front riders. "I am entitled by treaty with my friends the white knives to a toll. A horse or cow will be paid by any party passing through my land. I have been fighting those cowards the Sioux, who passed through the Three Forks after their battle at a place you know as Little Big Horn. These are not good Indians. They kill many whites, many of my people too."

Father Wimberley extended a hand and the chief surprised everyone when he shook it. "We will gladly honor your treaty. Thank you for your friendship. Give us a minute to talk."

He turned around to look for Bonnie, spoke to his daughter instead. "Claire, get some food for our guest."

Shaking, Claire stepped down from the wagon and walked to the rear to find the lunches Bonnie had made earlier. She held onto the side of the wagon, breathing deeply. Finally she stilled the shaking long enough to lift the covered tin plate and hold it against her chest as she walked unsteadily over to the strange man and his odd horse. If only Bonnie were here when she needed her. Claire could imagine how happy the girl would be to carry the food and get to speak to a real Indian.

Channeling her friend's courage, Claire stepped forward and lifted the plate to him, looking down at the ground as she did so. "Please enjoy."

As soon as he took the tin plates, she backed away. He smiled down at the skittish girl who made him think of his white horse with blue eyes, then he looked up in astonishment. The men were leading the tallest horse he had ever seen and offering him the reins. Balancing the plate on one knee, he took the reins, shook his lance and turned his pony around to ride off.

It was not until the wagon train was three miles down the trail and stopping for lunch that they realized Bonnie was gone. The search went on for two hours but no trace of the girl was found. When one of the boys and his dog found the scrap of blue shirt with its brass button, all despaired that she was lost.

Everyone was terrified to stay in the area any longer and the search was abandoned. Then there was a debate as to whether a rider should be sent to Ft. McPherson for help.

Henry Lambton raised the winning argument. "If a troop of trained soldiers weren't safe from Indian attack, who among us has any chance of getting there alive." They all agreed they were better off making as many miles as they could to reach the fort and safety themselves. They were still nearly two weeks away at best.

Mary Anne and Claire wept openly, the others wanted to. No one talked about their fears, but each man and woman felt exposed and vulnerable. If the Indians could take a woman as fit as Bonnie, who among them was safe. What would they do to her?

Bonnie woke, confused and disoriented. Heat rose up from the ground far below her feet and smacked her face in waves. Her head throbbed and there was a hard pain in her stomach but she couldn't move her hands or feet to relieve it. She raised her head up to get some of the blood to flow back down and fainted.

The band were already twenty miles from the wagon trail headed north toward home. When the chief saw the woman move he halted the horses and had one of the men untie her. When she stayed draped over the back of the tall mare, the chief had her taken down and laid on the ground. He himself checked the bloody side of her head, satisfied that it was not a killing blow as Wolf Dog had told him.

Next he checked the big brown horse, pleased that the mare did not move under his hand or try to back away. Again he grunted as he leaned his bare head against her wither and laughed. Each of his men did the same. He would guess this strange animal was six feet at the shoulder. While the woman slept, the chief shared the strange white men's food and they ate and said it was good.

There were many jokes about where the strange woman and horse had come from. Men there must be seven or eight feet tall to ride such creatures.

Bonnie woke to laughing voices and listened to the musical words and more laughter. Groaning, she opened her eyes and saw the brown mare that belonged to the Indiana wheat farmer looking down at her. The fool had bought her from a neighbor who claimed she could pull the biggest load put to her. "She'll work all day and never complain about anything you ask her to do. If I were going west, she's the first animal I'd want to take."

But the farmer complained about the animal all the time. The horse was always hungry, eating two or three times what the others did. The farmer had lost two horses he tried to harness with her. He'd made poor trades for both as they wore out along the trail trying to keep up with the powerful mare. Finally he bought a team of oxen, but kept her, thinking she would make a good saddle horse. But the mare couldn't abide a saddle, even if he'd had one big enough.

When the mare snuffled over her, Bonnie raised a hand to the big head and snagged her halter to let the mare pull her up as she pulled back. "Thank you Brown Bess, that's a good girl."

Startled, Bonnie turned as the old Indian addressed her. "Sit, eat, then we ride."

Feeling numb, she sank back down on the ground. One of the braves passed her a dish. She took it and automatically took a bite. Surprise flooded through her with the food. She grabbed the metal plate, recognized it from this morning. She lifted the tin plate and hit the man with it. "What did you do to them? Did you kill my friends? What are you going to do to me?"

In a second she was flat on the ground, her arms pinned to her side, the man sitting astraddle her. Grinning he said something to the other men and they laughed.

The old Indian spoke, his voice strained. "I am Washakie, Shoshoni chief, friend to white men, enemy of Sioux and Blackfeet. We killed no whites."

Bonnie stared at the man grinning at her and relaxed for a second then twisted violently, almost pulling free. The brave raised a hand to strike her and the old Indian quickly grabbed the man's fist and put his foot on her neck. "Enough," he said. "Eat, foolish woman. I collect toll for use of wagon road. I get a giant horse and a crazy woman. I think your people cheat me."

The brave moved away carefully. The chief stared at her, noting the strange eyes and how they changed color with her mood. When they were no longer lit with yellow light he removed his foot and gracefully folded down beside her. He picked up the biscuit, brushed off the dirt and did the same with the meat, handing both to her.

"Eat, is good."

Bonnie looked at the biscuit and repeated his actions, putting the meat inside before taking a bite. Slowly she chewed while all the men watched her. When she had trouble swallowing the man who had just wrestled her to the ground held out a pouch that changed shape. Cautiously she reached out and took the water bag. He motioned and she copied his motions and drank.

The man beside her gave orders and as she handed the water pouch back the man pulled her to her feet and gave her a boost onto the tall horse. All those words and they meant "Let's ride."

Taking the reins handed her, Bonnie worked at her skirt until her legs were both covered while the mounted Indians talked to each other. Gripping the tall mare with her knees, Bonnie clucked to get her to walk. The trail headed downhill and Bonnie had all she could do to stay seated and hang on to the big barreled horse. As soon as they reached level land she urged Bess forward. In a minute she was riding abreast of the old chief.

Suddenly there was a torrent of Indian words which she didn't know but she assumed were profanity. Instantly she was pulled down from the mare and told by hand gestures to walk behind.

Annoyed but undaunted, she struck out to keep up with the ponies, leaving Bess to follow behind. When they came to a stream she again came up even with the chief. "I don't believe my people would ever give me up to you."

The chief grunted and two of the braves rode up and held her while the third tied her hands. Bonnie glared at them holding her hands forward without a struggle. "Tell me the truth. If you hurt my friends or the children, I'll…"

The chief stared at her where she stood angrily yelling at him. For the first time he smiled and the others seemed to relax as well. "You are captive. Horse is toll. Ride behind, or they tie you on horse again."

Bonnie walked back and looked at the short man beside her, waiting impatiently beside Bess. The man cupped his hands and Bonnie stepped up, snagging the horse's mane with her joined fingers. The Indian mounted and held the reins to her horse. They all entered the water and started across.

"Why did you take me captive, Chief Washakie, friend of white men? Why me?"

The chief turned his horse on the other side of the river and stared at the angry woman. The sun struck her and he could see copper gleaming in her hair and how her eyes had green and yellow both in them.

"Mistake. Go back, get yellow hair with sky eyes."

"Claire?" Bonnie shook her head, instantly afraid for her friend.

The chief struggled not to smile. "Woman with good nose?"

"Not Bella, her little boy is very sick, you couldn't take her."

"White men have sickness?" This time he sounded afraid.

For a moment she wondered if she could lie to him and frighten them away. "No, the child is weak. The dust and the heat from the trail hurt his chest."

The chief nodded, then shrugged. "Pretty little one with stormy eyes."

Bonnie's eyes filled with horror and she shook her head furiously. Never, she could never let them take Mary Anne.

"Little men with mirror faces."

She shuddered, "Tom and Jim are just boys."

"Then I take you as captive. Now no more talk or I have them cut out your tongue." He turned around, grinning.

Bonnie felt frightened for a moment, then heard the others laughing.

CHAPTER FORTY-ONE

The Indian camp looked just like the ones on the stereograph images. Dozens of teepees were spread out over an area near a slow meandering river. Bonnie sat atop the big horse and rolled her shoulders to relieve her tension and fear. She knew it was rude to stare, but she could not look away. Neither could the Indians in the village. They gathered to stare at her, forming a path for the returning chief and his strange captive.

Everywhere Bonnie turned was interesting. The faces and dresses of the Indians. The smell of the campfires and the cooking foods made her crinkle her nose. The sound of the Indians as they talked, made her strain to listen as the language ran like music over her. Children rushed about barely covered, splashing in and out of the water and laughing. She wished the children on the wagon train could see it.

The chief raised his hand and the small band stopped. Chief Washakie looked up at the strange woman. He had brought many prisoners to his village before, most crying and moaning in terror. None had sat regally looking like they were honored visitors, with eyes that changed color with every thought. He spoke to his braves and they rushed to pull her down from the tall horse. He scolded her in his tongue so his people could hear. She stood straight and stared directly at him. He scolded even louder. The men threw her into a nearby tent.

◇◇◇

Bonnie felt fear return. Whatever she had done to make the Indian so angry, she would have to not do it again. During their time on the long drive, the women had sometimes whispered stories to each other about the atrocities that Indians did to women prisoners. She already knew how a man could make a woman suffer. What would they do to someone who wasn't even their kind? If Tarn could be so brutal to her after vowing to love and protect her, what could she expect from savages?"

It was cool and dark inside the teepee and a small fire sent up a single strand of smoke toward an opening at the top. As her eyes adjusted, Bonnie stared around her strange surroundings. Her hands were still bound but she managed to raise them to touch her throbbing head. Her nose filled with the rank smells inside the tent and she sneezed, then sneezed again.

From the corner of the tent she heard a moan. Was this tent some sort of brothel? Was that another victim in the corner? The woman uttered a louder moan and Bonnie saw the pile of furs move. Was she being ravaged while Bonnie stood by and watched?

Bonnie felt her fear replaced by anger. Hadn't she vowed to never willingly let a man hurt her without fighting back? Men resented women who spoke up, who voiced an opinion, who stood up to them, but she didn't care. She was never again going to be a submissive victim.

Stumbling, lurching her way across the crowded tent she reached the writhing figure. Leaning forward she pulled the furs back and gagged. The stench was clearly coming from here.

◇◇◇

Bonnie moved to throw back the tent flap to allow light into the fetid tent, looking outside for someone to help. Instead she saw a dozen Indians standing about admiring Brown Bess. She watched as first one, then another, then another climbed onto the mare's big back. Only when there were four seated along the length of her did she shake her massive head and pound a hoof in objection. When one more started to jump on she spun and moved her head to nip at him, then arched her back and shook the laughing Indians off.

Bonnie looked to her left and saw the Chief standing there, laughing with his men. Furious, Bonnie stomped up to him and held her bound hands out to him. "Who is responsible for that poor woman inside?"

She saw his laugh turn into an angry scowl and one of the braves who had helped man-handle her on the way here stepped forward to grab her. Bonnie swung her bound arms and struck his chest. She looked back at the chief, then knelt and raised her arms in supplication. "Please, untie me so I can help her."

The chief smiled at the kneeling woman and took his own knife to slice her bonds. He spoke rapidly and two Indian women ran up. Soon Bonnie had the woman in her arms and was carrying her with the two women running ahead.

Bonnie followed the young women to a part of the bank overgrown with willow trees. She was astonished when both the Indian women shed their shoes and clothes to dive naked into the brown water. She started into the water dressed but one of the girls pointed to her shoes and made a lot of noise and motions with her hands.

Bonnie leaned down to ease her moaning burden into the waiting arms of one of the girls. She looked around, searching for any men lurking about. Satisfied, she removed her blouse, split skirt, shoes and socks but waded into the water still wearing her chemise and drawers, her tiny pouch of money tucked securely under the plain edge of her bindings underneath. The women giggled about the strange panties, the ruffled ones she had made from the old pantaloons.

It took all three of them, using a special weed that made soap, to gently wash and clean the sick woman and then clean her hair. One of the women brought down a padded blanket, spreading it out on a flat rock beside the deep pool. Bonnie eased the woman out of the water and onto the blanket, then covered her. The heat from the rock and from the sun helped the woman to relax and sleep.

Already wet, Bonnie took the time to bathe and wash her own hair. She was relieved the woman wasn't sick from cholera or smallpox since she had no fever or marks. But her emaciated body had a large irregular bulge on one side. Bonnie had heard of cancer, where people had massive growths or tumors that killed them. If this was why she had been captured, Washakie would be disappointed. She had no nursing skills or magic to cure her.

Bonnie climbed out of the water to sit on a smaller rock to wash away the mud that had squished between her toes. The two girls who had helped her were gone. Bonnie finger combed her own tangled hair, then picked up the comb they had used on the sick Indian and washed it with the weed before rinsing it in the water. She looked about in vain for her clothes. She groaned in outrage, and then realized the woman on the rock was awake and staring at her.

"Who are you, tall woman?"

"You're a white woman?" Bonnie said, lowering her arm and the comb.

The woman panted as though she had been running. Between every couple of words she would gasp for air. "I don't remember my white name. I became part of this tribe as a child. My parents were killed by Apache. These people saved me. Washakie wooed and married me twenty summers ago. My name is Half Moon. What is yours?"

While she listened, her eyes intent on the woman's dark eyes and labored breath, Bonnie worked the comb through her knotted and tangled hair. "Bonnie Magee, but sometimes my friends call me willow."

"Willow is good. I'm sorry, but I asked for one of my people to be here at my dying."

A breeze blew through the leaves overhead and the sound mingled with Bonnie's prayer. She felt cold and wondered how she would be able to move this woman back inside her tent without her own clothes.

Suddenly the girls came running, giggling and hiding something behind their backs. Bonnie stood on top of the rock, towering over them and scowling. Before she could begin to berate them for stealing her clothes the girls set down a bundle at the foot of the rock.

Bonnie opened it and found a pair of men's moccasins. She slipped one foot in and was relieved when it fit. Then she unfolded the bundle. It was a misshapen leather dress, well-worn and stained. Bonnie sniffed it and it made her sneeze. The girls stared at her, reading her disappointment. Again there was their incomprehensible chatter. Desperate, Bonnie raised her arms and worked her way into the smelly garment.

When she gave a tug, she managed to pull it down over her wet underwear. It was tight across her chest, loose and misshapen over her stomach and hips. Worse, it barely covered her legs, the uneven hem and fringe struck and tickled her knee. Too annoyed to speak, Bonnie tugged on the other shoe. Lifting the sick woman, Half Moon, she followed the girls back to the teepee.

Inside, the worst of the stench was gone. The fire still smoked feebly. These two must have removed the soiled bedding. Bonnie held Half Moon as gently as she could but the woman still moaned. Finally one of the girl's returned with the blanket and padded bedroll from the rock. Bonnie thanked them both and they darted back through the open tent.

Bonnie knelt as she put the woman down. She strained to hear the gasping words.

"It is good here. I no longer miss my white family. These are my people." Half Moon sighed and then collapsed in exhaustion.

For a minute Bonnie hung her head and fought the urge to cry. Twenty years. There was no way that she could live in this ugly, smelly place or wear this stinky tight dress for twenty years. Nor did she want to be wooed by or married to an Indian. She needed to get to Utah, then on to Montana. She had to claim her own free land. Once she had it, she could earn enough to afford to send for her family to join her.

For now, she had to figure out some way to let the children and the Wimberleys know she was safe. Her heart beat a little louder. If she could only get word to Fort McPherson, someone might come to rescue her. Not her brothers. She didn't want them traipsing across the plains among wild Indians to search for her, but someone. An image of a handsome man in a double-breasted uniform filled her thoughts.

Thinking of Calum Douglas, Bonnie relaxed for the first time all day. Collapsing onto a pile of furs beside Half Moon, she was soon asleep.

CHAPTER FORTY-TWO

The bedraggled platoon rode into the courtyard, looking disappointed at the absence of fortifications. Fort McPherson barracks had been the army's solution to cutting back on the western war five years ago. Now that Fort Kearney had been dismantled, this outpost at the conjunction of the Platte Rivers alongside the Union Pacific railroad was where the trail passed before dividing to head to Utah or California. The soldiers stationed here were charged with controlling the Indians and protecting most of the immigrants on the trail.

The incoming forty soldiers had been ten days on the move and they had had to fight off Indians on two occasions. While waiting for their interview with the commander, a soldier remembered and pulled out a note that Bonnie had sent to her brothers. The aide took the note and promised to deliver it to the Magee boys.

Inside the commanders office, Calum listened to them describe their journey to General Crook. As the men described members of one wagon train party, Calum was sure the tall, fierce woman who sent word to her brothers was Bonnie. The woman had filled his dreams every night since he had left her behind in Ohio.

The man's voice interrupted his memories. "We were barely out of Independence. We had passed this small wagon train moving with oxen, maybe a dozen wagons. Nice people and a couple of pretty gals so we weren't in a hurry to leave. They were traveling along at a good clip, enjoying the high prairie grass and easy water. But we knew we were needed here. So we hit a lick and made about thirty miles before letting our horses blow.

"Then we got slowed down by a larger train, with closer to forty wagons and some pretty good horse and mule teams. Few more gals, but they weren't so nice and friendly. Nobody had any trouble or complaints and didn't seem as though they wanted us hanging around. So we let the horses out and made maybe another ten miles. It was near the end of the day when we were attacked."

Calum stared at the man, tried to hold his temper. While the Lieutenant reported on their run in with a Sioux raiding party, so cavalierly, Calum was filled with alarm. The man was an idiot. Hadn't he worried about the poor pilgrims following along behind him on the trail? If he and his men were taken at a disadvantage, what happened to the people in the wagon trains? He grew even angrier when the man reported they had killed at least one of the Indians and wounded two others but only had one of their own men captured.

Calum stared at the short dark man and wondered what kind of soldier would leave another man behind to the mercies of his enemies? Not for the first time he stared at the yellow stripe on the side of the man's trousers and wondered if it shouldn't be sewn down the back of his shirt.

The second scrape had been a day out of this base and the man was bragging that they had fired on the Indians and been able to rout them without them even shooting at his men. Calum wondered if they were renegade Indians or some poor reservation souls that had been scattered by this sorry excuse of a trooper.

At dawn, Lieutenant Douglas left with a party of twenty-four men and two Indian scouts to find the trail of the Indians that had

attacked the fresh troops. At noon, they met the forty wagon party and
ascertained that all were safe and unharmed. In case the Indians the
troopers had shot at were hostiles, Calum asked for volunteers to
escort the wagon train back to base. He noticed both Magee boys
backed out of sight while ten of his men moved forward to volunteer.
He sent six back with them.

The platoon ate as they rode, staying roughly in formation with
all soldiers warned to stay alert. A short distance further they saw a
small band of defeated looking Indians. Calum ordered his men to
stand down but there was no need. By now they had seen enough
reservation Indians to know the difference between those and the ones
wanting to fight. This time he sent the Magee boys back with orders to
hand them over to his six men for safe escort into the Indian agent's
compound.

He wasn't surprised when an hour later the boys came up riding
hell-for-leather to catch the troop. Clearly they were as interested in
finding out about Bonnie as he was. He called them up to ride beside
him.

"Men, I expected you to escort those Indians into the fort. No
sense having that little lieutenant shoot at them two days in a row."

"Yes sir," Ian answered with a salute. "We told the men headed
back that's what you wanted. Wagon train folks weren't too pleased to
have them following them in, no sir. Figure our men will be protecting
the Indians more than the settlers."

Calum smiled. "I imagine so. Did you get your new letter from
your sister?"

Shawn pulled it out of his shirt and started to read it. Both knew
their Lieutenant had a special interest in how the train with Bonnie was

doing, and Calum was glad they didn't seem to disapprove. In the first letter she had sent from St. Louis, she had folded a *billet doux* addressed to him. He hated to admit it, but he had read the paper thin. The words were short and simple, he hoped chosen so her brothers could read it too.

Lt. Douglas,

"I am trusting you with the lives and well-being of my dear brothers. Knowing you are there to care for them gives me all the reassurance I need to rest peacefully each night. God bless you and keep you safe."

Special Regards,

Bonnie Magee Micheals

To find the comfort he needed, he had to read between each line. Shawn finished and Calum realized he hadn't heard a word of the new letter.

The brothers exchanged a wink and Calum sat up and extended a hand. "May I read it?"

"Honest Lieutenant, that was every word," the boy teased. Calum growled and the boy passed the note over.

Ian and Shawn,

I pray all goes as well with you as with us on our journey. Since selling two wagons in Independence, we now have to use the tent. As you can imagine, the McKinney lads are delighted. Father Wimberley found he was unable to sleep on the ground so I volunteered to sleep with the boys again. We shared the second wagon during the trip and are used to each other by now.

Not sure if I wrote last time, but the twins found two dogs when we passed through Indiana. The other night we heard a lot of howling and it upset the dogs. Although I can abide the smell of wet boy, sleeping with wet and smelly dogs is a good deal harder. Glad they are back outside tonight, plan to sleep well.

So much more to write you. Each day reveals a new and grander vista and I can never get enough of this beautiful, gently rolling land.

Now traveling with nine other wagons so feel a good deal safer. It makes me uneasy about how well everything is going. No sickness or problems of any kind.

Sending my prayers and love to all of you.

Love and kisses, Bonnie

Although he read the letter twice, he could find only one three letter word to give him any comfort. She had sent prayers and love to 'all' of you. Surely if she were only writing her brothers, she would have sent them to 'both' of you. Did that mean she had sent love and kisses to him too? The question tortured him. Well, if they rode hard, in a day they would overtake the small wagon train and he could get his answer from her lips.

CHAPTER FORTY-THREE

Bonnie adjusted to tending the sick woman. Though her pain must have been terrible, Half Moon tried to stay silent. But when she slept sharp whines and moans would escape to reveal how much she suffered.

When awake, Half Moon would talk, remembering her parents and their journey from Iowa. When she grew winded, she would look pleadingly at Bonnie. Bonnie knew she was supposed to tell her about her own people. At first she resisted, but after the first time or two the telling didn't make her as sad. She talked about her parents and little sisters and brothers to get Half Moon to eat, slowly feeding her broth.

Living with the Indians wasn't that different than camping with the wagon train. The day consisted of rising, making food, tending to others, and preparing food for mid-day. At the evening meal when the men came home with meat, a second meal was made around it. Since they were not on the move, there seemed no rush to do any of it. It felt as though life flowed as easily and naturally as the river.

When the Chief made no sexual advances toward her, Bonnie relaxed, adjusting to her role as nurse and maid. She focused on keeping Half Moon clean and well fed. She enjoyed talking to her, listening to her halting English spattered with Indian words.

Bonnie's first upsetting moment was when she saw her shirt being worn by a fat woman. Her first impulse was to rush over and rip it off her, but it was already stained and torn. The way the woman stared at her made Bonnie realize she was wearing the squaw's deerskin dress and the woman probably felt the same way. They smiled foolishly at the same time.

It was a day later when she spotted the split skirt. She tried not to, but laughed out loud, when she saw one of the braves prancing around to make the others laugh. A different brave was wearing her shoes and she knew she must be wearing his moccasins. Her happiest moment was four days after arriving when the young women helping her with Half Moon brought a different dress. Made of tan buckskin, this one fit her perfectly and had fringe that reached to brush the tops of her moccasins.

At night, she grew used to hearing the chief talk tenderly to the woman Half Moon before leaving her to go sleep in his half of the tent. At first Bonnie thought he left her alone because he was too old to need a woman or out of kindness because of her pain. But during the night she had heard him coupling with the young Indian captives and felt disappointed. It was clear he loved his wife, but no one seemed to think he should be faithful to her. Later, Bonnie was shocked to learn both of the young women were his wives as well.

At first, Half Moon grew stronger. She enjoyed going out into the sunshine. Bonnie learned to love taking long baths while the sick woman slept.

The pool was a good place to socialize. The women in camp all bathed frequently and shared the same pool. The camp had a large number of captives. Most were survivors from atrocities by other Indian tribes. There was also another white woman and her small son, and a black man and woman.

Mattie, the black woman, was a run-away slave from Missouri and had lived here ten years. Her family had fled with their children when Lincoln freed the slaves, but her master didn't. Along the way, all had died of cholera but Mattie. She could not remember how she came to live with Chief Washakie's band, but was glad they found her. Her new husband had been a free man, forced to fight for the Union Army. He was a buffalo soldier who had been scalped and left for dead by the Sioux. Washakie's braves had found him and brought him to the camp where the woman nursed him back to health. Married by the Indians, she was now pregnant and happy.

The other white woman was also pregnant but not happy. She cried a lot and wanted to go home. She told Bonnie the Indians had raped her. She rolled her eyes and Bonnie wasn't sure if she meant the raiding Indians or her present captors. The woman begged Bonnie to take her with her when she was ready to leave. The black woman didn't want to go. She said they still had to work for others, but the Indians never beat them without reason or just for fun.

A week, then a second week passed. Bonnie's fear faded. Most surprising was how free Bonnie was to move around. She could easily escape, but had no idea where to go that would be as safe. There were several children captives, all were captured Indians but the white woman's son. The giggling young women who helped her bathe Half Moon the first day had been survivors of raiding parties of other Indians. One woman was a Navaho, the other a Flathead. Neither woman wanted to ever leave. They were wives of an important chief. Soon when the old woman died, they would be first and second wives. Often they argued with each other about which would become the first wife.

Bonnie missed her family, and worried about her brothers and whether they had been in combat yet. Once at night she was awakened by a dream that the people she loved on the wagon train were in danger. The dream was vivid and she despaired for their safety without her there to protect them.

Bonnie's second upsetting moment came when one of the brawny braves who brought meat to the chief grabbed her. She wiggled out of his arms and rebuffed him. He complained loudly and Half-Moon heard them and spoke sharply in Indian to the brave, gasping while she spoke.

Bonnie was ashamed for upsetting the sweet woman. When they sat down to eat, Half Moon told Washakie what had happened. The Chief grunted and later gathered the men together. He ordered all his warriors to leave the tall woman alone. Half-Moon translated what was being said to Bonnie.

Satisfied, Bonnie carried the sick woman to bed. The warriors continued to complain. After the women were gone, the Chief promised the men he would decide what to do with the girl. But not until his wife Half Moon was gone and no longer needed her help.

It was two days later, when Bonnie woke and found Half-Moon moaning and burning with fever. Hurriedly she ran to the river to fetch cold water to bathe and quench the fever. She also pulled some bark from a willow tree to make the hot tea that seemed to always help her. Even as she made the tea, she wondered how long anyone could live when their insides were filled with such a massive growth.

She was suddenly aware of the young wives filing out of the tent, shaking their heads at her as though in pity. Bonnie had learned only a word or two of the language, but she could read in their face and bodies that they were sorry for her. When she straightened with a clay bowl of the hot liquid she saw Chief Washakie coming out of the tent, scratching and flapping his arms to restore their circulation.

He too stood and stared at her as though seeing something written above her head. For a moment, Bonnie felt like he was working out a price to write there. She gave a cold shudder and hurried inside to tend her only link in this world.

Bonnie berated herself as she settled beside the dying woman and tried to get her to drink the willow bark tea. She could not perform last rites. She was a good enough Catholic to know only a priest could hear penance, anoint the dying, or perform the last sacraments.

What she could do was offer this poor woman comfort and pray for her soul. Was that enough to justify her staying when she should run?

CHAPTER FORTY-FOUR

It was dusk of the second day before the soldiers met the small wagon train with its eleven wagons. When the children ran forward to greet them Calum was relieved. All three of the McKinney children looked healthy and excited to see them. The Magee boys dismounted and Shawn swung the little girl up on his pony while Ian held his horse for the twins to mount.

Though he searched, there was no sign of Bonnie in the welcoming crowd. Mr. Wimberley rode up to greet and welcome him next, and others in the party cheered and yelled in excitement. When Calum looked at the wagon with the two Wimberley women riding on the seat he felt a strange unease at their solemn faces. It was only when he noticed the second wagon, the Lambton's, with its arrow sticking out from one of the side-boards that his heart failed him.

Shaking, he looked from the smiling children to the sad women and forced himself to the task at hand. In minutes they had the wagons circled, the troopers and their animals added to the lowing herd inside.

He noticed Mrs. Wimberley and her daughter Claire were busy making a fire and starting supper. With trepidation, Calum asked the question, "Where is Bonnie?"

It was then that Calum learned of their tragedies.

◇◇◇

"It happened when we were out of Independence, on the main trail. This Indian appeared out of nowhere," Mr. Wimberley said.

"Awesome, big Indian Chief, with a war bonnet, spear, and everything," Tom interrupted, pantomiming.

"Chief Washakie, a Shoshoni," Jim added.

"He said he was a friend of the white men, chasing the Sioux who had killed some of his people and a lot of white soldiers," Mr. Wimberley continued.

"He demanded a toll, and we paid him," Henry Lambton said. Calum noticed for the first time how much the dapper young man had changed. His eyes looked haunted and he looked dirty and disheveled. The most striking thing was that he now carried the small boy on the saddle in front of him. Calum stared at the pale face, noting the dark shadows around the boy's eyes and the blueness of his skin. He stood and walked forward to take the little boy and let the man dismount. The child seemed to have no weight, his breath escaping in a tiny whisper.

Calum shivered, certain that he held a dead boy in his arms and the breath was that of his ghost.

Henry reached for the boy, then stood stiff and whispered, "Hold him for a minute, I'll be right back."

The small blonde woman cooking moved forward as though she would take the boy but Calum held onto him. She too seemed to have lost some of her polish and poise. She didn't protest, just walked back to the campfire.

"Then they attacked the wagon train?" Calum asked.

Mr. Wimberley shook his head and so did the boys. "No, we gave him a horse that one of the men had bought but couldn't figure out how to use. If you'd seen the mare, you'd understand. Anyway, we all agreed to pay ten dollars so he would just be out twenty on the deal.

He would have complained, but the other Indians started showing up alongside us and he agreed to the deal."

"The Chief looked surprised ... but took the horse ... and turned... and they all rode away," Tom and Jim alternated telling the story.

"We realized Bonnie was gone when we stopped to eat," Claire said from over the fire. She held out a plate and raised her spoon in the air. She looked so sad or Calum would have asked if it was because she finally had to do some work that she missed Bonnie. Instead he looked around at all of them, squinting in rage.

Ian and Shawn stepped forward, crowding the men beside him. "You just noticed she was gone and did nothing."

"All the men went out to search for her, we looked up and down the trail for a couple of miles in either direction. We looked for hours. The boys took the dogs and ran the brush along the trail and then a mile behind it," Mr. Wimberley said.

"Then Tip found the shirt and button," Jim said.

"Show him," Mr. Wimberley said. Tom jumped up and pulled the scrap from under the wagon seat.

Calum took the rag of uniform, noting how neatly it was cut along one edge. Even though there was no blood stain, no sign of violence, the piece of garment meant only one thing. Wherever the body of the missing trooper was, it wasn't alive.

"We studied on it, came to an agreement that if they could attack a large group of troopers so easily, our little party didn't have a chance. We decided to hurry the oxen and get as far down the trail as possible. Our hope was to catch up to the bigger wagon train or maybe reach some Fort ahead to take shelter."

Calum returned the sick boy to his father and pocketed the sad trophy. He didn't know the name of the lost soldier, but looking across at the suddenly pale faces of troopers Ian and Shawn, he knew somewhere he would be sorely missed.

He nodded at the women and men. "At Fort McPherson there are over four hundred soldiers. I'd say you made the right decision. So Bonnie has been missing a week?" He tried to control his voice, keep his hand from shaking as he visualized all the terrible things that could have happened to her in that time.

"Over twelve days," Claire said in a dead voice. "Dinner is ready."

No one had much of an appetite, but they ate stew anyway. Calum's troops were camped in a circle around the outside of the wagons eating their usual rations, all except Bonnie's brothers. They sat with the McKinney children, occasionally taking comfort from one of them sliding in closer to share a hug.

When he had returned Bonnie to the train he had noticed how close she was to the children in their small party. He tried, but could not imagine how they had survived without her all these days.

"Did she have a gun or knife with her?" Ian asked as the food was finished and the group became quiet.

Tom shook his head. "She went to walk around, before lunch, like usual. She said it was too late to surprise game, especially following such a big wagon train."

"How long after she disappeared did you see the Indian?"

Calum tried to ask the question as though it were unimportant but they all heard the emotion in it.

"Not sure, we didn't realize she wasn't back until we had walked on and stopped for lunch. After the boys came back with proof about dangerous Indians, we moved on."

"I wanted to stay and hunt for her, but they wouldn't leave me," Tom said.

"I wanted to stay too," Jim added.

"Boys we've been over and over that. You're not good with guns and you wouldn't stand a chance alone. Besides, we need you to help move the teams. We needed you to help protect the little ones and the women."

Henry made a barking sound. Calum stared at the man, not sure if it were a laugh or a sob. Claire Wimberley rose from where she sat between her parents and stared at him. "What is it, Henry? Do you want me to put Barney to bed?"

Again there was the explosive sound. In the dark, the man shook his head violently, crushing the small boy in his arms. "I couldn't protect them, I couldn't protect either of them."

"When?" Calum asked.

Claire answered, extending a hand but not touching either the man or the boy. "Yesterday morning, Indians came racing toward us. The Lambton's wagon was in the lead, free of the dust for the first time in days. Father and Henry were on horseback and they shouted and started the wagons into a circle as soon as they saw the first one."

"We were lucky, the terrain was flat. We'd just passed a big hill where they could have fired down on us. As soon as we got the first wagons started circling, we turned and fired at the Indians," Father Wimberley said.

"Did they look like the Shoshoni chief? Were they the same type of Indians," Calum asked.

Wimberley shook his head and then answered, "No, I don't think they were. These had paint on their faces and horses and wore no shirts. They looked terrifying. We started firing on them, Henry and I."

"We shot at them too," the boys shouted.

"We rehearse what to do if we're attacked. The women crawled in the back of the wagons with the children and all the men stood behind the wagon seats to fire, taking our time about aiming."

"We shot two and they fell," Henry said.

"I shot one of their horses and blew its leg off," Tom said without excitement. Calum heard the regret every good man felt when his terrible shot went home.

"It was afterward, after they were gone, that I realized Bella had been hit," Henry said. "Poor Bella. We buried her along that God-forsaken hill. There were no other graves or people nearby. She was all alone." His voice broke and this time there was no doubt that he was crying.

Calum waited, but no one reached out to comfort the man. It was August, over ninety in the morning shade. Of course they had buried her right away. In a minute the tear choked voice continued.

"She made me promise to take care of Barney, to take care of him the way we had agreed if anything happened to her. I couldn't do it. She wanted him buried with her, but I couldn't do it."

Suddenly Claire sank beside him, leaned to wrap an arm around the sobbing man. "I thought, I heard you promise her to take care of him, then I saw you put your hand over his face." She leaned against him. "Oh Henry, I thought you wanted to kill him."

The weeping man rose as though scalded by her touch. "At first I resented him. He took all her time and attention. It left her nothing for herself or for me. He was her son, not my child, but her son from a previous marriage. But seeing them together, day after day on this endless trip, I saw, I saw things differently. I never wanted to hurt him, to …" the words faded into a gasp of horror.

Onto the lap of the shocked girl he let the lifeless body of the child fall. "And now, now he is dead and we are days and miles from her grave. They both will be buried alone."

The girl screamed and fainted and the grieving man walked out of the circle of light into the dark. Calum whistled and one of the two Indian scouts ran up. Calum said something to him in Indian and the scout disappeared.

Mother and Father Wimberley rushed forward, Mother to take the dead child and Father to sweep his daughter into his arms and carry her to their wagon.

In the dark they heard a thud. Minutes later the scout returned with a body over his shoulder.

"Tie him up and put him in his wagon," Calum ordered. He spoke to the four boys staring accusingly at him. "Guilt and grief have killed many a man."

He turned to look down at the woman praying over the dead boy. Strangely, the other children were gathered in a circle around him, each touching a hand or foot of the little boy. Tenderly Calum leaned down and closed the dark staring eyes. "If you'll prepare him for burial, my men and I will find the grave and bury him beside his mother. Hopefully it will provide some solace to Mr. Lambton."

"Yes, yes, I'll see to it now."

When Father Wimberley returned, he offered no explanation for his daughter's reaction. Calum could guess what the source of the girl's problems were. He told the older man what he planned to do the next day, promising to send ten of his troops with the wagon train to ensure they arrived safely at Fort McPherson.

"That doesn't leave you many to move forward with."

"A half dozen, plus my scouts are both Shoshoni. They will help me find this Chief's camp. If Bonnie is still alive, we'll bring her back."

CHAPTER FORTY-FIVE

At dawn, Calum sorted his men out, emphasizing the importance of being on guard. Whoever was leading the band of Indians harassing the wagon trains, they were bold enough to attack a far larger troop of soldiers than these ten men. When he had them prepared to follow the sergeant back to headquarters while protecting the settlers, he turned to deal with the survivors.

First, he rode up and took time to remove the arrow from the side of the Lambton's wagon. Even without it there, he knew Henry would always see it. He handed it to his scouts and listened to them talk. He wasn't surprised when they decided it was an arrow of the Lakota, one of the most war-like of the Sioux.

He wanted to trust the settlers to deal with Henry Lambton. Instead, he opened the drawn canvas at the rear of the wagon and looked inside. He was shocked to see the man was awake, staring calmly at him. "We're leaving. I wanted you to know that we're taking the boy back to bury beside his mother."

Henry nodded, his eyes betraying his emotions. "Elizabeth Wimberley told me last night that she was preparing his body. Thank you. I know Bella will rest easier once he is beside her. You know, I told her not to bring him, that it would kill him. But thank God she didn't listen to me. It gave them both so much joy, just sitting and smiling at each other each day. He wasn't long for this world anyway, but he had a good soul and it was full of love for his Mother."

Calum leaned in and tugged the end of the rope to pull the knot free. "A lot of people are counting on you to be strong and brave. I hope I can trust you to buck up."

Henry Lambton freed his arms and feet from the tangle of rope. "The silence gave me a lot of time to think and put things into perspective. You can trust me."

The McKinney boys were up, struggling to fold their tent despite the help of two energetic black and white dogs. Calum remembered the last letter from Bonnie, and exchanged a salute with the boys and then laughed when the dogs stood on their hind legs and barked as though saluting as well.

Calum stopped by the Wimberley wagon, not surprised to see the older couple up and sharing the chore of preparing the breakfast. Calum accepted a cup of coffee but apologized for not stepping down. He felt such an urgent need to be in pursuit. Behind them, he was shocked to see the Magee's arguing about who would carry the body of Barney Lambton. Finally they agreed to share the duty. If he kept them alive long enough, those boys were going to make fine men.

Some of his men grumbled about the burial duty and the horror of carrying the dead child. They accused Ian and Shawn of being ghouls for wanting to carry him. After Calum scolded them, they subsided. By noon they reached the scene of the attack.

While the stern Lieutenant and his red-headed ghouls located the grave, the other men sat in the shade to eat and grumble. When the boys moved the rocks on top of the grave, gases of decay blew their way and despite his scowl the men swore and complained. Ignoring them, the boys laid the little child in his mother's arms, then recovered the bodies.

They stared at Calum and waited, holding their breath while he started and ended the short service with the words of Henry Lambton. "This child was fated to a short, hard life, but he had a generous soul and was full of love for his mother. May you welcome them both into heaven together. Amen. The boys lowered their scarfs and moved upwind of the grave to begin singing. The words were clear and high in their young tenors.

Calum had never heard the hymn but the last words rang true to him.

Blest are the pure in heart
For they shall see our God,

The secret of the Lord is theirs
Their soul is his abode.

As soon as they mounted, he turned to his Indian Scouts and followed his instincts. After twelve days, there was nothing to be gained by traveling to the site where Bonnie had been taken. If raiding Sioux had found her, well he couldn't think about it. There would be no point in knowing. He preferred to believe she was alive and that the Shoshoni Chief, his scouts described as some kind of God-like man, had taken her for some noble reason and was protecting her. He set the scouts in front with orders to find Washakie.

Two days later, Calum and his men approached the Shoshoni village. The scouts entered first, and Calum mounted and rode forward, halting at the tree line. "I know some of you men are afraid to enter this village, maybe you fear you'll get your throats cut or end up scalped. Stay here, wait until dark. If we're not back, then make your way due south. You'll cut the wagon trail and can follow it west into North Platte."

He emerged from the trees across the plain toward the village, Bonnie's brothers riding at his heels. The other men remained behind, hidden, and shook their heads.

◇◇◇

Chief Washakie sat in the shade thrown by a hide hung from the top of his tent. He was bored already with the bickering. The whole village knew his wife was dying. Braves had been pestering him about who would get the white woman when she was no longer needed in his tent.

When the scouts arrived, they were welcomed by friends and family. The chief slowly got to his feet at the happy commotion. The whole village was celebrating the arrival of their kin and then suddenly, there was silence.

◇◇◇

Bonnie sat beside Half-Moon, unable to ease her pain or suffering, settling for holding her hand in the stifling shadows of the tent. Her fingers felt permanently crippled from the frequent tightening as pain would tear through the woman. Bonnie recited the Lord's Prayer in an endless lament and the dying woman would join in on a word each time she gripped her hands.

Outside they could hear the raised voices, the men arguing and bargaining for her. She did not need Half-Moon to translate in order to understand. She had known when she woke at dawn that it was time for her to escape. She could have taken Brown Bess and raced out of camp. She figured when the mare tired, the Indian ponies would as well and she had faith that the big horse would continue to carry her far away.

That was the problem. She had no idea how to get back to any area with white people. What if she found the warlike Indians instead? Most of the time, these Shoshoni were like sweet and playful children. In the two weeks she had lived here, she had not seen them torture or kill anyone, Indian or white. She remembered Washakie telling her that they were chasing and trying to kill the Sioux who were the enemy of whites and Indians. If they were, they didn't seem to be working at it very hard.

There was that, and the fact that Half-Moon needed her. She could not bear to leave the woman to suffer alone. Who would whisper a prayer over her fleeing soul? Who would pray for her safe return into the arms of her lost family?

No, whoever Chief Washakie chose to be her husband, she had decided to accept. First, he could not be any worse than the one she had chosen. Second, one man would be better than many. Third, at her first chance, she would escape.

The tone of the voices outside changed and Half-Moon released her hand and made a waving motion. Bonnie crawled around the fire pit and rose to stand at the teepee entrance. Timidly she held the rawhide flap. But when the world outside became silent, she flung the hide back and stepped out into the light.

CHAPTER FORTY-SIX

Bonnie squealed in delight to see her brothers and Calum riding down the tunnel quickly formed by the Indians. Flapping her hands to work the blood back into her fingers she raced past the chief and the arguing braves straight toward the riders.

Immediately, Calum and the boys dismounted. She flew into his arms then reached out to snag each of the red-headed lads and pull them all into a tight hug. Frantically she kissed Ian, then Shawn, then smiled up into the astonished eyes of the Lieutenant. Swallowing her fear, she leaned in closer and placed her cheek against his own. Calum hungrily wrapped his long arms around her.

Behind them there was an angry roar and Bonnie quickly turned back to face the mad Indians. She raised her hand in the sign for peace and tugged the suddenly frightened men forward.

Smiling radiantly, she kept walking forward until all four stood there, the men still leading their horses. The curious Indians now moved to form a circle around the chief's tent and these strange white men. Even as Bonnie watched, they began to fold down to sit like spectators at a major event.

Bonnie remembered how angry the Indian had become the first time she stood eye-to-eye with him in front of his men. Summoning her old timidity, she bowed her head and knelt before him.

She felt a little amusement and fear for the men behind her who remained standing. "Chief Washakie, my family have come for me.

These are my brothers, Ian Magee and Shawn Magee, and their commander, Lieutenant Calum Douglas."

Calum studied the old chief with admiration as the man stood eyeing their group. Calum looked around, saw one of the scouts smiling, another nodding as though they were there to back him up if needed. Yet neither man moved forward.

"This your husband?"

Bonnie swallowed. If she said he was she would be lying, if she denied him, all three might be tortured or burned at the stake. Just because she hadn't witnessed it, didn't mean these Indians were any less savage than the ones she had read about.

"He is the man I love," she answered raising her eyes to smile at the Chief.

Calum gasped and ignored the throng watching. Instead he reached out to pull the girl to her feet by one long brown pigtail. If she hadn't raced toward them, he would have mistaken her for one of the other Indian squaws. Bonnie looked up at him, her eyes questioning, begging him to not reveal the half-truth she had just told.

Shyly she tucked her head, lowering her eyes as she whispered, "You are my true love, aren't you?"

He reached out to tilt her chin up so he could stare into her eyes. "Look at me," he growled.

Bonnie opened her eyes and stared at him, her breath held until he answered. "When I see those shamrocks blooming in your eyes, how can I ever love another?"

Then he pulled her in with a hand on each braid and kissed her, softly at first, then as deeply and hungrily as he had each night in his dreams. As his hands dropped from her hair, he ran them along her strong shoulders and straight back, finally putting hands on her hips to pull her into an even deeper kiss.

Shouting and pandemonium broke out as the braves bartering for her moved in to shove them apart.

Chief Washakie stared at the woman, clearly wondering if he had misjudged her. Finally, he managed to calm the outraged braves. Standing up, he demanded his headdress and one of the women came to set the prized war bonnet on his head. The other wife handed him his feathered spear. In clear English he spoke to the soldiers.

"These braves have waited for this woman, Willow. Now Half-Moon is dying, I have promised to decide whose teepee she will sleep under."

One by one he named the man and what he had offered for the woman. When he reached Calum, he stared fiercely. Calum reluctantly drew out his Remington and held it out to the chief. For several minutes the Indians gathered around and admired the weapon. The Chief looked pleased and raised it to fire at a distant tree. All seemed impressed when he hit a branch and the leaves vibrated.

Bonnie started walking over to the tall man but the brawny brave who had pursued her before grabbed her arm and raised a long and angry complaint.

Chief Washakie listened to him and nodded. "Red Badger has offered three horses. This rifle is fine, but is not enough for woman who out walks horses and has eyes like mountain lion. Not enough."

Calum eyed Bonnie and shook his head. He unbelted his holster and passed it and the Colt pistol over to the chief.

Another debate ensued and the Chief looked offended by what the man was saying. Bonnie had learned some words but not enough to follow the conversation. She stared at Calum, watched him furiously shake his head. He again looked toward the Indian Scouts but both men were laughing.

The Chief walked over to the Lieutenant and stroked his horse. The stallion raised his head and snorted. Calum brought the reins up short and talked to the big animal. His voice was tight and controlled as though he were talking to himself, but she heard him clearly. "I've had Champ for nine years, ridden him during two western campaigns. This horse has never failed me. He has saved my life a dozen times."

The words she didn't hear aloud she heard in her head. 'I love this big horse. That kiss had been good, but Bonnie was another man's wife.' Bonnie felt his pain and watched in disbelief as he handed the reins of the stallion over to the chief.

The Chief nodded. Bonnie ran over and put her arms around the man who only made a surly growl in return.

The crazy white woman and her child ran up, begging them to take them too. Calum started to speak, but her brothers moved forward to hand the Chief the reins to their mounts and point to the white prisoners. Chief Washakie grunted in assent and took the two horses. Bonnie wanted to shake the boys. The Indians would probably have given them the troublesome woman and boy for free.

Calum shook his head in disbelief. "Take all your gear off them, especially your guns, and keep them. These Indians have no use for harness. Now. Start walking back down the trail with them and don't look back. I'll bring Bonnie." He turned and looked at the Indian Scouts and spoke to them in Indian. The older one stood with his arm around a squaw and shook his head. The younger man shook his head and called an answer back to them.

"Great, they're not ready to go yet." He looked at the two Magee lads but they were already unsaddling the army horses.

Ian lifted the shaggy headed lad who was about the age of Clyde, and Shawn took the hand of the pregnant woman. Each lad hefted his saddle, bedroll, and guns and headed back the way they had entered the village. Calum peeled their sister's arms free and turned to remove the saddle from his stallion. When he turned to take her hand, Bonnie was gone.

Calum entered the darkened teepee, the laughter of the Indians still ringing in his ears. The smells were strong and unmistakable. Something or someone had died in here. He found the expensive girl kneeling beside a moaning mound and realized he was wrong. The horrible moans were coming from a woman who was still dying. He squatted down beside Bonnie.

"We need to go now. The lads are almost back at the tree line, but heaven knows if those cowards I left behind will be there to protect them."

Bonnie leaned over, pressing against him. "I promised her I would not leave her alone to die. I cannot leave yet. Go on if you need to, I'll catch up to you."

He laughed, swore softly. "I guess that'd be easy for a woman who out walks horses. I suppose if it gets dark before then, you can see with those mountain lion eyes."

There was a brief glow of light, then the thick darkness surrounded them again.

"I'm sorry I cost you so much. I can't believe he took Champ. I don't think I'm worth that much."

"Oh, I don't know. They seem to think a lot of you. Tall, and strong as you are with your big beautiful breasts, long white legs and fire-colored..."

"What?" she whispered in outrage.

"Yeah, and a whole lot more old Red Badger had inventoried up."

Half-Moon moaned and Bonnie leaned forward to sponge her face and neck. "That vile skunk. He must have hidden and watched when we bathed."

Calum collapsed to sit on the soft furs beside her, buried his head in his hands. "I guess that's one explanation for it."

Bonnie looked over her shoulder to glare at him. "I give you my word, no one has touched me."

He cleared his throat and she was grateful for the dark that hid her blush. "I've had relations with only one man, and he was my husband."

Calum sat there in the dark, heard the breathless moan of the dying woman and used it to cover his own sigh. Struggling to control the emotion that suddenly overwhelmed him he extended a hand and placed it on Bonnie's back. Leaving it there, he stretched out and relaxed for the first time in days. All he had feared, all he had imagined, all had been wasted pain.

He rubbed a hand across his face, no longer even smelling the strong scents. All he was aware of was the warm beating heart beneath his hand. In minutes, he was asleep.

◇◇◇

In the dark, Bonnie felt a strange sense of peace sweep through her. She felt it in Calum's heavy hand on her back and then minutes later in his even breathing. He had believed her. Bowing her head, she took the hand of the woman suffering beside her and began to pray out loud.

Minutes later she began to sing *Rock of Ages*, the song strong and full of joy as it rose through the opening at the top of the teepee. In the dark, someone struck a flint and a small fire glimmered beside her. A deep male voice joined in her song, the words transformed into grunts and rhythmic sounds.

When the hymn ended she leaned down to listen to Half-Moon's chest, held her hand over her mouth to feel for her breath. Carefully she recited the prayer she had heard at the funeral of Lynne's mother. She made the sign of the cross and stared across into Chief Washakie's eyes.

"She is gone," Bonnie whispered.

"It is good. Now, you and your man must go."

CHAPTER FORTY-SEVEN

Bonnie shook Calum's shoulder and he startled awake, grabbing for the handgun that was no longer there. "Come, it is time for us to go," she whispered.

As they rose and exited the tent, she looked back and saw a plume of black smoke appear at the top. In the distance she heard a voice begin to keen the death chant. They stood in the Indian camp, the shadows forming around them, hearing other voices join in. Calum strode forward to heft his saddle and pack onto his back, this time making sure he had her hand in his.

The brave who had been such a problem made an obscene gesture and Calum slowly put the saddle down. "Oh no," Bonnie said, "we can leave, you don't have to do this."

"Sit down on it," he whispered angrily. "Unless you want them to skin us and then your brothers alive, stay there and stay quiet."

Threats, the same kind the Chief had used to frighten her into being quiet just weeks ago. Bonnie sat, watched in awe as the handsome man shed his doublet and pulled off one boot then started on the other.

Red Badger came at him, and suddenly one of the Indian Scouts grabbed his arm and took away his knife. The man protested, but all heard the Chief speak and the angry Indian gave up the weapon and no longer seemed so eager to fight with the taller, fitter man.

Calum wasn't fooled. He pulled off the second boot, then nodded at the scout. He bent at the waist into a wrestling stance and Bonnie smiled in amusement. It hadn't been that long since she saw her brother's playing at wrestling with the same grand poses.

This time when the Indian came forward, Calum caught and threw the man over his head. The brave landed in the dust with a loud grunt. In seconds he was back on his feet and coming in low again. This time Calum extended his leg but the Indian jumped over it and tumbled to land back on his feet. There was a scattered cheer from the Indians on the smoothness of the move. Now those gathered from their evening meals began to chant and taunt both men.

The next round both men caught the other's arms, but neither could flip the other man. After grunting and pushing they moved about in a circle and stopped, shoulder to shoulder glaring at each other. The Indian made a hard, stabbing motion with his fist and hammered Calum over his hip. The tall soldier grunted and then shoved, breaking free of the other man's hold. This time when the Indian came grappling in, Calum brought him up into the air with a solid blow to the gut.

The Indian backed, rubbing at his belly. Calum stood and swung his shoulders as though to loosen them and brought both arms up, fists ready. Again they circled. If they were back home in the alley behind the tenements, Bonnie would have been egging the combatants on. Now she thought it wiser to sit quietly as the officer had commanded her to do.

Finally, the annoying peeping Tom charged and Calum hit him solidly on the chin with a right and then the nose with a left. The Indian went down on his seat in the dust. He sat there for a minute, than instead of getting up, collapsed on his back into the dust. A nice bit of drama, but if it had been Shawn, the brave would have had to cry uncle.

Bonnie tried to look impressed as Calum walked up to her. For a second she was tempted to call him a big ham. Instead she rose and held his shirt while he slid one arm into it, then the other. Soon he had his feet in his boots. As he started to walk away, Chief Washakie called his name. Calum stopped.

◇◇◇

They rode into the shelter of the trees laughing. The chief had kept the guns, but they had Champ and Brown Bess as presents from the chief. Actually, he had given them both to Bonnie for her help with Half-Moon. Bonnie had no intention of pointing this out to Calum.

In the dark, the Lieutenant called to his men. When there was no answer he led the way down the trail looking for them. They heard someone or something moving beside them. The horses snorted and reared and an animal bounded out across the gravel. It was too fast to be anything but a startled deer. As soon as they had the horses under control he cautiously let his stallion lead the way along the path. Another mile, and the moon finally rose. In the dust of the deer path there was one deep imprint of a shod hoof.

Calum held up a hand and Bonnie stopped behind him. To her right, she could hear the music of the slow-moving river, in front, only silence. Calum motioned to his right and Bonnie followed his direction. Ahead was a small cleared space under the trees, just beyond it, moonlight bounced off the surface of the river.

"Our own little Eden," Calum said, quickly dismounting.

Bonnie's face darkened and all her joy fled. This was too much like the path beside the river in Boston. She shuddered as she dismounted. "Aren't we going to find the boys and your men?"

Calum caught both reins in his hands. "There's plenty of time to catch up with them in the morning. Since we're unarmed, probably safer if we just bed down for the night here. No sense risking the horses."

"I thought you saw their hoof prints on the trail?"

Calum was walking toward her, the horses pulling against the reins, wanting to reach the water. He released them, let them spring over to get a drink. From their snorting, Bonnie was sure they had realized they were too high above the river to drink safely.

"I thought it might be nice to have a little privacy."

Bonnie raised a hand, planted it firmly against his chest. "I told you I'm a married woman," she said fiercely, her voice loud in the dark.

"You told the chief I was the man you loved, everyone heard you," he barked.

"You said I was your one true love," she answered, her voice shaking with emotion.

"I fought for your honor."

"I've seen my brothers playing at fighting the same way."

"Damn you, it wasn't play. Why do you think boys practice fighting?"

She glared at him but didn't answer.

Bonnie relaxed a little and Calum reached out to take her shoulders, wanting to pull her in for another passionate kiss. Instead, she pushed against his chest harder, her breath coming in quick panicked little bursts.

"Shh, we're over here." Bonnie recognized the voice. She moved into Calum's arms, instinctively squeezing closer as she heard someone moving through the brush toward them.

"We're over here, Ian," Bonnie called.

"Damn it," Calum swore, more angry at the woman tormenting him then the interruption by the boy.

Suddenly both boys burst through the thicket and ran into Brown Bess. The mare snickered and swung her big head down to be petted and it was Shawn who laughed. "What the he--?"

Bonnie shivered, her panic forgotten. Holding onto Calum she turned to call softly to the boys. "Thank God we found you. Are you all right?"

They quickly ran toward her voice and she caught them close, once again holding all three men she loved.

"We're camped just around the bend. That woman, something's happening with her. I'm so glad we found you Bonnie. Are you all right? Are you all right too, sir?" Ian asked.

"How'd you get the horses? Did you wait until dark and steal them sir? Were you able to take the guns as well?" Shawn asked.

Disgusted, Calum called his horse and the mare followed. "Come on, let's just follow the trail. How far ahead are you?"

In minutes they reached the cold camp of the disgruntled men. In the moonlight Bonnie saw the bawling child, the men staring at the woman thrashing on the ground twisting in pain. Well, life had a way of happening. It wasn't always convenient, but babies had a way of deciding when they were going to be born.

"Take care of the boy Shawn. Ian start a fire. I'll need plenty of hot water."

The horses walked through the crowd to push into the river and drink.

"You men, if you don't want to watch this babe come into the world, best move down a ways to camp," Bonnie called.

When they ignored her, she simply bent and lifted the woman in her arms and carried her into the shelter of the trees.

"What about the Indians, isn't it too dangerous to have a fire near all them savages?" One of the men protested.

"Those are the civilized ones," Calum answered. "Move to it, let's get this done so we can all get some sleep. Anybody do anything about supper?"

The other men shook their heads, clearly ashamed of riding off and leaving them. "What happened to our scouts?" one demanded.

"Guess they're enjoying home cooking tonight. Probably catch up to us in the morning."

By the time they had the water boiling over the fire, Calum had caught three trout and they were wrapped in mud and roasting in the ashes as the fire blazed merrily against the clear sky. One of the men mixed up bread and had it in a covered skillet in the same fire. Another opened his pack and found the last of his bacon. Cut in strips, they were laid on the hot lid of the skillet, the grease sending up tempting smells as it sizzled into the fire.

Bonnie yelled to her brothers and one carried the hot water to her. Minutes later they heard the mewing sound of a new baby. The men all smiled at one another, a universal feeling of peace at the miracle in the dark.

CHAPTER FORTY-EIGHT

Later, Bonnie stopped to fill the kettle with water for coffee, and washed her hands thoroughly in the cool river. She handed the kettle to Calum and he added grounds and put it on the empty rock. He handed Bonnie his plate and she finished the bit of fish, bread and bacon he had left for her. She smiled at him in gratitude and reached for the other plates but Calum handed them off to the complainer in the crew. "Don't worry, Tiller will wash them."

She beamed and took a cup of coffee as Ian passed it to her. "It was a boy, not that small either."

"A half-breed," one of the men sneered.

"A beautiful baby boy," she answered. "A miracle after all she's survived. She and her son hid in a root cellar when Blackfeet raided and burned their cabin. Her husband and older son were butchered in front of her. They raped her, threatened to kill her baby boy if she fought them, that little one over there. She was rescued by Washakie's band and kept safe all this time."

"Yeah, bet they kept real good care of her," the man Tiller said as he returned with the clean metal plates. Bonnie didn't know what to answer. Was the new baby from the raiders or the saviors? For that woman, did it make a difference?

Bonnie rose, "I'll be sleeping with her tonight. Is there a spare blanket?"

Shawn rose and brought his bedroll and handed it to her. "Ian and I can share. Take mine."

She leaned forward as though to kiss him but he backed up and instead she caught his hand and shook it. "Thank you brother," she turned and smiled at Ian and touched his shoulder and he caught her hand.

As she turned to walk back to the thicket, the fringe on the end of her skirt and along her sleeves swung as the moonlight lit the lush curves of her body beneath the soft leather. Calum watched, hypnotized by the beauty of her movements. Apparently the others watched as well.

"Don't take them bucks long to turn any woman into a squaw," Tiller said.

Calum half rose and held the boys back. The last thing he needed tonight was another fight.

"Mrs. Micheals wasn't any man's squaw. The chief captured her to tend to his wife, a white captive, who was dying and wanted one of her own people to tend her. She was kept safe under his protection."

"Well, if she was kept under the Chief, reckon that don't make her no squaw," the man said and suddenly found himself jerked up by Calum and held with his feet over the fire.

"The chief had other wives, she wasn't any man's squaw. You say another word against either of these women and I'll see you flogged when we get back to camp. You got that."

"Yes sir," the man said and Calum set him down carefully on his feet without giving him a shove back into the fire or a fist in the face onto the rocky ground. Using all the restraint he could muster, he led his horse down beside the thicket with the river close beside him. Carefully he spread out his bedroll, shook out his blankets and shed his boots.

He pulled the blanket up over his shoulder, but the moonlight bouncing off the ripples made it hard to sleep. He rolled over, his face turned toward the woods. Softly he heard her call.

"Good night, Calum," her mouth moved softly around his name.

He closed his eyes, imagined kissing her again. But in his mind he still heard Tiller's goading voice and the boasting, nasty words of the Indian Red Badger.

What had Bonnie said about the other woman? A miracle after all she had survived. What about Bonnie, what had she survived? If it was nothing, why had she pushed him away when they were alone earlier. He had been eager, hungry to make love to her. From her response to his earlier kiss, she had seemed just as eager. But when the time came, all he felt was her panicked fear.

"Calum," she whispered.

He grunted in answer, heard the other woman moan and the new baby start to cry. Silently he mouthed the words, goodnight my love.

Both women joined them for breakfast. The Magee boys seemed eager to help with the rescued boy and newborn. The other men took their food and moved away to eat it. Calum stared at the little baby. He was red all right, but weren't all newborns. He smiled as Ian unwrapped the baby to look at his little feet and tiny toes.

Calum watched Bonnie smile as she put down her food for the first time. It was hard tack and jerky plus hot coffee but she had been eating it like it was steak and potatoes. If they didn't get a move on, the last day of their ride everyone would be eating roots and tree bark.

The lads had their saddles, but nothing to carry them unless Bonnie used one on the mare. The big horse had refused the first time he tried to saddle her. He looked toward the mule. Maybe they could divide up its load and the boys could go double on it. That still left the woman and her children.

Bonnie smiled as she watched her brothers playing with the little boy, getting him to touch his new brother. Shawn lifted the lad's bare foot and Ian touched the baby's to it. The child smiled. "He's beautiful isn't he, and so perfect," Ian said. The little boy nodded.

"He's Indian," the woman said with a shudder. "I should just walk over and throw him in the river. Be kinder for us all."

"Don't talk crazy, you can't mean that," Bonnie protested. "What if he were the last child you could ever have?"

"I would rather be barren, than cursed with such an abomination."

Bonnie started to argue more but Calum pulled her up and away from the conversation. "I need your help saddling the mare."

They walked over toward the horses, out of hearing but still in full view of the men. "Brown Bess won't wear a saddle. She'll pull or tote whatever you give her, but she hates saddles." Bonnie pulled away to go back to argue with the new mother.

Calum captured her arms. "You already said it all. She's crazy, and after all she's had to survive, who can blame her."

"Yes, but she doesn't know what it means to be barren, to know you can never have children."

He held her fast, his heart beating in fear. "But you know what it's like?"

Bonnie looked like she would scream if he didn't release her. Instead, slowly she raised her eyes to see the horror in his own. What was the point in fooling herself that she could ever have this man or a happy marriage? She needed to tell him all the ugly truth. She heard the other troopers saddling up and stammered out the worst part of it. "After I lost my baby, the doctor said I would probably never have another."

This time when she pulled away, he released her.

Bonnie walked back to the fire to tell her brothers what she needed. Calum turned to order the Magees to put their saddle on the mule and divide the supplies but heard her already giving orders.

Annoyed, he still managed to get the words out. "She's right, the travois makes sense. Then see if you can saddle the mule. I'll divide out the remaining supplies and each man can carry some in his saddlebags. Come on, let's hurry."

Ian and Shawn cut saplings and tied Shawns' bedding between the two poles to form a travois to carry the new mother and baby. Once it was secured behind the big mare, Bonnie made sure the mother and baby were secure riding there. Shawn helped her mount and Ian handed up the little boy.

Calum abandoned the pack saddle and one of the lad's army saddles. Hopefully their scouts would find them as they came along the trail to rejoin them. He just hoped they would bring them along.

Tiller started off the day by complaining how dragging women along was going to get them scalped. Bonnie kicked Brown Bess into motion and would have taken the lead down the trail but Calum put out a hand to slow her. "Remember your passengers." The Magee lads moved up behind her and Calum looked at the complaining troopers.

"You men get your eyes open and your guns ready. The Shoshoni may be our allies, but we know there are plenty of hostiles around." He rode forward onto the well-used Indian and game trail. When he reached the crest of the hill he looked back and waved as he saw his scouts coming out of the woods.

The mule who had been antsy brayed and shook off one of the Magee lads. Luckily Ian backed the kicking animal in the opposite direction, trying to see his brother. Swearing, Calum ordered Shawn to the front. Champ danced a little and the boy couldn't pull up.

"There's plenty of room on Bess," Bonnie said.

Calum backed and gave the lad a lift up onto the big mare. The mare stomped her foot and a ripple ran along her back. Shawn circled his sister's waist and asked. "How do you stay on up here, the damn thing is as round as a barrel?"

"Don't be swearing at Brown Bess, or she'll shake you off on purpose. Just use those bowed Irish legs of yours to grip her and hang on to me. I'll not let you fall."

The little captive looked around and grinned at the soldier. Shawn stuck his tongue out and the boy giggled and pulled back out of sight. For several minutes, the little one continued to play peek-a-boo beneath Bonnie's raised arms and Shawn kept him giggling by making faces.

Well his mother might be bitter and scarred by her time with the Indians, but this little one wasn't. Bonnie had never seen happier or more care-free children than among the Indians. Maybe the new mother was right about the life this half-breed would have among white people. If he had remained with the Indians, would he have been welcomed and loved by all, the same as the others?

Suddenly the scouts pushed ahead and talked rapidly in Indian with Calum. The Lieutenant halted his horse and stared back at his tightly bunched men. "We're getting off into the brush here. Dismount, hold your horse's nose to keep it from calling out and giving us away. We need to be as quiet and as quick as possible. Keep your guns ready and your mouths closed until these men give us the all safe signal."

As Bonnie and Shawn slid to the ground, Calum placed a hand around the terrified new mother's mouth. She was already rolling her head. Quickly Bonnie tugged his kerchief from around his neck and they wadded the yellow cloth into her mouth and Shawn handed his own over to tie it into place.

Calum took the woman over his shoulder while Bonnie took the two children. Shawn freed Bess of the travois and the scouts helped hide it in the weeds.

As they crouched down in the weeds and vines, she watched the brave scouts sweeping the hoof prints down the trail before stopping and climbing up onto the top of the cliff. They sent their horses into the brush and Bonnie noticed it was her brave brother Ian who snagged their bridles and led them into the hiding place.

Paralyzed with fear, Bonnie held the little ones close against her and closed her eyes to pray.

CHAPTER FORTY-NINE

Calum laid the new mother on the ground and whispered in Bonnie's ear, "Sit on her."

Instantly Bonnie did, pressing the woman's arms into the earth beneath her knees. The woman's eyes were frantic, white all around. When the newborn made a tiny noise, Bonnie opened the woman's dress and pressed her nipple into the infant's mouth. The woman and child grew quiet. The little boy pressed against Bonnie turned to wrap an arm around his mother's neck and squeeze his face against hers. Everything was silent, even the birds and the wind.

Calum took the rifle abandoned in its saddle sheath by Tiller and inched closer to the trail, the gun ready. Shawn held out his revolver and his rifle. Bonnie took the rifle and slid the safety off, raising it to sight just to the right of the Lieutenant.

A small party of Indians appeared on the trail. From the strange hair of the shirtless riders, Bonnie knew they were not Shoshoni. Suddenly the group of seven paused and stared at the trail ahead as though they could sense the troopers waiting there. The leader raised an arm and waved and three quickly sprinted from their ponies and started to mount the cliff.

When the scouts fired, Calum and the soldiers opened fire as well. Bonnie shot at the leader. The woman beneath her bucked and Bonnie lowered her rifle to give the woman a light tap on the forehead.

Instantly the woman stopped. When Bonnie sighted along the gun, all she could see was smoke. The firing ceased.

Calum bounded out of the brush and stood in the road, feet firmly planted as he continued to fire at the fleeing Indians until his gun was empty.

Bonnie followed him from her hiding spot and stared at the ground. There were two bleeding Indians and she watched in disbelief as the blue-coated troopers quickly dispatched them. One horse was dead on the ground, another was screaming in agony and thrashing about. Calum shot him.

From down the trail they heard a tremolo of victory. The two scouts ran up leading three horses. Bonnie grinned as Shawn raced to claim the reins of the palomino but arrived too late. Ian led out the mule and held its reins out instead, as he checked the strange red waves and hands pressed onto his new horse's coat.

In minutes their caravan was reassembled, the new horse saddled and the unconscious woman and children carefully settled in the travois. But Bess refused to let anyone near her to attach the poles. Bonnie started to mount but the big mare was having none of it and tried to bite her.

To Shawn's annoyance, the travois was transferred to his mule and Calum held out a hand to Bonnie. He emptied one stirrup and shaking her head in frustration, she used it to step up, working to slide her leg across the saddle in front of him. She was very aware that the leather dress was pushing up to expose her bare leg. From the voices of the other men she knew they were aware as well.

As though he did it every day, Calum ran a hand down her bare leg and reached under to pull the skirt down. Bonnie's face flamed red as he tucked it under her and scooped her bottom up to rest neatly against his crotch. One of the men gave a big laugh and Bonnie wanted to fight her way free but Calum wrapped an arm around her and said "hush".

One of the Indians shouted in triumph and Calum swiveled his horse around. The uncomplaining mare had dropped a red mass onto the blood spattered road. The Indian ran up to help and in minutes a wobbly foal was struggling to its feet, the big horse washing its white face with her big tongue. Unlike its mother, the new colt had white legs, a white blaze and a large white patch on his chest.

The troopers were strung out along the road, guns ready. Tiller yelled, Hurry up."

Calum's deep voice bellowed, "Shut up and move back against the cliff wall if you men don't want to be a target. Or if you don't want to wait until I give the order, go ahead on your own."

All the men fell back against the protective overhang and the Indians guided the new colt to his first meal.

"I thought your horse must be part Clydesdale. Nothing else in the world looks like 'em. See his feet?" Calum said. Bonnie looked and noticed the down on the shaky legs.

In a few minutes the baby stopped nursing. "You ready Bess?" Calum called. The big brown mare swung her head up and snorted and the Lieutenant fanned his arm down. The scared troops moved out with the scouts shifting to the front and the Magee brothers running drag behind the mare and new horse. Both kept an eye on their special cargo behind them.

◇◇◇

It took over a day to reach the main wagon trail. It had been a slow, uneventful journey. Whenever the mare would stop for the foal to nurse or so she could graze, the whole caravan would pause for a few minutes of needed rest. When the little horse grew too weary to move, they rested their horses and the troopers lay down for brief naps as well.

But as they started down the main wagon road, they all heard the angry sound of gunfire. Calum dropped Bonnie from his horse. "You two, stay here and protect these women," he ordered the Magee boys.

Bonnie ran to her brother's horse and he handed her the rifle again as they took the animals and children to cover.

Calum led the men forward in a charge, firing at the Indians attacking two wagons. With heavy fire from the wagons and the surprise fire from their rear, it quickly sent the Indians running.

As they rejoined the troops, Bonnie stared at one of the wagons full of bearded men. In horror she recognized the thieves from St. Louis in the party. She leaned down to stay partially hidden behind the travois being drug by the mule as they passed by.

One of the men hooted as the captured women passed, making a crude remark about the Army carrying along the right kind of supplies.

Calum took the opportunity to ask if the wagon had any supplies they could share, explaining how they had been delayed long enough to outrun their grub.

Suddenly one of the animals in front of the wagon collapsed. A man rushed forward to unyoke the other ox.

"Well, looks like we've got a right smart of beef we can sell you," the man answered.

◇◇◇

The animal was butchered and loaded into the back of one wagon, the women and children into the rear of the other. Shawn's mule was harnessed with lots of complaints beside the remaining ox and the wagons set in motion with their new nervous escorts alert in case the raiding Indians might return.

Bonnie arranged the saddle to form a pillow and urged her companion to relax now they were safe.

"Safe, didn't you see how those men looked at us. Didn't you hear what they said? They wanted the soldiers to share their whores. They meant us."

"They thought we were captured Indians."

The woman shook her head. "Maybe you were lucky, but it's what I've been for the last two years. Guess there's not much difference being shared among a bunch of braves or rode by troopers or settlers. But I'm not doing it for free for this crowd. I need money to take care of my boys, especially 'spawn of Satan' here."

"Oh no," Bonnie sighed. "Don't talk about your son that way. All babies are born innocent."

"Hell no, read your Bible," the woman swore.

"Christ said we must become as children to enter heaven. That means children are innocent of sin."

"It's also writ in Psalms somewhere, 'Behold, I was shapen in iniquity; and in sin did my mother conceive me.'"

"You know your Bible so well. You know there are many verses that talk of the innocence of children."

"More talk of being conceived in sin. Don't talk Bible to me. My father was a preacher and my husband believed he'd been called to the word. That's what we were doing in the wilderness. But where was God when the heathens came to butcher that good man and my innocent son? Don't talk God to me. He has forsaken us all."

Bonnie shook her head, stretched out on the hard bed of the wagon. Calum had told her not to argue with this crazy woman but Bonnie felt tears fill her eyes as she prayed for her and her little boys. As she relaxed the wagon hit a pot hole and she bounced off the box beneath her. The corner of the canvas covering the boxes bounced up too. Bonnie saw the brown mouth of a jar and heard something slosh. Whiskey. She rolled so she was facing the rear of the covered wagon and stared out at her brothers. The boys rode double on Ian's nervous new horse.

Cautiously so as not to have anyone in the front of the wagon notice, she scooted the canvas up from the cases in front of her. One of them was clearly labeled, 'Henry.'

They made camp early when they came on a half-burned tree. One half of the dead ox was wrapped in its hide and buried beneath the log which was set on fire. The rest of the animal was set to cooking over it and one of the travelers made fried corn cakes and stacked them for when the beef would be ready. Several of the men didn't wait, especially their scouts. They sliced thin strips of the raw meat and ate it before it even began to smoke.

When Bonnie heard a couple of men giggling beside the wagon her and the woman had shared, she walked up to Calum and took his arm with a smile and nodded toward the river. The men watching all grinned and whispered while her brother's glared after them angrily.

Calum wasn't sure what was going on, but he let her lead him until they were out of sight and earshot of the others. "This really isn't safe, those Indians might return at any time. I don't know why, but my scouts and men don't seem too worried about it."

"I know why." Then she told him about the whiskey, and the rifle cases. "I recognized two of those men. They tried to steal our oxen teams when we were camped in St. Louis. At the time we thought they were just taking something of value since they didn't find the money that was hidden in the wagon boxes. Now, I don't think we were right, they really wanted our oxen."

"To haul their wagons full of guns to sell the Indians. One reason Custer was wiped out was they were outgunned. Some of the Indians had repeating rifles, our troops had single shot Springfields."

"The men are acting so crazy because he is giving them whiskey and promising them turns with the two women. I don't want to be a victim. I know my brothers are sober, who else can you count on? You need to act quickly, before he gets them all drunk."

"I like to give the orders," Calum snarled.

"Please, I'm terrified."

"Well you don't seem it." When he heard a noise in the brush he pulled Bonnie into his arms, hissing, "make it look good, they're watching." Then he kissed her.

Just like the time in the Indian camp, she melted into his arms and kissed him back. They both heard a nasty laugh and the brush rustling again.

"As soon as we're back in camp, get your hands on a rifle. I'll do the same and see who I can get to help. You get your brothers." He pulled her in closer for another long kiss.

This time they did it for themselves because they knew no one was watching. Maybe it was the fear and danger, but Bonnie thought it was the most exciting, sweetest kiss she'd ever had.

CHAPTER FIFTY

When they returned to the campfire, a blushing Bonnie slipped over and sat between her brothers. When a red-faced Ian started to get up she grabbed his hand. Fiercely she squeezed it and whispered, "Act like we're fighting about the Lieutenant."

"We don't have to pretend. What the hell are you walking off into the woods with him like some trollop?"

One of the bearded men said something to a soldier and she heard him answer something that sounded like 'brothers.' She turned to stare up at her little brother Shawn and noticed he was just as angry as Ian. "Listen, keep scolding me, but listen," she whispered. While they went on, she continued to whisper as though protesting for their ears only. "These men are gun runners and they are feeding the others whiskey and promising they can take turns with me and the other woman. We have to get to our rifles and be ready to fight before it's too late. Who have you seen going back to the wagon?"

"Tiller and Clarence, at least just those two so far," Ian whispered while Shawn talked loudly about how disappointed their parents would be in her.

"Is that the same Clarence from Ohio?"

"Yeah, ever since Tiller joined he's stayed drunk and ornery."

"The scouts were over there, then they snuck off like they had business elsewhere," Ian snarled "They took some more raw cow meat to eat with them." His voice rose as he continued to complain. "I'm so hungry I'm about to give it a try. At least it's stopped mooing. You want some too, sis?"

"Cut me some that looks burned around the edges," she answered.

As men lined up to get the food, Bonnie stood and walked over to where the woman huddled with her two small children. "Are you all right?"

Fear shown in the woman's eyes, but she nodded, and Bonnie gave her a hug, and then slipped her a long knife. "Just in case."

As the woman gripped it behind her, Bonnie worried that she might have made a terrible mistake. When people were distraught, they often did harm to themselves and their families. The infant and child were so helpless.

"Don't worry, I know who to use it on," she said to the unspoken question. "But if anything happens to me, what will become of my babies?"

"I promise, I will see they are cared for. God has a plan for all of us, we just have to trust in his wisdom." At the skepticism in the other woman's eyes, Bonnie added, "And be ready to do your part."

The woman nodded and slid the blade into the side of her moccasin. Bonnie took the plate of beef and corn cakes from Shawn and turned to share them with her new friend.

Calum rolled his bed out beside hers away from the fire. Men made remarks, but he ignored them. He stood his rifle ready at the tree behind them, slid another gun from under the top blanket of the roll. He looked down and saw the white gleam of her eyes.

She could hear the voices of the thieves from the wagon talking with the troopers beside the fire. One of the voices rose, "been used by lots of braves, one more shouldn't matter to them."

Bonnie gripped the rifle he'd slid her and looked to the blanket with children beside her. Her new friend was shaking. Bonnie forced herself to relax enough to reach out a hand to the woman. The baby started to cry and from the fire she heard one man complain.

"The one's just had a baby. I don't want none of that."

"Well, what about the tall, young one. She looks mighty ripe to me."

"I've wanted that woman since I saw her in Boston. Believe the Lieutenant's got her staked out, and she's got those devilish brothers."

She heard a crude remark from one of the other thieves and rolled her eyes to stare at Calum. So it was the thieves who had followed them.

"Those pups," one of the thieves answered. "They don't need to know, they're out on guard duty anyway. I've got something that will put lead in your pencil. Come on over to the wagons with me." Bonnie looked around but couldn't see her brothers.

Calum sat upright, with his hand on the grip of his rifle.

In the dark, Bonnie heard an owl call. From far away, there floated an answer.

"Indians?" she whispered in terror.

"Hopefully ours. Ready to do some acting?"

Bonnie gasped as he rolled over on top of her and roughly kissed her. One of the men at the fire yelled and pointed their way. Calum raised his head to look at the man in mock anger. Then he made a big deal of trying to lift his blanket up to screen them. "You two, move and get the children over behind the rocks. Stay down but be ready."

Cautiously Bonnie used the raised blanket as cover and took boy and rifle behind the tree and below the rock. The woman quickly copied her actions.

Bonnie looked back to see Calum doing energetic push-ups and covered her mouth to smother a giggle. At the noise, she saw the gleam of his teeth and a wink in her direction. As he continued, the men still at the campfire began to whoop. Bonnie heard his heavy breathing and felt her stomach clinching in rhythm and her breath coming in answering pants. As soon as he stopped she sighed in disappointment. Shaking, she took the safety off the rifle and placed it on the lower edge of the big rock.

As she watched, the two troopers by the fire suddenly rose and clubbed the two from the wagon party. She fought the urge to climb out from behind the rock, but she saw Calum's men quickly and quietly tie and gag the thieves. Calum rose and disappeared.

Behind the wagons she heard an oath, a grunt and a single gunshot. When she thought she could stand the waiting no longer. Calum appeared with the two troopers who had gone around the wagon. They emerged with one of the bearded thieves trussed like the beef over the fire and being carried the same way. They dropped their burden on top of the ones already there. Someone in the pile grunted.

Bonnie sprang from behind the rock, putting the safety back on the gun as she ran. "You're all right?" she asked, breathlessly running into his arms. "What about Shawn and Ian?"

As if conjured by their names, the two walked in prodding the two problem soldiers, Tiller and Clarence, in front of them. The drunken soldiers had their hands tied behind their backs. They glared at the Lieutenant and the woman clapping her hands beside him.

"We heard a shot, Lieutenant?" one of the troopers said.

"Their leader pulled a gun on my men so I had to shoot him. I wanted to take him into headquarters and let them sweat information from him, but hopefully one of these three can give us answers."

Calum stood in front of the staggering drunks. "You two traitors will be cashiered out of the army if I have anything to say about it. You were willing to betray your comrades for a jug of whiskey and a chance to rape two helpless women." Tiller started to say something about Bonnie and Calum slugged him.

"Tie these men in the second wagon for tonight. We have to wait for our other men to report, but it should be soon. Then we have to get in motion."

Calum walked over to cut some of the beef still dripping over the flames. Bonnie followed him over and he cut her a piece of meat and handed it to her on the tip of his knife. "I'm sorry, I couldn't eat earlier. Ever since you told me about the repeating rifles, I've been imagining the men who would die if they were traded into the hands of our enemies."

Bonnie poured a cup of coffee, took a sip of the bitter liquid and handed it to the handsome man beside her. She raised her hands to rub her bare arms, making the fringe stir over them.

"I'm going to hate when we get you back into regular clothes. You make such a beautiful Indian."

Bonnie dimpled and blushed before him.

"When we get back to headquarters, you and I are going to have a long talk," he said with a deep, gravelly voice.

"Are you going to sweat the answers out of me?"

Suddenly the Indian scouts rode up on horseback, shouting. "Big hunting. Heard your shot."

"Had to shoot. Anyone coming?"

The scout shook his head and Bonnie was surprised to see both men look happy. For the first time, she noticed the six Indian ponies behind them.

CHAPTER FIFTY-ONE

"My men. They each took a jug. Said they'd left it by the trail for the Indians who had been following us."

General Crook stared incredulously at the young officer before him. Apparently with six men and two Indian scouts, he had rescued one wagon train, recovered two white women captives, and captured the largest gun runner supplying repeating rifles to the warring tribes.

"You say 'my men.' You're telling me those Indian Scouts didn't drink the whiskey but left it to lure a Sioux war party to get drunk. Where are they?" he paused, then interrupted Calum's answer. "The scouts thought of the plan themselves."

"All six dead. Yes, it was their plan. They had helped us earlier when we left the Shoshoni camp to rout a band of raiding Blackfeet. Anyway, we rode the captured horses so we could use our mounts to pull the wagons. It wasn't easy, but we knew we didn't have much time to get back and the oxen were too slow," Calum answered. "We turned all the cattle loose."

The General paced back to stare out of the window. The two wagons were being unloaded. From one wagon two young troopers were helping down a woman with a small boy and a new baby. She looked better than most of the women recovered from captivity, but she still had that bitter, defeated look. But it was the woman dropping down from the tall brown horse that drew his attention. She petted the big mare and her fuzzy colt and then moved to the first wagon to help unhook the Calvary horses and turn them over to two of the troopers from this strange mission.

The tall, slender woman had all his troops gawking as she strode back and forth to help the men. She looked anything but defeated. They were unloading the second wagon and she sent them with a wrapped beef toward the kitchen and then stood toe-to-toe with the two troopers whom the Lieutenant was accusing of treason. When one made some remark she didn't like, she reached out and gave the man a stinging slap.

In astonishment, he saw her turn to stare in the window at him. He pulled back when he thought he saw her eyes shooting sparks his way. "And that is the young woman the Wimberley party were so worried about?"

Calum stepped up to the window and stared out at her. "Yes, that is Mrs. Bonnie Magee Micheals, the woman I hope to marry. With your permission, I'd love to introduce you."

Without waiting for an answer he opened the door and the girl bounded up the steps into the man's arms.

"And you were a captive of Chief Washakie?"

"Yes, because he needed a white woman to comfort his wife, Half-Moon, while she was dying. There was another white woman in the camp, but she refused to go near her. You have to understand that she had been through a lot and confused the Indians who now held her in gentle captivity with those who originally killed her family and took her captive."

"Gentle Captivity?"

Bonnie smiled. "They were kind to me. The Chief made sure I was protected and safe. His wife was actually a white woman and they had lived together for twenty years before her death. Both were Christians and wanted someone to offer her spiritual comfort as the end."

Suddenly Bonnie rose, unable to sit and answer another question. "Please, I'm sorry, but I need to take a break. It has been such a long and tedious journey."

The General sprang to his feet and stared at the girl, apologizing as he did so. He walked to the door and as he opened it a woman stepped back. Bonnie exchanged a smile with Calum. Clearly the woman had been listening to every word. "Mary, could you please escort Miss Magee…"

"Mrs. Micheals." Bonnie made a deep and graceful curtsy to the amazed man and then beamed at the curious woman staring at her. "Good-day Mrs. Crook," she curtsied again and the woman waved an arm to usher her through the door.

"I'm sorry, but we don't visit the latrines, they are for the troops only. I have a chair and the Indian girl empties it each day."

Bonnie ducked behind the screen in the bedroom without any further civilities. As she emerged, she caught a glimpse of herself in the mirror and laughed. "My goodness, no wonder Mr. Douglas thought I was an Indian. I do look the part." She rubbed at her dusty face with her hand and stopped to look at the shocked woman.

"It has been three days since I last had a chance to bathe and so much has happened."

The woman threw up her hands and said, "Of course, I will have Mini draw you a bath immediately."

"Mrs. Crook," Bonnie raised her brows and turned to look at her lovely fringed dress one last time. "Do you think anyone would have something that would fit me? I really had a very sensible traveling dress but the Indians took it away."

"They took your clothes," she said with a touch of frost.

"Yes, and gave me this to wear instead. I need, well, I need everything."

"Were you ..." the woman asked, wide-eyed.

Bonnie shook her head. "No, I was treated honorably. The women just took my clothes and gave me this to wear."

"I see. Excuse me," she bowed out of the room and Bonnie stood at the mirror and began to unbraid her long hair, dropping the beaded leather ties onto the shiny dresser. The girl who entered frowned at her and Bonnie wasn't surprised. The portable hip bath was covered with dust and the poor girl had to make four trips to get enough water to fill it. Then Bonnie requested soap and hot water before it was too full. She disrobed completely and sank into the water as soon as the girl left.

She had scrubbed until her skin was pink and her hair clean before the plump Mrs. Crook returned with a variety of garments for her surprising guest.

Bonnie sat shyly in the tub but it was clear Mrs. Crook was not going to grant her any more privacy. Bonnie rose as gracefully as she could, wrapping herself in a towel so quickly she doubted the studious woman could have seen all her birthmarks.

The underwear was difficult. Bonnie determined to wash out her old ones and save them to wear later. She dropped them into the tub and then pulled on the split crotch white ones. Claire would have known the name for the ugly garment but Bonnie was just grateful there was a string that she could tighten enough to keep them from dropping off.

The chemise was part of the petticoat and came over her head but she had to leave the top partially unlaced with her bosom spilling out above the top to get it over her chest. She tried to imagine the woman who owned these disproportionate garments.

Next came the dresses. She tried, but the first dress belonged to the same flat chested creature and she struggled back out of it before she split a seam.

The next was a black widow's crepe for a much stouter figure but at least it fit over her chest. The extra fullness in the skirt let it drop down farther over her flat stomach so the waist band circled her now slender hips. She tugged it down as far as she could, however the bottom hem didn't come close to reaching her ankles and revealed a broad swath of the rather plain petticoat below.

There were no shoes so Bonnie pounded the dusty moccasins before slipping them back on. The toes only showed if she took wide strides. She decided to take mincing steps. Dressed, she was afraid to look in the mirror.

"May I borrow your comb?"

The woman looked indignant. Bonnie took the time while she was reaching a decision to suds out her own underwear and wrap them in the towel to press dry.

She took the reluctantly offered black comb. Without considering if she was being offensive, she dipped it under the soapy water to wash the white scaly dust and hair away. Sitting in the vacated chair she began to work her way through her own long, now wavy strands.

As she did, she smiled, remembering how often her mother and sisters had worked out her tangles for her. For that matter, so had Claire and Mother Wimberley. Even the Indian women had combed and braided it. But not this stiffly proper General's wife.

Bonnie decided to make another attempt. She stared across to where the woman sat on the edge of her bed. "Thank you for being so gracious. I feel so much better after that lovely bath. Please thank Mini for me."

"Thank Mini, good heavens. That little savage probably spat in the water. It's a miracle she hasn't stabbed me in my sleep. George insists it's customary for the staff to include the natives, but at times she looks at me so. It gives me the willies."

Bonnie held her tongue and moved the comb to the other side of her head to start again untangling. "You know the woman I just came in with. Stella Jamison, I believe is her name. She would make an excellent maid."

"The white captive?"

"Yes, the one with the new baby and small child. She was a minister's daughter you know, and married to a preacher before he was killed by the Indians. I know she hates and fears all the natives herself. And she has suffered, don't you know." Bonnie said the last with a whisper and raised brows.

"Oh," Mrs. Crook said.

Bonnie took her time, separating and twisting different strands to loop and form a more elegant hairstyle, trying to guess what Claire would have done if she had been there. Mrs. Crook was very complimentary of the effect and offered Bonnie some of her toilet water. Bonnie hesitated since the woman reeked of lilacs but took and dabbed a drop at her throat and behind each ear.

Satisfied that it was the best she could accomplish, she followed the woman out of the bedroom, through a sparse parlor, and into the dining room. Mrs. Crook said she had to see if Mini had made anything edible for the General and his guests.

CHAPTER FIFTY-TWO

Bonnie stood nervously staring at the strange woman in the wavy glass of the mirror over the sideboard. Suddenly a tall man appeared behind her. She felt his eyes appraising every change and held her breath until he smiled. He leaned closer and whispered. "You are always the most striking woman. Each time I see you, you seem to be even lovelier, no matter what you wear. I can only imagine how you would look..."

Sighing, she turned toward Calum, but froze and stepped away as the cloud of fragrance warned her the General's wife was back. Three other officers and their wives or friends had been invited to join the table in honor of Calum's return. In seconds, the others began to arrive. Bonnie was grateful that they were all seated immediately and she didn't have to parade around with her petticoat exposed. The Crook's took their seats at the ends and the officers sat across from their partners with the guests staggered, man, woman, man, woman down each side. Bonnie looked up nervously to see Calum point to the correct fork.

Bowing her head, Bonnie waited for the prayer. Suddenly there was a cough and the General said a perfunctory blessing.

The General cleared his throat as they waited for the dinner to appear. "I've written up a commendation for your bravery, Lieutenant, or should I say, Major Douglas."

Calum looked embarrassed and the other men looked unsettled by the news.

Bonnie sat with her hands folded in her lap, waiting for the endless questions to resume. Instead, the Indian girl carried in the largest platter of meat Bonnie had ever seen. When she set the large roast in front of the General she saw his eyes roll and watched him nervously reach up to comb his funny, separated beard to each side. Mary was beaming with pride. Bonnie stared at Calum and they both laughed.

After the story of the ox all relaxed. "We were rather crowded and the horses were difficult to manage since none of the Indian ponies had ever been saddled before. The ox was roasted and we didn't want to leave the meat behind since we'd make Fort McPherson by evening if we pushed hard," Calum explained.

"The captives were loaded in the second wagon with the roasted meat," Bonnie added. "Well, five big men and a hot ox made an uncomfortable ride."

Everyone laughed at the image.

"They accused us of trying to cook them too, since the meat gave off heat for quite some time." Calum said.

"We ate it for dinner, breakfast and lunch. So it surprised us to have it again for supper. But thank you, it is a most delicious animal," Bonnie said.

The officer beside her spoke. "Most amusing. We heard that many travelers on the trail have been attacked lately. The people you traveled with, 'The Williams'?"

"Wimberleys," Bonnie said, suddenly uncomfortable next to the oily haired little man. "I thought they were okay and had already resumed their journey."

"Yes, they had a military escort here, so of course they arrived safely, but they were most upset about your being taken and one of their passengers being killed in a later attack."

"And a child," Mary Crook added with a sad shake of her head.

Bonnie's eyes darkened and her face paled. She raised a hand to her throat.

Calum reached a hand across the table toward her. "Mrs. Lambton was shot with an arrow. Her son died of natural causes a day later."

Bonnie crossed herself and took a deep breath.

As though it were a matter of no consequence, the obnoxious little man continued to talk. "The Wimberleys were a very pleasant couple, their lovely daughter was most charming."

Bonnie stared at the company but could only see the face of Bella sitting in the wagon talking to her son and him smiling up and babbling back.

"We were able to find her grave the next day on the way to rescue you. Ian and Shawn carried the body and helped bury him in her arms," Calum said.

Bonnie looked up and smiled sadly. "Thank you for that extraordinary kindness, Lieutenant."

General Crook spoke from his end of the table. "Remarkable man, your Mr. Wimberley. They were restocked and ready to leave the next day when a second group of five wagons arrived. They had also been attacked, two of their teams stolen and one of the wagons burned. Mr. Wimberley and those boys of his rebuilt the burned wagon in one day. I've never seen anything like it."

The other officer finally joined the conversation. "All of them left together that way, don't you see. Both trains united. Although still, fifteen is a small group with so many Indians about."

"When was that?" Bonnie asked.

"Day before yesterday," he answered. "They were friends of yours?

"The dearest. Claire is one of my closest friends and the three children are not Wimberleys, but McKinneys. Claire and I were taking them to meet their sister Lynne in Ogden. We told her mid-September."

"That sounds ambitious, doubt it can be done," the General said.

"Two days," Bonnie spoke, ignoring him. "I could ride Brown Bess and catch up with them tomorrow. This is wonderful news."

"You can't think you can leave here alone? Didn't you hear what happened to the last two wagon trains? One of your party was murdered by Indians just days from this outpost," Calum's voice grew angrier and louder as he talked.

Bonnie looked up at him but he saw her eyes darken in resistance. Mrs. Crook tutted at him and Calum apologized to his host but glared at the girl who meekly bowed her head in submission.

As all rose from the table, Bonnie stood, leaning against the back of her chair.

"I am sorry, but after such a rich meal, I find I am exhausted. Do you know where I am to sleep?"

"We have an apartment for stranded travelers and rescued settlers. Lieutenant Douglas can escort you there." General Crook bowed over her hand as Bonnie curtsied.

Bonnie felt the strange tickle of his beard and resisted the urge to giggle at the ridiculous moment. Did the man not recognize a poor Irish factory girl when he saw one? Maybe she had channeled Claire too well.

Calum gallantly held out his arm and Bonnie accepted it, looking back to her hostess. "I had some things I left in your room."

The little Indian girl ran up and bowed before her and Bonnie put a hand on the young girl's head as she took the bundled dress and damp garments. "Thank you, Mini."

Feeling regal despite her borrowed dress Bonnie smiled at the company as Calum said goodnight.

General Crook called after them, "We'll take care of the trials in the morning, should be able to shoot the lot by noon."

Calum picked up his hat and settled it on his head. "I'll be there. Will you need Mrs. Micheals to testify?"

"I shouldn't think so, but you will be available madam, if we do?"

Bonnie nodded, and together the handsome couple escaped into the night.

They strolled across the porch, Calum raising a hand to acknowledge salutes as they passed soldiers in the night. After the second of the long buildings there was an alley running between the barracks and the supply store. Bonnie heard a woman's giggle in the night and shuddered. The world wasn't so different here than the poor tenements in Boston. People like the General and his wife lived in comfortable isolation while the poor and desperate did whatever they could to survive. She thought of the McPherson girls.

At the next alley Calum pulled her into the empty darkness. Bonnie felt her heart thud with her panic. Silently she begged him not to do this. If he did want to take her against the side of the building like one of the whores, would she have the courage to refuse him?

Calum raised his hands to rest against her bared throat, feeling the heavy pulse in her neck. Did she feel the same desire he did, or was it fear again? Unable to resist, he bent his head and gently kissed her.

Bonnie raised her own hands to tug at his yet moaned in surrender at his tenderness. Trembling she let him pull her into his arms, felt the wonderful thrill of his excited body pressed against her own. Was that what the mysterious undergarment was for, this sort of wild coupling in the shadows?

"Darling," he growled against her mouth. "I don't want to take you to that room of lost souls."

Bonnie tried to breathe, fought to regain her self-control. "Lost souls?"

"That's what the men call it, the room with the women who have been rescued. Many are mad from what was done to them. Not always by Indians. There are other men like our thieves and gun-runners. Desperate men who will do desperate things to helpless women and children."

"To children?"

He felt her pull away, heard the shock and anger in her voice. Gently he tugged, trying to bring her back into his embrace.

"Did I mention how delightful you are in widows' weeds?"

Bonnie remembered the tremor she had felt when she pulled the black dress on and thought the same thought. Was it possible that she was already a widow? What if she never saw Tarn again, never knew if she had a living husband? Or, horrors, what if she did see him? What would she do then?

"Tis a borrowed dress. I am still married to another man."

"Not here, not now, not in this place. You could just take up your maiden name. Then you would be free to wed again, to marry the one you love."

Hungrily he pulled her into his arms, reached up between their bodies to trace the pale whiteness of her lovely breasts beneath the thin gauze of the garment. He felt her nipples harden at his touch and growled. "Come to my room tonight Bonnie. I want to make love to you. You're not an untried girl. I know you want me too."

He leaned down to kiss her and she shocked them both by pushing him away and rushing out of the alley and up onto the boardwalk. A man made a lewd call and then backed up and saluted as the frustrated Lieutenant emerged from the shadows.

Without another word he escorted her to the women's apartment. A guard saluted and backed to open the door. Calum stood there, heard the crazed moans and cries of the women and children inside. In the flickering light of a lamp, he looked at Bonnie's frightened face. "I will see you in the morning, Mrs. Micheals. Good-night."

Bonnie reached out a hand to grip his, horror at what she might find inside making her regret her choice for a moment. Then she straightened up and brought his hand to her lips. "Try to forgive me. I can't become one of those creatures of the night. Try to understand."

For a minute he fought the urge to jerk his hand away, then from afar he heard the same soldier call to a different woman and heard her answering giggle.

Calum took off his hat and held it up as he leaned forward to shield her as they softly kissed goodnight.

CHAPTER FIFTY-THREE

Into the shadowed light of the room full of fear Bonnie stepped, gathering her courage with each step. She began by picking up the lantern and walking down the row of straw mats, seeing to the needs of anyone who was crying. In the corner she found her new friend and her small children.

She squatted down beside her and welcomed the weight of the little boy rushing into her arms. She laughed as he hugged her neck tightly. The strange sound startled the room into silence.

"I'd worried about you. Afraid the Indians or some man had grabbed you."

Bonnie extended her hand to pat the frightened woman's hand. "No, quite the contrary. I've just come from supper with the General and his wife."

"Go on, you don't need to lie. What did you do? You look different."

Bonnie laughed again the sound loud in the breathless silence surrounding her. "It's the truth. She let me take a bath and found these clothes, though I don't think much of them. What do you think of the fancy hair? I did it myself."

The woman didn't answer and Bonnie sat down beside her and moved her hand to touch the downy head of her baby who was suckling. "He has a lusty appetite. Will be as tall as your other son in no time."

"Draining me dry."

"Did you have anything to eat or drink for supper?"

"Oh yes, they brought us all a big plate with beef and corn. I had a cup of water but I am right parched."

Bonnie pried the little boy from her arms and left him with his mother, leaving the lantern with her as she walked to the front and found the bucket of clean water on the table. She drank a dipper of it first, then carried it back, stopping to share a drink with two women along the way before returning to her new friend. She gave the boy a drink first, and then handed the woman a full dipper.

After the second cup full, the woman returned it. "It don't look so bad from behind, but it hides too much of your face in the front."

Bonnie raised a hand and patted her hair. "One of the women in our wagon train wore hers this way, I just thought I'd try it when I got mine unbraided and washed. Turn around and I'll take your braids out as well."

A woman scurried from the shadow toward the bucket and Bonnie handed her a dipper of water. The woman drank, making little gasping sounds with each swallow. "Good and sweet, isn't it?" Bonnie asked.

The woman nodded then started to take the bucket. Bonnie reclaimed it and carried it back to the table, again sharing a drink with children on the other side of the room.

When she returned to the corner, the gasping woman was still there along with two of the older children, clustered around the lantern on the floor like moths around a flame. Bonnie cautiously threaded her way past without brushing the lantern and took a seat against the wall so she could reach her new friend's hair.

As she loosened the thin braids, she hummed, the words of the tune forgotten. The woman in front of her relaxed with the motion of Bonnie's fingers on her head and began to hum the tune as well. One of the women on the cot on the other side began to hum. Finally a voice nearer the front of the room began to softly sing the words of *"Praise God from whom all blessings flow,"* and other voices joined in.

Bonnie ran her fingers through the unbound hair to words from another chorus. Bonnie whispered. "I think the General's wife might need a new maid. I recommended you to her. I wasn't sure of your name, was it Stella?"

Bonnie heard a woman in the dark whimper and the voices begin to falter. Boldly she sang the old tune, wishing her voice were sweet and high like Lynne's or as soft and even as Claire's. It didn't matter, the words had the right effect.

My times of sorrow and of joy,
Great God, are in thy hand;

Other voices in the dark fumbled around the words and joined in with,

My choicest comforts come from thee,
and go at thy command."

When they reached the end, Bonnie started a new song before the fear could return. Even the children knew the words to *Rock of Ages*. As more and more voices joined in the woman in front of her answered, "Yeah, Stella Jamison."

"Good, that's what I thought you said. What were your son's names?"

"Sean and David, my eldest was named Sean," her voice broke on the word and Bonnie patted her shoulder.

"My best friend lost a brother named Sean. What are you going to call the new boy?" Bonnie asked. "For when he's baptized?"

The child had finally stopped nursing and as he rolled away, a white bubble of milk showed on his pursed mouth. Stella's hand shook as she looked at her child. "What name do you think?"

"John, he looks like a little Johnny to me."

The woman nodded and while she was distracted Bonnie leaned forward and touched the woman's moccasin. "Do you still have my knife in your shoe? I need to see if I can let out the hem on this dress."

Confused, the woman shook her head and Bonnie leaned forward and removed the dangerous looking Bowie knife. There was a gasp and one of the children drew back. Holding the knife carefully, Bonnie flipped up the edge of her skirt and pricked the thread in the hem. Silently she slid the knife into her own shoe and carefully pulled the thread from the cloth while humming again.

As Stella lay down with her children, others began to move back into the shadows, no longer crying as Stella sang softly the words for, *When Johnny Comes Marching Home.* Other women joined in, singing it like a lullaby to their children.

Calum hadn't reached his quarters when thoughts of Bonnie's face pulled him back. Maybe he could convince her to use his bed while he slept in the outer room. He shook his head at the nonsense. He knew he wanted to try to convince her to join him. Perhaps if he talked marriage again, she would come around.

When he reached the women's quarters he heard the guard humming a hymn as he approached. The man abruptly stood at attention. The man saluted, but before he could ask what he needed, Calum held up his hand. In the dark instead of whimpers and cries the men smiled as they heard the words of an old song every soldier knew. It was Bonnie, there was something almost magical about her ability to comfort others.

In place of the heavy lust he had walked over with, he walked back with a heart beating with a deeper love and a bottomless need to claim this woman for his own.

◇◇◇

In the early hours before dawn, Bonnie searched her bundle of clothes and was thrilled to not only find her underwear, but her precious bag of coins. She used the last of the darkness to wrap and bind her full breasts and then worked the slip and dress back on. She rearranged her hair that was mussed from sleeping into its usual loose bun on top.

After searching through the bag of clothes the army had provided for the rescued women, she finally found something suitable for Stella to wear.

As breakfast was served, she made a point of trying to talk to each of the survivors, introducing herself and Stella and asking each for a name.

She turned and asked the soldier who had brought the morning food. "Can we walk around outside, it seems a beautiful day?"

He stared at the tall woman, surprised by the question. "I think so, I guess I'll need to ask."

Bonnie smiled, "Of course we can, I'm sorry for being so silly. It's just children need sunshine and I wanted to walk my friend Stella over to the General's quarters. I promised I would present her and her children to Mary Crook."

The soldier stood aside and Bonnie led the way, encouraging the women out the door and into the courtyard of the large complex of barracks. Everyone stood in a frightened huddle until Bonnie spotted the corral and the head of a tall brown horse. Laughing, she asked if anyone would like to go see her giant horse. Afterwards, she led her party of hen and chicks around the area between the big train tracks and the buildings.

By the time they returned, they had attracted quite a lot of attention. When they passed by the Indian agent's headquarters and spotted an Indian one of the women started to cry and a couple of women began to whimper. Bonnie took the woman by the hand and talked to her all the way back to the barracks until the whimpering stopped.

While Mary talked at the dining room table with Stella, Bonnie slipped to stand by the door into the general's office, eavesdropping as his wife had the day before. She wanted to hear the arguments and testimony. Surprised, she raised her hand to her heart as she heard Calum's deep voice making accusations.

Although she had been busy with the women last night, when all were quiet and asleep she had tossed and turned. The torture came from reliving the press of his lips, the intoxicating feel of his arousal against her in the dark. She knew saying no to him had been the right answer, but her body had its own arguments to make. If he asked again, she wasn't sure she would have the strength to say no.

Suddenly she heard excited voices from the military court inside and the General's announcement. She felt surprised at how blessedly free and relaxed she felt on hearing the verdict. Execution for all had been set for the following morning.

She looked on in amazement as Mrs. Crook led Stella into the kitchen, talking about what she needed from her. Mini stood holding the baby in her arms and the hand of the small child. She looked worried, clearly aware that she was being replaced.

When the General's wife emerged, Bonnie smiled and walked up to do some convincing. When she left with Stella, Mrs. Crook had boasted that George would be no problem. It was clear as head of the western division his wife needed more servants than the other officers.

CHAPTER FIFTY-FOUR

Back at the women's quarters, Bonnie demanded to meet with whoever was in charge of the survivors. A crusty old sergeant arrived and Bonnie asked him to explain what the army was doing to aid and provide for the comfort of these women and children. The man had blustered and fumed, but when he left, Bonnie had a table, paper, and pen and ink, as well as two chairs.

All afternoon she sat talking to a woman one on one, asking questions about her name, her family, her point of origin. Carefully she recorded each response. It was difficult at first, but the act of writing down the answer made the women sit up a little straighter, open up a little more. By late afternoon, the women were all sitting on the cots in small groups talking or out on the wide boardwalk as they watched the children play tag in the dust beyond.

Although all had been abused and suffered the tragedy and horror of losing loved ones, there was something truly liberating at being able to talk about it at long last. The fact that the other women had suffered the same or worse fates, seemed to give each woman courage.

There were two more to interview, although one woman who had remained in the room all day seemed almost catatonic. Bonnie despaired of being able to reach what was left of the poor woman's mind.

Later, when the sergeant returned with Calum in tow, Bonnie called Stella and explained the information needed. She left the woman in charge of interviewing the next survivor. The look on the woman's face as she was placed in charge was amazing. Stella called and the woman she had just been talking to came forward to take Stella's children to watch, her back straightening a little too as she took them.

◇◇◇

"Mrs. Micheals, the sergeant has brought it to my attention that you've been intruding in army matters and have set yourself up in charge of these women he has been…"

The sergeant who had been staring at the talking women with disbelief, turned from the children playing tag to look at the tall woman in black who had given him such a blistering this morning. Gruffly he interrupted, reaching out a big paw toward her. Bonnie stared at him, and then took his hand to shake. "Ma'am, ma'am…" He clearly was speechless, just shaking her hand. Bonnie smiled and nodded, "You are welcome sergeant. Now do you think you could find some suitable clothes for these little children, and perhaps some toy or ball for them to play with?"

"Yes, ma'am, yes, right away, ma'am." He saluted her as he backed off the porch.

Calum stared at Bonnie who turned back to him, her chin a little higher, her hands set firmly on her hips in case he wanted to argue further. He noted the yellow sparkles in her hazel eyes and laughed.

"It's a damn fine thing they don't let women in the army. You would all want to give orders and be saluted all the time."

Bonnie smiled and let her hands relax. "Perhaps someday they will come to their senses and do that. Then maybe we can do away with all this war and suffering."

She looked back inside, watched the transformed Stella gently asking the woman beside her questions, stopping to commiserate when the woman looked ready to cry. Just as Bonnie had done earlier, she wrote everything down that the woman told her and that woman snuffled back her tears, her eyes widening.

Bonnie stepped into the doorway. "When you finish the interviews, hand the papers to the sergeant when he returns. And Stella, do you think you could lead the women in a prayer service before supper tonight?"

Stella nodded and Bonnie turned, linking her hand in the crook of Calum's elbow as he escorted where she led him. Back at the corral they both watched the little red colt scurry around his mother.

"Did you only come to scold me?" she asked, rolling her now light brown eyes toward him.

As they stood there, the tall mare walked over and extended her head to be petted. Satisfied Bonnie hadn't brought a treat, she walked away, swishing her tail. Bonnie barely got to touch the soft baby before he scampered after his mother.

Aware that they were being watched but unable to resist her, Calum slipped an arm around her beautiful, strong back. "I came to report on our trial. The military court found them all guilty. They face a firing squad in the morning."

"Even your men?" Bonnie asked, already knowing the answer and glad of it.

"Yes," Calum sighed. "It's what they deserve, but some of the men in the platoon are upset by it, thinking death is a pretty stiff penalty for getting drunk."

"They didn't just get drunk. They planned to rape me and Stella, perhaps shoot their own comrades, and help those gun runners escape."

He caught her waving arms and pulled her hands between his own. "I know darling, I know. But you don't have to be afraid any longer. In the morning they will face the firing squad and it will all be over."

Bonnie tried to smile up at him, but in her heart she knew it would not be over until she saw their bloody bodies. The stories the women had shared today filled her with dread for her friends traveling on without her.

"Calum, I still need to leave with the next wagon train through here. I have friends who need me, children who are counting on me to help protect them. I cannot stay here any longer."

Calum was called back to his duties and Bonnie entered the women's quarters just as Stella finished her prayer. All the women watched as a pair of soldiers carried in a kettle and bowls. Only after the women were served and the men departed did Bonnie move over to take Stella's position and sit down.

Bonnie ate the soup, listened as Stella recounted the last poor soul's trials and reported she had handed everything over to the sergeant.

"Good, now the army will be able to contact any family members and help reunite them with these brave women. Hopefully now we've lanced the boil, it should drain some of the poison away. With time and help, maybe it will let them move forward in life. They may not look it, but most are young women."

Stella stared at her, looked away. Then lifted up her small son and looked back. "What about you? Are you ever going to tell your story? Heal yourself?"

◇◇◇

When Calum entered his quarters, he had expected some catastrophe, not his blustery sergeant wiping his eyes and nose.

"The men said you need to see me? Sergeant, are you crying?"

The ugly brute rolled his eyes, got up and held the chair for the Lieutenant. He gave another honk into his handkerchief and then walked over to sit in the other chair. "Think it's easy, you read them."

Calum sat and picked up the first record which already had a pool of ink where the big baby's tears had struck the paper. Scoffing, he spread them out, saw all were in the same hand but one. The writing was tight and stiff, the stories all began the same: name, relatives/friends, place originally from, where attacked, what happened. All but one he knew had been recorded by Bonnie.

After he put the last letter down, Calum wiped his eyes, blew his nose and rose unsteadily. "Damn it, Sergeant, where the hell are my papers and writing materials."

Calum stomped across the compound, blaming the waning light for his poor eye-sight. Twice he snuffled and spat, then coughed to swallow the rest. As he bounded up onto the boardwalk outside the women's quarters he saw the young guard pacing nervously.

"Go on trooper. Take your break. I'll guard them until you return."

The young man nodded and sprinted toward the canteen, not the outhouse. Calum turned toward the closed door and stopped, his heart in his throat as he heard the trembling voice inside.

◇◇◇

"Today, you women, you brave survivors, made the first difficult step on your journey toward recovery. As Stella just told me, it is time I tell you my story." She looked to her new friend who now traded the three year old for the fussing baby.

"I have been more fortunate than most of you. I have loving parents, four sisters and three brothers. Two brothers, Ian and Shawn are troopers posted here. I have two friends who are as near and dear as sisters to me. Although like many of you, I was taken by the Indians, I was not tortured or raped."

The group who had been focused before began to mumble angrily and Bonnie cleared her throat and raised her voice to continue. "Not by the Indians, but I was led up the garden path by a man I loved and trusted. When I picked myself up from the ground, I realized I was ruined for any decent man."

The room was dark except for the lamp on the table and Bonnie stood above it, her face ghoulish in the shadowed light. "Later, I realized I was in the family way. I told my parents what he had done, they told the magistrate, and Tarn Micheals married me."

"In Boston, where I'm from, the men have been out of work and desperate for the most part. It has been hard on my family too. My Da couldn't get work, so I went to work in the mills. My Da had a problem with the drink. He would sometimes beat Mum and take all our money to the pub. But I knew Da loved Mum. So when Tarn did the same to me, slapped me about and took the money I earned at the Mill, I accepted it."

Bonnie's face was red, her voice strained. One of the women in the back shouted, "Write it down, you there, put that baby down and write it."

Bonnie smiled and turned to pat Stella's shoulder. "No, it's all right," she shook her head and Stella raised the baby a little to burp.

"Go on," a woman with two little girls said. Bonnie stared at them, remembering the terrible things this woman had shared today.

"When I was far along, Tarn took up with another woman. When I complained, he beat me," her voice faltered, "so badly. I lost the baby. When my father went to the law again, Tarn fled and headed west."

"He's still out there, waiting?" a woman asked.

Bonnie straightened her shoulders and held her head high. "If he is, I'm prepared to shoot him on sight."

The women cheered. Standing on the other side of the door the Lieutenant smiled.

"I just want you to know. If we stand together, we can help each other. We all have stories, things that want to fill our minds with dark and tortured thoughts. If we sit idly, brooding, looking back and thinking only of those things, we are lost. Tomorrow we will change that. 'Idle hands are the devil's workshop.' We will ask for work. Tonight, we will pray."

Calum turned as the guard returned to his post. They heard the women inside begin to sing. Saluting, the men moved apart.

What he had heard helped him understand her fear of intimacy with him, but it didn't explain why she had thrown her husband up as a barrier between them. If the man were such a devil, why did she stay married to him? Surely desertion would be grounds for divorce in Massachusetts. Perhaps it wasn't the missing Mr. Micheals, maybe she just didn't want him.

Calum walked on toward the General's quarters, shaking his head. Reluctant or not, he had no doubt her desire was coursing as hotly as his own. Later, he would call on Mrs. Bonnie Micheals and try a little persuasion. First he was going to try to help her with her crusade for the other women. If he could get his commander and his wife to read these records, he knew they would want to help. If he had that pair working on the problem, he had no doubt it would get solved. Then Bonnie could return her focus to him.

CHAPTER FIFTY-FIVE

Calum sat at the General's desk, addressing another envelope. As the General read them, Calum wrote letters addressed to families/friends of and filled in the woman's name, sending it to their original address. Mary Crook hovered behind him, taking the documents as soon as Calum finished with them.

Suddenly the men heard the distant sound of gunfire. There was the answering fire of several guns in answer. As the men jumped up and ran out, Mary sat down at the desk and continued the task.

Calum and the General stood over the bleeding soldier. The General called for men to carry the wounded man to the surgery.

Calum swore at the stupid waste. This was the same recruit who had complained the loudest about the unfairness of the trial. "He was a friend of Clarence. Thought he'd been given a raw deal, that Tiller was the only one at fault. Apparently he made the mistake of trying to help Clarence escape."

Inside the cell they found the second body, Clarence. This one was dead, shot through the head. No doubt with the gun the fool had smuggled in for his friend. "If I had to guess, the bleeding boy smuggled the gun to Clarence. When Tiller tried to grab it from him, the boy was shot accidentally," Calum said.

"And then Tiller shot the protesting Clarence," the General added. "A vicious cowardly villain, this man Tiller."

In the second cell they faced two chained bearded men angrily staring at them. How had the lead gun smuggler managed to be unchained? Worse, why had Tiller helped him escape? "Can anyone explain to me why these men were chained but the most dangerous one was not?" General Crook demanded.

A frightened young man spoke up. "The old man complained of feeling dizzy when we locked them up. He fainted and we just laid him out on the cot and locked the cell. With the door locked and a guard on duty, we figured he'd be safe enough," the soldier who had guarded earlier explained. "He was still unconscious when my relief arrived, the wounded man they just took away."

"Tiller was the last man we recruited. I added him in St. Louis, Sir. He came in as a volunteer when we camped outside town. Asked if he could join up to go kill Indians?"

"Don't blame yourself man, that's what you were sent for, to find more men to fight this bloody war."

Several of the men who had gathered outside the jail were Calum's own. When they carried out Clarence's body, Ian said to Shawn, "Poor Clarence, he didn't deserve that. I know he was obsessed with Bonnie, but he would never have done any of this without Tiller's egging him on and keeping him drunk."

Shawn answered, "Wasn't St. Louis the place where Bonnie's oxen were stolen."

Calum heard them and nodded to the worried boys. "Maybe Tiller was a plant among the troops to help the gun-smuggler. Knowing where the army was moving helped him elude the troops."

Calum looked at his commander, the one man out of uniform. "It's your call General, should we pursue tonight or wait until daylight? They could be getting away?"

"Or waiting in ambush for whoever rides after them. Do you know how they're armed?"

The guard who had been supplying most of the information answered. "They have the guard's rifle and the dead soldier's handgun."

"What about changing out our rifles tonight like we talked about?" Calum asked.

"Good enough, I was waiting on word from headquarters. But no sense letting the Indians and renegades be better armed than us when we have cases of Henrys sitting with the quartermaster," General Crook answered. He started to walk away and then turned back.

"Start the chase bright and early in the morning. Sergeant call every man to assembly. Lieutenant Douglas, exchange the guns but make sure the quartermaster records all serial numbers. Those for the new guns as well as the old."

"Yes sir, General. With your permission sir, can we test them at dawn?" Calum asked.

"Fine, make sure the men clean and check them out tonight. Guess a volley is a good enough way to sound reveille. If you want to stand the two prisoners up for target practice, be my guest."

"I'd rather leave that detail up to you, General. Don't want them so tattered their kin folk won't know them," Calum answered.

While the men were hauling out the rifles and the angry quartermaster was setting up to record numbers, Calum ran back to the women's quarters. The guard grinned at the tall Lieutenant but said nothing as the man knocked on the door. Once again the door opened to the voices of women and children singing hymns.

"Holding revival every night?" he asked.

Bonnie came to the door and the baffled woman who had opened it moved away without answering. Bonnie put a hand on the door as though to hold it closed and Calum touched her hand to pull her outside. She drew it back as though burned by his touch.

Annoyed, he spoke more brusquely than he intended. "I need to talk to you about the gun fire earlier."

Bonnie slipped through the door and they both walked toward the shadows without touching.

"Tiller and Monroe have escaped. One soldier was killed, another badly wounded during the escape," Calum said rapidly.

Suddenly Bonnie grabbed at his hands. "Shawn and Ian?"

"Both are safe. We're issuing the new rifles to my men tonight, all the others tomorrow."

"Why tonight? Who is Monroe?"

"He's the leader of the gun smugglers. We're going after them in the morning."

"My brothers too?"

Calum nodded, swept her off her feet and around the corner of the building. He set her down when he had her in the dark beside him. "I couldn't leave with things the way they are between us. I hope you know how I feel about you. I need to hear…"

Bonnie put her slender fingers over his lips to hush him. He felt her trembling emotion in her cool touch and held his breath waiting for her to speak.

"I'm leaving in the morning with the new wagon train that's camped on the other side of the railroad tracks. There are forty-two wagons and the girl who never speaks had family come in to find her. They agreed I could ride with them and tend to her until they catch up to the oxen train my friends are on."

"But your work here, your brothers?"

"Stella will be able to minister to them, she already does. Mary Crook has agreed to use her as a cook so she can be here to help and look after the women the rest of the time. I have to go. The Wimberleys and the McKinney children need me to protect them and help see they reach Utah. You met them. I can't sleep for worrying about what's happened to them."

He broke his promise to them both in pulling her against him. When he leaned down to kiss her she didn't stop him but took his breath away with her passionate response. When he drew back, breathing heavily she ran those trembling fingers over his face, tracing the curve of each feature as though memorizing it in the dark. She cupped and ran her fingers over his ears at the last.

"I love you," she whispered. "I cannot stay and resist you any longer. I must go."

"I know it's not that damn husband you are denying me for. Why, when you could stay and marry me?"

"But I can't be your wife and I won't be your whore. I'm married, in the eyes of the state and the church. When I'm free, I'll return to you."

Furious, he pulled away and left her standing there in the dark, alone.

CHAPTER FIFTY-SIX

Bonnie saddled the Palomino Ian had been given outside Washakie's camp. She put a halter on the oversized Brown Bess and then turned to her brothers. It was so early, the camp still seemed asleep although both boys had told her last night that they would be up and leaving by dawn.

She had run to find them as soon as Calum stomped off last night. It seemed she was always saying goodbye to those she loved. But she didn't want them to chase the killers, maybe be wounded and shot like the soldiers last night, without a goodbye hug and kiss.

"It's your birthday tomorrow, I can't believe you're giving me your horse, I should be giving you a present." Ian would be sixteen tomorrow, Shawn had already turned fourteen. Just babies, these two brave men in their blue uniforms.

"The army replaced our mounts, since they were reported stolen by enemies. The new wagon train you'll be on will move a lot faster. You'd never be able to keep up on foot the way you could with the oxen," Ian said.

"Besides, riding that big barrel without a saddle would make you more bow-legged than me. Anyway, Bess seems busy enough minding little Clyde."

"Is that what you've named him, Shawn? I noticed you both playing with him the other day."

From the barracks they heard the bugle and the boys kissed her cheeks and disappeared.

Calum led his troop of twenty men with the same two Indian Scouts who had proven themselves on their last foray. It didn't sit well with him that he now had two men dead, another wounded, and one man a convicted traitor and murderer. Either this Indian war was fiercer or he no longer had what it took to lead and keep his men safe. As he rode ahead to where his scouts had dismounted, he looked all around, pulling the new Henry rifle from his saddle scabbard nervously.

He needed to stay focused on his duty to the army and his men, but his mind was still on that tall, obstinate woman. One of the scouts held up horse dung and said eight hours ahead. But instead of seeing the dry droppings he visualized the hazel eyed witch with copper lights in her hair.

"Hey, Lieutenant," the other scout said.

Calum nodded, "Let's close the gap." He turned to wave the platoon back into motion.

The tracks of the two horses were plainly visible in the center of the narrow ruts of the road. The sign meant the two fugitives were determined. They had stayed in the saddle throughout the night and all day, stopping only once to water their tired animals and fill their canteens. The scouts had pointed out the imprint of one man's knee in the mud to Calum. Why not follow the wagon trail, it was a wide path? Buffalo had formed the trail, Indians had followed the animals, and now white men drove down it. The path followed near the water in the places of least resistance it had cut through the rugged land.

After waking with rifle practice at dawn, the men had saddled and ridden out with cold biscuits and beef to eat as they rode. None complained. They didn't think Clarence and Tiller deserved their sentence, but now Tiller had killed Clarence and wounded another comrade, they were ready to ride to hell to execute the tribunal's sentence.

He had been part of an army before during the war. There were three things that determined the outcome. Motivation – whoever wanted it most would fight hardest to triumph. For the moment, the men running away had to move or die. They had the advantage.

Condition – who had the best horses and food. The soldier who had packed and saddled had put most of the food in two saddlebags, and these idiots had chosen to escape on only two mounts. Most of the food was on the horses that had been abandoned. That advantage would go to his men. There were three packed mules and his men and their horses were well rested.

The third factor was weapons – if the guard could be trusted, they had the sentries rifle (a single shot Springfield) and the man's colt revolver. Two shots had been fired from it inside the jail and the holster with bullets was still around the dead man's waist.

Calum stroked the stock of the new rifle and grinned. All they had to do was not lose the trail and pursue relentlessly. Today they would gain a couple of hours, tomorrow another two. By the third, these two men were his.

Relaxing for the first time all morning, Calum's thoughts returned to Bonnie. Ever since he had first seen the striking woman she had been in his dreams. Maybe it was the two Magee lads kissing their Mum for the little ones and giving a handshake and kiss on the cheeks for their Da and Bonnie. Such a strange thing, that total respect and love for their sister.

Then he had seen her standing on the railroad platform like some statue. Tall and proud, her brown hair gleaming in the sun like it was lit with flame and those remarkable eyes, not brown, not green. He could stare into her eyes and never grow weary of them with their changing sparks of yellow and green and their unwavering honesty. Proud, practical, and principled, she was too strong for a woman. Yet she had the alluring figure of a goddess and was more woman than he had ever kissed.

Their second day out of Fort McPherson, Monroe told Tiller they had a big enough lead on any pursuers. Crossing at a shallows in the rambling river, they rode across without wetting their boots, then followed the river back until they saw advance scouts for a massive wagon train. They were nearly at the end of the train when it began to stop for lunch. The two found a place where they could cross by swimming the tired horses and splashed up and through a grove of trees. Now all they needed was to talk these fools into trading horses and giving them some food and they would be on their way.

The two men on horseback rode quickly toward the large wagon train where it had paused to water the stock and eat a midday meal. Bonnie peeked out of the canvas wagon to stare at the intruders. Immediately she jerked back inside.

As soon as she heard them ride past, she snuck out of the back of the wagon and ran to find Mr. Searle. He in turn raced to warn the wagon master that the duo were escaped army prisoners and murderers. He waited, listening to them talk pleasantly about being separated from their party and needing horses and food, and then Mr. Searle worked his way up to whisper to the wagon master.

Bonnie kept out of sight until she reached the wagon again. Beverly still slept, but each day they traveled, the girl seemed to become more curious about her surroundings and the noises. Bonnie figured they might catch up with the train that carried the Wimberleys by tomorrow and she hoped the woman would begin to interact with her parents before then. Losing her husband and children had shattered her mind but there were times when her mother spoke that she now made little monosyllabic answers.

When Bonnie heard riders again, she peeked out and saw the two men angrily riding away, their hands on their guns as the curious people resting after lunch watched their rapid progress.

She couldn't hear anything they said, but she noticed the blue coated traitor point toward the remuda of grazing horses. She didn't have to look out to know that they had noticed Brown Bess. Would they just assume someone on the train had bought the mare or suspect that she was in the caravan somewhere? What had Tiller threatened?

"You'll pay, squaw woman."

CHAPTER FIFTY-SEVEN

The troopers rode all afternoon of the second day, expecting to catch the escaped men but seeing no trace of them. The wagon trail was dry and a light hot wind blew and stirred the dust constantly. Leading the column, the lieutenant looked intense but tired. When they came upon a small train pulled by oxen, Calum was almost as excited as the Magee boys to spot the familiar twins walking beside their teams. Seated on each wagon were one of the blonde Wimberley women and riding alongside each was a man on one of the perfect bays that were the only things that looked unworn by the long trek.

Calum rode up with a big long hi-oh and watched as the weary travelers all stopped to look his way.

"What is it? More Indians?" the boys running toward him asked.

Calum grinned at the handsome boys and shook his head. "Nope, we're chasing a couple of renegades that escaped from jail." He looked past them to the second wagon where the pretty blonde was busy sponging some of the dust from her face. A small gray-eyed girl climbed over the seat beside her, the book she had been reading still in hand.

"Good afternoon ladies. I need to warn you all that we are in pursuit of some pretty desperate men. They should be looking for horses and food by now. Have you seen them?"

"Good-day to you, Lieutenant Douglas." She looked past him to see Bonnie's brothers and smiled for the first time. "Shawn and Ian,

I'm so happy to see you both looking so well. Have you any word of Bonnie? Has she been found?"

Calum sent the scouts and half his men ahead of the train to clear the area and locate a good campsite. He and the other half walked along and talked, filling in Bonnie's friends of her amazing rescue and activities since her recovery.

By the time they made camp, even the children had run out of questions. The settlers were so excited by the presence of the troopers and already the women had planned what they would cook and what they would do to make the boys in blue feel welcome.

The scouts returned with bad news. No sign of the escapees. Calum was frustrated. Three days hard riding had done nothing but raise blisters on their seats and turned their uniforms gray with dust. Had he been naïve in following the trail instead of fanning out to search for clues. They had passed only two ranches and he had sent men out to carefully search for any sign of the missing men but found none.

Behind them they saw the cloud of dust from the large train that was carrying Bonnie. The small caravan circled the wagons between the cliffs and trail, and then men walked the animals across the road to the shallow bed of the Platte. By the time they had tended the animals and set them to grazing, the women had their beans cooking over the scattered fires along the shale ledges.

Coming along, passing them on the trail were the lead wagons of the second, larger wagon train. Their horses wanted to balk and protest when they spotted the grazing animals up on the plain. Forgetting his weariness and the warm welcome of his friends, Calum sprang into the saddle and rode out to meet and talk with the wagon master and lead riders.

When the man began to describe the two men who had visited the train around noon and been chased away, Calum knew they were his men. It was his corporal who asked the most important question. "How did you know who they were?"

"Mr. Searle warned us. He has a woman in his wagon, she's come along to guard and protect his daughter. She ran and warned him who they were or we would have…"

But he was talking to the air where the Lieutenant had been as Calum galloped his horse along the train asking for Searle. At the tenth wagon he pulled Champ up so short the stallion reared in protest. The woman driving the wagon yelled in fright and her husband shouted at the excited young soldier.

"I'm looking for a woman, Bonnie Magee Micheals," but Bonnie herself was tearing out of the back of the wagon and reaching up to him. Calum pulled her into his arms and into his lap despite his prancing horse.

"Madam, sir," Calum doffed his hat to the astonished couple. "I came to carry her over to her friend's wagons. They have been frantic with worry about her. Please excuse my haste."

He set his hat on at an angle and stared at the woman in his arms. "Do you have anything we need to carry with us?"

Bonnie raised the slim pack containing her Indian dress and whispered. "All I own is inside here." She astonished herself at how much she wanted to say or 'holding me in his arms.' Just because she had thought of him every minute since leaving Fort McPherson, didn't mean he had spent those three days thinking of her. She hastened to remind herself, 'besides, I am a married woman.'

Struggling, she managed to sit erect, holding back from circling his neck with her arms and giving him the passionate kiss she wanted to.

Calum stiffened at the frosty reception and hurried to reach the Wimberley campsite. For a moment, he felt consumed with disappointment. Maybe her denial was what he needed. He already loved her more than anyone he had ever known and she regarded him with controlled disdain. Upon seeing her tearful welcome into the camp site, he swallowed his jealousy.

When Ian and Shawn shouted at Bonnie she was glad she had resisted. It was not right to worry them that she was carrying on with their commander. Calum released her into her brother's arms and they hugged as though it had been more than three days since they'd parted. "Where are your horses?" Ian asked.

When Mary Anne and the twins flew up to grab her, Bonnie felt the tears start to flow despite her best intentions. Mother and Father Wimberley waited, letting Claire rush in next. Then they hugged Bonnie as though she were a long lost child. Only Henry Lambton seemed withdrawn.

Bonnie nodded at the handsome but aloof young man, and then stared questioningly from his face to Claire's. She had expected him to be standing as close to Claire as she was to Calum. At least her friend and the widowed man could openly explore their attraction to each other.

They would betray no one if they were to fall in love and marry. At the thought she turned to stare at Calum. For an instant she read all the same thoughts in his eyes, then he turned away from her and mounted to ride out to oversee settling his own men.

◇◇◇

Bonnie and Claire were still talking, long after the children had been sent to bed and the Wimberleys gave up and left the fire. Dark clouds suddenly hid the moon and stars. "Thank heavens you are back. That's the first decent meal we've had all month."

Bonnie laughed. "You two had everything going when I arrived. Besides, the little I know of cooking I learned from my Mum and yours." She grabbed her friends hand and gave it a little squeeze. "Now tell me what's really wrong. Where's my sunny little canary, chirping about fashion and what everybody's doing?"

Claire's lower lip began to tremble and she blurted out, "Oh Bonnie, I've done everything wrong."

Bonnie's laugh was hollow as she rolled the young woman in for a tight hug. "You're not the only one who has done everything wrong. I've finally found the perfect man but I'm afraid to accept what he's offering because of my past with Tarn and the fear that I'm not worthy of his love."

"It's too late, I've hurt him and destroyed any chance we'd have to ever be happy."

Bonnie knew not to laugh this time, the words had rung with truth and as she listened to Claire confess her sins, Bonnie stared into the dying flames behind her. Had she done the same thing? Turned aside the man she wanted and admired for a moral obligation to one she hated?

"Oh Bonnie, what can I do? Some days I feel as though my chest has been hollowed out and filled with jagged rocks. Henry never even looks at me. If I'm standing in front of him, he looks through me like he is still seeing Bella and Barney. Oh Bonnie, he really loved her. I don't think he ever noticed me the way I did him. And after she died, I accused him of trying to smother Barney."

Suddenly Bonnie raised the blubbering girl from her arms to look at her. "You what?"

Bonnie listened as Claire revealed what she saw and heard and how she misinterpreted things. Then she confessed that she had been cruel and cold to Henry when he was grieving and needed her most. When she told him she was sorry, he said it was too late. "Now, I've lost him forever. Bonnie, I don't know what I'm going to do?"

Bonnie shook Claire and the little blonde's eyes rolled open and shut like one of her fashion dolls' glass eyes.

"Stop crying. If you're going to give up than there's no reason to cry. If you want to change things, than you have to change how you're behaving. I mean, I was shocked when I saw you. Your hair is dirty and unstyled. So is your dress. It's like you don't care at all how you look."

Claire sniffed but sat up a little straighter. "I've been broken-hearted," her lip began to tremble again.

"Pooh. Stop thinking about your own problems. Clean up and straighten up. If you think about what you can do to help him, the man will notice you. Then you can work on the rest. Once he's looking at you, if you apologize and ask for forgiveness, he'll hear you."

For the first time in a week, Claire looked hopeful. As usual, her mood changed instantly. "All right, now tell me what you've done wrong, lately?"

Smiling, Bonnie hugged the sweet blonde beside her, holding back nothing. She told about her rescue and each of the heated kisses. "I just don't know if I can continue to resist him." She described the temptation and her fears of surrendering. At her protest that she was still a married woman, Claire scolded her. "To that animal Tarn."

"Right, I guess I can change my religion and do it, divorce him. But I don't know how my family and friends will view my abandoning my faith. Besides, Calum is Catholic too."

"Did you ever just want to shoot him?" Claire asked.

Bonnie laughed. "Only a thousand times. Each time I feel so guilty. I mean, who can I confess to or do penance. I haven't been in a church since St. Louis. You can't imagine all the guilt."

"Oh, I understand guilt. All the times I've imagined..." her voice broke. "I haven't even had one tempting kiss, but oh, how I've wanted them."

Bonnie stared around at the deserted campfire. The sky was overcast and the air smelled like rain. "Go on, hurry and get your soap and things and we'll go down to the river to clean up before it rains."

CHAPTER FIFTY-EIGHT

Calum stared at the woman he loved where she sat watching the burning embers of the fire. The small blonde sat beside her, making Bonnie look even taller and stronger. He didn't mean to listen, but as he sank beside the wagon wheel to wait for the other girl to leave, he heard a lot.

It was after Claire left that Bonnie realized he had returned. There was an awareness of him, his scent, maybe his heartbeat that sent her pulse pounding and her own heart racing. How long had he been there?

He stepped into view. Bonnie stared at him, her body instantly awake. Calum held his arms open and for all her arguments to Claire, she knew she couldn't remain distant again. Instead she ran into his arms. Hungrily he folded her against him and they kissed deeply. They both heard Claire clambering over the tail of the wagon and stepped apart.

Claire froze, startled. It was clear where she was going as she pulled her wrapper closed. Calum cleared his throat. "I must remind you that we're here pursuing two dangerous men. With your permission I will escort you both to and from the river. On my honor, I will only look for intruders."

"Where's your fathers rifle?" Bonnie whispered to Claire. She stared up at Calum. "I trust you Lieutenant, but two guns are better than one."

"Here, is this it?" Claire asked.

Bonnie accepted the heavy shotgun and said, "It will do." They walked past the guards on duty on the outside circle of the large wagon train. Calum responded to each challenge, asked and was directed to a shallow area that other bathers had been using.

Bonnie was relieved that it was a moonless night. Unlike Claire, she quickly shed her dress, slip, and moccasins and unpinned her hair. Eagerly she dove out into the pool of water.

Calum stared intently where he heard her movements, unashamedly struggling to see her and bitterly disappointed when all he caught were the white of her discarded petticoat and the narrow white of her underwear. After a little coaxing, Claire waded out into the stream to join her.

Calum heard a branch snap and whirled to face an angry Henry Lambton, also carrying a rifle. "What are you doing out here," he hissed.

Calum smiled, obviously he hadn't been the only one eavesdropping on the girls' conversation. "I'm standing guard so the ladies can bathe."

"I don't think looking at them is the way you said you would be guarding them," Henry said.

"You can't see anything." Calum said. But suddenly the clouds swept past and in the pale moonlight the two men were transfixed as they saw the girls revealed, Bonnie was standing behind Claire and shampooing the giggling girls hair.

In the distance they heard the pop of a rifle, waited but heard no more shots and relaxed. But when they looked back, the shadows again had wrapped the moon and the bathers were hidden.

Tiller and Monroe crept closer to the big remuda of the wagon train. They were down to a single shot in the colt Tiller had taken from the dead trooper. Three had been wasted shooting at and missing rabbits. Without ammo, they carried the rifle like a talisman since it was useless as a weapon. When Tiller's horse gave out yesterday, they had cursed and then dared a fire and eaten steak. They were two miles south of the river and the steady slow creak of the oxen and travelers worried them, but they were too hungry and had made a guarded fire and ate all they could swallow of the barely cooked meat. They cut a haunch and abandoned the rest of the carcass.

Monroe's horse was too weak to carry double so they had taken turns walking beside it. From a distance they had watched the troopers greet the oxen train. Then the big wagon train that had chased them off showed up.

Desperate, they were going to steal two good mounts. They had argued about taking the big mare and Indian horse they had seen in the herd. Tiller wanted them to hurt the squaw girl. Monroe wanted something that they could ride and that would cover ground. If he'd had a choice, he would have waited until the troopers and the big wagon train moved on and then they could have handled the farmers and their slow-moving oxen.

Tiller had argued that they couldn't steal from either one if they were still afoot.

So now they crouched in the shadows at the edge of the picket-line and waited for the horses to settle back down and ignore them again. It might take all night, but sooner or later one of the guards would nod off and they would grab two nags and take off. With luck, they might even get another weapon.

Ian and Shawn asked permission, then walked over to the big remuda to claim Bonnie's horses. Both were eager to see the big mare and frisky colt. When the guard called halt, they both froze, but quickly called a greeting and introduced themselves and stated their mission.

The guard had been in the wagon behind the Searle's and knew Bonnie. He had seen her riding both animals and it was easy to see a family resemblance between the girl and these lanky blue-coated soldiers. The guard warned it would take some doing to catch the mare, they might want to wait until morning.

Ian called, "Here Bess, here pretty lady." The mare trotted up, the palomino gelding on her heels almost as closely as the big colt.

Shawn held out the apple the boys had stolen to tempt the gentle mare. Ian slipped a halter on her and the guard chuckled. "Never would of believed it if I hadn't seen it. I wasted a whole day trying to catch her to saddle up. Wanted to see what the world looked like from up there but she would have none of it. Big as she is, she's good at slipping the noose."

Ian nodded as he petted the friendly colt nuzzling up against him then laughed as it jerked away with shrill little whinnies. "She's good if you let her do what she wants to do. Don't think she's ever been saddled."

Shawn wiped the slobbers from his hand on the big brown shoulder then swung up. He extended a hand and Ian scrambled up behind him. "Thank you, mister. Be on your guard. Doubt they're around here, but we're chasing a couple of desperate men."

"Yeah, I was riding lead with the wagon master when Searle came up and warned us. You know we were about to give them fellows a meal and a couple of fresh horses. If your sister hadn't sent him to warn us, we would have too."

The mare snorted impatiently and the boys waved to the guard. "Thanks, believe she's telling us it's time to go.

The guard lowered the picket line to let the three animals pass, then hazed back the others that crowded forward.

The two men crouched in the weeds scowled at each other. One lifted the empty rifle, the other the pistol with the single shot. Seething, they remained hidden and watched the boys ride happily back toward the smaller wagon train.

An hour later they saw their chance and Tiller used the rifle butt to knock out the guard. Quickly they grabbed gear left beside the temporary paddock and saddled a pair of likely animals. Taking the unconscious man's rifle and finding only a couple of bullets in his pocket, they left the picket line down and rode out toward the distant wagon train.

The new guard coming on duty saw the riders and the scattered horses and fired a shot. The thieves raced into the night and sleepy travelers poured forth to try to catch the escaping mules and horses.

Monroe and Tiller sped along the river between the two camps leaning close to their mounts as the shot rang out behind them. So far, nothing they had tried had brought them luck. As they ran parallel to the river looking for a more sheltered spot to cross, they blinked in amazement. In front of them were two barely dressed females and as

Monroe recognized the taller one he yelled to his partner. "Now's our time to get even. You grab one and I'll get the other."

CHAPTER FIFTY-NINE

Bonnie heard the shot and listened, hushing the giggling girl. When she heard riders she was already urging her friend toward the bank. At the yell of the men behind her she dove across the water throwing Claire with her.

Even as the horses splashed into the river she saw a gun on the bank flash. On the muddy shore, she picked up and pumped the heavy shotgun as she turned. But before she could fire a second shot rang out. This time from one of the riders. Bonnie raised the shotgun and fired and the second rider disappeared.

Only when she was sure both men were down, did she stand and wade farther up the bank, stopping to drop the semi-conscious Claire beside their discarded clothes.

Standing, she heard a voice call. "Are you all right?" Bonnie set the shotgun down and then struggled into the slip and dress, stuffing her feet into her shoes as she stumbled forward.

"Fine, now," she muttered as she straightened the dress over her wet body, "thanks. Was that Tiller and the oxen thief?"

Instead of answering, she heard a groan and rushed forward. "Calum, Calum, are you hurt?"

As she dropped beside him, she felt the sticky, wet patch on his chest and screamed for help. In the dark, men were coming. She looked past where she knelt when she heard another voice moan. "Who's there?"

"I killed a man."

Bonnie recognized Henry Lambton's voice. "Henry, thank God. Run and cover Claire before the others arrive. Hurry."

"Claire, my beautiful Claire," he whispered then ran toward the girl.

Awkwardly he picked up her wrapper and tried to lift her to slide it over her damp gown. "Oh no, Henry, don't look at me. I wanted to get clean for you, but now I'm all muddy again."

For the first time Henry laughed and crushed her to him. "You goose, you beautiful goose, thank God you are all right."

Bonnie pressed against the wound, heard Calum moan again. The bullet had struck high on his shoulder near the top left button. In horror, she realized how lucky he was to have the two rows of buttons. She spread her fingers across to touch the one beside his heart and closed her eyes in prayer.

Men were there, urging her back to examine the fallen soldier. As they pulled him from her, one man ordered the others. "Bring a light, I'm a doctor."

Bonnie drew back, making room, stepping forward to where Henry was holding and rocking Claire, cradling her barely covered body in his arms. Bonnie pushed her heavy wet hair back from her face and moved forward to lift the shotgun and stare where the renegades had been pulled and plopped onto the bank.

"Are they dead?" she asked.

"This one is, he pointed to the one in blue. Think the other is still alive."

Bonnie stared down at Tiller, the one who had threatened and insulted her so many times. His body looked unmarked, until one man held a lantern down and she saw the hole through his neck.

The other man was still unconscious but Bonnie noted the ragged rise and fall of his chest. His shirt was splattered with small holes and both arms were bleeding. "Best tie his hands and feet. If he doesn't die, the army plans to take him home to execute," she said.

One of the man laughed. "Are you kidding?"

Suddenly two soldiers were standing beside her. "No, do as she says. Then we'll take him."

Bonnie reached out a hand to either side of her and clutched her brother's hands. "Calum was shot."

"Is he going to be all right?"

"He has to be."

They moved Calum Douglas to the Lambton's wagon after the doctor removed the bullet and partially embedded brass button from his shoulder.

The corporal stood beside Bonnie. "I don't think we should be moving him just yet. He lost a lot of blood."

Bonnie nodded, staring at the pale face and then touching the warm skin. A fever was never a good sign.

"Figure he would want me to get the men back to headquarters, now we've captured that gun runner and done for Tiller. That was our mission, you know."

Bonnie nodded again, wondering what this man was trying to say. The sergeant behind him butted in. "Monroe wasn't as bad hurt as we thought. Know the General wants to personally see him shot. He could take a turn for the worst or maybe even escape again, lest we head on back."

Bonnie looked at the mounted troopers behind them. The other wagons were getting ready to move out, just waiting for the last of the larger train to clear out first. The twins walked back with the oxen and she watched Father Wimberley and Henry Lambton yoking the teams.

"Figure if the Lieutenant is going to make it, he'll need some nursing," the sergeant said.

"Don't worry, we'll assign a couple of men to stay behind so he doesn't have to return to camp alone. Figure maybe if they follow your wagons on in, they can take the train back to Fort McPherson. Only going to be another week or so," the corporal said.

"Three weeks," Bonnie said.

"Really, that long," the corporal said as he scratched his head. The sergeant elbowed him.

"Probably take about that long for them cattle to make it at that. Reckon the Lieutenant there ought to be fit as a fiddle time he gets back to headquarters with all that rest and recreation," the corporal said with a grin.

The sergeant was scowling and shaking his head and Bonnie wondered what the two men were up to. But Calum moaned and she forgot everyone else as she bent to wipe his face with a cool cloth.

The two men grinned at each other. The sergeant turned to the mounted men and their moaning prisoner. "Hey, you two pups fall out," he jabbed a thumb at them but the Magee boys were already spurring their horses out of line.

"Your orders are to keep an eye on the Lieutenant. When you see he's fit enough, you're to bring him back to headquarters. Just ride up to the track and signal the train. They know to stop for military. They'll bring you all three back to Fort McPherson."

Shawn started to argue but Ian shot him a look and Shawn swallowed the words. "Yes sir, sergeant. You can count on us, sir, I mean sergeant."

The corporal rode to the head of the line, the two scouts grinned and waved and soon the whole platoon was out of sight.

Bonnie looked up at her puzzled brothers. "Well, if you're to stay with us, best earn your keep. Help Tom and Jim with the oxen. I'd ask you to keep your eyes peeled for something to shoot for the dinner pot but following all that ruckus ahead of us, would be no use today and probably the next. Go on with you."

As soon as they were out of sight she watched Henry Lambton climb onto the bench beside a pale but happy Claire as he moved his wagon into position. He asked Ian if he or Shawn would mind riding post for him today so he could keep an eye on Claire. Ahead she watched the Wimberleys sharing the seat with Mary Anne wedged between them, busily working on her lace work.

When the hand touched her breast, Bonnie's eyes widened in shock. As Calum moaned she felt ashamed of her suspicions and leaned closer, looking at the stained cloth covering his wound. She felt his other hand from the wounded arm reach out to stroke the other breast and she grinned widely.

"You sir, are incorrigible."

"Please, kiss me, I'm dying."

"Dying, you faker," but the words died as his right hand circled her breast and his thumb brushed across her nipple.

His eyes opened a slit and he stared up at her. "I love watching the shamrocks bloom in your eyes. I love you. I want to make you my wife."

All the usual arguments were still there between them but she didn't say anything. Slowly Bonnie lowered her mouth to his, felt the swollen, fever warmed skin of his lips.

When she raised her head from the kiss, both his hands had fallen away and she knew he had passed out again. The wagon wheel hit a rut and his head rolled against the wagon bed. As though it were what she had been made to do, Bonnie curved into the space between his head and the wagon seat ahead and cushioned his body with the curves of her own.

When he woke again, then she would argue. He had an enlistment to serve. Another year she knew, one full of danger. She wanted him for herself, but until the boy's terms were up, she wanted him there in charge to protect the lads as well.

Besides she wanted to buy property and set up her own claim, a house to bring her family west to join her. That would take time and work. Maybe by the time his term was ended, she would have it all worked out.

As the wagon rolled forward, slow mile by mile, she dozed with the man she loved rolling softly against her breasts with each bounce. In a week they would be in Utah. The state where Brigham Young had argued there was no such thing as bigamy. Well if a man like Young could have multiple wives, the latest rumors were he had fifty-five, surely a woman could have two husbands. One a devil and brute, the other a loving, kind man.

They would have to talk again about the children. She didn't want to deny this wonderful man the opportunity to have sons and daughters.

CHAPTER SIXTY

The benches had been removed from the front of the wagons to sit around the fire again. As usual now Bonnie was back to do all the work, Claire held court. She had on her best mint green cotton dress with the pseudo bustle of flounces and had arranged her hair in multiple twists and loops, with a few curls escaping to frame her face.

The two men who had courted her casually in the past were there, especially now Bonnie's brothers seemed to make such a fuss about the girl. Tonight, they were all busy testing their musical skills, tuning a fiddle and blowing the juice from a small harmonica. When they got going, the two dogs set up a howl.

Mother Wimberley raised her hands over her ears and Bonnie laughed. In protest, Ian and Shawn stood up and challenged the disharmonious pair to play Barbara Allan. Silenced, they sat vexed while the boys sang the sweet song in their lilting tenors. Even the cattle mooed in satisfaction and the travelers in the circled wagons stopped their children playing so all could listen.

Claire clapped each time they reached the chorus and sang Bonny Barbara Allan, but the boys continued until they ran out of verses and the other suitors were called home to dinner. Then the young lads abandoned Claire to Henry Lambton's company and sat with the McKinley twins to eat and joke around before bedtime. Already the twins had pitched both tents, the one for their favorite soldiers and one for the two boys and Bonnie. Calum and Henry remained bunk mates and Bonnie found herself falling to sleep at night listening to their deep muffled voices as they talked of their plans.

When Henry rose and stomped off, Bonnie remained seated with the Wimberleys and let Mary Anne slip over to hear Claire vent. Bonnie had heard her complaints too many times. 'Henry was never going to give her another chance. He was still grieving over his wife and the boy. Not sure what she could do to convince him she was sorry.' Bonnie always gave her the same advice. 'Stop being a ninny. Tell him how you feel and how sorry you are. The way you flirt and carry on all the time, he has no idea.' But the girl refused to listen.

In a minute Bonnie smiled as she heard Claire loudly protest to Mary Anne. "I've never worn hand-me-down clothes or shoes. I certainly don't want to begin my life in the west with a hand-me down husband."

Using her hand for cover, Bonnie looked past the fire and saw Henry puffing angrily on his pipe as he turned to complain some more to Calum. She watched the handsome soldier lean forward and lift his hat for a moment to shield his face as he rolled his eyes in horror.

Bonnie covered her mouth and laughed and as she stared at him, Calum put his hat back into place and grinned at her. Suddenly she blushed and looked at the Wimberleys to see if they had noticed.

Today as they walked beside the wagon, Calum had teased and tormented her as he told her of the customs from his grandparent's homeland in Scotland. He had described a special courting couch where the couple sat facing in opposite directions with a barrier between them. They would be left alone in the room with the understanding that both pair of feet had to remain flat on the floor at all times or the chaperone would be back immediately. Of course the chaperone was outside, listening and peeking beneath the door at the pair of feet.

The first week, he had been too weak to leave or to be any danger to her peace of mind. They had merely talked about their plans. Bonnie shared her thoughts about Mormon territory. He had agreed it was difficult to be a bigamist in a state where it wasn't illegal. But both were Catholic and they were surrounded by friends and even though a temporary one, a community that would never approve. They had agreed to wait until his and the boys' enlistment ended. She would pursue her plans to grab a claim and prepare for her family to join them. The McKinney children had volunteered to stay and help her get it started. But she wasn't sure if Lynne would be able to spare them.

This whole week, now that he was back on his feet again and gaining strength each day, he had been a torment to her. Sneaking caresses and stealing kisses at every opportunity. Yesterday he told her he was leaving. In two days they would be within a mile of the train track. He and her brothers had already stayed a week too long.

He dared her to stay out late tonight after the others went to bed and to court with him like in the old country. She had finally agreed, if Claire's parents would permit her and Henry to stay out as well. They had shocked her by quickly giving their permission. There would be no point to having permission if the couple continued to quarrel.

Tonight, Henry's wagon had been moved after dinner and now their wagons were parked side-by-side. It was dark without the fading campfire. The benches were placed between the two wagons at different ends but sheltered from the eyes of those in the tents or in the distant wagons. Bonnie knew the Wimberleys would be awake inside, listening.

Her blood was pounding and she trembled as Calum led her to the bench. Carefully he helped her sit facing toward Claire now on the other bench. The girl giggled but Bonnie felt paralyzed with fear. It was too dark for anyone to see what they were doing, she could see the light color of Claire's dress but not make out her features. She knew in her dark dress, she would be invisible to the other girl except for her face.

Had Calum explained all this in detail to Henry and the Wimberleys? Suddenly Bonnie stiffened her spine and gripped the bench to calm her nerves. Poor Claire must be terrified, but Bonnie had been married. She knew what happened between a man and woman and for the life of her she couldn't imagine how it could ever happen with both seated side-by-side facing in opposite directions.

Calum walked around and whispered something to Henry before passing him a full cup of wine. Humming, he walked back around and took his place beside Bonnie. He heard her startled breath as his shoulder brushed hers and grinned in satisfaction. He filled his own cup with wine and spoke loud enough for the other couple to hear. "We will share a toast to the old country and to the women we love. Drink."

He held the cup and Bonnie breathed in the rich scent of the sweet wine and took a long swallow. Calum sat with his body facing away but his face turned to stare at her. She heard him do the same steps, breathe, sip, then swallow greedily. She wanted to raise a finger and trace the bob of his Adam's apple as he swallowed. He handed her the cup again and she started to refuse.

He held it there and repeated, "Drink." She swung her head away and then back to face him. Leaning backward a little as he leaned back the other way, she raised both hands to grasp the cup and his hand. He left it there, imprisoned as she drank, raising her eyes to his as she swallowed.

This time as they shifted the cup to his mouth she surrendered to the temptation and placed her palm on his throat as he swallowed. He gasped in surprise, then coughed and sputtered. A moment later he drank the wine.

The empty cup was discarded and Bonnie waited with a mixture of annoyance and anticipation. If they were going to kiss and cuddle, why had he made such a production of it instead of slipping away for a night stroll around the wagons as usual? She wanted him to get on with it.

Yet at the feel of his right hand on the back of her bare neck, she shuddered. Breathless she turned to face him, eager to surrender her lips to his. The fruity scent of the wine as their breaths mingled made her feel instantly drunk. Softly, teasingly he kissed her. Bonnie made a little hum of pleasure at the contact and he grunted in return.

The hand that reached around to touch her breast did not surprise her, the fact that he slipped it beneath her dress and chemise did. For a breathless moment she felt the rough scrape of his palm over her sensitive nipple, the next she was ready to move around to sit on his lap facing the opposite direction. She wanted his mouth on her breast, his manhood pulsing inside her.

Calum's hand on her neck was firm, commanding. He held her prisoner to his touch. Frantically she leaned closer, tore her lips away to whisper against his ear. "I want you to make love to me."

This time he shuddered. His lips moved to her ear and he whispered. "We agreed to wait a year to marry. I've no intention of leaving you alone and pregnant, trying to establish a home on your own."

She tried to interrupt up but he continued, the words annoyed but still for her ears alone.

"There's no way that I want my child born with another man's name. Besides, you're the one who insisted we wait. We will do this the right way. Trust me."

"I might be unable to, to get that way again. If I can't give you children?"

"In this wild land, I'll just find you a dozen that need a mother for us to raise."

Bonnie sighed. Kissed him softly to bless the words. For a minute she relaxed, let his hand roam as it would, coaxing each nipple into a perfect point, molding each breast into a full globe. Bonnie felt her blood singing through her veins, her heart pounding.

When he whispered, "scoot your hips forward. Remember to keep your feet flat on the ground." She did and almost scooted off the narrow bench but his arm had circled her waist and moved her back to where he wanted her.

When he took his hand away from her breast and slipped it beneath the band of her skirt she swallowed in anticipation. But at the tight string tying her drawers at her waist he met an impenetrable barrier. "Hold still, I'll use my knife," he growled in her ear.

"No, wait." Feverishly Bonnie worked at the tight knot until his hand slipped beneath the waist band. For a moment he let the warm weight of his hand rest on her cool, flat belly. As she leaned back against his arm she wanted his mouth against hers again. She gasped as his strong hand began to explore and create amazing sensations but when he swallowed the sounds she was making she was startled to feel his tongue slip inside her mouth.

Moaning, she felt first one, then two fingers enter her and as his tongue entered her mouth, his fingers copied each motion. She caught his hand, shocked at what he was doing. He waited, holding his breath until she pressed his hand tighter against her. He moved his arm enough to capture and pull her right arm across his body, working two, then three buttons open and inserting her hand.

As soon as her fingers closed around him, Bonnie felt a thrill shudder through her. For several delicious minutes they were locked in giving each other pleasure. All the time there was the fear that the chaperones in the wagon might storm out and shout at them. But each moan and sigh was swallowed by the other. Suddenly like a rocket burst, she wanted to scream and her body gave an exultant spasm of pleasure. Trembling they clung together as Calum carefully dried her hand.

She curled into him, tucking her face so her lips were pressed against the pulse beneath his ear. Her eyelashes flicking against his jaw.

His arms tightened around her, then his hands worked busily to tidy all that he had disordered. Bonnie moved, limp and docile beneath his touch, letting him retie the string at her waist. Surrendered to the comfortable cupping of his hands on her breasts as he fastened her chemise, then lifted and smoothed the front of her dress.

All was restored but her peace of mind as he said, "Now that we are betrothed, let us take one last stroll together my beloved Bonnie."

He pulled her to her feet and took her hand, struggling not to shout in exultation. An experienced married woman of eighteen she might be, but he knew now her foolish husband had never taken the time to give her real pleasure.

As they walked, long legged and loose jointed with their arms wrapped around each other they circled the long chain of wagons. "Tell me how much you will miss me," he pleaded.

"I'll write every day, first thing in the morning, last thing at night. You will be part of my prayers and thoughts all day." She hugged him tighter, breathed in the cool night air full of the scent of him. "Don't go. In a week we'll be in Ogden and we can wed."

Calum stopped and cupped her face to try and see her clearly. It was too dark and all the campfires seemed to have died out. "Remind me to never make love to you again in the dark. I want to see your face, look at your amazing eyes each time."

Bonnie laughed and leaned closer to kiss him. "Silly, no one does that."

"We will," he whispered. "Only when you've screamed my name will I put out the light."

Bonnie shook and moved closer into his embrace. "I didn't scream, I didn't move my feet."

He laughed, snuggling closer and rubbing his face in her soft hair. "I know darling, you were marvelous. But I heard you in my mind."

She gave a playful pat at him, let him pull her close beside him so they were walking with their arms around each other's waists again.

"You will keep yourself safe, and my brothers. I'm counting on you."

"And you and all those splendid children, take no chances."

"I promise. But I will only have them a month, then they have to go home with Lynne, that is, if she'll let them stay that long."

"Then your family will come?"

"That's the plan. Didn't the boys share the letter? Da is building a boat for them to come down the rivers. He and the girls have been planning it out, every detail. They'll follow the coast, enter on the Hudson, and navigate the rivers down into the Missouri and Platte until the river is too small. Then they'll come by cattle-car."

"Cattle-car?"

"Aye, Da says it's the only way he can afford to bring all the cailins and Clyde and me Mum. Besides, the girls are daft over their sheep and pigs and chickens. He has to bring all that lot and the furniture as well."

"I would think it would be too expensive to build a boat."

"He has friends who build them all the time. When it's done, they'll let Da bring it to St. Louis, maybe Independence or North Platte, to sell and wire them the money back. He gets to keep enough for the cattle-car."

"Sounds like he has it worked out."

"Aye, now he's sober again, my Da's more than able."

They were back at the wagons and the two tents along the outside edge. Calum pulled her into his arms, this time pressing her against the long hard length of him. She moaned and when he kissed her and slipped his tongue between her lips she felt an inner, answering quiver. The power of desire devoured her like a prairie fire and her knees buckled. Calum turned her so her back was against the wagon wheel and her front was pressed tight against him. He rocked against her and she moaned louder.

One of the dogs barked, then the other began to yip frantically as well. One of the twins called sleepily, "Hey, is that you Bonnie."

Slowly they separated, aware of all they had shared and all they had not. Bonnie was glad it was so dark. Her face, her whole body, felt hot and flushed. Softly Bonnie called to the boy. "Aye, tis me. I'll be there in a minute. Go back to sleep."

She reached for Calum but on the other side they heard the small girl whine, "Claire."

"Shh, I'm here, I'm right here," a husky woman's voice answered. Bonnie and Calum shared a knowing smile. After one last quick kiss, she slipped into the tent while he took another frustrated walk around the wagons.

He heard Henry say good night and stopped to wait.

"Not waiting for a proper year of mourning."

Henry laughed and Calum was certain it was the first he had heard from the man.

"I had to insist she go to bed with her parents and promise to wait until we reached Ogden and a priest."

After a minute, he turned to ask. "How did your campaign go?"

"She now wants to wait until her Da builds a boat and sails from Boston to here. Although a minute ago, she told me not to go. That we could wed in Ogden next week."

"Well, there you go," Henry whispered excitedly. "We can have a double wedding."

Calum sighed and looked at the man, seeing his outline. "It's Bonnie. She's so damn sensible, so practical. If we don't wait, if she doesn't get her land, she'll always blame me. She has to want me more than all the rest."

"So, you're going to wait a year?"

"Or until she decides I'm the only thing she wants."

CHAPTER SIXTY-ONE

The city of Ogden was busy. Junction City as most people called it was the meeting for the Union and Pacific railroads as well as the Virginia City-Corinne Road. Bonnie was glad to be at the end of the journey, but heartsick still at missing Calum. Was it just a week ago that he and her brothers had left to ride back to Fort McPherson. The skunks had ridden away before dawn, before she stirred from her warm dreams.

When she came out of the tent, it was to the smell of coffee, bacon, and biscuits. She and Claire had made the journey into the bushes together, laughing, and whispering. Neither was surprised to learn the other was betrothed. Bonnie was shocked to learn Claire and Henry had decided to wed as soon as they reached town and a church. She had asked Bonnie to help break the news to her mother and father.

Bonnie had laughed as they both came to the campfire and heard cries of Congratulations. Henry was beaming and the twins were jumping up and down.

So today they had spent a long time dressing and styling each other's hair. Although Bonnie wore the remade black and white maids' uniform, Mary Anne had supplied lace collars and cuffs for the blouse and attached a little lace trim to the skirt pockets and along the hem. Bonnie felt beautiful and sad.

Claire looked especially radiant in her own lace adorned gown, the light-weight purple flowered wool she had purchased in Boston.

Her hair had been restored to its old style of golden ringlets and Mary Anne had created a lace scarf to tie beneath the curls but not hide their beauty.

The day was one of those golden days, where the air was warm and the air sweet. Along the trail into town they had noted the yellow leaves of the aspen, vivid gold against the tall dark evergreens.

One of the wagons had stopped, the oxen yoke held on either side by the twins. Bonnie and Claire were swinging their hands as they strode down the dusty street. Tyler and Tip were racing about eager to get the team back in motion as all heard a woman scream.

Bonnie stared as a young woman in lavender screamed again. Just as she recognized Lynne she heard Claire scream her name as well. Before either of them could move a tiny blur ran and leaped into her arms. Bonnie let go of Claire's hands as they both started running for their friend. Even as they gained ground the twins Tom and Jim bolted for her.

By the time Bonnie reached her, Lynne was laughing and crying as she kissed first Mary Anne, then Tom and Jim. Bonnie laughed as she heard her friend's happy voice saying over and over again how much they had changed. In the six months since they had last seen her, Lynne had been transformed as well.

As Lynne released her family, the children stood back a step to let the three women embrace. Behind her short friend Bonnie saw a tall rancher let his hands drop down from his guns. As his face softened with a smile and he started toward them Bonnie realized it was Lynne's tall, well-formed veteran. The little ad had undersold him, he was breathtaking. Behind them Henry and Father Wimberley had dismounted to steady the oxen.

Lynne drew back just enough to stare at her two friends and all three said the same words together. "You look so beautiful." Lynne laughed and whispered, "I can't believe you're here. Safe and strong and healthy."

Claire blurted out. "We're both engaged. She turned to point to the handsome blonde man beside the gigantic oxen. Henry brushed his trimmed mustache and smiled shyly. "This is Henry Lambton, my betrothed. We're going to get married today. Where's the church?"

◇◇◇

The church was Episcopalian. "I think they call themselves the Protestant Catholics. But they do have priests and a Bishop," Lynne said.

"Just be glad they're not Mormons," Bonnie said. "You don't want to have to compete with several other wives."

"I guess not. It's hard enough competing with Bella's ghost," the nervous bride said.

"Bella?"

"Henry's wife was killed by Indians between here and North Platte," Bonnie answered. "It happened while I was living with the Indians who had captured me."

"You were captured by Indians? Oh Willow, are you okay, did they…?"

"No, they treated me like a guest. The chief captured me so I could tend his wife while she died of cancer. The army sent men to rescue me."

"Her Lieutenant Calum Douglas rode in to save her. Traded his favorite horse and all his guns for her," Claire said while raising her eyebrows suggestively and giggling.

Bonnie reached out to pinch her friend's waist as though peeved. "It's a long story, I'll tell you everything later."

"Am I doing the right thing girls? His wife has been dead less than a month. Maybe I should wait."

Bonnie took her nervous friend's hand and gave it a little squeeze. "I thought you told me you couldn't stand the wait. If it took any longer to get here, you were going to climb into his wagon and become a sinner," she whispered.

"Is this Lieutenant your betrothed?" Lynne whispered as they pushed Claire in front of them to where her father waited to hold her arm.

The girls followed sedately behind her. On the Bride's side of the aisle sat Mother Wimberley with the McKinney children. Mary Anne reached out to hand Claire a bouquet of wild flowers she had picked along the route. Mostly Hyssop and Pye weed, the love in the wilting purple and pink blooms made Claire smile and her eyes water. On the left side sat three dusky Indians and a couple of strange looking trail drivers, one tall and thin, the other short and round.

"I love him, Lynne. He is tall and handsome and all that is kind. But since I'm married, he returned to the Fort and his duties while I look for land and a house. I hope to find something off the railroad right of way so I can move my family out here to join me. In a year..."

The priest hissed in annoyance at the whispering women as Claire's father gave her a last kiss and placed her hand in Henry's. The two girls, one tall and the other petite looked guiltily at each other and held hands silently while Claire and Henry exchanged their vows.

Afterwards, Phillip left Henry's side to claim the arm of his own bride. He swept all the members of the wedding party toward the hotel and the large dining room he had reserved for an early supper.

"Did you tell your friends your big news, darling?" Phillip asked.

Lynne looked up at her handsome husband and blushed. Bonnie clapped her hands and looked at Mary Anne who jumped at the sound. "She's expecting. Your sister is going to have a baby. Right?"

Lynne laughed and blushed even redder as all the guests in the hotel turned to stare at the wedding party.

Once again the children crowded around their sister and Henry took the opportunity to kiss his bride again. Her father finally tutted to break up the kiss.

Everyone was so happy, but as the families followed a bell boy toward the dining room Bonnie felt another wave of sadness. It had been her idea that they wait. She had things she wanted to do and Calum still had his duty. But if it was the right decision, why was she so miserable?

Lynne stood beside her husband, making introductions as she assigned everyone to a seat like the perfect hostess. She chose to sit the three girls together at one end of the table, her husband and the children at the other end. When she saw Bonnie's eyes take on the sad, muddy brown she used to have, Lynne called her name.

"Up here."

Phillip Gant hesitated, then took his seat at the other end between his two mining buddies and the three McKinney children. Henry Lambton sat beside his new bride and the Wimberleys sat across from them, watching their happy daughter and her new husband.

"Why so gloomy? Did you just hear the news?"

Bonnie looked up, tried to smile and shook her head.

Lynne gave a wry, sad smile of her own. "That Tarn Micheals is dead, and how he died. It was horrible, but the inquest acquitted me of all charges for shooting him. You see, he had attacked Phillip before and injured him severely and since I was the only one armed, I had to shoot him. If you don't want to sit next to me, I'll understand. But with the way things were between you..."

Bonnie stared at her friend, her eyes suddenly turning lighter with sparks of yellow excitement. "Tarn is actually dead. I'm free. I'm a widow and can marry Calum." Her voice rose with each sentence.

She leaned over to hug her friend and kiss her. "Oh Lynne, oh you beautiful smart friend. I owe you so much, so very much. But before you tell me more, where is the telegraph office?"

Phillip Gant rose and bowed. "I'll take her and be right back darling. Guests order anything you like. My treat for the happy couple. Order for me, sweetheart."

Lynne nodded and laughingly tried to make conversation with the deliriously happy couple beside her.

◇◇◇

Bonnie wrote the words frantically. "Widowed, Tarn Micheals dead. Ready to wed."

Phillip stared at the lovely tall girl as she signed and filled in the rest of the form. He tendered the payment before she could look for where her money was pinned "Send word to the Union hotel if you get a return message," Phillip said as he paid.

He held out an elbow for her. "Let's rejoin the party. I know my wife has a great deal to share. In fact she has filled pages and pages with her news."

Bonnie smiled into his flashing dark eyes. It was foolish to stand around a telegraph office when it might be days before Calum received the message and got back to her.

"Thank you. I am so happy Lynne found a perfect gentleman in such a wild place."

"Well, interestingly enough, our marriage started in a telegraph office too."

◇◇◇

The telegram came as they were served a flaming French dish called cherries jubilee. The children were yelling and clapping in delight at the burning dessert when the messenger arrived.

Bonnie's hands shook so much that she had trouble opening the yellow paper without tearing it. Lynne and Carrie ran to her sides, each bracing her arms as she gently tore the edge of the envelope and opened the message. The room was so silent they could all hear the paper rattle.

Silently she scanned the telegram. The messenger who had been waiting, spoke. "Reply was requested."

Claire was the one to insist, "Read it out loud, please Bonnie."

"Will send ticket. Return to me, Fort McPherson. Leave with General Miles two weeks, Major at Fort Keogh. Bringing cubs. Officer's quarters ready for wife."

While she read the message out loud, Phillip and Henry had risen to join their wives.

Suddenly none of Bonnie's earlier decisions mattered. She had planned to buy land and make a new home before she married, to wait until Calum and the lads served their enlistment time, and wait until the rest of her family could save enough money, and finish the boat to come and join her. And wait, and wait, and wait…

Bonnie's whole body shook as she realized. None of that mattered. She loved Calum Douglas and tomorrow she could be his wife. She didn't have to wait.

"Yes, yes." Bonnie yelled.

Phillip paid the man and repeated the message. "She said, 'Yes, Yes.'" When the man started to protest, Phillip grinned, "He'll want that extra word."

EPILOGUE

Bonnie Douglas tried to smile. The boys on the floor were wrestling, with four year old David Jamison Douglas rolling beneath two-year old Johnny Jamison Douglas and hollering 'Uncle.' The two boys had arrived special delivery three months after she and Calum wed. The carrier from Fort McPherson had stuffed one boy in each side of his supply pack and ignored their complaints until he arrived at Fort Keogh.

Stella Jamison had pinned a note to Johnny's diaper before taking her own life. It still hurt to think about. The woman had seemed the strongest of the rescued women at Fort McPherson. But when two men attacked her in an alley, it had been more than she could bear. She had sent the boys to Bonnie, who had promised before to raise them if anything ever happened to their mother.

Calum entered the room, taking in the boys and the sad look in Bonnie's eyes. So she had lost another. The third time in their two year marriage. The first pregnancy they had shared everything, their dreams, their hopes, their excitement. She had miscarried at three months, with little Johnny in her arms.

These last two times, she had said nothing, but he had known from the first moment. Her eyes were the window to her soul. They changed from the light muddy brown to hazel with green dreamy highlights. When the pregnancy ended, they became the sad, muddy brown again. Only when they made love could he get the happy shamrocks to bloom there. Fortunately, Bonnie was as passionate as he.

He stooped to pull the wrestling boys apart, hoisting one under each arm as he walked over to kiss her. It worked, as she stopped in mid-fluster to kiss him back. Then she kissed each little boy as he tilted first one, then the other giggling face up to her.

"Sillies, I don't have time for this. The train will arrive in," she looked at the clock and flapped her arms. "Oh no, they'll be here in less than an hour. I have so much to do."

Calum set the boys down and waved his arms up and down as well, making chicken noises. She slapped at him while the little boys laughed. Before she could grow angrier, he wrapped her in his arms and pressed her head beneath his chin. "I love you, Bonnie, you wonderful nut. The house is perfect, you've been cooking for two days, calm down. Your family will love everything."

For the first time all day, Bonnie felt at peace. She raised her face to kiss him, loving the tender way he held her. He was right. The cabin on her land beside the Great Northern spur was built and even had a stove. The lads had brought back the wood stove from a burned cabin along the Bozeman trail. As sad as it was for the family chased out by renegades, her Irish brothers usually found something worthwhile to bring home.

"I know, well, I think you're right. I haven't told Da you're a Scott. He doesn't think much of them, you know."

Calum straightened, lifting one, then the other boy, as they hung one from each forearm.

"No, funny you never mentioned that. What does he have against Scotts?"

"Well, you know my grandmother, on my Mum's side, was a Scott. Da always said she was a tight-fisted terror. Says it's a flaw all the Scottish have. When I annoy him, he always says I'm just like her."

"He does, does he? Not sure about tight-fisted, but you can be a holy terror."

The little boys giggled and repeated the words. Bonnie moved back to her stove.

"Well, I'll just have to be my charming self and change his mind." She watched her smiling husband finish a sixth set of arm raises and then bring his hands together in front. It brought the little boys nose to nose and they both hollered, 'ugh.' and dropped off at the same time.

Bonnie looked nervously around for her brothers. Ian and Shawn had left on patrol yesterday, but had promised to be back to help her welcome the family to their new home. She had bought the land just as she intended when setting out for the west. With the help of her friends, the Wimberleys and Gants, and her husband's troops, they had raised the large cabin and barn on the property within sight of the fort. But as Calum had wired her so long ago, there was room in his officer's quarters for a wife. Even room for a wife and two boisterous boys.

With the work of rounding up all the Indians in Montana and the Dakotas and keeping them peacefully on the new reservations, he had not felt it was time to surrender his commission and become a farmer. When he reenlisted, so did her brothers and most of the men who had come west as new recruits.

Calum hadn't made a lot of arguments. They had both known he had been a soldier most of his life. It was what he was meant to do, all he knew to do. Bonnie was proud to be a Major's wife and would follow this man to the ends of the earth. He was the other half of her heart and always would be.

Besides, when her parents and the rest of the family moved in, she would have her home in the west. Anxiously she twisted around Calum, looking up the tracks where the train was due to arrive, then back toward the barracks. The little boys stood perfectly still beside them, only their eyes moving as Calum stood at attention and Bonnie fidgeted.

The black smoke from the small engine appeared first. Bonnie bounced on her feet and the boys tilted their heads back to look at their father. Calum felt their questions against his knees and slowly relaxed his stance. "At ease men. Prepare to welcome your relatives." He leaned closer to Bonnie to whisper, "The ones who don't like Scotts."

She laughed nervously. He noticed her eyes were abloom with colorful green and yellow sparks of excitement. He wrapped an arm around her strong back and asked himself again what he loved most about this tall woman. It had to be her loving nature. There was no end to how deeply she felt things or how many people she loved.

His boys were jumping up and down as steam spewed from around the big metal wheels and the train ground to a noisy stop. Minutes later, the side of one of the cattle cars opened and a short, dusty man emerged swearing a salty oath. Minutes later a woman appeared who stood a little taller than him but bent over as she coughed into her handkerchief. Her face was worn and thin and as he saw Bonnie's expression change, he knew her dear Mum was ill.

A crowd of children came forward to join them. Four girls, in stair-step order, the oldest three each a little taller and more like Bonnie with each year. All week she had been telling him their names. Brigid, Darcey, and Meara. The youngest girl, red-headed and defiant, would be little Reagan. A young boy stood there, taking his Da's hand, his expression fierce. He recognized the same strong chin and clear blue eyes of the Magee lads. This would be five-year old Clyde. Not the big Clydesdale namesake that never stopped eating.

But Bonnie was running toward them, screaming names and pulling their faces toward her. Then she was kissing and hugging her dear hearts as she called them. Calum waited a few minutes for her to greet each and then lifted his boys to walk forward and meet his in-laws.

With the help of a few of his troopers, they moved the whole Magee clan and menagerie to their new home. In no time, all the furniture was arranged and the women gone to tour Bonnie's quarters. Calum had introduced his sons to Clyde and the three little boys had immediately disappeared. Seven-year old Reagan had remained at the new cabin to 'supervise' and had washed the plates as they were unpacked and already had the long table set.

The women and girls emerged from the quarters freshened and carrying food. His departing troopers stared at the pretty young girls walking down the road. He knew he and Bonnie would have their hands full in a few years helping her Da keep the beaus from the door.

The food was on the table, everyone seated with two empty places at the ends of the bench. Calum studied his beautiful wife and saw the tension in her lean face. He was about to rise and go get a patrol together to ride off after the lads when they heard the clatter of horses outside the cabin.

Everyone rose and stood as Bonnie burst through the door.

Minutes later they entered, all three laughing and crying as they were engulfed by the noisy Irish family. It was a minute before he realized Bonnie was holding a new addition.

She walked over toward him, her eyes overflowing with love. "We have room, don't we darling. She's such a wee cailin. The boys arrived too late to save the family, but they found her hiding with her dolly in the corn-crib."

Calum held his arms open and hugged them both. Somehow, God always knew when she needed a child. "Of course there's room." He smiled down at the little girl, blonde and blue-eyed like her friend Claire. "What are you going to call her?"

"There's time enough for that, we'll have to find out who she is before then." She held the child, who looked about two, in her arms and rocked her back and forth, humming softly. When the girl smiled back, Bonnie relaxed.

"Come on, let's eat before the food gets cold." She stared at the two tall troopers beside her who were smoothing their red mustaches. "You two, the pumps outside. Wash off that dust if you want to eat with all these pretty girls."

Calum bowed his head and Bonnie pulled his hat off, brushing a hand across his ear before walking to sit at the other end of the table. The children were all excited but she kept the little girl close and hidden against her. There would be time for her to learn all the members of her wild Irish family soon enough.

Calum realized the thing he might like best about his wife. She was always so sensible.

THE END

ABOUT THE AUTHOR

J.R Biery, is a retired teacher who loves to write fiction. "I enjoy stories about wonderful people, especially in more difficult times, as they rise to overcome a challenge."

DEAR READER

I hope that you enjoy this historical romance, Valley of Shadows. The characters and incidents are composites from stories of the west and the imagination of the author.

I have done my best to edit this text, but if you find errors, I apologize. Please send me your comments or suggestions at biery35@gmail.com

Would love to hear from you.

If you enjoyed this novel, I would appreciate your help. Please post your kind review at http://www.amazon.com/dp/ B00RPTXMU4

OTHER WORK BY J.R.BIERY

Romance Novels
WESTERN WIVES SERIES
The Milch Bride, http://www.amazon.com/dp/B00JC6DOLK
From Darkness to Glory, http://www.amazon.com/dp/B00LG1ZPMK
Valley of Darkness, http://www.amazon.com/dp/B00RPTXMU4
CONTEMPORARIES
He's My Baby Now, http://www.amazon.com/dp/B00N1X6ZFW
Happy Girl, http://www.amazon.com/dp/B00MHHXMEA
Mystery Novels
Potter's Field, http://www.amazon.com/dp/B00KH7Q8C0
Killing the Darlings, http://www.amazon.com/dp/B00IRRMO2A
Edge of Night, http://www.amazon.com/dp/B00J0LLQC6
Others
Will Henry, http://www.amazon.com/dp/B00K5POM0O
Chimera Pass, http://www.amazon.com/dp/B00KALJYRY
Ghost Warrior, http://www.amazon.com/dp/B00M62NBEC

Made in United States
North Haven, CT
05 May 2023

36282339R00251